*"You certainly experienced
a miraculous recovery,"
Elizabeth said.*

But she didn't look at all pleased about his good
health. Her features were taut with controlled
emotion. And it was then Drew noticed the gun
at her side.

"Tell me one thing," she said. "How long have
you been able to walk on that leg?"

Drew considered lying. But after reading her
journal he was certain he had nothing to fear
from Elizabeth. "Since yesterday afternoon,"
he admitted. He stood and walked across the
bare wooden floor until he faced her. The gun
was still held loosely at her side, and he took
heart from the fact that she hadn't pointed it at
him. "It's not what you think," he began. "I
didn't come here to—"

"What kind of game are you playing
with me?"

Dear Reader,

For years, Silhouette Intimate Moments has worked to bring you the most exciting books available in category romance. We were the first to introduce mainstream elements, to make our books themselves something out of the ordinary for romance publishing. Next month we'll take another step in that direction when we introduce an extraordinary new cover design. At last our books will "look as big as they read." Our commitment to quality novels hasn't changed, but now we've come up with a package that we think does our stories justice. I'm hoping you'll think so, too, and that you'll share your thoughts on our new cover with me just as, all along, you've been sharing your thoughts on our books themselves.

But let's not forget the excitement this month in the middle of anticipating next month's big change. Veterans Jennifer Greene, Alexandra Sellers and Kate Bradley are in this month's lineup, along with talented newcomer Joyce McGill. Actually, Joyce has written young-adult novels before, but this is her first foray into adult fiction, and I know you'll be glad to hear that it won't be her last.

That's it for now, but keep your eyes open next month for the newest look in romance—only in Silhouette Intimate Moments.

Yours,

Leslie J. Wainger
Senior Editor and Editorial Coordinator

Sheep's Clothing

KATE BRADLEY

Silhouette Intimate Moments

Published by Silhouette Books New York

America's Publisher of Contemporary Romance

SILHOUETTE BOOKS
300 East 42nd St., New York, N.Y. 10017

ISBN: 0-373-07346-1

First Silhouette Books printing August 1990

Books by Kate Bradley

Silhouette Intimate Moments

Ancient Secrets #231
Sheep's Clothing #346

KATE BRADLEY

has written everything from poetry to news releases to instruction manuals. Before starting her first romance novel, she worked as a corporate writer for a high tech company. She says, "Writing about people is much more fun than writing about computers!" Besides writing, Kate loves reading, eating and listening to her Billie Holiday albums.

Chapter 1

Drew felt the mist fall like a wet curtain on his face. Beneath him was cold, hard ground. He'd connected with a rock on his way down, and his skull still reverberated from the blow and the sound of thunder—and gunshot. How long had it been since the gun had fired and he'd started running? Two hours? Four?

The mist, the pounding and the pain were the only things that made him feel as if he were still in the land of the living. If he didn't know better, he'd be certain that he'd walked off the edge of the earth into space. Only, instead of blackness and stars, he was cloaked in a blanket of relentless gray. Gray skies, gray mist.

He realized he must have been unconscious for a while, and he wondered again how long he'd been lying here on the sodden ground. The dampness had seeped under his clothes until he was chilled to the core. But then he'd been soaked long before he'd stumbled and fallen, even before the gunshot and the headlong dash through the woods. Soaked, tired, hungry, and now he was also in pain. Every bone, every muscle in his body ached, and his head was one throbbing hurt.

He reached up to touch his forehead, wincing at the sharp sting. He brought his fingers close to his eyes and saw the watery red stain. Blood. Had he been struck by the lone bullet?

No. He remembered hearing it tear through the leafy bushes behind him, remembered fleeing through the woods like a hunted animal, racing across open meadow until he'd tripped and hit his head.

Must have been a gopher hole, he thought, and grinned weakly. At least his brain was still working. Apparently his thick skull had protected him this time. If it didn't hurt so much, he would have laughed at the irony of the situation. He'd been to every trouble spot in the world, dodged bullets and shrapnel and survived a handful of tropical ailments. It had taken a cow pasture in Wisconsin and an industrious ground squirrel to finally bring him down.

He tried to concentrate on the reason he was out here in the middle of nowhere, hoping it would help him gather the strength to stand up, but all he could think of was how stupid he'd been. He should have known better than to leave Chicago in the middle of the night. He should have known better than to take that narrow cowpath people here in the northwoods called a road, while driving a pocket-size truck that had never been any farther out of the city than the Lincoln Tollway. And he should have known better than to leave the stalled vehicle and start out walking when he was already more than half lost.

But when a man manages to pick up the trail of whoever murdered his best friend, caution is the last thing on his mind.

What was meant to be a quick investigative foray had turned into a several-hours-long nightmare. He'd left the cowpath-road long ago, wandering up the first driveway that he'd seen, hoping to find help. Instead he got a bullet. He'd run like hell, trees blurring before his eyes, his heart pumping. He vaguely remembered coming to a sturdy fence of woven wire, although he couldn't remember how he'd crossed it. Somehow adrenaline had spurred him over to the other side.

A fence meant there had to be people nearby, didn't it?

But then he remembered just what sort of people lived in these woods, and he decided he was probably better off out here flat on his back in the rain. At least this way he didn't present much of a target.

Another wave of pain swept over him, and he groaned aloud. If only he could go to sleep. Maybe he would wake up in his cramped apartment in Chicago, and this would all be some bad dream. Then he heard it.

Laughter?

The high-pitched, mocking sounds surrounded him, suffocatingly close in the thick mist. Maybe he'd slipped into another world after all. His mind conjured up a picture of hellish griffins and gargoyles circling him and tittering at the stubborn recklessness that had led to his folly. He closed his eyes, but the sounds came closer still.

Then a bell tinkled sweetly, and he opened his eyes to see an incredibly lovely vision in the shape of a woman. Her pale hair looked like a nimbus in the fog as she bent over him. For one crazy moment he wondered if he was dead, then he realized that a man like him would more likely end up in the netherworld he'd first imagined than in cloudlike vapor populated by angels such as this one.

He laughed aloud at his cynical thought, and the resulting pain almost sent him over the edge into unconsciousness. The woman smiled and bent closer, her blond hair the single bright spot in the murky gray. She touched his face with her hand, and with the light feel of her warm fingers on his skin, he knew he was alive.

Elizabeth looked at the man lying in her brass bed. He'd slept most of the evening without stirring once. Worry made her fingers fumble, and she dropped the sweater she was knitting into the basket next to her. *Maybe I should have driven to Doc Wilson's after all,* she thought, biting her lip.

At the time, she didn't think the man's injuries were serious enough to warrant driving through six miles of mist and muck to Doc's small cabin. It would have taken at least the better part of an hour to put chains on her old truck in the dark, and who would have watched him while she was outside in the shed? For that matter, how could she have gotten him into the truck? He wasn't a tall man, but he was solid. She never would have made it from the pasture without his help, weak as he was. He'd conveniently delayed passing out until the moment they'd reached the bed. Besides, knowing Doc, he'd probably chosen to weather the rain with a fifth of his favorite whiskey. He most likely wouldn't have been in any shape to do much more for the man than she had done herself, Elizabeth justified further.

But it had been a long time since she'd made that decision, and the man was still unconscious.

She left her position by the bedside to check on the time. Her cabin featured only one clock and that was in the kitchen, the only place where time occasionally mattered. Hours and minutes weren't as important to her as they used to be. She judged time's passage by her surroundings; long ago she'd relegated her expensive gold watch to a shoebox filled with other needless bits of the past and shoved it under the bed.

That bed had now been occupied by the masculine interloper for three hours and fifteen minutes, she noted as she checked the antique ship clock on the windowsill. The morning's thunderclouds had evolved into mist, which in turn had given way to drizzle—the same slow, steady, unrelenting drizzle that had fallen yesterday and the day before that.

Summer had ended abruptly in the woods this year, and looking out into the dark night, Elizabeth found it hard to believe that it was only September. It was an odd time for visitors: too late for the summer tourists who populated the area lake resorts, now closed for the season, and too early for hunters. She had good reason to be wary after the incident last fall. Silas Freeman's men had rescued her that time.

When she found the man in the low pasture this afternoon, she'd thought he might be another one of Silas's strays, like Cal Hoskin or Lewis Cole. But no one from the Colony would be walking around in the damp woods unarmed and lightly dressed. The man's clothing had given him away: a jacket of a light, breathable and therefore not waterproof fabric favored by joggers; jeans that, even though faded, were cut to be flattering as well as serviceable; and a navy blue chamois shirt that looked as though it had come right off the pages of a preppy New England catalog. His silvertone watch looked merely practical, until she'd spotted the name of its high-priced German manufacturer. He was altogether too cosmopolitan to belong here in the woods.

She'd hesitated over the eelskin wallet now sitting on her dresser, finally deciding that she wouldn't open it unless she needed to contact his next of kin. And since he was injured only slightly—she hoped—she certainly wouldn't need to violate his privacy. Prying was not part of her nature.

But it had been impossible to leave the man with *all* his privacy intact. Elizabeth chided herself for blushing as she looked at the masculine clothing strung across the clothesline in front of the fireplace. Almost-thirty-year-old women weren't supposed to blush, not even when they hadn't seen that much male skin since catching Lily Freeman's little brother Luke skinny-dipping in the sheep pond. And she'd had to rub down every inch of that skin to prevent hypothermia.

Exposure was a real danger, since she had no idea how long this man had been lying outside in the rain. She checked his condition again. He still hadn't moved, but at least some color had returned to his high cheekbones. When she'd half dragged him across the room and dumped him on her bed, his face had been as white as the cotton pillowcase. His shadowed jaw and heavy brows stood in marked contrast to his paleness. She'd had a brief impression of remarkably dark brown eyes before they'd been hidden by lids edged with thick black lashes.

Now she looked at his features more critically. His hair was grizzled heavily with silver, glinting brightly through the thick dark strands. His bone structure was rough and craggy, his mouth wide, his nose slightly askew. A thin scar on his left temple showed white against his olive skin and sliced the edge of one dark eyebrow, giving him a slightly sardonic expression even in sleep.

All in all, he wasn't a pretty picture, especially considering the gash that marred his forehead above the other eyebrow. Elizabeth had cleaned it carefully and bandaged it, deciding against stitches even though it would probably leave him with another scar. She didn't think that would bother him, judging from the scars that crisscrossed his abdomen. She looked away quickly when she realized her gaze had drifted down to the silver pendant he wore around his neck, then lower still to his bare torso. Her interest in an unconscious man was unseemly—and unusual, considering her lack of interest in any man.

She took up her knitting again and wondered what would bring a man like this one into the woods, the clacking needles lending a rhythm to her distracted thoughts. This was a place where people came to be private and apart from the madding crowd, and it was a habit of hers not to ask too many questions. Some things were better left unexplored.

Still, she was curious about how a man with an odd combination of designer clothing and rugged scars could end up here. Anyone else might be frightened at being isolated in a cabin with a tough-looking stranger, but Elizabeth was calm. She'd been through the worst, and nothing or no one could shake her ever again. If the man's intentions were unpleasant, she was prepared. But something told her she could trust him.

His breathing changed, and she looked up from her knitting to find his gaze on her. "And here my Sunday school teachers always told me angels played harps," he said.

His voice was rusty, his smile weak, and Elizabeth didn't even try to suppress her relieved laughter. She judged his condition carefully. He was talking and smiling, but she could tell by the lines bracketing his mouth and the frown between his brows that he was still in pain. She also noted with surprise that he was much younger than she had first suspected—probably still in his thirties, although his gray hair and gravelly voice made it difficult to tell.

"You're a long way from heaven," she assured him. "How do you feel?"

He grimaced at her question. "I feel like hell, actually. How long have I been out?"

"About three and a half hours. Are you hungry?"

"Starving."

"Then I'll get you something to eat," Elizabeth told him before leaving his bedside.

Actually Drew had been too busy watching the angel that rescued him to give a thought to such mundane matters as food, until she mentioned it. As soon as she'd said the words, the rumbling in his stomach joined the pounding of his head and throbbing in his right ankle. His body's clamoring was uncomfortable, but reassuring.

He was able to keep track of her actions through the open bookcase that partially screened off the sleeping alcove from the kitchen area. Judging from the rugged walls, her home was a log cabin. The bookcase was the only partition in the room, save for a waist-high countertop that defined the kitchen.

He saw her ladle something into a bowl, her movements hurried but graceful. He couldn't help remembering how serene she'd looked in the rocking chair by his bedside. The heavy oak had dwarfed her slight figure. She was simply dressed in jeans and a sweater the color of an apple's blush. Corn silk blond hair spilled down her back in one thick braid, nearly reaching a waist he guessed he could circle with his hands.

She walked toward him, carrying the bowl on a wooden breadboard that served as a tray. He reached to take the board out of her hands, hiding a smile when he noticed that the kerosene lamp on the nightstand highlighted a pale dusting of freckles on her ivory skin. Her eyes were a lavender blue that reminded him of woodland flowers. Everything about her implied delicacy. He could vaguely remember walking through the mist with her help, and he found it hard to believe that this petite package of femininity had practically hauled him to bed.

As he shifted to set the board on his lap, he realized that not only had she put him to bed, she'd undressed him—completely. She'd left him nothing but his watch and the silver Saint Christopher medallion he wore on a chain around his neck. A quick glance beyond the alcove to the left, where he could see a clothesline in front of the fireplace, confirmed the sensation of cotton sheets against bare skin.

She noted the direction of his glance, and when he looked back again, her eyes didn't quite meet his. Her cheeks turned the barest shade of pink, and he couldn't resist the urge to deepen the color. "I feel like we know each other already—" he grinned suggestively "—but my name is Drew Carter."

Her reaction to his teasing disappointed him. The trace of rose in her cheeks had disappeared, and she looked as serene and unruffled as she did when he'd awakened. "I'm Elizabeth Johnson."

The name came as a surprise, even though he'd guessed that she must be the one he was looking for. From what the waitress in the café had told him, he'd expected a crusty individualist—a white-haired old crone who'd turned her back on the world. Instead he'd found an angel with a face right out of a quattrocento canvas.

She spoke again, and he braced himself for the inevitable questions. Instead she told him, "Your clothes are almost dry."

When she didn't ask any of the things he expected, he felt oddly compelled to tell her more. He was tempted to ask about her neighbors, but that would have to wait until he was sure he could trust her. He carefully omitted any reference to the gunshot, or to his mission.

"I'm usually not this stupid," he said. "My truck stalled just off the main road, and I decided to walk. Then the storm hit, and..." He let his words trail away. No matter how he explained this, he would look foolish, and for some reason he didn't want her to think of him as a city slicker who couldn't get along with cab drivers and fast-food restaurants.

She nodded toward the bowl in front of him. "Don't you like chicken soup?"

At least it was a question. "Oh, yeah, sure." He lifted the spoon. "This is great. You know, my Greek grandmother always said that chicken soup was the best remedy for a chill." He stopped, realizing he was babbling stupidly.

She smiled, and he didn't feel stupid anymore. "My grandmother was Bohemian and she told me the same thing."

"I think it must be a universal prescription. They probably say the same things to little kids on Jupiter." He knew he was talking too much, so he finished the soup, relishing the thick, chewy noodles. The simple meal tasted far better than anything the chef at his favorite four-star restaurant on Lakeshore Drive could have offered. "Thanks," he said. His hand cautiously checked the bandage on his forehead. "And thanks for fixing me up."

"Your injuries aren't as serious as they seem right now. Do you feel nauseated?"

Drew shook his head.

"Good. I don't think you're concussed, and your ankle's only lightly strained. I put some liniment on it and wrapped it, which should help the swelling go down. You'll be able to leave in the morning."

Dismay froze the smile on his face. He hadn't gotten the information he'd come for yet and already she was trying to rush him out the door. A thousand questions rebounded in his aching head, questions that couldn't wait. He had little more than eight weeks until the election—fifty-nine days to expose the man who'd ordered Paul Brewster's death. But first he had to figure out whose side she was on.

"I suppose you don't get many visitors," he began. "Have you lived here long?" He knew it wasn't the most subtle of interview openings, but he was still surprised when she ignored it completely. She stood and reached for the makeshift tray.

"I'll see you in the morning, Mr. Carter. The bathroom is over there, in case you need to use it." She gestured past the bookcase to the right. "There's a walking stick leaning on the wall on the other side of the bed." He glanced over at the long, heavy stick that looked surprisingly like a shepherd's staff.

"You can go to sleep if you like," she continued, "or I can get you something to read."

The thought of reading made his head ache even more. "Looks like you've thought of just about everything. I think I'll pass on the reading for tonight, but thanks anyway. And call me Drew."

He smiled. She didn't, and he wondered why a simple little question had changed her attitude from cautiously cordial to downright cool. He was tempted to suggest that she stay and chat until the fire went out, but he knew that was the wrong approach. So instead he'd use the time to contemplate his next move. Elizabeth Johnson would talk. He'd never come up empty yet.

He crossed his arms behind his head, still smiling. "Good night, Elizabeth." She didn't even flicker an eyelash.

He watched as she rinsed out the bowl, turned out the lamp in the kitchen and carried a block of wood to the fireplace. The flames limned her hair with brilliant highlights, and he remembered again how she'd appeared like an angel out of the mist. Now she stepped out of sight. Drew waited several minutes for her to return, until he heard a muffled noise from above. He wondered about the doorway or stairs he couldn't see. He felt an irrational sense of pique at being left alone, but then his reporter's curiosity took hold. If Elizabeth Johnson wouldn't talk about herself, he'd find out what he needed to know on his own. Being an ex-journalist had its advantages.

He tested his ankle by moving it under the blankets, and the resulting jab of pain made him decide to stay put for the time being. He began to take careful inventory of the large room, or at least what he could see of it from the bed. The ceiling in the living area was lower than in the kitchen and alcove, suggesting the cabin had been extended in recent years. A jog in the rear wall formed the sleeping alcove and marked the line where old met new. Past the screening bookcase to the left was a sitting area, the furnishings utilitarian rather than decorative.

Beyond that were a round oak table and chairs in front of a low window. The front door separated the dining area from the kitchen. It was there that his gaze lingered. On one side was an old black iron range, across from it a modern stove—or somewhat modern, he amended. He put the aqua-blue finish at about 1950s vintage. A scarred wooden countertop formed a U with the open side facing him. Through the bookcase he could see a wide window set between wooden cupboards, and beneath the window was a sink.

At least there's running water, he thought as he let his swimming head fall back against the pillow. He couldn't see what was to the right of the kitchen and alcove, so he concentrated on the "bedroom" itself. The walls, like the rest of the cabin, were unfinished logs. The elegant bird's-eye maple dresser looked out of place in the rustic surroundings. The top was bare of perfume bottles or cosmetics. Somehow that didn't surprise him. Not only did Elizabeth not need them, he could see by the rest of the cabin that she cared more for comfort than for appearances.

The room-dividing bookshelves at the foot of the bed provided the cabin's only clutter. Almost five feet high, the top shelf was a forest of potted plants. The shelves below were filled with books, but not so much so that he couldn't see past them into the rest of the room.

He squinted, trying to read some of the titles in the dim light. He'd hoped to learn more about her by examining her library, but the books told him nothing except that her tastes were diverse. The upper shelves contained everything from paperback thrillers to cookbooks to the latest pop psychology bestseller. Even when he propped himself on his elbows, the bottom shelves remained hidden by the foot of the massive brass bedstead.

He gave up and stared at the beamed ceiling overhead. Not a sound came from the floor above. It was as though she'd vanished, leaving him here alone with the fire and a reading lamp for company. He felt a moment of panic at his unaccustomed helplessness and moved to get out of bed. Pain, mingled with nausea, stopped him short. In order to take his mind off his frustrating condition, he forced himself to analyze what he'd found during his brief survey of the cabin.

From the bare dresser and aging furniture and appliances, he'd already concluded that she didn't care much for appearances. The small cabin was full without appearing crowded, so she was organized and tidy. The books told him that she was intelligent, the knitting that she was industrious. Her reluctance to answer his questions proved she was reserved. And his own eyes told him that she was the loveliest woman he had ever seen.

Perhaps there'd be some good in this project after all, he thought. He smiled grimly and turned out the lamp beside him, falling asleep surrounded by the wildflower scent that clung to the sheets and pillowcase. It reminded him of Elizabeth.

He awoke to the smell of frying eggs. Dark gray still lingered outside the windows, but his watch read eight o'clock. He sat up in bed. The sudden movement made his head ache, but the pain subsided to a dull throb, and he was able to swing his legs over the side.

"Good morning." The lyrical greeting came from the other side of the bookshelf.

He snatched at the quilt to cover himself just as she entered the alcove. Wearing the rose-colored sweater with her hair neatly braided, she looked as composed and lovely as she had the night before, while he felt like death warmed over. She tossed a small bundle at him, and he realized it was his clothing.

"Bathroom," he managed to croak.

She helped him stand and handed him the walking stick, lowering her eyes demurely when the quilt threatened to slip around his thighs. He winced as he put weight on his ankle. She must have noticed the sudden tension in his muscles, because she asked, "How is your leg?"

"Better than last night. But that's not saying much."

He tucked the bundle of clothing under his arm and allowed her to assist him to the bathroom. It was only a few feet away, just around the corner, but when he finally reached the doorway he felt as though he'd just completed a fast 10K. He wondered for a moment if his rapid heartbeat was due more to Elizabeth's nearness than it was to exertion. Her arm circled his waist, and she placed her other hand against his chest to balance him whenever he threatened to stumble. Her hands were small and warm against his skin, and their strength astonished him.

He gripped the edge of the pedestal sink as though it were a lifeline, and she removed her hands from his bare torso.

"I think you can take it from here."

He nodded, and she closed the door behind her. She'd looked as calm and cool as a plaster saint, while his insides were stirred to the point that he'd practically forgotten his headache and

sore ankle. He grimaced at his reflection in the medicine cabinet mirror, then laughed at his affronted vanity. He was lucky
she hadn't run in the other direction. His face was stubbled in
black; his salt-and-pepper hair looked wild. A bluish lump had
appeared beneath the gash on his forehead. He splashed his
face with cold water, and gingerly completed the rest of his
toilette. Holding on to the edge of the sink, he managed to pull
on his jeans before leaving the closetlike room.

He used the doorknob to support himself until she came over
to assist him. And that was when he noticed the one item he had
missed last night.

There, propped behind the kitchen counter, was a deadly-
looking rifle, a twin to the one in the evidence room of the
Chicago Police Department. He wondered if the waitress who
had directed him here was wrong after all. Was Elizabeth
Johnson as innocent as she appeared? Or was she a member of
the group that called itself ASP?

"Just how dangerous is a man without his pants?" he asked,
his voice raspy with sleep. Sleep and disappointment he
couldn't crush.

Elizabeth followed his gaze to the gun she'd taken down last
night and then forgotten. *Extremely dangerous,* she could have
answered. Thank God he'd at least put on his jeans. Touching
his bare skin had sent tremors up her arms, and her palm still
tingled where it had come in contact with Drew Carter's gen-
erously haired chest. Even his rough voice did funny things to
her equilibrium.

While he was in the bathroom, she'd busied herself with
breakfast and berated herself at the same time. By the time she
heard the bathroom latch click, she'd reined in her galloping
senses—or so she'd thought.

"Would you like to amend that statement?" she asked,
coolly raising an eyebrow. Keeping her voice even was a chore
when once again her hand grazed his naked chest. This time he
leaned on her shoulder, as though he, too, was anxious to avoid
the earlier closeness. The maneuver was difficult with the difference in their size. She guessed he was about average height,
but her own five feet four inches were pretty inadequate for
such a task. She managed to get him to the oak table, and he
settled into the closest chair.

His breakfast, a cheese omelet made from the precious fresh eggs her neighbor Lily had brought the day before, was already on the table. She'd eaten earlier, before going out to do chores. She went back to the kitchen for the plate of toast and the mug keeping warm next to the old cast-iron teakettle. Somehow she managed to keep amusement from showing on her face as he bit into the omelet.

"Kasseri."

He looked at her, clearly puzzled.

"The cheese," she explained. "It's Greek—made from sheep's milk. I'm surprised your grandmother didn't tell you about it."

"She must have forgotten." He reached gratefully for the mug, his expression changing back to puzzlement when he inhaled deeply. He eyed its contents suspiciously. Displeased surprise registered on his face after he took a cautious swallow. "This isn't coffee."

"Considering your head injury, I thought you'd be better off with some herbal tea."

"I'd be better off with some coffee," he nearly growled.

"I'm afraid I don't have any. But I do have coffee substitute."

"What's in it?" he asked, doubt edging his voice.

"Roasted grains, chicory root—"

He held up a hand. "I'll stick to the tea, thanks." He muttered something under his breath about health nuts, then said, "I suppose you threw away my cigarettes."

"You must have dropped them in the pasture. I didn't notice any in your pockets." Realizing she'd just admitted to going through his clothing, Elizabeth flushed. She felt unaccountably embarrassed, even though she hadn't looked through his wallet.

Instead of showing the anger she suspected, Drew grinned. "That's all right. I quit—or tried to—six months ago."

Bemused by that flash of charm, Elizabeth sat down across from him and watched as he ate. There was certainly nothing wrong with his appetite. In fact, she suspected he was a man of many appetites. Even injured, he managed to exude an energy that fascinated her. He ate with gusto, polishing off every last piece of toast after coating them thickly with jam. So the man had a sweet tooth, she thought. She'd have to bake more bread later in the day, after he had gone. The unexpected work didn't

bother her as much as it should have. For a moment she actually felt regret at the thought of his leaving. But only for a
moment.

His presence managed to make the cabin seem less lonely and
isolated, and Elizabeth had to remind herself forcefully that it
was loneliness she sought. Drew Carter was very clearly a man
of the world, and she didn't want him bringing that world in
with him. The sooner he was gone, the better.

"If you'll tell me where you left your vehicle," she began, "I
could put chains on it and drive it here so you can leave this
afternoon."

Drew looked up from the mug he was lifting to his mouth,
not bothering to hide his surprise. He was so stiff from yesterday's little excursion through the trees that he could hardly
hobble, yet she was ready to throw him out. Did her eagerness
to be rid of him mean that she was hiding something? "This
afternoon? In kind of a hurry to get rid of me, aren't you?" he
asked laconically.

Elizabeth's lavender gaze met his with surprising firmness.
"There's no reason why you can't drive once I bring your truck
here. There's no sign of concussion this morning."

"No," he allowed. "But my truck is stalled, not just stuck,
and even if you could manage to get it here in this—" he gestured to the rain streaming across the window "—I couldn't
drive it. It's got a stick shift, and my ankle's injured. Remember?"

"You probably flooded the engine by revving it to get un-
stuck." She ignored his snort of impatience and continued.
"Your sore ankle just needs rewrapping and exercise. If
you'll—"

"Just how stupid do you think I am?" Drew couldn't hold
back his protests any longer. "I know what a flooded engine
sounds like, and I know how to start one. The engine *wasn't*
flooded," he said. She stared back at him and he went on, even
though he knew he sounded like a testy child. "And my ankle
isn't sore. It hurts like hell."

Elizabeth's lips firmed, but she showed no other reaction. In
a calm voice, she said, "In that case, I'd better help you back
to bed."

"Thanks for your generous offer," he said without hiding his
sarcasm, "but I'll manage myself."

He did manage, barely. Every step caused a shooting fire to go up the back of his calf, but he wouldn't let her see that. The exercise was probably good for him, he admitted as he unwrapped the bandage around his ankle. The swelling had gone down, the pain had localized, and he decided it wasn't broken or sprained. A minor strain, just as she'd said.

She was right about another thing, too. The knock on the head wasn't a concussion. He knew because he'd suffered one before, six years ago in Beirut. That was after the cracked ribs in Ulster, the broken nose in Tehran, and the fever in Phnom Penh. After three injury-free years of covering domestic corruption instead of international violence, he'd gone soft. Considering the fact that a bullet had whizzed by mere inches from his head just yesterday morning, he'd actually gotten off lightly.

The most troubling injury was his calf. It was probably just a strained muscle from his encounter with the gopher hole, just as Elizabeth had said. And the best thing for it would be rewrapping and gentle exercise. She was right again.

He hated to be wrong. He knew that he was angry, not because he was wrong about the ankle, but because he might be wrong about Elizabeth. She was too private, too controlled. Not once did she bang a dish or clatter the silverware to show that she was upset. He watched as she calmly lifted the iron teakettle and poured steaming water over the sinkful of dishes. Her fragile appearance hid stores of strength. What did her cool attitude hide? he wondered as he rewrapped his ankle.

By the time he made the last awkward turn of the bandage, she had already finished the dishes. She took a wet slicker from a peg on back of the door and left without another word.

Fine, he told himself, but he couldn't tamp down his frustration as she closed the door quietly behind her.

Chapter 2

Elizabeth took a deep breath of cool, damp air. It helped, but not much. It would be a long time before she forgot how Drew Carter's hard-muscled body had felt leaning against hers. Even through the solid wood door she could still feel his dark eyes glowering at her. She crossed the porch and stepped down, putting even more distance between them.

She'd finished her morning chores before *he* woke up. If it wasn't for the unwanted, irascible man occupying the cabin, she'd be quietly knitting by the fireside, enjoying the warmth and crackle as it contrasted with the heavy gray mist outside. Frustration started to creep over her again, and she walked briskly down the trail that led away from the homestead.

Why *her* cabin? she demanded silently, kicking at an exposed tree root on the path in front of her. Why couldn't his truck have stalled in front of Doc's? Or the Colony? She shuddered involuntarily and put up the hood of her slicker to protect her from the encroaching dampness.

No, she was glad he hadn't gone all the way to Silas Freeman's small settlement. The people living there guarded their privacy even more fiercely then she did hers, with equally good reason. Lily Freeman had been with her last fall when three men attacked them in the woods. Since then, the Colony viewed any outsider with suspicion. They would have seen Drew—even injured—as an interloper, a threat to their rigid self-sufficient community.

And he would have found them just as odd. She had, too, at first, but isolation and adversity forge strong links among neighbors, even strange ones. And she supposed she was considered a pretty odd bird herself—an almost-thirty-year-old woman, living alone in the middle of nowhere without telephone or electricity.

As she walked, the trees grew denser around her. No one traveling the dead-end road that edged the forest would guess that a small homestead lay beyond the pine and hardwoods, but somehow Drew had known. For the first time, she wished it wasn't so difficult to get into town. The dead-end road turned into mud every time it rained, and her narrow driveway, a trail that cut a half mile through the woods, was even worse.

Above her, the tops of the dark evergreens disappeared into gray clouds of moisture. If the wet conditions kept up, she might have a houseguest for much longer than she wanted. Not even during the fiercest January blizzard had she felt so trapped by nature: a man, a woman, a remote cabin cut off from the world by weather. A city slicker and a country innocent. Elizabeth knew the ending to the scenario too well. But what had happened to her mother wouldn't happen to her, she vowed as she ducked beneath a branch.

When she glimpsed the flash of red through the low-hanging evergreen boughs, she wasn't surprised that it had been her destination all along. The boxy little truck on the other side of the trees didn't look as though it had enough power to keep up with freeway traffic, let alone fight its way over rough country roads. The wheels were inches deep in the soft mud. She groaned with dismay. She'd have to tow it out with her own truck. *If* her balky, thirty-year-old rust bucket could make it through the muddy trail between the road and her cabin. And if Drew's smaller truck would even start.

Both doors resisted every attempt to open. The license plate was missing, and the Illinois license application taped to the back window was so faded she couldn't read it. Impatiently she slapped her hand against the window, then paused. Curiosity got the better of her, and she rubbed the glass free of moisture so she could look inside. Wedged tightly behind the passenger seat, almost invisible, were a faded green army duffel bag...and an official-looking leather briefcase with brass combination locks.

She could think of only one reason for a visit from an outsider who carried a briefcase, and the thought chilled her. Silas Freeman had boasted often enough that he'd never pay taxes as long as he was able to barter for everything he needed—and she'd bartered with him. She'd reported every transaction correctly in her own tax forms, but she'd always dreaded a visit from the IRS when they got around to realizing that the other half of the transaction wasn't being reported on Silas Freeman's.

Less than three miles away, the Colony had two four-wheel-drive pickups, in addition to several sturdy farm vehicles and a telephone. They could tow Drew Carter's truck or phone for help. But if Drew was a tax man, Freeman and his people wouldn't lift a finger—unless it was to chase him off their land. No, she didn't dare go there for help. As she turned away, she wondered who she was protecting—her neighbors or Drew Carter.

Drew looked up the ladder to the loft above. All he could see was a rooftop skylight splattered with rain. Climbing the ladder with his gimpy ankle was out of the question.

The long walking stick, along with the foul-smelling liniment he'd found on the nightstand, had helped him make it from the bed to the living room without too much pain. He wished now that he'd accepted Elizabeth's offer to rewrap his ankle. He'd done a damn poor job of it, and he could feel the elastic bandage slipping with every step.

Something snapped loudly, and he spun around, nearly losing his balance. He realized the noise was just a log burning in the fireplace, but the memory of yesterday's gunshot was still fresh, and Elizabeth's continued absence was making him edgy. *Where the hell had she gone anyway?* It had been almost three hours since she'd slammed out the door. He forced aside his concern. If anyone could take care of herself, it was Elizabeth Johnson. When a sharp needle of pain froze his calf muscle, he retreated back to the sleeping alcove, sparing one last look for the ladder stairs that led up to the loft.

"Damn it," he said, partly to relieve his frustration, partly just to hear a human voice. At least he could read, he thought, and paused at the bookcase for a closer look. He rejected title after title until he came to the bottom two shelves that he'd missed last night. He scanned several nonfiction volumes until two in particular caught his eye, their titles and the author's name leaping out at him from the spines and making him forget all about the throbbing in his leg. *A. J. Carter.* He grinned. The lady had good taste.

But then panic filled him. What if she figured out who he was? It was clear she didn't like to answer questions, and once she found out that she was sharing her cabin with an investigative author . . . Well, he wouldn't be surprised if he ended up out in the rain, sore leg or not.

He couldn't take a chance by leaving the books on the shelf. Somehow he would have to dispose of them. He looked at the fireplace speculatively. But what if she returned before they burned completely? That thought was answered by the sound of footsteps approaching the door, and he realized that he didn't have time to debate the issue. He grabbed the books, and ignoring the pain in his leg, he headed for the sofa.

He was sitting on the faded challis sofa looking completely bored, Elizabeth noted guiltily as she came into the room. She could have at least found something for him to read. He stood up then, and she allowed her gaze to travel from the tousled silver and black hair on his head down to the midnight-dark hair that covered his broad chest. She paused at the silver medallion for a moment before stopping completely at the waistband of his jeans. He still hadn't put on his shirt, darn him.

She bent to remove her muddy boots, hiding her expression, taking far longer than the task required. When she was composed, she stood to shake the droplets of water from her slicker before hanging it back on the door. All the while she could feel him silently watching her movements. Just when she thought she couldn't stand it anymore, he spoke.

"You were gone a long time."

His smile was friendly, but she thought she detected a note of something else in his voice. Boredom? Sulkiness, perhaps? She decided that the role of Good Samaritan didn't include entertaining him. He had a roof over his head and food to eat, and that was plenty.

"Hungry?" she asked, turning away before he could answer. She moved to the kitchen cupboards and checked their contents. "Will canned soup and crackers be okay?"

"Sounds fine. Can I help?"

His voice came from directly behind her, and she almost dropped the can of soup she was holding. How could he have crossed the room that quickly and quietly with his injured leg? She turned to face him, and found herself struggling to keep from staring at his muscular torso with its network of scars, only inches away.

"You could put on your shirt," she suggested, meeting his eyes with what she hoped was calm detachment. Apparently her coolness didn't fool him. He shot her a devilish grin before limping away to retrieve his shirt from the bathroom where he'd left it that morning.

By the time he returned, his navy blue chamois shirt neatly buttoned, Elizabeth had set the table and had heated the soup on the gas range. They ate in uncomfortable silence, until she remembered her intention to start asking questions. It was against her nature to be so openly curious, but she had to start somewhere. "Where are you from, Mr. Carter?" she began awkwardly. She regretted her prim-sounding words the moment she spoke, and doubly so when she saw Drew's amused grin.

"I think we got beyond that stage last night, Elizabeth." His eyes crinkled at the corners, and her name sounded surprisingly soft spoken in his rough voice. "I'm from Chicago. And please call me Drew."

Chicago. For a moment she panicked. But then she reminded herself that Chicago was an awfully big city where tragedy and scandal were commonplace. Maybe he didn't remember all those headlines five years ago. Or perhaps he hadn't even been living in Chicago then.

"Have you lived there long . . . Drew?"

He smiled at her use of his name. "All my life." She tensed, then relaxed when he went on to explain. "I haven't been there much during the past fifteen years or so. I move around a lot."

Without understanding why, she was relieved that he would have no memory of the events that changed her life. Surely it didn't matter what a stranger thought of her. Especially if he was hoping to throw her in jail for tax fraud. She continued to probe. "For your work?"

His eyes narrowed. "Sometimes. Why do you ask?"

She swallowed a spoonful of soup and shrugged, hoping she looked more nonchalant than she felt. "You don't look like a tourist, and we don't get many visitors on this road. I thought your being here might have something to do with work. I saw a briefcase in your truck."

Emotions she couldn't begin to read chased across his face. "You were there? Then the roads must be clear."

"The road's a mess, so I walked through the woods. I would have brought your things with me, but the doors were locked." She asked him again, "Are you here to work?"

His gaze was long and assessing, and for a while she thought he wouldn't answer at all. Finally he said, "Yes. I'm writing a book about the area."

"Are you a naturalist of some sort?" she asked doubtfully. She couldn't see him picking flowers—he looked more like a street brawler.

He laughed. "Hardly. I thought I'd interview you and your neighbors about living here in the woods. It must be quite an adventure." He nodded toward the gun that she'd restored to its usual spot above the door.

She swallowed her last spoonful of soup too quickly, and it went down the wrong way. After clearing her throat she told him briskly, "I don't want to be interviewed." She stood and started to clear the table. "What do you write? Fiction? Non-fiction?"

He didn't answer, and she ventured, "Let me guess. You write adventure novels—the kind men read, with a gun battle in one chapter and a sexual conquest in the next. Secret agents, private eyes, that kind of thing."

He leaned back in his chair. "The book I'm working on now definitely has those elements. Good guys, bad guys. Guns." His gaze went back to the rifle.

"Are you married?" she asked.

He threw her a measuring look that prompted her to take the dishes quickly into the kitchen. "No, I'm not."

"Then there's no one worried over your whereabouts?" She pretended that was the only reason for her interest, keeping her attention fixed on stacking the dishes in the sink and covering them with water from the kettle heating on the gas range.

"Not a soul," he confirmed. "Is your concern an admission that I might be here a little longer than you expected?" He stood then, leaving the table to face her across the countertop, gripping the edge for support.

Her heart skipped as she considered the implications of his continued presence. But she allowed none of her concern to show as she looked him in the eye and said, "Your truck is in mud almost to the axle. I could tow it out, but it won't be easy because I don't have a four-wheel drive. My neighbors do, though, and I could walk there for help," she offered reluctantly. "They also have a telephone. If someone is expecting you, I could call."

"No, not yet," he said quickly. "I mean, don't go to all that trouble on my account. I'll be better in the morning." He smiled. "I'd offer to help with the dishes, but . . ." He looked down in the direction of his ankle.

Elizabeth's lips firmed. "Enjoy it while you can. This isn't exactly a guest operation."

"Are you suggesting that I'm malingering?"

He acted affronted, but Elizabeth knew he was teasing her by the telltale crinkles around his eyes. She flushed with sudden heat—from the steaming water in the sink, she told herself. She tried to think of something for him to do, so he wouldn't be standing around watching her every move. "Do you think you could knead bread dough?" she asked doubtfully.

He grinned. "Remember my Greek grandmother? She showed me how when I was about as high as this counter."

"Carter's hardly a Greek name," Elizabeth commented as she rinsed the dishes with more hot water. "Was she your mother's mother?"

"No. My father's. When he emigrated he anglicized his name," he explained briefly. "My mother's maiden name was Lapinski."

"Ah—Greek and Polish, then."

"And French and Irish and Italian." He grinned. "My mother's family has been here in the States for a long time. I guess you could say I'm all American. How about you? Johnson sounds Scandinavian."

"It's a Swedish name," she answered. *But not mine.* His questions were getting too close. She wiped her hands on the dish towel and asked brightly, "Do you prefer whole wheat or rye?"

Less than a half an hour later he was seated at the table, his injured leg propped on a chair and a mound of whole wheat dough in front of him. While she finished putting away the dinner dishes, Elizabeth watched him out of the corner of her eye until she was certain he had the knack. The rhythmic motions of his strong fingers mesmerized her. A vision of those same strong hands kneading her skin caught her completely off guard. Abruptly she pulled her attention back to the plate she was holding. She put it away and immediately looked around for something else to occupy her.

Her gaze settled on the hulking black iron range. The lingering rain had brought a dampness that seemed to penetrate the cabin's log walls, and another fire would help combat the humidity. She'd only used the old range once or twice since spring, so she checked the stovepipe to make sure it was clear before kneeling to clean the ash drawer, a chore she normally dreaded.

She hadn't yet finished when Drew covered the kneaded bread dough with a towel and walked over to watch. His presence made a routine she'd performed a million times suddenly foreign to her, forcing her to concentrate on each step. Somehow she managed to dispose of the ashes, then fill the reservoir and load the firebox without fumbling. She removed one of the stove lids to light the kindling on top of the wood stacked in the firebox below. When she was sure the fire had caught, she replaced the lid and adjusted the sliding draft on the side of the range.

"Wouldn't it be a lot easier just to use the gas stove?" Drew asked.

"I thought a second fire would take some of the damp out of the air," she explained. "Besides—" she admitted with a smile "—bread tastes better baked in here."

"I bet it does. Why don't you have electricity?"

"I chose not to."

"Then why is the cabin wired? I see electrical outlets on every wall."

"I had a generator for a while. It broke down in the middle of a blizzard, and by the time I could get out to have it repaired or buy a new one, I didn't need it anymore. Why grow to depend on something if it isn't available when you need it?"

"An independent woman."

"That's right." Her words were clipped. She sensed that the conversation had slipped to a different level of meaning, and she wanted to make sure Drew understood her position.

He changed tack smoothly. "I've still got one hell of a headache." He rubbed a hand over his forehead, scowling. "You wouldn't happen to have aspirin around?"

"In the bathroom—I'll get it. And maybe I should have another look at that cut while we're at it." When she returned, he was seated at the table again, his face drawn with tension. She filled a glass with water from the stoneware jug in the corner and brought it to him with the tablets. "By the way, I hope you didn't drink any water from the tap this morning."

"No, why?" He reached for the aspirin, and she sat down on the other chair.

"It's pumped in from the lake. The water looks crystal clean, but you really shouldn't drink it."

He looked at the glass she handed him, his expression doubting.

"Oh, that water's okay," she informed him. "I carry in enough spring water for drinking and cooking." She leaned toward him to check the cut on his forehead. The surrounding skin was red and puffy, so she decided to cover it with gauze again. She worked quickly, ignoring the urge to let her fingers linger and soothe away his headache. "Done," she announced briskly and started to move away.

"Wait." The word was too hesitant to be a command, but she paused anyway. She understood the reason for his reticence when he admitted, "I didn't do a very good job of wrapping my ankle this morning. Would you mind . . . ?"

Elizabeth shook her head. "Of course not."

She gestured for him to put his leg up, and he complied, gingerly setting it down across her thighs. Instantly, she did mind. A lot. His foot was bare, giving him an aura of vulnerability that didn't fit her earlier impression of him. Her thighs turned to liquid as she rolled up the blue denim a few inches, exposing his skin to her careful touch. She didn't realize Drew had spoken until he repeated his question a second time.

"How do you pump the water and heat it without electricity?"

"I have a windmill for pumping. I heat the water on the stove for dishes, and in the winter there's plenty of hot water in the range reservoir for baths." She dropped the unwound bandage on the floor.

"And in the summer?" His voice deepened as she gently probed around his ankle. His skin was warm beneath her fingers and rough with dark hair. She concentrated on his words and ignored the tingle in her hands.

"I use the shower in the bathroom. The lake water is very—" she looked up and discovered the intense expression on his face "—refreshing," she finished weakly. Did he guess how she was reacting to him? She swallowed and her hands stilled.

"You mean *cold*." The look in his eyes was anything but. His dark gaze had moved to her lips, and it took conscious effort to keep from dampening them with her tongue.

He was a stranger, she reminded herself. He didn't belong here in the woods, in her life—not even for an afternoon or a night. She quickly turned her attention back to his ankle. "Your ankle doesn't look swollen. I'll just put more liniment on it and rewrap it."

He nodded his approval and helped her lower his leg back to the floor. While she retrieved the bottle of liniment from the nightstand, she tried to collect herself. It wouldn't do to let Drew see how easily he affected her. She wasn't as helpless as a lamb, and she wasn't about to become this wolf's next meal. Or a chapter in his next trashy novel.

She carried the small bottle over to the table and resumed her seat. With a quirk of his eyebrow, Drew settled his bare leg back onto her lap. Somehow he made the gesture both trusting and challenging, and her resolve wavered like a frail branch in a windstorm.

She smoothed the liniment over his ankle and calf, knowing that its tingling warmth penetrated his skin the way it did her fingertips. The strong medicinal smell should have reminded her that she was simply treating an injury. But she fumbled with the long bandage until Drew finally had to help her. Between the two of them they at last managed to wrap it around his leg.

She started to roll his jeans back down, but his hand reached out and caught hers. "Thank you," he said quietly. Their gazes locked, and the message she read in his was unmistakable. And unthinkable. It was ridiculous to have feelings like this for a man she didn't know, she protested inwardly.

Drew ignored the silent plea in her eyes. The pressure of his hand on hers increased, and he was drawing her closer a bare millimeter at a time while she did nothing to stop him.

Outside the mist obscured the late-afternoon sun, and the only light in the cabin came from the warm glow of the fire-place across the room. Her senses leaped into awareness, noting the familiar scent of wood smoke, the muted crackling of both fires, the faint ticking of the kitchen clock. But all were background to the fire in Drew's eyes and the touch of his hand on hers.

She was on the verge of giving in to his silent seduction when a noise from outside broke the spell. It came again: the melodious tinkling of bells.

"What the—" Drew turned toward the window, and Elizabeth used the distraction to pull her hand free of his.

"I have to go." Abruptly she stood, barely pausing at the door to pull on her boots. She felt as though she were fleeing from the devil himself, although she recognized that the real danger lay in her own churning emotions. She'd been saved by the bell, literally. Grateful, she escaped outside.

Drew recognized the sound immediately as the one he'd heard yesterday just before Elizabeth rescued him from the mist and its imaginary demons. "So, I wasn't hallucinating after all," he murmured. He walked to the window, his leg already feeling the benefit of the liniment, and looked out.

Of course. He should have put two and two together sooner. The shepherd's staff, the cheese, the basket of homespun yarn by the rocking chair. Elizabeth was a shepherdess. The quaintness of the term made him smile. It suited her. And it answered at least one of his questions, providing another piece to the puzzle of what she was doing here in the backwoods.

Quietly he stepped outside onto the porch so he could see the paddock to the right. He ignored the roughness of the boards against his bare feet as he watched, entranced. Several sheep— white-faced, lop-eared and fat with wool—followed trustingly behind Elizabeth.

The scene was tranquil and uncomplicated, like the woman herself. Then he rejected the notion. Elizabeth might seem like an innocent, but he sensed that she kept much hidden behind that angelic face. For one thing, that rifle still needed explaining. He was certain she'd obtained it through the people he sought. She wasn't the kind of woman to go out on her own and buy an assassin's rifle.

Or maybe that was only what he wanted to believe. Thinking about Elizabeth being a part of the ugliness that killed Paul Brewster turned his stomach. He'd been disillusioned often enough to take people's duplicity for granted, but the thought of being wrong this time was disturbing.

He realized what was happening. He was attracted to her—
but that was as far as he intended it to go. All he needed were a
few answers, enough so he wouldn't have to step into the snake
pit down the road without being prepared. With any luck, she
wouldn't even realize she was helping him. And the attraction
that pinged between them like a taut guitar string would probably help his cause . . . unless he let it get out of hand.

Elizabeth smiled indulgently as Genevieve, her oldest Corriedale ewe, edged out the sheep next to her so that her seven-
month-old daughter could eat beside her at the feeder. Even
though the ewe lamb, Dorcas, had been weaned months ago,
Genevieve still watched her solicitously.

The hay in the feeder supplemented the grass from Elizabeth's twenty acres of wooded pasture. Another twenty acres
of land to the north and west, between the cabin and Eagle
Lake, were too wooded for anything except privacy and her
own personal source of wild plants. Bloodroot, nettles, ferns
and more were what she used to dye her handspun yarn before
turning it into exquisitely crafted sweaters and shawls.

The small flock of six adults and three lambs was her liveli-
hood, and she pampered the sheep so that they would produce
the fine-textured, clean wool she needed to earn her living. They
were as precious to her as children, and the cabin, once merely
a refuge, was now more home than she'd ever known. Together, they were the means of her self-reliance, the independence she'd earned over the past five years.

When she left Chicago, disgraced, she'd lost everything—a
promising career, the man she loved, her mother and her reputation. It had taken years for her to heal and rebuild. With the
help of an old friend of her mother's, Claire Johnson, she'd
learned how to live in the woods. And then, a year ago last
spring, Claire had died and Elizabeth was on her own again.

It seemed that whenever she was finally able to deal with one
change in her life, fate threw her another one. She hoped that
fate had nothing to do with Drew's sudden appearance. She
wasn't ready for another change, and she had a feeling that if
she allowed him to get to her emotions, nothing would ever be
the same.

She breathed deeply, and the sharp odor of sheep dung reminded her that by most people's standards her life wasn't

much. Even so, she would fight to protect it. When Genevieve looked up at her and baa-ed softly, Elizabeth rubbed the ewe's poll. "Don't worry, sweetie," she said. "I'm smart enough to know that a sweater from your wool will keep me a lot warmer than that man's arms."

She left the barn through the wide outside doors rather than the door that connected with the cabin. The single building had been constructed in European fashion by Claire's grandfather, the barn and living quarters sharing a wall to conserve heat. Cold rain soaked into her clothing when she stepped into the paddock. Her slicker was still hanging on the backside of the cabin door where she'd left it in her haste to get away from Drew.

The sky was getting darker all the time, and she decided to check the garden for supper ingredients while it was still light enough to see. Without electricity for refrigeration, she relied on in-season vegetables. The spring house and a small root cellar under the pantry allowed her a few fresh things during other months. She walked down a muddy row, the wet black earth tugging at her boots. She bent to pick tomatoes, bell peppers and eggplant and placed them, their skins glowing jewel-like with rainwater, in the basket she'd brought from the barn.

She paused to check the string beans, hoping the rains had brought a bumper crop, but it was getting too dark to tell the beans from the vines. Finally she admitted that she was simply stalling, and that she couldn't postpone going back to the cabin any longer.

She opened the door quietly. He was in bed again. He'd lit the Aladdin lamp on the nightstand, but he appeared to be asleep. She bent down to remove her boots, then looked up to find him regarding her, his dark eyes enigmatic and his hair silver in the lamplight. She shivered, partly from the cold and wet, but mostly from reaction to the man lying in her brass bed.

"Looks like you could use a shower," he said.

"No thanks." She wrinkled her nose in distaste. "I've already had my cold shower for the day."

"A hot bath, then."

"I don't think so."

"Why not? Afraid I'll peek?"

"No," she answered, hoping he couldn't see the flush creeping up from the neckline of her sodden sweater. While her face was hot, the rest of her body felt as though it had been tossed in a snowdrift. The odor of wet wool clung to her, and water from her heavy braid trickled under her collar and down her spine. She shivered again, and the teasing expression on his face was replaced by impatience.

"Listen, from a purely selfish standpoint, I don't want you catching pneumonia. My leg's better, but not so much so that I want to end up as nurse, shepherd, chef and bottle washer. I assure you I won't be sneaking glances at your body, however delectable it might be under all that baggy denim and wool."

A flash of anger warmed Elizabeth, but only temporarily. Her impulse to argue was quashed by another icy raindrop dribbling down her spine. Refusing to take a bath because he was here would be simply admitting that he affected her. Maybe if she denied the attraction, it would go away. Resolutely she placed the basket of vegetables on the table and crossed to the alcove. He watched as she took dry clothes from the maple dresser, but she steadfastly ignored him. Or at least she did until right before she left for her bath. Then she stopped at the food of the bed, picked up the shepherd's staff that was propped there and looked him dead in the eye.

"If you so much as breathe in my direction, I will use this—" she brandished the staff threateningly "—wherever it hurts the most."

She didn't wait for his response before stalking off to get the tub.

Chapter 3

Funny, the galvanized steel tub had always seemed cramped before. But now, as Elizabeth stood looking at it, hands on her hips, it seemed huge, too big to fit into the cabin's tiny bathroom, and much too big to drag to the loft upstairs. She could hardly use it in front of the iron range as she usually did. The open bookcase only partially screened the alcove; Drew would practically have a front row seat.

The tub barely fit in the short hallway between the bathroom and the pantry, completely blocking both doors. It was just out of Drew's line of vision, and she'd have to climb over it to use the bathroom as a dressing room. It would have to do. Drew wouldn't be able to tell that the tub wasn't actually in the bathroom—unless he cheated.

Aware of Drew's interested gaze as she passed through the kitchen, she filled the tub with steaming water from the range's reservoir, adding enough tap water until it was just the right temperature. She checked one more time to be sure the tub was completely shielded from Drew's line of vision. Then she tossed in a handful of herbs, enjoying the subtle aroma as she peeled off her wet clothes and unbraided her hair. She inched herself slowly into the water, letting it swirl over her like warm satin.

She sat still for several minutes, breathing in the fragrant steam and letting the warm water work its magic on her tired limbs. Slowly the silky heat began to relax her mind as well. The idea of taking a bath while Drew lounged in her bed only a few feet away lost its strange awkwardness, and she realized that fighting against her attraction to him only pulled her more deeply under his spell. It was as futile as struggling against quicksand. After all, her body's response to him was only natural—she'd hadn't been with a man since Barry's betrayal.

Impatiently she drove that memory from her mind before it could surface completely. Instead she concentrated on the present. She was here alone with an attractive, unattached male who didn't bother to hide his interest in her. And her response to that interest was as inevitable as the seasons. Proximity intensified the attraction; their isolation multiplied it. But that didn't mean she couldn't beat it.

Strength and purpose flowed around her like the scented water, and she grew ever more certain that she could handle Drew Carter for another twelve hours or so. Besides, she remembered with an utterly feminine smile, until his leg healed she could always outrun him.

Drew stifled another groan. Whatever had possessed him to goad Elizabeth into taking a bath? He admitted that he enjoyed her blushes, enjoyed causing ripples over her surface calm. But his enjoyment had backfired, and now he was forced to lie here immobile while his imagination ran rampant.

The scent of her bathwater wafted across the room, and he realized it was the same scent that enveloped the bed linens. The fragrance surrounded him, somehow linking him to Elizabeth, and it carried him off on a carpet ride of fantasy. He closed his eyes, but couldn't close his mind to the pictures created by the occasional splashes of water. He toyed with the idea of joining her, but he had a feeling her threat to use the shepherd's staff wasn't an idle one. His leg felt much better, but he'd just as soon wait a while before risking the rest of his anatomy to any further punishment.

He joined her instead through imagination. He smoothed his hand over the cotton sheet until it lapped against his skin. Another splash from the direction of the bathroom made his breath catch in his throat because his mind's eye saw Elizabeth, her cupped hands filled with water, rinsing soap from his body as he bathed with her in the steel tub. He moved against the pillows, and he was leaning back into the softness of her breasts. Her hands trailed over his chest, and lower, beneath the lapping water. The touch was only imaginary, but his response was very real.

He clenched the sheet at his sides, his knuckles almost as white as the cotton. She wasn't even near him—he couldn't even see her, for heaven's sake—and his body was reacting as it would to a lover's touch. His loss of control baffled him, and worried him. He had to keep his thoughts clear, to be alert for the danger he knew lay ahead. He willed the sensuous images to disappear, but they returned in detail. The paleness of her skin against his, the luscious fullness of her lower lip, the feel of her long wet hair trailing in slick ropes over his bare skin.

He tried to control the vision by replacing Elizabeth with one of the undemanding women he dated whenever he was in Chicago. But for some reason he couldn't call any particular face to mind. His brow wrinkled in concentration. It had been a long time since he'd gone out with anyone—months, in fact.

Of course, during the past five months he'd been busy investigating the circumstances surrounding Paul Brewster's death. But even before that, he realized, he'd been slipping. The last book, which required a return trip to the Middle East, had taken a lot out of him. He'd been happy to get back to the States, almost glad to see the cramped apartment he kept in Chicago.

Was he burning out? Or drying up? The next thing he knew, he'd be in a retirement home looking forward to a nightly game of whist. No, he protested. He needed his work—the challenge of using his mind, of sifting through bits of information until he found the truth, even the occasional fillip of unexpected danger that made him appreciate the simple fact of being alive.

The same way a beautiful woman could make him feel. And yet the only woman he could picture right now was Elizabeth.

It was proximity, he told himself. Proximity and abstinence. Lately his mind had simply been too preoccupied to notice the demands of his body. Now he was definitely preoccupied, only this time it was his body that was taking the initiative. Images of Elizabeth in her bath continued to taunt him until he thought he would go mad. He gave up the fight, closed his eyes and let the visions take over until reality slipped a little further away.

It seemed like hours later when he heard her voice call him softly.

"You're awake." She was eyeing him with surprise, and he nearly laughed. If only she knew. He may have been dreaming, but sleep had been the farthest thing from his mind.

Her skin glowed from her bath, and her hair, pulled back loosely, was just starting to dry in tendrils around her face. Her pale lavender sweater turned her eyes to amethyst. She was unlike any woman he'd ever known—innocent, yet with an earthy, primeval beauty that descended straight from Eve.

But he couldn't afford to be as easily tempted as Adam. He needed every ounce of his concentration to find out what linked the gun that killed Paul to the shot that had missed him yesterday. And just how Elizabeth fit into the picture.

He followed her to the table and sat down, swallowing back a compliment on her appearance. He transferred his praise to the table setting, even though he guessed by Elizabeth's blush that he wasn't supposed to notice how much trouble she'd gone to on his behalf. The dinnerware was cracked and unmatched, but the old-fashioned floral designs complemented each other, and candles gave everything a soft glow. She explained that she was trying to save on kerosene, but Drew knew Elizabeth wouldn't have bothered with a linen tablecloth or a centerpiece of dried flowers if she'd been eating alone. Her expression challenged him to comment, and he felt a twinkle of amusement as he accepted the serving dish she handed across the table.

"You must have guessed that I have a weakness for ratatouille," he said after heaping his plate. The flavor of garlic and tomatoes brought back memories of one of the few times his mother had dared to cook traditional food. He couldn't remember where his father had been that day. Seeing that he'd embarrassed her again, he resorted to teasing. "Now, if only the sommelier would bring us a bottle of Chianti."

She smiled as he'd hoped, but when she stood up he thought he'd offended her. "I was only joking," he explained hastily.

"I know." She headed for the pantry. "I'll be back in a minute," she called out. When she reappeared, she was holding a vintage bottle of a California merlot. "One of my concessions to civilization. I hope it will do, because it's my last bottle. I've been hoarding it in the root cellar."

He was about to refuse when she insisted, "Please. I'll be getting some more with my winter supplies in a week or two. It will be nice not having to drink alone."

He accepted the bottle with a sense of surprise at Elizabeth's new attitude toward him. Since he'd joined her for supper she seemed less prickly, more relaxed. Maybe he'd finally be able to get some answers, he thought, then immediately felt like a louse. He wished that he could forget, just for a few hours, that he was here for a purpose. But he couldn't. And if fulfilling that purpose required charm . . . well, then he'd be a regular prince.

He opened the bottle with the corkscrew she handed him, and they made a laughing ceremony of pouring and tasting.

"To civilization," he toasted, and she barely hesitated before clinking her glass against his.

They talked while they ate, Drew never letting on that he was waiting tensely for the right moment to start asking questions. After a second glass of wine Elizabeth was smiling and relaxed, and he decided the time was right. "At the risk of sounding terribly clichéd, what's a woman like you—"

"—doing in a place like this," she finished for him. For a moment he thought she was going to refuse to say anything, but then he realized that she was choosing her words carefully before answering.

"I came here almost five years ago to visit an old friend of my mother's," she began. "My mother had just died a few weeks before."

"I'm sorry."

She acknowledged his words of sympathy with a small nod. "It was a long time ago. Claire—my mother's friend—taught me how to live in the woods. I've never left." She shrugged as if to say that's all there was to it, but Drew suspected there was far more that she wasn't saying.

"Where's Claire now?"

"She died last year."

He caught a brief glimpse of sorrow on her face before it was controlled. "It must be difficult to adjust to being alone."

"Not really." She reached for her glass and refilled it, as though signalling that particular subject was now closed.

He tried another tack. "Did Claire raise sheep?"

That brought a smile. "Yes, she did. She willed everything she owned to me—the sheep, the cabin, her truck. She was the one who taught me to spin and knit. She gave me a chance to start over."

Start over from what, Drew wanted to ask, but he knew that the question was too bold. She was hiding something. But did her secrets have anything to do with his investigation?

Elizabeth knew she hadn't imagined the sudden heightened interest in Drew's eyes. She'd already told him more than he needed to know, but the rich-tasting wine had subtly taken over where her bath left off—she was too relaxed to let wariness spoil her evening.

Drew wouldn't discover her most important secret, however. That part of her past was so well guarded that she needed no extra vigilance to keep from referring to it. She hid a wine-reckless smile. Let Drew ask what he wanted. He'd probably never met a woman like herself, and the fact that she could pique his interest was almost flattering. Or—her sense of power fled—had she been right all along? Was he here to investigate her barter arrangement with Silas Freeman's Colony?

"You made the sweater you're wearing."

Elizabeth nodded in confirmation. His gaze lingered just seconds too long on her breasts to be interested purely in the textured design, and she felt a response stir deep inside her—a response that had become all too familiar during the past twenty-four hours.

"Something like that would fetch a hundred dollars in Chicago," he said.

"Yes, I know." She smiled, even though the comment sounded more like it came from the tax man she'd thought he was than the writer he claimed to be. "Some have sold for much more than that," she admitted. "It's an honest way to make a living."

He didn't look surprised, nor did he comment on her challenging comeback. If anything, he appeared amused. "So that's how you can afford—" he paused and looked around him "—all this."

Drew barely managed to hide his puzzlement at her life-style. How could she make him understand the satisfaction she gained from living with the land, the web of interdependence between humans and nature? "My needs are simple," she explained. "Money isn't that important to my way of life. I buy only what I can't make or grow myself. Or," she added carefully, "I trade with my neighbors."

"Tell me about your neighbors, the ones who live across the road."

She was startled by his question. "No one lives there. Kurt Kresge died several months ago, and the farm's been deserted ever since."

Drew appeared to be equally startled by her answer, but he quickly recovered. "What about the rest of your neighbors? Do you think any of them would agree to an interview?"

"I doubt it. This is a very isolated area, and the people who live here chose it for that reason."

"Why? I'd like to understand what makes people stay here," he explained.

She doubted she could make him understand, this man with his city ways and his convenient life-style. Words couldn't convey the deep appreciation she had for nature's gifts, or how she reciprocated by being a steward to the land and to her animals.

"Well, there's Doc Wilson," she began. "He was a small-town surgeon until the town decided to throw him out. Too much liquor," was her blunt explanation. "Then there's Tom Wheeler. He was a hotshot corporate attorney in Chicago who got tired of the rat race. He and his wife wanted to get away from the city and bring up their kids in a more wholesome environment."

"Anyone else?" he persisted. When she hesitated, he added, "I heard there's a commune near here."

She smiled wryly. "The farm down the road supports several families. I guess you could call it a commune, but if you're looking for granola and free love, you'll be disappointed. The people who live there are very religious and very old-fashioned."

"Are they the ones who call themselves ASP?"

"Asp? As in the snake?"

"No. It's an acronym for the American Society of Patriots. Ever hear of it?"

"Never." She shook her head. She wasn't sure where Drew's questions were leading, but they were definitely making her uncomfortable. "They're just farmers. Homesteaders like I am. We try to live off the land as much as we can. It's not as adventurous as it sounds, and I'm sure it wouldn't fit in the kind of books you write." Unwilling to answer more questions, she stood and started to clear the table.

"I'm sorry I don't have dessert," she apologized abruptly.

"We'll finish the wine instead." He stood, too, filling the glasses while holding both in the palm of one large hand. It was a practiced gesture, and if she'd had stemmed goblets instead of plain glass tumblers, it would have been almost courtly. Another example of his worldliness. If he was trying to impress her, he was going about it the wrong way. She tried not to smile as he set the glass next to her on the counter.

"Let me help this time," he said.

"What about your leg?"

"I can prop myself against the counter if it gets tired."

He moved next to her and demonstrated, leaning one hip against the wooden countertop. The kitchen felt suddenly crowded, and she nearly faltered in the act of pouring hot water from the heavy kettle into the sink.

"Here, let me take that." He smiled at her.

He knew, she realized. He knew what he did to her, and he was enjoying every minute of it. Then the tense moment of sexual challenge was forgotten as he smoothly changed tack, asking if she'd seen the latest Hollywood blockbuster.

"Here?" she asked dryly. They both laughed at the ridiculousness of his question, and Elizabeth admitted that she did miss movies. "Nisswa has one theater, and I think it's still showing *Gone with the Wind,*" she complained.

Drew responded by relating the plots of several recent films, making her smile with stories about Hollywood antics and egos as she washed the dishes and put them in his side of the sink to be dried.

She noticed that he wasn't leaning against the counter for support and wondered if he felt better. If he could walk to his truck and get it started.... She was about to ask, but he left to take the sack of rice to the pantry, and by the time he came back, she'd thought of several practical reasons why she couldn't ask him to leave. And all of them were lies, except for a single *impractical* reason. She wanted him to stay.

When he returned to the kitchen he was grinning widely and hiding something behind his back. "I thought you said you didn't have dessert," he accused. At her questioning look, he produced a plastic bag of marshmallows.

She smiled at this second glimpse of Drew's sweet tooth. "I'd forgotten all about them."

"Shall we?" He gestured toward the fire.

"Why not?"

She brought their glasses of wine and a long-handled fork for the marshmallows. He'd already removed the cushions from the sofa and placed them on the floor in front of the fireplace. She held out the fork. "I'll let you do the honors."

"You're not one of those people who like their marshmallows thrust into the fire until they're burnt black on the outside, are you?" His comment, with an accompanying grimace that told her what he thought of "those people," promised to keep the conversation moving lightly along.

"Nope. I like to go slowly and wait until everything is all melted on the inside."

"So do I," he said with a quirk of one eyebrow. His teasing glance instantly brought home to her the second, sensual meaning behind her words, and she felt something like a marshmallow herself as her insides melted.

The crinkles at the corners of his eyes appeared then, but he didn't try to twist her comment further. Instead he continued their easy conversation of moments earlier, bringing up inconsequential topics such as food and music. Elizabeth confessed her weakness for elaborate Eastern Indian dishes, and Drew told her about the time he'd started a fire in his college dorm room by using a contraband hotplate. They ate the sticky marshmallows, drank the rest of the wine and laughed frequently.

When Drew admitted that he liked jazz, Elizabeth jumped up to get her battery-powered cassette player. The mellow, yearning sounds of an alto sax filled the cabin. The light from the dying fire gave Drew's skin a deep burnished glow, and silver highlights glinted in his hair. His expression was serious, considering, and Elizabeth realized all at once that the mood in the room had changed.

"Fusion jazz, fine wine, the latest in books—you really are quite civilized, you know," he told her before turning back to the forkful of marshmallows he was holding over the area of red-hot embers.

Drew's perceptiveness unsettled her. She'd never intended to cut herself off from civilization, only from the people who wanted to use her. It was easy to forget, sitting here and talking like old friends, that Drew was practically a stranger. She dismissed the possibility that he might be a tax investigator, here only to question her about Silas Freeman. Her mistrust seemed paranoic now. In retrospect, the evening's moments of awkwardness and exploration were more like the atmosphere of a first date than an interrogation. He hadn't told her much about his personal life, and she wondered if they might have even more in common.

"Tell me more about the book you're working on," she invited as he turned back to her with the forkful of marshmallows. For a moment she thought he wouldn't answer. Was it her imagination, or had his smile faltered for an instant?

She decided she was being paranoid again when he laughed and said, "I never talk about what I'm working on. It jinxes it for me. Here's your marshmallow."

He pulled it from the fork and held it up to her mouth for her to eat, and she forgot all about her question. Forgot everything except for the fact that the sticky marshmallow held inches from her lips was oozing down his index finger, and that he apparently expected her to remove it somehow.

She remembered her vow not to let him rile her, and she reached for his hand and steadied it between them. She scraped her teeth along his skin, letting the sticky sweetness dissolve in her mouth. It only took a second, but she knew she was blushing furiously when she finished and his finger was clean.

When she unwrapped her fingers from his knuckles, he didn't move his hand away. He reached out to touch her cheek, then smoothed his fingers over her hair until he was cradling her head.

"My turn," he said, so close that his breath teased her lips. "You missed some yourself." His gaze was directed toward her mouth, and his boldness made her part her lips in shock—and in anticipation. He touched his lips to hers, delicately licking the stickiness from the corner of her mouth, setting off flares of excitement wherever his tongue touched. "You are so sweet."

"It's the marshmallow," she said, wondering what had happened to her voice. Her throat felt all tight and hot, and her words were barely a whisper. She ached for him to take all of her lips, even as she reminded herself of the danger.

"No. Sweeter than marshmallow." The denial was a murmur against her lips, vibrating through to the center of her. One kiss couldn't hurt, she thought. As though guessing her thoughts, he tasted her more deeply this time, and Elizabeth's lips parted to accommodate him.

"Much sweeter." He moved his hand to her chin and used it to fit her mouth more firmly beneath his.

The whisker-roughness of his cheeks scraped against her skin, a harsh contrast to the silky sensuality of his mouth and tongue. The room started to swirl around her, and she gripped his shoulders for support. Heat from the fireplace intensified until her skin was burning and the crackling of the fire became a roaring in her ears. Still held tightly in Drew's arms, she tore her mouth from his and looked wildly over her shoulder.

"The fire . . ." she cried, then stopped, seeing the fireplace held mostly embers. The burning came from inside her, and she felt like a very small child who'd just been caught playing with matches.

"What about the fire?" Drew asked gently, his hands stroking over her back in soothing circles.

She pulled out of his arms, breathless with response to a man she barely knew and shocked to her toes by it. She couldn't blame it on heady wine or soft music or a glowing fire. The key to her response lay within her. And him. And it had to stop before it went any further. "Er, I have to stoke it now. The fire. Before I go up to bed." Her words jerked out, as uneven as her breaths.

"There's room down here for two." He nodded toward the alcove and the brass bed, his voice a husky promise.

"I don't think so." She pulled out of his arms and stood, her breathing steady once more.

He leaned back against the sofa, watching her with measured dark eyes. She turned her back on him to put more wood on the fire, telling herself as she did how glad she was that he couldn't follow her upstairs.

Gray light was beginning to creep in through the windows when Drew heard Elizabeth shut the front door behind her the next morning. He pulled back the covers and tested his leg by putting his full weight on it as he stood up. Almost as good as new, he decided with a mixture of relief and regret.

He'd spent half the night soaking it in cold water. His ankle wasn't the only reason he'd needed the cold water, nor was it the only thing keeping him awake all night. Actually, the liniment had eased his muscles yesterday afternoon. He could have followed her up to her loft with very little trouble at all. For a while he'd even been tempted, against all arguments.

But she'd been uncertain, and he hadn't wanted to force the issue. And then there was the investigation. It stood between them like a concrete wall. Was she completely uninvolved, as innocent as she appeared to be? Or was he blinded by his attraction to her?

Even innocent, she was dangerous, he'd realized. That was the final and most convincing argument that had kept him downstairs. He'd never come so close to losing control with so little provocation. A single kiss had nearly made him forget everything: his principles about mixing work with pleasure, his need for constant vigilance, even the very reason he was here in the first place.

He was certain that the man who killed Paul Brewster was one of Elizabeth's neighbors. He was just as certain that there was some connection between the rifle hanging over Elizabeth's front door and the one that killed Paul. He figured she'd be gone for at least a couple hours, just like she had been the morning before. And this time the opportunity wouldn't go to waste, he vowed as he pulled on his jeans. He waited until the sound of the sheep's bells faded in the distance before heading toward his goal.

The loft was the only part of the cabin he had yet to explore. The steps were steep—more ladder than stairs. He climbed cautiously, his leg still a bit stiff. When he pulled himself through the square opening in the ceiling he looked around curiously.

The room was small, and the slope of the roof met the floor on two sides. The corners were dark, but the skylight above him faced the east, and already pinkish dawn light was streaming into the room. He wasn't sure what he'd expected, certainly not the feminine boudoir or a crowded attic, but the small space surprised him with its austerity.

He realized the loft's sole function was as a workroom. In the far corner stood a wooden spinning wheel. Another took up the room's center, although he probably couldn't have identified the squarish contraption if it hadn't been for the wool yarn that stretched around the bobbin.

The opposite wall was covered with cupboards, the wall behind him with row upon row of odd-looking utensils that he recognized as spindles. He'd watched a Bedouin woman spin once, and these were similar to the sticklike spindle she had used. Half of one side of the ceiling was hung with bulky bundles. He walked over to examine one more closely, pulling back a corner of brown paper wrapping and discovering woolly fleece rolled into a cylinder.

On the floor in front of the cupboards was a pallet of quilts and blankets. He realized guiltily that Elizabeth had spent the past two nights sleeping here on the floor. He told himself that he would correct that tonight by offering to use the sofa. *If* he could convince her that his leg was still too sore to drive, and *if* the rain kept up. If not, he'd have to find a place to stay in town, then keep driving back here until Elizabeth told him what he needed to know about her neighbors. He glanced up toward the skylight, hoping that the gray clouds would produce several inches of rain.

After his silent prayer he methodically began opening the doors of the plain pine cupboards. Inside, shelves were lined with wool and garments in a rainbow of soft, earthy colors. He trailed his hand over a sweater the shade of autumn leaves, appreciating its softness and textured design before going on to the next cupboard where he found bobbins and reels of undyed yarn. Below that shelf were bottles labelled with chemical-sounding names such as Alum and Chrome and a row of larger glass jars. He picked one up and held it toward the skylight, realizing the jar held bits and pieces of lichen. He grimaced and put it back, taking out a second jar, filled with dried flowers. Another one held pinecones, and yet another contained tree bark.

As his gaze moved downward, a stack of heavy books on the bottom shelf caught his attention. He put the glass jar back with a clink and pulled out one of the books, opening it to a random page where he found a chart with several headings. He matched one heading, Mordant, to the chemical salts stored on the shelf above. Written underneath Dye Stuff in a spidery scrawl was the word Marigolds. Drew assumed the handwriting belonged to Claire, Elizabeth's friend and mentor. Bits of yarn were glued across the columns, a different shade for every mordant across a range of times and quantities.

The second heavy volume was similar to the first with its colorful samples and charts. It was the third and last volume, tucked away as though meant to be hidden, that caught Drew's attention. This one was Elizabeth's. Even without ever seeing her handwriting, he knew the clear, graceful lettering was hers.

This volume continued the meticulous work begun by Claire, but its loose-leaf pages contained much more than dye records. It was a treasury of Elizabeth's life at the cabin. Drew found detailed sketches of plants, pressed wildflowers and bits of prose and poetry. It was an elaborate journal, and he gave in to the temptation to read. One passage began:

The first snowfall came today and we had to postpone our trip to town. Claire, who can always tell these things, says it will melt by Friday. I look out at the white blanket covering everything, and for the first time in months I feel truly safe. Once the snow is here to say, no one will be able to follow me.

There it was again—the suggestion that something in Elizabeth's past had sent her into exile. Drew felt his heart pounding faster as he read. He searched for the date of that passage and quickly calculated. It was written almost five years ago. Who, or what, was she afraid of?

He paged backward, trying to find an earlier entry, but all he saw were sketches and notes about woodland flora. He noted the fact that she hadn't begun to record her feelings until she felt "truly safe." He paged ahead then, losing track of time as he searched for clues. He read about Elizabeth's frustration at learning how to spin, her sudden triumph when she mastered it, her awe at seeing a lamb being born. There was no word about the gun, nor even about her neighbors.

Later on, poetry began to appear along with the sketches and the prose, and Drew felt like a Peeping Tom as he read lines filled with stark emotion, written in her clear hand. He realized he was watching as a woman healed from an experience so traumatic it was never mentioned directly, only referred to obliquely as "that time," or "in my life before this one."

The last entry, a brief paragraph, was dated two days ago. He read:

I found a man injured in the low pasture this afternoon. I knew it was unwise to bring him home with me, but I couldn't do otherwise. Something about him made me want to trust him....

He got no further. A small sound from behind distracted him. He looked up from the page and saw Elizabeth. She was dressed in a fuzzy white sweater that made her look like an angel. An avenging one, he amended as he saw her expression.

"You've certainly experienced a miraculous recovery," she said. But she didn't look pleased at all over his good health. Her features were taut with controlled emotion, her breast heaving with contained rage. It was then that Drew noticed the gun at her side. "Just tell me one thing," she continued, "how long have you been able to walk on that leg?"

Drew considered lying. But after reading the journal he was certain he had nothing to fear from Elizabeth. "Since yesterday afternoon," he admitted. He waited for her reaction. At the least he expected her to deliver an indignant lecture about violating her personal domain. At the most... he braced himself for scathing anger. Instead she spoke so quietly he had to strain to hear her words.

"You could have climbed the ladder last night?"

"Yes."

"Why didn't you?"

"I didn't think you wanted me to," he said. It was only part of the truth, but the rest, he decided, would have to wait until later. She was in no mood to listen to wild stories about secret societies and an assassination.

"What kind of game are you playing with me?"

He stood and walked across the bare wooden floor until he faced her. The gun was still held loosely at her side, and he took heart from the fact that she hadn't pointed it at him. "It's not what you think," he began. "I didn't come here to—"

"Get out." She spun away from him and started down the steps.

Chapter 4

As she climbed down the monkey-ladder stairs, questions and reactions surged through Elizabeth like bubbling lava. Who was he? Why was he snooping through her things? And why had he been so solicitous of her wishes last night when he didn't hesitate to violate her privacy this morning?

She thought again about his reason for not following her up these same stairs the night before: *I didn't think you wanted me to.* The words nagged at her, reminding her just how much she *had* wanted him, how many hours she'd lain awake because of it. She didn't want to believe it was his restraint, not hers, that had kept them apart. The words were another lie, just as he'd lied about his injury in order to stay longer.

She was almost certain that he didn't know who she was. That left only one possible motive for his malingering, and she didn't like it at all—no matter how willing she'd been last night.

She heard Drew on the stairs behind her, his steps awkward, and she realized he wasn't quite as recovered as he claimed. She turned her back on the sound of his cautious progress, crossing the room to stare out the window. She wondered if poor judgment where men were concerned was an inherited trait. Her mother had picked the wrong man, too, and had ended up pregnant and alone. Like her father, and like the characters in his adventure books, Drew apparently lived for the next conquest. But at least her father had come back occasionally. She had a feeling Drew would never return. She could hear him crossing the floor to stand behind her, and she tensed.

"It's not what you think" he said again. "Let me explain."
She stepped away quickly and walked to the door, leaning the gun in the corner before taking his jacket from the hook beside her slicker. She held it toward him, but he didn't reach for it. He just looked at her, his eyes dark with a concern that infuriated her at the same time that it made her want to run crying into his arms.

Don't forget that he tried to use his injury to get into your bed, she argued against the automatic softening his expression caused. And he'd been awfully close to getting her in that bed with him. So why hadn't he? A little more persuasion on his part last night, and . . . But he didn't know that. And she had no intention of telling him how close she had come to abandoning her usual caution.

"No." Her voice quavered and nearly gave her away. "No," she said with more force. "I want you to leave." She tossed his jacket toward him. "Here."

He stood, unmoving, letting the jacket drop to the floor. The sight made her anger rise again.

"Listen," she told him, "your seduction scene didn't work." It took every ounce of strength she had, but she managed to dredge up a note of sarcasm to mask her hurt. "I'll give you credit, though. Pretending to be injured was certainly a lot more creative than 'Hey, baby, haven't I met you somewhere before?'"

"I didn't come here to seduce you, Elizabeth."

"But that's why you stayed, isn't it? Your leg was better. You could have walked into town to find a mechanic. But you didn't. You stayed. And you made me . . . made me—" She stopped when she realized what she was about to reveal. He held out a hand, but she spun away and went outside.

Drew paused for one last look around the cabin's interior, reluctant to leave it for some reason that had nothing to do with his unfinished investigation, before following Elizabeth. She was standing on the porch, leaning against a rough wooden column, her back toward him.

"Elizabeth," he began, then halted. He didn't know what to say. He certainly hadn't set out to seduce her, for heaven's sake, just to make her trust him enough to confide in him. But things had gotten out of hand. He'd be lying through his teeth if he told her that he hadn't thought about taking her to bed.

She turned to face him, and he saw that her eyes were shining with unshed tears. She was on the verge of losing control of her emotions, and he realized that he didn't want to see that happen. At least not now, not unwillingly. He had a sudden vision of her underneath him in bed, responding passionately to his lovemaking, and he banished it just as quickly. Leaving began to look like a very good idea.

He realized that this was the first time in years he'd let control over a situation slip out of his hands. Oh, he'd backed down before, but only when he wanted to, when he knew it was the best way to get what he needed. This time he backed down because it was what she wanted. A little distance would do them both good. But that didn't mean he wouldn't come back.

"What about my truck?" he reminded her. "I can hardly make it into town without a vehicle."

"Why not? It's only ten miles. Seeing as your leg is so much better, I think it would do you good to walk."

Drew matched Elizabeth's glare. He was willing to back down about leaving, but he was damned if he would back down over this. The sky was overcast, and the smell of rain was still in the air. It'd be a cold walk to town. Not that the ride was going to be much warmer, he realized when he caught a look at Elizabeth's chilly expression.

At last she looked away. "Oh, all right. But I'll have to put chains on my tires to get you out of here. Even then it won't be easy." He followed as she headed for the three-sided shed, which sheltered a pickup so old and rusty that he couldn't even tell what color it was.

"Here, let me do that." He reached for the heavy set of chains Elizabeth was preparing to maneuver under one of the pickup's rear wheels.

"I don't need your help."

"All right. Have it your way." Drew gave in easily because he didn't want her upset again. But after watching several more moments, he conceded that Elizabeth was right. She *didn't* need his help. He no longer wondered how she had gotten him from her pasture to the cabin the day she'd found him. She worked quickly and efficiently, with a strength that belied her slight build. If she were trying to prove her independence, she had succeeded, and something about her ability bothered him. He felt as though she'd slammed a door shut in his face.

He had an overwhelming urge to tell her everything. That his friend Paul Brewster had been shot down in cold blood. That the man behind bars for the crime couldn't possibly have committed it. That the trail of evidence led to this piece of woods in Wisconsin. But another look at her closed expression convinced him that now wasn't the time. In a day or two, when she'd had time to calm down, he would come back. *If* he needed to.

What he didn't need were more complications—such as one Elizabeth Johnson. The fact was, if he could carry out his investigation without Elizabeth's help, he'd be better off.

"Ready?" Elizabeth wondered if Drew even heard her. When she'd gone in the cabin to wash up a few minutes ago, he'd stayed outside in spite of the light mist that was settling over the hollow where the cabin nestled. Now he was looking across the pasture toward the woods that separated her homestead from the road.

"We can go now," she said a little louder.

This time he turned, and for a brief moment Elizabeth felt the warmth of his dark gaze, and her pulse leaped in response. Then his expression became neutral again. "Good," was all he said.

"Here." She thrust a paper bag at him before she went around to the driver's door. She already regretted the impulse that had spurred her to fix the sandwiches it contained. She tried to explain away the gesture. "You didn't eat breakfast or lunch. I thought you might be hungry."

"The condemned man's last meal?"

His sardonic words brought a flush to her cheeks. She felt a twinge of regret that was totally uncalled for. It was getting harder and harder to remind herself what a heel Drew Carter was when all she could remember was the warmth he'd brought to the cabin during the past forty-odd hours. She decided the rain was making her crazy. The drive to town was just the cure she needed.

The half-mile-long stretch to the dead-end gravel road took even longer than she expected. Twice, the pickup's wheels nearly slid off the soggy track, and both times Elizabeth sighed with relief when she was able to straighten the pickup out. The third time she wasn't so lucky. Even with the chains, the tires sunk into the mire at the side of the track.

Reluctantly she accepted Drew's help. He got out and pushed while she rocked the truck back and forth, shifting into first gear, then back into reverse. Sometime during the process, the rain began in earnest. At last she felt the tires grab purchase. She hated to stop, fearing she would end up mired again as soon as she lost momentum, but Drew had anticipated that problem. Before she could lean over to open his door, he had it open himself, jumping into the crawling pickup so that she wouldn't have to come to a halt.

Apparently his leg had recovered very nicely indeed, Elizabeth thought acidly. She was immediately contrite when she caught the quick grimace on his face as he shifted his leg into a more comfortable position. She squelched the rush of sympathy that made her want to reach out and smooth away the lines of pain underneath the dark growth of his beard.

The pickup's cab felt cramped and hot. She opened her window a crack, just enough to let some of the warm air fogging the windows escape without letting the drizzle in. The silence between them was nearly as oppressive as the humidity.

She breathed in the cool air from the window with a sense of relief that doubled at the sight of the dead-end road a few yards ahead. The gravel road would be soft, especially in the low spots, but at least it was better than the trail behind them.

"Can we stop at my truck for a minute?" Drew's question broke the silence. "It wouldn't hurt to try and start it again. There it is," he added as the rain-slick red finish came into view.

Elizabeth slowed down, wiping the steam from her window so that she could see well enough to avoid the road's soft shoulder. She jumped out of the pickup after Drew, fervently hoping that between the two of them they could restart the stalled vehicle. If so, she could be rid of him that much sooner, with less chance that she'd change her mind about being rid of him at all.

An early twilight settled around them as Drew's attempts to start the pint-size truck failed time after time. Finally, he got out and held the truck's door open for her. "Here. You try it while I look under the hood."

Their hands brushed on the doorframe as she got in, and a jolt of warmth rushed through her, strong enough to make her forget about the rain and the dark. Elizabeth looked down to hide her startled expression. She knew the touch was completely innocuous, and still she couldn't stop her pulse from jumping at the feel of his fingers against her skin. The knowledge of her weakness irritated her. She jammed the key into the ignition and turned it fiercely at Drew's signal. Again the engine strained but failed to catch.

"That's enough!" Drew yelled from the front of the truck. He slammed the hood, then went around to the passenger door and gestured for her to unlock it. He retrieved his things from behind the seat next to her, his movements jerky and his face set. When she handed him his keys this time, she made sure their fingers didn't touch.

"You can just drop me off at the nearest motel," Drew told her several minutes after they turned onto the asphalt county road that led to Nisswa.

"There isn't one," she informed him. "Not in Nisswa, anyway."

"No hotel, either?"

"The Nisswa Astoria went out of business years ago. There are a couple resorts about ten miles on the east side of town, but they're closed until hunting season opens. That's a few weeks away," she told him as she slowed down to cross the abandoned railroad tracks on the edge of town. "We could try Forest City, the county seat. It's about thirty miles from here."

"Too far. Isn't there anything closer?"

"No, Nisswa's about the biggest town around. Three hundred people at the last census. From here to the Michigan border it's mostly parkland or Indian reservation."

"How about a boarding house?"

"Sorry." Elizabeth's sense of satisfaction was tempered by unwilling concern until she reminded herself what a slick operator Drew Carter was. "I'm sure a resourceful type like yourself will come up with something," she said. She spotted a single empty space in front of the Nisswa Café's bright picture window and pulled into it smoothly.

"Maybe I will at that."

Elizabeth followed Drew's gaze to the window where she could see Janice Lindstrom, one of the café's two waitresses, waving to Drew as though he were a long lost friend. When he returned the wave with a nonchalant salute of his own, Elizabeth felt an unexpected twinge of annoyance.

Trust a man like Drew Carter to land on his feet. She had no doubt that he'd just found another woman willing to take him in. Of course it didn't matter to her, she reminded herself as he left the pickup. She was glad to be rid of him. *Wasn't she?* The truck's gears clashed as she pulled the stick into reverse. Before she could back away, Drew walked around to her window and gestured for her to roll it down.

"Yes?" she prompted, acutely aware of the curious stares through the café's front window.

He smiled and rested his arm along the top of her door. Before she could guess at his intentions, he leaned forward and kissed her. Elizabeth tried to dredge up a sense of outrage, but the feel of Drew's mouth on hers, the brush of his three-day beard against her skin, crowded out every thought. The kiss was hard and swift, and when his lips left hers, Elizabeth felt as bereft as an orphaned lamb.

"Thanks for the…hospitality. You're wrong about me," he added quietly before stepping back onto the sidewalk.

She stared at him blankly for a moment. Then thought returned, and she realized that she was parked in front of Nisswa's only restaurant, underneath one of the town's few streetlights, with half the populace looking on. She yanked her foot off the clutch and pulled away from the curb. The gears ground again when she changed roughly to first. She refused to look in her rearview mirror, knowing that Drew was standing on the sidewalk in the rain, watching her drive away.

The curiosity that greeted Drew when he entered the café was almost tangible. So much for keeping a low profile, he thought with disgust. But he had no one but himself to blame. He wasn't sure what had driven him to kiss Elizabeth in front of so many witnesses. All he knew was that for a few brief moments, his usual logic had deserted him, leaving him with a need to prove to Elizabeth—and himself—that she still reacted to him. Now, sane again, he realized that he could have just as well announced his arrival in Nisswa by hanging a sign around his neck or shouting through a bullhorn.

On the other hand, Nisswa was so small that any stranger would be noticeable no matter what he did or didn't do. He wiped his muddy shoes on the mat by the door and walked with as much dignity as possible to the counter at the front of the restaurant. He deliberately sat at the far end, where he could see most of the room's occupants and the front door.

The waitress, Janice, was there to pour him a cup of coffee before he even removed his mud-splattered jacket. Drew breathed in the aroma of the fresh brew with a grateful sigh and smiled at the tall brunette. She smiled back slowly, as though he were a lover instead of a customer who'd stopped in at the café for only ten minutes two days before. She wasted no time taking his order and introducing him to the man seated at his left.

"Drew Carter, this is Jed Smith. He's the sheriff of Potawatomi County."

"Pleased to meet you, Sheriff." Smith was in his late fifties but still handsome, his thick brown hair brushed back above a wide forehead. His smile seemed genuine enough, but his hazel eyes were cold as he regarded Drew's extended hand. His reaction was hardly surprising, Drew thought as he glanced down at himself. With mud covering his clothes and his hands dirty and greasy, he looked like the worst kind of drifter.

Smith wiped his hands on a paper napkin before responding. "Welcome to Nisswa. What brings you to town?"

Drew had expected the question, and he'd decided to embellish the story Elizabeth had accepted. It was too bad he'd already used his real name, but Carter was common enough, and since he'd borrowed the truck, anyone trying to trace him through the license application would find a dead end. "I'm looking around for some property," he explained. "Something rustic for a weekend getaway. I'm a writer, and I like my privacy."

"You'll find privacy here. As long as you steer clear of the café," the sheriff joked, the smile never reaching his eyes. "Most of the land for sale is farmland, though. Not too many that can make a living around here anymore, so now we've got to take in city folk looking for a hobby or an investment."

He smiled again, but Drew wasn't fooled. The temperature of Smith's gaze had lowered a few more degrees, if possible. The message was clear: outsiders weren't welcome.

Drew responded genially and sipped at his coffee, but all the while his mind was working. Perhaps later he would enlist Smith's help, but for now it was best to be cautious. Something told him the sheriff wouldn't be a willing ally.

"Excuse me for a minute, Mr. Carter," Jed Smith said as he glanced at his watch. "I should be checking in right about now. It's a small county, and the sheriff has to be everything from dogcatcher on up the line."

Drew watched the man cross the room to the vintage pay phone at the café's entrance. His attention was withdrawn when Janice returned with his meal.

"I see that you found Elizabeth Johnson," she said with a coyness to her voice that Drew found irritating.

He shrugged with what he hoped looked like worldly nonchalance. "My truck stalled about a mile from her cabin. I spent all day yesterday working on it, but didn't have any luck." He changed the subject smoothly. "You wouldn't happen to know the name of a good mechanic, would you?"

"Well, there's Mel Bofry." She gestured to a booth across the café where a dark, nervous-looking man in his thirties was sitting with a woman and two small children. "He's the only mechanic in Nisswa. He's good, too," she assured him.

"Thanks, I'll take your word for it." Drew smiled wryly. No motels, one mechanic and a county sheriff who didn't like outsiders. He hadn't known there were still places like this in the U.S.—rural enclaves where life went on much the way it had fifty years ago.

His gaze traveled from Bofry's booth to the café's other patrons. Women fussed over their children's plates, while men talked to each other over the backs of booths or across aisles. The men wore plaid shirts with blue jeans, and many sported billed caps that touted a seed company or a brand of motor oil. The women were also simply dressed, in jeans or slacks with basic sweaters—nothing like Elizabeth's creations.

For Drew, who was raised in a large city, the café scene was like something out of a Norman Rockwell illustration, more foreign to him than Bangkok or Peshawar or any of the other Third World cities where he'd lived and worked as a journalist. His own clothing—the chamois shirt and jeans he was wearing when Elizabeth found him—didn't differ much from those of the other men, but Drew could tell he stood out by the furtive glances directed his way. The curiosity directed toward him wasn't unfriendly, however. The atmosphere in the café was warm, almost welcoming. Apparently not everyone felt the same way about newcomers as Sheriff Smith.

And yet only a few miles away, a murderer hid.

At that thought, the meatloaf and mashed potato special suddenly tasted like sawdust. Drew set down his fork and looked around him. The killer probably didn't look any different than these men: honest, hardworking.

Drew realized that his mission wouldn't be as simple as he'd expected. He'd left Chicago hell-bent for leather, with a borrowed truck and a change of clothes, certain that all he needed to do was show up at the address he'd found in Paul's notes, knock on the door and be face-to-face with the murderer.

But it wasn't going to be easy at all. He suspected ASP and the "commune" Janice had told him about the other morning were one and the same. That meant he had a group of suspects, not just one. Janice had also told him only one person around Nisswa knew their habits. *Elizabeth Johnson*. And he'd botched everything by getting tossed out of her cabin.

Drew's thoughts came to a halt when he saw that one of the men was walking toward him. He recognized Mel Bofry, the mechanic, and stood to greet him.

"Janice told me you were looking for a mechanic, sir." The man's voice was an irritating whine that grated on Drew's nerves, but he wasn't about to reject the only mechanic in town. He clenched his teeth and smiled.

"That's right. My truck conked out on the dead-end road about ten miles from town. I'm not sure what's wrong with it, but—" Drew glanced at his watch "—if we left now, we could—"

"Excuse me, Mr. Carter," Bofry interrupted. He looked toward his wife and sons, now waiting by the door. "If I don't get home to my family . . ."

"I'll pay you extra for your trouble." Drew named a figure that was bound to convince even the most dedicated of family men. Bofry looked toward the door again, twisting his cap in his hands, then shook his head.

"How about first thing tomorrow morning?" Drew asked impatiently.

"I don't think so, Mr. Carter. I have to finish up a job for the sheriff, and naturally I don't want to keep him waiting." He laughed thinly.

"But this is an emergency," Drew stressed. "I'm sure the sheriff will understand." He looked around for Smith, but the man had already left. As his gaze swept the room he saw that people were staring at him openly now. He lowered his voice. "Listen, I don't even have a place to stay tonight."

But Bofry would not be convinced. He left, telling Drew to call him around noon the next day, and Drew sat back down at the counter in disgust. The first thing in the morning he'd call all the garages in neighboring towns. Right now, what he needed was a bed to sleep in. He thought of Elizabeth's brass bed, realizing that tonight she'd sleep between those scented sheets herself, then pushed the thought right out of his mind. He had work to do, and the sooner he remembered it, the better. Right now he needed a place to stay for a few nights. One with more amenities—and fewer complications—than Elizabeth's cabin.

He'd barely completed the thought when Janice appeared in front of him. "Hi, again." She smiled and refilled his coffee cup. "I couldn't help overhearing you tell Mel that you need a place to stay tonight." She tried to look embarrassed and failed. Her smile was just a shade too bold.

Drew knew what was coming next. He smiled in encouragement. After all, this might just be the answer to his prayers—a room and a means of forgetting Elizabeth in one fell swoop. And Janice was a good-looking woman; he'd always liked brunettes. *So why did he keep picturing Elizabeth's pale hair?*

". . . and I've got plenty of room at my place," she was saying. "You'd be more than welcome." She leaned forward to take Drew's plate, and her arm not-so-accidentally brushed his chest. Drew could smell her perfume. Sharp and spicy, it was nothing like Elizabeth's soft scent.

Before he could even think about it, Drew refused. "Thànks, Janice, but I couldn't put you out like that," he said. And once again, he pictured Elizabeth's brass bed.

Elizabeth pulled into the garage with a heavy sigh. She'd been tempted to leave the old truck at the foot of the driveway and walk the rest of the way to her cabin, but the drive was too muddy for walking and the woods too dark. Besides, she was anxious to get back to her sheep, even though it had meant another bout with the truck's ancient transmission and toilsome steering. It was hours past the time for the ewes' special feed, and the paddock gate and barn doors were open to any predators.

She still couldn't believe that she'd left this afternoon without a thought for her flock. But Drew was the kind of man to make a woman forget a lot of things. "Like common sense," she muttered into the darkness as she slammed the pickup's door.

An unfamiliar sense of loneliness jolted her at the sight of the cabin's unlit windows, and she decided to go directly to the barn. She switched on the battery lamp she kept by the doorway and smiled in relief to find every member of the flock present and accounted for, and complaining volubly at her neglect.

"All right, ladies," she said as the ewes butted against her while she distributed hay in the feeder. "And gentleman," she added, although the old Karakul wether that nipped at her jeans was hardly that. By virtue of his age and status as the only male, Whiskey Jack was the flock's leader. His gray wool was stringy and lusterless, good only for weaving into rugs, and he was nasty tempered. Like Claire's old truck, he'd outlived his use, but Elizabeth couldn't bear to part with him because he'd been one of Claire's original flock.

She went through the rest of her chores automatically before going into the dark cabin. When two large shapes loomed out of the shadows, Elizabeth nearly dropped her flashlight in shock, until she recognized Silas Freeman's slightly stooped figure. She barely spared a glance for Cal Hoskin, the tall man next to him.

"Good Lord, you startled me," she exclaimed, then quickly added before the carpenter-turned-homesteader could deliver a lecture about using God's name in vain, "What are you doing here? Has something happened to Lily?"

Silas assured her that all was well with his wife as Elizabeth led the way inside and lit a lamp with shaking fingers. His booming voice erased her initial unease. "We stopped to make sure you were all right," he told Elizabeth.

"I don't understand." She looked from one man to the other. Hoskin stood unmoving and silent, but she could feel his keen gaze on her. Slung over one shoulder of his faded army jacket was a gun—he was rarely without one. She'd been grateful for that once, the time he'd saved her and Lily, but now she felt uncomfortably like an animal in his sights.

"We found an abandoned truck about a half mile from your approach," Freeman said. "We wondered if anyone had been around here."

"Yes," Elizabeth admitted, thinking quickly. She couldn't lie to them, but she didn't want them to know about Drew. She realized she was protecting him—from what, she didn't know. Something about the way Hoskin and Freeman had waited for her in the darkness made her uneasy.

"The man was injured, and I let him stay here until he recovered. I just got back from taking him into town."

"How was he injured?" Cal Hoskin asked with his slight drawl. Until now, he'd never spoken more than three words to her. He'd always seemed content to let Silas speak for him, and Silas seemed just as content to let Hoskin back up his words. She had nothing to fear from them, Elizabeth reminded herself.

"He told me he stepped in a gopher hole and struck his head. He had a mild concussion, a bruised ankle and he pulled a muscle in his leg." She ended the list of Drew's injuries. "I figured I didn't need Doc Wilson's help," she added, trying to keep the defensive note from her voice. "I didn't want to move him until the risk of concussion was gone. Besides, it was too muddy to drive anywhere."

"You drove today," Freeman pointed out.

"Yes, well..." Elizabeth flushed, hoping the flickering lamplight masked her unease. "It wasn't easy." She didn't add that she'd been so angry at Drew that a raging blizzard, never mind a couple inches of mud, wouldn't have stopped her from taking him to town.

"What was he doing here?" Freeman asked.

"He's a writer. He's trying to get some local color for his next book."

The men seemed satisfied with her answer, and soon left. Elizabeth heard their truck start up and realized she must have driven right by the camouflage pickup without seeing it. The sound of the engine faded, but it was a long time before her heartbeat returned to normal.

Janice Lindstrom provided Drew with a bed for the night after all, but not in the small rambler she rented. No, this *bed*, for lack of a better word, was around the corner from the café in an aging bungalow that belonged to Janice's cousin, Albert Knutson. Albert was eighty, deaf and as ornery as an old pack mule. According to Janice, his last roommate left because Albert had used the man's denture glass for a spittoon, while Albert swore he kicked the man out because he cheated at cards.

Either way, Drew was Albert's newest renter. After declining his landlord's offer of a game of pinochle, Drew had said good-night. The bed in the low-ceilinged guest room upstairs was little more than a cot, with a sagging mattress and a thin pillow that didn't boast enough feathers to cover a single goose. But it wasn't the lack of comfort that kept Drew awake. He couldn't sleep because every time he shut his eyes he saw Elizabeth. He pounded the pillow, but the visions stayed.

She was too good, too sweet to be real, but, oh, how he wanted to believe she was.

Chapter 5

Elizabeth wound the ship clock for what must have been the tenth time since noon, looking past its permanently furled metal sails to her front yard, where a real wind raced through grass and swayed treetops. The constant movement mirrored a restlessness within her, and she hesitated only long enough to put on her boots and pull a denim jacket over her sweater before going outside to check on her flock.

At the top of the hill she stopped to catch her breath, the scent of wet earth and crushed grass filling her lungs. Halfway down she could see the grazing sheep, but she admitted they weren't the reason she'd come outside after all. From here she could see the dead-end road—and Drew's truck.

Her breath caught in her throat when she realized Drew was there, too, standing next to a man bent over the engine. The open hood hid the man's torso, but she recognized Mel Bofry's '57 Chevy parked down the road. Judging by Drew's impatient, hands-on-hips stance, he was already tired of waiting.

Although a good hundred yards separated them, she saw that the white gauze bandage was gone from his forehead. When he smiled at something Mel said, her memory pictured the lines at the corners of his eyes. She watched with a curiosity so strong it shocked her. She realized she wanted to know everything about him. How he got the scars that crisscrossed his abdomen, who gave him the Saint Christopher medal he always wore . . . *what he would be like in bed*.

She made a small sound of dismay, and while Drew couldn't possibly have heard her so far away, he looked up. His gaze found her immediately, but he didn't wave or smile. He simply returned her stare until the distance between them contracted and the wind rushed past her ears. The spell was broken when a strand of hair pulled free from her braid and blew across her face.

She turned away, and her gaze caught a fluff of white at the base of the hill, thirty or forty feet from where Drew was standing. The white blob wriggled, and Elizabeth saw it was one of the ewe lambs, probably Dorcas. She'd lost count of the times she'd caught the troublemaker poking her head through the fence in order to reach the grass on the other side.

She started down the hill toward Dorcas, who was now struggling and baa-ing insistently. When she dropped to her knees beside the ewe lamb she realized that Drew had walked through the ditch to join her. He stood on the other side of the fence, and a quick look told her he was dressed in jeans and a dark plaid shirt, and that his jaw was clean shaven and smooth. He didn't look nearly as disreputable as he had the day before, but he was every inch as dangerous to her equilibrium.

"Need some help?" he asked.

"I think I can manage." She didn't look up as she gently pulled the ewe lamb's front legs back through the fence wire. As soon as Dorcas was free, Elizabeth scrambled to her feet and brushed the clinging grass from her jeans. Dorcas was already poking around farther along the fence, where a particularly lush clump of green beckoned.

Drew chuckled, and the sound rippled through her. "Looks like she doesn't want to leave just yet," he said.

"She'll follow me when I go back up the hill," Elizabeth told him, then wondered why she wasn't already on her way. "That ditch you just walked through is loaded with poison ivy," she pointed out.

Drew glanced over his shoulder at the glossy red triplets of leaves standing out against the long grass between the fence and the dirt road.

"If you're allergic to it, even the sap caught on your pants will make you break out if it touches your skin," Elizabeth warned, flushing when she caught Mel Bofry's interested gaze.

"I'll be careful next time I take off my jeans," Drew said with a smile that brought the lines to the corners of his eyes. "I hate having an itch I can't scratch."

Elizabeth could feel her flush growing deeper, so deep that the brisk wind couldn't cool it. "Just think of it as a souvenir of your visit," she told him, keeping her voice as even as possible. She turned to leave, clapping her hand to signal Dorcas to follow.

"Oh, I will," Drew's voice rumbled behind her. "When I get around to leaving."

His words stopped her in her tracks. She turned, telling herself it was mere curiosity that made her ask. "You mean you're staying?"

"Yep. I found a place in Nisswa after all. We'll probably run into each other during the next couple of days, so it'd be nice to be friends. Think you could manage that?"

"I doubt it." But she couldn't help smiling at his persistent charm. Darn it, but he was trouble.

"I'd still like to interview you and your neighbors," he called after her as she started back up the hill. She ignored him, calling for Dorcas, but the ewe lamb stayed behind to gaze at Drew.

"Stupid female," Elizabeth muttered as Drew reached through the wires of the fence to rub the adoring creature on the head. She wasn't at all certain that her words were meant for the sheep.

Drew called out his thanks as the mechanic turned the '57 Chevy around and headed for town. The repairs had taken the better part of the day. Bofry went to Nisswa twice for tools and parts, and both times Drew had stayed behind in the truck, ostensibly to read the notes that filled his briefcase.

He didn't get much reading done. His attention kept straying to the hilltop where he'd spotted Elizabeth earlier. Yeah, he had an itch all right, he thought as he got into the truck and slammed the door.

He started back for Nisswa but turned around before he ever got to the blacktop county road. But not to go to Elizabeth's.

So far, all she'd done was distract him. Now it was time to get on with what he'd come here for. He was going to the Colony.

He'd picked up the town's term for the group he knew as ASP while playing pinochle with Albert and his friends. They'd told Drew everything they knew about Freeman and his followers. Unfortunately, that wasn't much, and Drew was able to conclude only one thing. Silas Freeman and his Colony had a passion for secrecy that made Elizabeth's pale by comparison. He knew they were hiding something. Something like murder.

Drew switched off the headlights, even though the twilight was fast changing to darkness. Minutes later, he parked down the road from the steel-barred gate that marked the Colony's driveway. On either side of the gate, a six-feet-high steel mesh fence was topped by several strands of barbed wire. Even in the darkness he could tell its design wasn't to keep animals in. It was to keep people out.

His footsteps sounded overly loud on the gravel road's surface, so he kept to the grassy ditch, ignoring the dampness that soaked his jeans. He thought of Elizabeth's warning about poison ivy and smiled briefly before shifting his attention back to the fence. Fog drifted around, settling into the low spots, and the crickets and frogs went eerily silent as he passed. He stopped twenty feet from the gate, crouching behind a broad-girthed oak, instinct telling him he should go no farther.

Then he heard it. It was a sound distinct from nature's night music—a hissing, crackling noise that increased in volume as it moved closer.

Drew strained to see in the darkness, every sense alert. A tiny orange light arced through the air. He knew what it was even before the acrid hint of cigarette smoke reached him. *The gate was guarded.*

The crackling noise ended abruptly as the guard spoke, and Drew realized he was using a two-way radio. Drew followed the burning cigarette's progress, closer and closer to his hiding place, until the guard's words came through clearly.

"I tell you, there ain't nuthin' here, man." Radio static disguised the reply, but the guard's response was too clear. "Yeah, sure, I'll check."

He rattled the gate, and Drew stopped breathing for a moment, waiting to be discovered. The muscles in his legs tensed as he prepared to slip to another hiding place . . . or to run. But the guard seemed satisfied that the gate was still secure, and Drew slowly exhaled with relief, watching the cigarette's glow fade as the guard walked away. Drew stayed behind the oak several minutes longer before creeping back to his truck to drive away.

He didn't breathe normally again until he was well past the Colony. He thought of Elizabeth, and a chill settled around his gut. He knew she wasn't involved in the Colony's dark political machinations, but she held their trust, and that made her vulnerable. He'd already placed her in danger. Small towns were no place to keep secrets, and half of Nisswa had seen them together outside the café the night before.

"Damn it!"

He pounded a fist against the steering wheel. Without her, he had no chance of getting beyond that gate. He had to find evidence that Paul's suspicions were truth, that these bastards did more than just line politician's pockets. He had to prove that they were men who had killed and would kill again for their beliefs. Until he did, the Chicago police and the FBI would continue to dismiss his allegations.

He reached down to switch on his headlights. The beams didn't penetrate very far in the fog, but he recognized the bushy sumacs that concealed the end of Elizabeth's driveway. The thought that he might be putting her in further danger made him hesitate, but only for a moment. He turned in.

This time, he told himself, he wouldn't forget why he was here.

When she heard a vehicle bumping up the track to her cabin, Elizabeth knew instantly that Drew had come.

She nervously pulled down the sleeves of her indigo and lavender sweater and fussed with the yarn tie that held back her hair before going to answer the door. Drew stood on her porch, looking unsure of his welcome.

"Hi," she said simply.

He leaned against the doorjamb. "Something smells good."

"Chili." Her gaze traveled over his lean form. Faded jeans hugged his lean hips and muscled thighs, and underneath his open jacket was the dark blue-and-black plaid flannel shirt she'd noticed earlier. He'd obviously been shopping at Nisswa's farm supply store. It was the sort of thing most of the

men around here wore, but on Drew it looked anything but ordinary. Her intentions wavered. "Would you like some?"

He straightened. "Sure. I'd love some." His voice rang with
a false heartiness, and she guessed that he was as uncomfortable as she was. They'd known each other for only four days,
yet they'd already shared an argument and an embrace. It gave
their relationship a curious intimacy, confirmed when Drew
slipped off his boots and set them on the mat by the door.

She went to the kitchen while he hung up his jacket. She
could feel his dark eyes watching her as she filled the bowls and
set them on the tray-cum-breadboard along with two glasses of
water. She was almost relieved to be out of the heady merlot.

"Here, let me get that." Drew rose from his chair to take the
tray from her. After he complimented her on the chili and she
thanked him politely, they ate in awkward silence for several
minutes. Finally he set down his spoon.

"I think we need to clear the air about what happened yesterday," he said.

"Don't. Please, I don't want to talk about it." She tried to
think of the words to explain, but simply shook her head.
"Let's just forget it, okay?"

Drew's gaze held hers for a long time before he turned his
attention back to his food. The awkward silence returned, and
the spicy chili tasted like chalk dust on Elizabeth's tongue.

"I think we're both finished eating," Drew said when she put
down her spoon. He stood and started to gather up the dishes.
"Do you want any more water?"

"No, thank you." As she spoke, Elizabeth realized they were
acting like strangers, polite and distant, as though everything
between them—the warmth, the kisses, even the argument—
had been erased. The omission echoed deep inside her.

She left the table and picked up the towel on the counter, remembering that the last time they'd stood here together, Drew
had made her laugh and smile.

"You're almost out of dish soap," he announced, inter-
rupting her thoughts. "Do you often go into town for supplies?"

Elizabeth welcomed the awkward attempt at making conversation. Anything was better than silence. "Two or three
times a month in the summer. In the winter, once a month,
maybe less. It depends on the weather."

"It must get pretty lonely out here. What about your neighbors—the Colony. Do you socialize with them?"

Her brow wrinkled at the question. Elizabeth was sure she hadn't mentioned the Colony by name, but he knew it now. Yesterday he'd been looking through her things, and before that he'd asked about her business and her neighbors. She set down the plate she'd just finished drying and turned to him.

"Are you an investigator?" she demanded.

"What?" Drew's mouth went dry at Elizabeth's question. Had she guessed what he was doing here?

"If you are," she went on, "you're talking to the wrong person. I've paid my taxes. And what other people do is none of my business."

Taxes? He frowned in confusion. And then it hit him. Elizabeth thought he was a tax collector. Drew nearly laughed in relief, until he realized that she'd inadvertently revealed an important clue. Was the nonprofit organization ASP a cover for tax evasion? Several supremacist groups like the Colony declared the federal government powerless to collect taxes; he didn't know why he hadn't thought of the angle himself.

She spoke before he could question her. "If you've lied to me—again—" she stressed "—I'd like to know about it right now. Are you a writer or not?"

"I'm a writer." It was the truth, Drew told himself, but he felt a stab of guilt anyway because he knew Elizabeth believed he wrote macho adventure novels. Someday he'd tell her the rest, but for now, the less she knew, the better.

"Good." She flashed him a challenging smile that played havoc with his heartbeat. "Then you can tell me the plot of your latest book while we have tea."

He watched her fill the teakettle from the bottle of spring water in the corner, wondering why one lie—or in this case, mistruth—always led to another. In the past, he'd been a master at spinning cover-ups and excuses, but the thought of lying to Elizabeth was distasteful.

"I don't like to talk about myself," he said finally.

"Neither do I." She slammed the teakettle onto a stove lid. "So what shall we talk about?"

She leaned back against the counter, her stance every bit as challenging as her smile. He swallowed a surprised laugh of admiration. Because she'd backed away from previous confrontations by escaping to the barn or her loft—or by driving into town—he hadn't realized how stubborn she could be.

She crossed her arms beneath the swell of her breasts and tilted her head back to meet his gaze, her golden hair slipping from the yarn tie at the nape of her neck. She wore a dark blue sweater with a lavender yoke, and the combination of colors made her eyes look like crushed violets. He wanted nothing more than to pull her into his arms and kiss her until she told him anything he asked. But if he did that, he knew that the last questions on his mind would be the very ones he'd come here to ask.

"Here." His voice was gruffer than usual as he handed her two mugs for the tea. "Since we can't talk about ourselves, you can tell me what's so bad about coffee that you won't drink it. Or is that too personal?"

She'd won this round, he conceded as she began to lecture him about the evil effects of caffeine on the human body. But he'd been a journalist for over a decade, and he knew how to ask questions. With a little more caution and a judicious amount of charm—since that was a dangerous element—he'd find out what he needed to know.

"You didn't really want to know about coffee, did you?" Elizabeth asked as she set her mug of tea on the floor next to her. She leaned back against the sofa and watched Drew add another log to the fireplace before he sat down beside her on the rug. She could tell he hadn't paid any attention to her diatribe on caffeine.

"No, I want to know about you."

She looked away, and her gaze landed on the workbasket sitting next to the sofa. It was piled with hanks of yarns in soft colors, sprouting with knitting needles, and the folds of the sweater she was currently working on spilled out the sides. She didn't want to talk about herself, but she could talk about her work.

She pulled the basket closer and took out a bobbin full of undyed yarn. "This is what handspun yarn looks like before it's dyed." She offered the tightly wound mass of yarn to Drew. "After I wind it into a loose hank, I'll dye it."

"Can I help you wind it?"

Surprised by his interest, she agreed. "Hold your hands about this far apart." She demonstrated. As soon as Drew complied, she started to unwind the yarn from the bobbin onto his outstretched hands, deciding not to tell him that she had a niddy noddy in the loft that wound a perfect yard-long hank of yarn. The task was relaxing, and she dared a personal question. "Is Drew short for Andrew?"

"Yep. Andrew Jackson Carter, to be exact. My older brothers are named Thomas Jefferson and James Madison. Dad was born in Greece, but he wanted his kids to be all-American."

There was an edge to his voice that Elizabeth didn't quite understand, so she asked carefully, "Do you have any sisters?"

"Three. Lucky for them, Ma picked their names." He grinned. "Diane, Mary and Juliet. At eighteen, she's the baby by more than twenty years."

"Six children." She tried to keep any wistfulness from creeping into her voice, but her hands slowed as she wound the yarn around Drew's palms. It would have been nice to have a big sister to confide in, someone to provide a counterpoint to her mother's overly suspicious views when it came to men.

"How about you? Any brothers and sisters?"

Drew's question startled her, even though she should have expected it. "No," she answered, feigning concentration on the yarn flowing between their fingers. People generally reacted with shock or pity to her illegitimacy, and she didn't want either from him. She quickly changed the subject. "It must have been fun living with so many people."

"Not always." The curt answer piqued her curiosity. "Anyway—" he looked pointedly around the rustic cabin "—I thought you preferred solitude."

"Not always." She repeated his own answer with a catch in her voice. This time she busied herself by securing the last yard or so of yarn, wrapping it around and through the middle of the hank stretched between Drew's fingers. "I'll take that now." She extended her palms to slip the yarn from his hands.

She looked up then, and caught her breath. Drew was watching her intently, his eyes almost black. Her fingers curled reflexively against his palms but before she could pull her hands away, he caught them with his own. The yarn fell unnoticed onto the floor.

"Elizabeth," he whispered. He moved his hands to frame her face. "Heaven knows I wasn't looking for a complication like you."

She tried to speak, but he stroked his thumbs over her throat and her words were trapped somewhere within. His touch was light, hesitant even, but it shafted through her like a beam of warm sunlight.

She knew he was giving her a chance to object or withdraw. He was so close that she could feel his breath on her face. If she leaned forward a little more, she would be able to feel the heat of his skin, she thought. Her mouth went dry and she swallowed, afraid to close the distance between them, but unable to pull away. Too close and she would melt like Icarus's wings, too far and she would wither like a plant without the sun.

Drew made the decision for both of them. He removed his hands from her face, leaving her bereft for a moment, until he pulled her onto his lap.

"We shouldn't do this," he said, his voice rough.

"I know." But Elizabeth had no intention of stopping him. She was wrapped in his strength, surrounded by his warmth, and it felt like coming home. Drew kissed her lightly on her throat, and she wanted more. He stroked his hands across her back, and she arched into his chest. He captured her lips, and she forgot everything except the feel of his mouth on hers.

He seemed to know exactly how to kiss her, when to be gentle and when to be bold. His lips teased hers unbearably, and when he pulled her lower lip into his mouth and sucked on it lightly, she made a sound of pleasure and tried to pull him even closer. Elizabeth wanted to fuse herself to him, and with the heat between them, it almost seemed possible.

Her breasts pressed against his chest, and heat radiated through her. He lifted the back of her sweater and slid his hand over her skin with a slow, sultry motion that made her senses sizzle.

She tugged at his shirt, reaching for the taut skin of his back. He groaned when her hands touched him. She smiled against his lips and smoothed her hand around his lower rib cage, pausing to run her fingers over the pattern of scars. She heard him suck in his breath, and felt his abdomen contract beneath her fingertips.

Without moving his lips from hers, he fell back against the rug so that she was lying fully on top of him. Their bodies touched from lips to entwined legs. It was heaven until, somehow, they tipped over the basket of yarn. Knitting needles skittered over the floor like a game of pick-up sticks.

The noise shattered the mood. Elizabeth moved away to lean back against the sofa and close her eyes. She realized with shock that they had been wrestling on the floor like a pair of animals. Her eyes snapped open, but she carefully avoided looking at Drew. Instead she began to gather up the mess on the floor, wishing fervently that her scattered thoughts and emotions could be dealt with as simply.

She felt Drew's gaze on her as she pulled at a strand of yarn that led under the challis sofa. She reached, expecting the touch of soft wool. Instead her hand closed over a solid rectangular object that felt like . . . a book?

Drew inhaled raggedly, already regretting his lack of control. Thank God Elizabeth had withdrawn before he'd broken his vow not to become personally involved. He'd forgotten everything except the feel of her hands on his skin.

His thoughts came to an abrupt halt as she saw her reach under the sofa. With growing dread, he watched her shamed expression change to puzzlement as she pulled out the books from underneath. When he'd hidden them the day before yesterday, he'd intended to go back later and move them to a safer spot. He'd never had that chance, and now it was too late.

"What are these doing—" Elizabeth stopped, staring at the book in her hand as though it were a deadly snake. As he watched, she turned it over to the photograph on the cover. It was an old picture—his hair was darker then and he'd worn a full beard, but he saw the recognition in her eyes.

The books had been best-sellers two and four years ago. One was an account of the CIA's attempt to cover up illegal arms shipments to a Third World country. The other told about political machinations within the U.S. automobile industry. They were a far cry from fiction.

"A reporter." She sounded shell-shocked. "This says you're a reporter."

"Used to be," he corrected. He realized he'd have to tell her the truth. "I'm an investigative author."

"It doesn't matter what you call yourself. The end result will be the same." She looked up accusingly. "And I thought I was safe here."

Her words rocked him. He opened his mouth to demand an explanation, but she kept talking, and he had to listen.

"What I can't understand is why anyone would be interested in something that happened over five years ago." She squeezed her eyes shut for a moment, missing the quizzical look that passed over Drew's face.

"What are you talking about?" He wanted to ask more, to tell her she was wrong, but she went on as though she hadn't heard him.

"I thought A. J. Carter wrote about major events—truth, justice and the American way," she mocked. "Who even cares about a five-year-old Chicago political race?"

He froze. Five years ago Elizabeth had come here . . . to escape? Was this her secret? The reason why she didn't like personal questions, why she guarded her privacy? He knew the past she alluded to had nothing to do with his investigation, knew he should tell her that right now, but an awful curiosity kept him silent.

"All those questions, your snooping. I should have guessed." She tossed the books on the floor. The disappointment in her eyes tore at him. "Please leave. And this time, don't come back." She stood, grabbing up the mugs of cold tea and taking them into the kitchen. Drew was right behind her.

"Damn it, will you listen to me? That's not the reason I'm here."

She spun and faced him. "I believe you said something similar yesterday when I accused you of trying to seduce me. You lied then, too. What a great story that would have made. I can almost see the headlines: *Gallagher's Whore Screws Reporter*."

"Stop it." Drew reached out and took her by the arm, using his other hand to force her chin up until she was looking into his eyes. "I didn't lie to you. I never told you what kind of books I wrote. You assumed that I was a novelist, just like you assumed I was still injured when I didn't follow you to the loft that night." Elizabeth flushed and tried to shake off his hold, but he wouldn't let her go until he'd finished with what he had to say.

"I'm not interested in your past." Her eyes mocked him, and he quickly corrected himself. "All right. I *am*, but not in the way you think. My interest has nothing to do with my investigation."

"So you admit that you *are* here to investigate a story."

"Yes, but not—" He got no further. With the speed of a cornered deer Elizabeth had eluded his grip.

She made it to the door where the rifle hung. She took it down and leveled it at him. "I've heard enough lies. Get out."

Drew walked toward her, his frustration so great that he didn't care about the gun. As he advanced, she retreated, until her back was pressed against the wooden door. Her eyes were shining with tears.

"Never point a gun at a man unless you're going to use it," Drew said. He ignored the way she cringed away from him as he pulled his jacket from behind her. He didn't bother to put it on before walking out.

The firm click of the door closing behind Drew released Elizabeth from her tight control. She dropped the gun to the floor—it wasn't loaded and never had been—and covered her face with her hands.

She couldn't believe she'd actually pointed a gun at another human being. That was the horror that claimed her for several moments, until the others forced themselves into her mind one by one. Drew had lied to her after all. He was a reporter. *He was here to resurrect the past.*

Oh, he'd been about to deny it, but she wasn't about to fall for yet another lie. Why else would he leave Chicago for Nisswa, Wisconsin? He wasn't a sportsman or tax man or a novelist. He was a muckraker, a contemporary Upton Sinclair. And he wanted to write about Chicago.

Even if he uncovered the truth—that she'd been a mere pawn sacrificed in order to destroy a man's political career—the end result would be the same. Her life was about to be destroyed for the second time.

She wrapped her arms around herself to ease the ache. She'd survived before, and she would again. She looked around the cabin that was her haven. During the past five years she'd slowly come back to life through the rhythms of the seasons and the solace of hard work. That way of life was now the very essence of her. And that was why she couldn't run this time.

The worst part of it all was that Drew had unearthed feelings that she couldn't just rebury. Even now her lips still felt swollen and tender, and her breasts ached. She told herself that it was just passion, her body's way of telling her to throw off the wintry cloak of abstinence and be warmed by a man's touch. It simply wasn't possible to fall in love with a man in only a few days, a man she barely knew. *A man who had lied to her.* She didn't love Drew; she *wanted* him, and there was a difference.

But could mere wanting hurt so much?

Chapter 6

Drew drove too fast for the rutted gravel road and foggy conditions, but right now he needed to put as much distance as possible between himself and the cabin in the woods. Wildly contradictory images flashed across his mind like a strobe. Elizabeth serenely knitting in the rocking chair. Elizabeth shyly nibbling marshmallow from his finger. Elizabeth telling him to leave, her lavender eyes shining with angry tears. But the image that kept coming back to him was the one of his own making, one that his imagination had supplied: Elizabeth, wet and lovely, sharing her bath with him.

Who was she? What happened five years ago? And why did he care so much?

A dark shape loomed out of the fog unexpectedly, and Drew slammed on the brakes. He came to a skidding stop on the gravel just in time to see a five-point buck trot into the fog at the side of the road. The near accident reminded him that danger came when a man's mind was somewhere else.

His heart beating like a tom-tom, Drew rested his head on the steering wheel until the dizzying circle of images slowed. He straightened and opened his window, letting the cool air sweep the rest of the confusion away.

When logic returned, he knew that the most important thing was to find out whether or not the Colony could be indicted for tax fraud. But that task had taken a back seat to Elizabeth's revelations about herself. She'd been involved in Chicago politics, and now she was hiding out next to a group who were backing one of Chicago's most promising politicians. Was there a connection? Or was he just making leaps of logic so that he had an excuse to look into Elizabeth's past?

Unable to find the answer, he rolled up the window and started back to town. He felt a vague sense of guilt for what he was about to do.

After parking the truck underneath the large elm in Albert's yard and going into the house, Drew picked up the old-fashioned princess phone in the front hall and impatiently dialed the Chicago number he'd already dialed once that day. The lack of privacy didn't bother him—Albert was as deaf as a post.

"Hullo?" The corner of Drew's mouth quirked at the sleep-dulled voice of Jim Levitz. Jim was a staff reporter for the *Banner*, the Chicago daily where Paul Brewster had worked.

"Jim, it's Drew. I need another favor."

After a short pause a groan filtered across the line. "Don't you know what time it is, for crying out loud? What's up that couldn't wait until tomorrow?"

"I think I know who killed Paul Brewster."

Drew listened to the shocked silence on the other end of the line, knowing what Jim must be feeling. The young journalist had idolized Paul, who'd taken Jim under his wing and shown him the ropes, the way he'd shown another young reporter nearly twenty years earlier. Then, Paul Brewster had been an army press officer stationed in Saigon, Drew a reporter so green that he'd wondered why the newsweekly had sent him to Southeast Asia.

Drew's journey back to the past was interrupted by Jim's wide-awake voice. "Who? This guy your roommate told you about, Silas Freeman?"

"Him or one of his men. Their farm is guarded like a fortress. I can't get in, but I found out there's a possibility that Freeman hasn't been paying his taxes. I want you to follow up on that."

"Jeez, Drew, I'm not a magician."

"What do you mean?"

"Silas Freeman is a ghost. I ran the name through a half-dozen different data bases today and came up with zip."

"Damn." Drew sighed. "Try again. Check court records, police files, everything."

"All right. I'll get on it first thing in the morning."

"What's wrong with right now?"

"For one thing, everyone is sleeping, including me—but I don't suppose that would matter to you. I can't start on this until business hours."

"Then there's something else you can do. I want you to find out all you can about a woman named Elizabeth Johnson. She'll be helping me with the investigation," Drew added optimistically.

"Sure." Jim's exasperation was clear even over the phone lines. "Do you know how many Johnsons are in the Midwest?"

"For this one you won't have to go any farther than the fourth floor."

"The morgue?"

Sensing Jim's confusion at being directed to the *Banner*'s file library, Drew explained. "She was involved in some kind of political scandal in Chicago five years ago. See what you can dig up on a guy named Gallagher."

"*Gallagher*. Wasn't he the alderman who had to drop out of his race for Congress?"

"I don't know. I was in the Middle East then. What happened?"

"I can't remember the details. This Elizabeth, is she a friend?"

The kid was quicker than he thought. Drew ignored the question. "How soon can you get this to me?"

"I'll phone you sometime tomorrow."

"No, don't call. Send me a hard copy, but don't send it to me here. An overnight letter at the Nisswa post office would be the talk of the town. I'll make other arrangements and call you back in the morning."

After hanging up, Drew climbed the stairs to his room and stripped off his shirt, careful not to bump his head on the bungalow's low ceiling. He stretched out on top of the sagging bed, knowing he wouldn't be able to sleep. He had too much to think about. He was afraid that if he closed his eyes, everything would shift again. Nothing was as it appeared here in little Nisswa, Wisconsin. Not even Elizabeth Johnson.

Drew parked the truck across the street from the courthouse-post office complex, where he'd rented a P.O. box. For two days he'd managed to stay away from Elizabeth's while he waited anxiously for information from Jim. During their last phone call all Jim said was, "You're not going to like it."

At the warning, a curl of dread had started in Drew's stomach and knotted tighter with each hour that passed. And the hours had passed slowly, even though he'd used them wisely, looking for Silas Freeman's name among the Potawatomi county records.

He walked up the broad steps to the imposing Richardsonian government buildings constructed decades ago, during the area's lumber boom. He accepted the stiff mailing envelope the clerk handed him and headed slowly toward the exit, knowing that his interest in Elizabeth's past had nothing to do with his investigation. It was a compulsion. He *needed* to know what had shaped her life, and that scared the hell out of him.

He paused in front of the post office's ornate exit. Between the massive glass and steel doors was a large trash can. His hand, clutching the envelope, hovered over the trash can as he debated with himself. He still hadn't made up his mind when the doors rattled ineffectually.

He looked up to see a young woman struggling to open the heavy doors as she balanced a pink-wrapped baby. He swept open the door for the encumbered woman, who smiled and thanked him. The next thing he knew, Drew found himself outside, the envelope still in his hand.

"Oh, what the hell," he thought. Elizabeth already had two reasons to detest him. Might as well make it three...

Elizabeth was outside with her sheep the next morning when Drew's truck pulled into the clearing. She could hear him walk up the porch steps on the other side of the cabin. She considered ignoring his knock, then decided that a closed door probably wouldn't stop him, especially once he realized the sheep were still here. Which would be any minute, she realized as Dorcas complained raucously about being put down on her rump.

She dug out the dried mud from Dorcas's hooves with a knife, then trimmed the pads, trying to shut out the loud knocking she could hear from the other side of the building. She knew mere inconvenience wouldn't stop Drew in pursuit of a story. She'd stayed up late last night to reread both of his books, and a relentless pursuit of the truth showed in every paragraph.

The insistent knocking ceased.

"There you go, love," Elizabeth soothed as she sprayed Dorcas's hooves with disinfectant and helped her up. The calm note of her voice belied her inner turmoil. She wiped her hands on the front of her jeans and returned the knife and disinfectant to the equipment closet inside the barn. When she could delay no longer she set off toward the front of the building, only to find Drew already on his way around to the paddock.

He was dressed in jeans and another new flannel shirt, this one a gray-and-black plaid that flattered his dark complexion and the silver and black mix of his hair. He looked too darned good for her peace of mind. He stopped on the other side of the fence and his gaze traveled over her from head to foot, as though he'd never seen her before. She felt uncomfortable in her baggy gray sweatshirt and soiled jeans. She'd bet the women he dated wore kidskin pumps, not mud-caked boots. And the mud wasn't the worst of it.

Her voice revealed her vexation. "You don't know when to give up, do you?" She climbed over the wooden fence and headed for the front door.

"I need to talk to you," he said, following behind her.

Refusal was on the tip of Elizabeth's tongue, but something told her that would only lead to another argument. She halted at the door, shrugging her shoulders in resignation. She couldn't battle his persistence, nor could she stop the sarcasm that edged her voice as she invited, "Won't you come in?"

She noticed that Drew didn't wait for a similar invitation to sit down. He pulled out a chair at the dining room table while she removed her boots and stood awkwardly in the doorway, delaying the inevitable.

"Tea?" she asked with false brightness.

Drew answered by pulling out the chair next to him. Elizabeth looked at the determination in his eyes and knew he wouldn't put up with any more delaying. In one last act of defiance, she ignored the chair Drew proffered and she sat down across the table.

"Do you know who this man is?" he asked without preamble, shoving a black-and-white photograph toward her.

Elizabeth picked it up. She recognized a publicity "head shot" when she saw one. The man was in his thirties, wearing a conservative suit and tie and a wide white smile. Very photogenic, very political. She knew the type—but she didn't know him.

"No, I don't." When she dropped the photograph onto the center of the table, Drew sighed and tiredly rubbed a hand across his face. "Disappointed?" she asked, sarcasm edging her voice again. "Were you planning to shock the nation with a whole new list of allegations about the politician's wh—"

"Stop." Drew half rose from his seat to reach across the table and grip her arm. The piercing blackness of his eyes told her that she had crossed the line. They faced each other like duelists.

"Listen to me," he said. His gaze pinned her as effectively as his strong fingers around her forearm. "This isn't about you. I don't give a damn if you seduced the entire Chicago city council, and neither does anyone else. I don't write smut." He released her arm, and his fists clenched on the tabletop. "I didn't know about Gallagher, not even when you mentioned his name the other night. And I wasn't planning on bringing it up today."

Elizabeth felt as though a pound of wool had been tamped down her throat. She struggled to keep her voice even. "This has nothing to do with Patrick Gallagher?" He shook his head. "Then what are you doing here?"

"I need your help." As she hesitated, he added, "I want you to know first that by helping me, you might be placing yourself in danger."

Curiosity urged her on, even as she wondered if she should help a man who believed the worst about her. "What do you want me to do?"

"Do you remember this man?" Drew asked, showing her a yellowed square of newspaper.

She immediately recognized the *Banner* columnist whose daily essays had turned him into a Chicago folk hero. His plain speaking and humorous style charmed everyone, except for the politicians he managed to offend with his witty satire. He was a pillar of the black community, and the pride of the city. "Yes. Paul Brewster is a columnist for the daily—"

"*Was*," Drew interrupted. "He was killed five months ago."

"I hadn't heard." Elizabeth sensed something more behind Drew's brief words. She asked carefully, "Did you know him?"

"Yes. We'd been friends for a long time."

"I'm sorry." She was. Paul Brewster had been one of the very few local journalists who hadn't joined the chorus condemning her. His stance had meant a great deal to her at the time, because she'd always admired the man and his work.

"He was shot outside an all-night café where he liked to stop after leaving the office. Everyone knew about the place. He made it a tourist attraction with his columns about the owners."

Elizabeth nodded. She remembered it well, a family-run coffee shop-cum-pub just off Dearborn.

"The police found the murder weapon in the possession of a transient named William Danzig, who was sleeping off a drunk in a nearby storefront. The case was cut-and-dried. The arraignment, the trial—everything was over within a few weeks. When Danzig went to prison everyone was satisfied."

"Except you," she guessed easily.

Drew nodded and continued, his voice matter-of-fact. "The police believed the shooting was random. Danzig was on Antabuse to control his alcoholism, but that night he had a pint of Scotch in his pocket. The police said the alcohol, combined with the drug, triggered a violent episode. According to them, Paul was simply in the wrong place at the wrong time."

She hadn't heard a flicker of emotion in Drew's voice as he told the story, but she noticed the way his hand gripped the edge of the table. "You don't believe that, do you?"

"No."

"What could this possibly have to do with me?"

"I'll get to that. First I want you to know the background of the case, so you'll understand how important—and dangerous—this investigation is."

Elizabeth nodded. "Go on."

"Before he died, Paul wrote a series of columns about the man in the first picture I showed you. His name is Phillip Prince, and he's running for Congress. Until five years ago, he was an avowed racist. He claims to have mended his ways, but

Paul believed that he still has ties to several radical white power groups across the country, including the Klan.''

"So you're saying Brewster's death wasn't random after all— that Danzig shot Brewster to keep him from writing another column? Or because he was black?''

"I'm saying that Danzig didn't shoot him. Someone else did.''

"What?" Instead of getting clearer, Drew's explanation seemed to be leading further and further away. He saw her confusion and leaned forward, the intensity of his face urging her to listen carefully.

"I talked to William Danzig in prison. He told me that a newcomer to the streets started hanging around with him a couple weeks before the shooting. The new man ate with him, slept where he did. Danzig looked through the guy's belongings one night and found a gun. A rifle. The police say Danzig stole it and used it to kill Paul. But Danzig told me the new man planted it on him after buying him a pint and getting him drunk. Then the man disappeared. No one can find him to deny or corroborate the story.''

"Why didn't you tell Danzig's story to the police?''

"I did. But they like things to tie up neatly, and the mystery man was a loose end they didn't want to pull on too hard in case the whole thing might unravel. They had a suspect, a weapon and a victim. End of investigation. The D.A. won't reopen the case without a new witness, so I'm going to find the man myself.''

"Here?'' Elizabeth's question revealed her skepticism.

"The gun was an expensive semi-automatic rifle, fully converted to automatic. Not the kind of gun a transient carries around on the streets with him. Except for the trigger sear piece that made it automatic, it was identical to yours.'' He nodded toward the gun hanging over the front door.

"You can't think that I—''

"Of course not,'' Drew interrupted. "Before Paul died he investigated several groups who'd contributed to Phillip Prince's campaign.'' He nodded toward the publicity photo. "Paul always kept good notes. The killer hadn't counted on that, or on the fact that Paul had prepared for just such an incident. He left a letter with an attorney instructing her to turn the notes over to me so I could continue the investigation.''

Drew's eyes were solemn, and Elizabeth knew she was about to hear the conclusion to his tale.

"Most of the questionable groups checked out. One didn't, and I traced it back to here. It's called the American Society of Patriots."

"ASP. And you think..." Elizabeth couldn't go on. She knew now why Drew had asked so many questions about her and her neighbors. He suspected one of the Colony members. But which one? "What did the mystery man look like?" she asked.

A loud pounding on the front door interrupted before Drew could answer. Elizabeth's gaze flew to the door and back to Drew. They sat frozen until the pounding resumed, more insistent than before, and a loud, unmistakable voice boomed, "Elizabeth, are you home?"

One look at Elizabeth's panicked expression told Drew who was outside. He quickly retrieved both photo and clipping from the table and stuffed them in his shirt pocket. He nodded to Elizabeth, and with an aura of calm, waited for her to open the door.

Inside, he was anything but calm. What if he was wrong about her innocence? What if she betrayed him? He could feel sweat bead on his forehead as he heard her greet Silas Freeman and someone named Cal. Freeman's voice carried clearly.

"Luke was out walking earlier," he was saying, "and he told us he saw that citified Illinois truck turn into your approach. We thought we'd stop by to make sure you were all right."

"I'm fine." Elizabeth directed a desperate glance over her shoulder to Drew. He nodded again, signalling his permission for her to do whatever she needed to do.

"Won't you come in?" he heard her say.

Drew watched as the men entered the cabin, stomping their heavy boots on the mat inside the door. He didn't miss the way the older man's gaze scanned the room, stopping when he spotted Drew at the table, or the way the younger man's expression hardened at Drew's relaxed smile.

"Silas, Cal, this is Drew Carter, the owner of the 'citified truck.' Drew, meet my neighbors, Silas Freeman and Cal Hoskin."

"How do you do?" Too bad he hadn't warned Elizabeth not to use his real name, but then Drew supposed it didn't matter since he'd introduced himself to half the population of Nis-

swa, from the county sheriff to the proprietor of Willie's Bar.
Even if Freeman managed to discover his identity, he wouldn't
guess why he was here. No one but Paul's attorney and Jim
Levitz—and now Elizabeth—knew he was investigating Prince.

"Howdy." Freeman took off his cap and stuck out his hand.
His grip was firm, his smile wide. Just a simple country sort,
Drew thought, then realized that was probably the very
impression he was supposed to have. Cal Hoskins, who was as
big and blond and shaggy as a mangy lion, stayed by the door.

"I was just about to make tea for Drew," Elizabeth said
brightly as the silence threatened to become uncomfortable.
"Should I put on extra water?" She sounded like a nervous
society hostess who'd just realized that her guests weren't
compatible, and Drew would have been amused if he didn't
know the real reason for her agitation. After a polite refusal
from Freeman, she went to the kitchen, leaving Drew to face the
men on his own.

"Well, now," Silas Freeman said pleasantly, "what brings
you to this neck of the woods, Mr. Carter?"

Drew composed his answer while keeping a surreptitious eye
on Hoskin, who was watching Elizabeth make tea. The man
stared at her like she was a three-course meal, Drew thought
disgustedly. He looked away, remembering that Silas Freeman
was waiting patiently for his answer.

"I'm looking for some peace and quiet," he said. He decided that the story he was using around town would do well,
explaining both his presence in Nisswa and his return to the
cabin. "I thought I might buy some land and build a cabin like
Elizabeth's here. We were just talking about homesteading
when you knocked on the door." He ignored the clatter as
Elizabeth dropped a spoon on the floor.

"Can't think of anything for sale in this area," Freeman said,
"but I bet you could find a couple farmers on the south side of
town looking to sell out." He smiled, revealing several gold
fillings. "Some folks think farming's easy until they wake up
one day and realize the bankers own everything but their wife
and kids. Ain't that right, Cal?"

The big man pulled his gaze slowly away from Elizabeth.
"Yep. That's right, Silas." He confirmed Freeman's attitude
with a voice that held a touch of a smooth drawl. His eyes
didn't match that hint of warmth. They were an expressionless
dark gray.

Elizabeth walked over to the table, two steaming mugs in her hands. "Are you sure you won't reconsider?" she asked the men as she set the mugs down.

"No, we have to get back," Freeman said. "Now that your driveway's dried out, Lily will probably be stopping by soon for her lessons," he added as he put his cap on over his thinning hair and stepped through the doorway.

As soon as the door shut behind them, Drew grasped Elizabeth's hand and squeezed it tightly. "Thank you," he said quietly, releasing her so she could sit down.

"For what?"

"For not telling them what I'm doing here."

"How could I? You haven't even finished telling *me* yet."

"But you've guessed by now, haven't you? I think one of the Colonists killed Paul Brewster."

"Who? What did Danzig's mystery man look like?"

Drew sighed. He knew she was skeptical, that she'd be even more skeptical when he told her the rest. "I don't know. Everyone I talked to described him differently. Blond, brown-haired, big, thin, blue eyes, brown eyes. Like most of the men on the street he wore a bulky coat and a hat. He didn't bathe regularly or shave, so his facial features were blurred."

"In other words, he could be anyone."

"Yes," Drew admitted tersely.

"What if you're wrong and the killer isn't connected to Prince or ASP?"

"Then I'll start over. But I'm not wrong." Elizabeth looked as though she still had doubts, and he told her, "Think about it. Your neighbors live behind a six-foot-high fence with a gate that's kept locked and guarded. They're obviously hiding something."

She shook her head. "You don't understand. A year ago Lily Freeman and I were walking in the woods when a group of drunken poachers attacked us. Fortunately, Cal Hoskin heard us screaming for help. He and a couple of the other men arrived before—" she looked away "—before anything happened."

Her voice quiet but intense, she added, "Lily, Silas's wife, is still very withdrawn because of the incident. That's why they built the fence, and that's why they gave me the gun. For *protection*," she stressed. "The gate is guarded so there's a man around in case something like that happens again."

"A man like Cal Hoskin?" Drew snorted. "That's like telling the fox to guard the henhouse."

"I don't think he would hurt me," Elizabeth said stubbornly.

"You're not going to help me, are you?" He kept his voice flat to hide his disapproval. "What if I told you Silas Freeman doesn't exist, at least not on paper? No birth certificate, no driver's license, no Social Security number. His name isn't even on the county plat books. The land is still registered to Robert and Richard Stoltz." He almost told her about the gunshot that had sent him fleeing for her pasture, but he decided to save that trump card for later. Instead he appealed to her sense of justice.

"Paul Brewster was murdered, Elizabeth. You have to help me find who did it."

Elizabeth shut her eyes to the persuasive look on Drew's face. She couldn't reconcile the idea of murderous racists with the people she knew. People who had rescued her from a traumatic experience, people with whom she traded and worked, people who'd shown her countless small kindnesses, such as bringing her mail in the winter when the snow blocked her driveway, or collecting rainwater for her so she had enough to dye her yarns.

She knew Drew was watching her, waiting for her to choose between him and the Colony. According to logic, the choice was an easy one. Side with the people like yourself, the people who will still be in your life a year—or ten—from now. But logic had already failed her, she thought as she opened her eyes and let her gaze run over Drew's salt-and-pepper hair. How else could this man have become so important to her in just one week?

"I can't turn on my neighbors, Drew," she said softly. "But I want to know the truth as much as you do."

"You'll help me then?"

Elizabeth hesitated. "I won't hurt them. No subterfuge, no snooping, no lying." The defeated look that crossed his face made her relent. "What exactly do you have in mind?"

"You know more about the Colony than anyone else in Nisswa. I want you to tell me about them, who they are, what they do. I need to know their comings and goings, especially during this past March and April."

She couldn't do it. She took another sip of cooling tea, but it didn't settle her churning stomach. She'd lived through betrayal, and she wouldn't betray her neighbors. She looked at Drew, knowing he could read the reluctance on her face.

"Okay," he said, leaning back in his chair. "I'll tell you about them. If I'm right, all you have to do is nod. Okay?" She murmured an agreement, and he began. "First of all, they're antigovernment and anti-authority in general. They avoid paying taxes by bartering or using cash."

"I practically told you that myself," she pointed out.

Ignoring her objection, he continued, "They don't trust bankers—"

"Which was pretty clear from the remarks Silas made while he was here."

He straightened in his chair and leaned forward. "Have you ever heard Freeman or any of the others say that the U.S. government is invalid?"

She nodded reluctantly, and he told her, "That's a common belief within the supremacist movement." He paused before continuing. "Many supremacists are religious fundamentalists."

"Some people would call them good Christians," she argued.

"*Good* Christians pay their taxes and love their fellow humans."

She flushed. "Go on."

"They often act as their own attorneys. They've filed court briefs and slapped liens on other people's property." Elizabeth nodded. Before Kurt Kresge died, Silas Freeman had placed a lien on his farm across the road.

"They collect guns and prophesy the end of the world."

Elizabeth nodded, and again at each terse description that followed. When Drew had finished, she realized he'd identified everything from the way the Colonists talked to the odd, noose-shaped lapel pin Silas sometimes wore.

When she asked Drew how he knew so much about the Colony, he told her, "These characteristics are shared by a number of groups on Paul's list. He took meticulous notes on the white supremacist movement before zeroing in on ASP. That's when he was murdered."

Elizabeth set the mug on the table, noticing she'd drained every last, tepid drop. "But they have good qualities, as well. They work hard, they help each other. And they've helped me, too. We all have quirks, individual beliefs that make us human," she insisted.

"When those beliefs harm someone else they become dangerous. I don't have to tell you that, Elizabeth."

"No." She thought again of Paul Brewster. If the Colony and ASP were one and the same, did that necessarily mean they killed a man in cold blood? Her information could just as easily clear them as convict them.

She kept that thought close during the next few hours as she answered Drew's questions. Some things he asked over and over again—even when she protested that she had no way of knowing every little detail. They'd stopped once, at her insistence, to let the sheep in the paddock and close the gate.

By the time they'd almost finished, the room was dark and Elizabeth was exhausted. She rolled her shoulders back to try to ease the tension in her neck from sitting for so long. She thought she caught a glint of sympathy in Drew's eyes, but then he looked down at the small notebook he'd pulled from his shirt pocket hours before. Elizabeth tried to see what he'd written, but she couldn't decipher the bold scrawls.

"So there are three families at the Colony, the Freemans and the two Stoltz brothers—who originally owned the farm, along with their wives and children." She nodded wearily. "And two single men, Cal Hoskin and Lewis Cole. Tell me more about the single woman—Jolene Fields."

Elizabeth sighed, trying to forget her tiredness and the fact that she'd already told Drew about the woman twice before. "Jolene is . . . different. She arrived last fall with Cal Hoskins. Sarah Stoltz was having a difficult pregnancy, and the Colony was glad to have an extra woman around to help. Shortly after Sarah was back on her feet, Jolene left the family quarters to live with the men in the smaller house next to the big farmhouse. I know that probably doesn't help much."

Drew straightened and set his elbows on the table, and she envied his alertness. "What about the other people on this mail route, the ones you told me about before?" he asked. "Do they have any contact with the Colony?"

"No. Tom Wheeler, the lawyer, stays on his side of the lake. The rest of the land on that side is owned by the reservation. You can't even get to Wheeler's place from the dead-end road—his turnoff is farther down the county highway. I've never met him personally."

Drew shot her a surprised look. "I told you I don't social-ize," she defended. "I just know what I hear in town."

"What about Wilson?"

"Doc uses his CB radio to keep tabs on the world. Once or twice he's helped with an accident after hearing about it on the police band. People aren't too fussy about his reputation as a drunk when it's an emergency," she said wryly, adding, "I don't think he's ever been to the Colony, unless it was to help with the livestock."

"A surgeon taking care of cows." Drew made a sound of scorn. "Seems like everyone around here is a dropout or a loser of some kind."

"I beg your pardon?" Drew's insensitive comment pierced Elizabeth's tiredness.

"Freeman came to build his own perfect little community, Wheeler couldn't take the big city and Wilson was drummed out of his medical practice. Everyone living in this corner of the woods couldn't hack the real world for some reason or an-other."

"Does that include me, too?" Elizabeth asked shortly, ris-ing to take the two mugs to the sink. She already knew what Drew thought of her—she didn't need another reminder. The feeling of being used returned, and Elizabeth scrubbed fiercely at the ceramic teapot that really only needed rinsing.

She heard Drew's footsteps behind her. "Elizabeth." His voice was rough, and she knew he was about to apologize.

She whirled to face him. "You can't possibly understand what draws people to a place like this. It's not an exile or a punishment like you seem to think it is."

"I didn't mean it that way at all, Elizabeth. I never pre-tended to be in my element here. That's why I need you." He put his hands on her shoulders and continued, "I'm just frus-trated, that's all. The election is only a month and a half away, and I've got to stop Prince in before then. I didn't mean to in-sult you, believe me."

Pretty words, she thought. And the way his hands soothed her shoulders.... Her fatigue returned full force, sapping her strength until she sagged against him.

During the past seven days this man had turned her world upside down time and time again. She'd considered herself safe here, hidden from a quiet road, a half mile in on a rugged track, protected by a gun. But her defenses weren't impregnable. Drew had proved that by worming his way into her life the way a burr embeds in sheep's wool.

He turned her to face him, and she didn't have time to rub away the wetness at the corner of her eyes.

"Don't," he said, his voice gentle. His fingers brushed a tear that hovered on her lashes, and she put her hands up to protect herself from the tender gesture. Drew ignored her resistance, taking her hands in his and pressing them to his cheek. His late-afternoon beard was rough against her fingertips.

"I can't get over how soft your skin is, like flower petals," he told her as he smoothed his fingers over her hands.

"It's the lanolin." She tried to be matter-of-fact, but her voice wavered. "Spinners' hands are always soft." She knew that Drew meant only to comfort her. But the comfort became an ache, and almost without realizing what she was doing, she tentatively rubbed her fingers over his skin. The gesture brought a passionate darkness to his eyes. She repeated it with a boldness foreign to her, this time allowing her thumbs to come dangerously close to the corners of his mouth.

He closed his eyes, and she knew he was struggling against the force that kept pulling them together despite their differences. She should be fighting it, too, she told herself. But her questing thumb didn't obey, stroking over his bottom lip until he opened his mouth with a groan.

Chapter 7

For an endless moment they hovered on the brink. Then hesitation disappeared, and Drew tilted Elizabeth's face up until their lips met in a slow, heated exchange. She couldn't have broken the kiss any more than the spring earth could have turned away raindrops, or a flower could have refused to bloom.

It was only a kiss, she told herself, but her legs went weak, as though every bit of energy was concentrated on the feel of Drew's lips moving over hers. She swayed and grasped his arms for support. Without ending the contact between their mouths, he moved his hands to her waist and lifted her up until she was sitting on the countertop.

Her hands stroked his muscled back while his traveled from her waist to her hips, then slid slowly down her thighs. Wherever he touched, she bloomed.

She wrapped her legs around Drew's waist, her hips nestling his. He groaned and pressed closer. His desire for her was unmistakable, shockingly hard against her thighs. He knew about her past, and she'd seen for herself the difference that knowledge had made. And yet he still wanted her in spite of it. *Or because of it,* a nasty little mental voice pointed out.

And then her arms, which only a few moments before had clung and pulled him closer, now pushed him away.

Instantly Drew stepped back. A shuttered look passed over his face, but Elizabeth could see the betraying heaving movement of his chest as he tried to control his breathing.

"I can't—" *make love with you,* she nearly blurted, proof of how quickly the kiss had escalated into passion. Drew stood silent and unmoving, making it harder for her to speak. "I can't let this happen," she said finally.

She picked out a spot on the wall behind him—a knotted log above his shoulder—and focused on it before continuing. "Because of what you've heard about my past, you probably think that I'd be agreeable to a quick affair. I'm not. You don't have to bed me to get me to help you. I won't be used like that, even—"

"Stop," he commanded roughly. "I already feel like a heel for involving you in something that could be dangerous. Don't make it any worse."

Without another word he turned, pausing only to pick up his notebook from the table before going out the door and into the night. She heard his truck driving away, and then nothing but silence.

Drew looked at the glowing numbers of his wristwatch. Midnight. He was back in Albert's spare bedroom, lying on the lumpy bed. He'd spent five hours at Willie's Bar after leaving Elizabeth's—five hours of playing pool and drinking and trying not to think. He'd managed to keep losing just so he'd have to keep buying beers for the other players. And himself—he'd hoped alcohol would erase Elizabeth from his mind.

It didn't work. He could still see the reproach in her lavender eyes, still feel the softness of her skin. And he could still taste her, dammit, even after countless cans of beer. Her past made no difference to his desire for her.

Drew retrieved the five-year-old picture from the wastebasket where he'd discarded the Chicago news articles before leaving for Elizabeth's that morning. The young woman in the photo didn't look like Elizabeth at all. She was harder, more polished, from the bottom of her elegant page boy to the carefully shaped eyebrows. Her name was Liz Eden, and she looked

every inch the successful, hard-driving achiever the articles said
she was.

They also said she was an adulteress. The headlines were
brutal, with the expected crude puns on Eden, the temptation
and the fall of man. It wasn't hard to see why she'd fled Chicago and changed her name. Or why she'd reacted the way she
had when she'd found out he was a journalist.

He'd excused Elizabeth by telling himself that she must have
been in love with Gallagher. But as soon as he'd seen her this
morning, with her jeans and sweatshirt streaked with dirt and
smelling of sheep, and her golden hair slipping from its braid,
he knew that she wasn't the kind of woman who could commit
adultery, not even for love.

Now he meticulously tore the most offensive articles into
shreds and tossed the pieces back into the trash, leaving a single clipping on the faded blue chenille bedspread. It was an
obituary, brief and matter-of-fact. Mary Anne Eden of Dan-
ville, Illinois, survived by her daughter, Elizabeth Jane Eden,
had passed away in a Chicago hospital two weeks after the
scandal broke. Only a few lines, but Drew read volumes between each one.

Elizabeth's past didn't matter, he told himself once again.
He'd found nothing to link her to his investigation. He wondered now if she would ever have trusted him enough to confide in him herself.

Spilt milk, Carter, he jeered. What she'd told him about the
Colony was enough to keep Jim Levitz busy checking files and
data bases for days. Once he wouldn't have hesitated to alert
Jim immediately. But now, with regrets and guilt clouding his
mind, the phone call didn't seem so urgent. From now on, he
vowed, he wouldn't involve her in his investigation.

It was late in the morning when Drew parked in front of the
Potawatomi County government complex. He was here to pick
up another package from Jim, the second since he'd called him
with the Colony's list of names two days before.

He stepped out of the truck and was almost surprised when
none of the shoppers leaving the grocery store across the street
even noticed. He was accustomed to Nisswa, where every head
would have snapped around to see who was driving the strange

truck. By comparison, Forest City, with a population of 5000, was downright cosmopolitan.

Drew was bounding back down the broad steps, envelope in hand, when he saw her. She was forty feet away, her back toward him and her cornsilk hair caught up in a tidy bun, but he recognized Elizabeth instantly. She stood next to the battered pickup, holding a bag of groceries and wearing a bulky light blue sweater that didn't begin to hide the graceful line of her back. He was unprepared for the delight that filled him. Then he realized she was deep in conversation with Jed Smith, the Potawatomi County Sheriff.

Delight vanished, replaced by near panic. What if she was telling Smith about his investigation? She might even think she was helping him. He stood awkwardly, trying to decide whether or not to approach them. The decision was made for him when the sheriff looked up and spotted him.

"Why, hello, Mr. Carter," Smith hailed. Drew returned the hearty greeting and started down the steps, comparing the sheriff's friendliness with his cold welcome at the café a week ago.

Elizabeth turned and Drew felt shock as her lavender eyes met his. Over the past forty-eight hours he'd convinced himself the improbable color was a trick of the firelit cabin or his memory. Was it possible for anyone to have eyes the shade of woodland violets?

"Hello, Elizabeth," he said.

"Drew." She nodded calmly, but her voice held an odd note. He hoped it wasn't guilt. Belatedly, he remembered Smith's presence and the gaudy envelope that felt like a flag clenched in his fist.

"Doing a little sightseeing, Mr. Carter?" Smith asked.

Drew cursed inwardly as Elizabeth looked down at the brightly colored envelope, and the sheriff's gaze followed. "I had to pick up some mail. My banker sent me some financial information in case I find that piece of property I'm looking for," he quickly bluffed, then dropped the subject by turning to Elizabeth. "What brings you to town?"

"Oh, several things. I needed some supplies I couldn't get in Nisswa, and I had to see the owner of the ram I put in with my ewes the other day."

"You're breeding them now?"

"Yes." Elizabeth flushed slightly. "In exchange for the use of Samson, I give Gene Larson all the ram lambs in the spring."

Sheriff Smith had stood quietly during their brief exchange, his gaze shifting from one to the other like a spectator at a tennis match. "Well, now," he said with a knowing chuckle, "since I work right here at the courthouse, I guess I don't need a reason to be here." He didn't seem to notice that the laughter of the others was a little forced.

He patted his flat stomach and added, "But if you're looking for a reason to stay for dinner—or lunch, as you city folks call it—" this in an aside to Drew "—the VFW down the street fixes a good meal." He put his hand on Elizabeth's shoulder, and Drew felt a quick surge of inexplicable anger. "If you don't need my help anymore," Smith told her, "I'd best be getting back to work."

"Thanks, Jed, for carrying that box for me." She smiled, and Drew felt his anger rise another notch.

"Anytime." Sheriff Smith left with a wave also meant for Drew. As soon as he'd disappeared inside the courthouse, Drew turned to Elizabeth.

"Jed?" He couldn't disguise the edge in his voice.

"It's a friendly community. People call each other by their first names."

"You weren't telling your friend Jed about me?"

"Of course not." She regarded him steadily. "By the way, what *are* you doing here?"

"I told you. I had some mail."

"From your banker?" she asked skeptically.

"No." He lowered his voice. "Information on the investigation. And next time I'd appreciate it if you didn't draw attention to it by gawking at it like that."

"I told you I wasn't very good at subterfuge." Elizabeth shifted the bag of groceries on her hip. "What have you found out so far?"

"Here, let me get those." The groceries were a good excuse to delay answering for a few moments. Drew put them in the truck bed next to the box of canned goods already there, trying to decide how much he should tell her. The smart answer was nothing. But a need to confide in someone—no, in Elizabeth—caught him off guard. He fought it, remembering his vow to protect her from further involvement.

He straightened and looked at her standing there, her hands in the pockets of her jeans, sunlight shining on the crown of hair. She was so lovely. "How about lunch?" he found himself asking. "We can talk about it then."

"Is having lunch with you my price for hearing about your progress or is it your payment for my information the other night?"

"It was just an invitation, dammit. Do you want to or not?"

She laughed then, and he realized how bad-tempered he'd sounded. "And such a charming invitation," she teased. He felt his exasperation evaporate as he admitted privately how much he'd missed the moments of easiness between them.

"All right." He pretended to be grudging. "But this is the last time I ask. Elizabeth Johnson—" he held a hand to his chest in mock formality "—would you do me the honor of sharing lunch with me?" At some point, he realized, the question had gone from teasing to hopeful sincerity.

Her smile faded. "I don't think that's a very good idea, Drew."

He saw the refusal coming, but he was disappointed, anyway. He wanted to persuade her. He knew he could, but he didn't relish an audience, and he was acutely aware of the attention they were beginning to attract standing next to a busy sidewalk. Forest City might be a whole lot larger than Nisswa, but it definitely wasn't as blasé as Chicago. Judging by the smiles on the faces of the shoppers who had paused to listen, a man pleading for a lunch date from an attractive woman was high entertainment.

"Then I'll help you run the rest of your errands," he offered. "I can load things into the truck for you."

"No." Elizabeth shook her head stubbornly. But her expression softened as she added, "Thanks, anyway."

Drew knew he wasn't imagining the wistfulness in her smile. He watched her climb into the ancient truck, wishing he could prolong their meeting, but she was right. Lunch, or anything else, would violate the distance he'd meant to keep between them. As he watched her drive away, he reminded himself that keeping his distance was for her safety as well as his peace of mind.

When he arrived back at the bungalow in Nisswa he made sure Albert was out before going up to his room and opening the envelope. Photos, clippings, notes, computer printouts scattered across the faded chenille bedspread. He went over every piece of paper carefully, then swore in frustration. Not a single word or picture concerned Silas Freeman.

He went downstairs to the hall telephone and dialed Jim Levitz's number. He got right to the point. "It's not enough, Jim. You've got to dig harder." Ignoring Jim's loud protests, he asked, "Are you still dating that policewoman—Diana or Dee, or something like that?"

"Dina. Yes, I am, but I've also got a full-time job, Drew. If I cross the line, I could lose it and end up killing my career."

"This investigation could *make* your career. Bend the rules if you have to. Look at it as on-the-job training." At Jim's considering silence, Drew added another enticement. "When this is over, I'll need a research assistant for the book. Maybe even a coauthor."

He could almost feel the waves of surprise over the line. Hell, he was surprised himself. But now that he thought about it, it wasn't such a bad idea. Before he could change his mind, he added the final inducement. It was a low blow, but he knew it would work. It sure would have worked on him when he was a fame-hungry twenty-five-year-old.

"Your name would look pretty good there on the cover, wouldn't it? I bet more than a few editors would be—"

"Okay, I'll do it." Jim's voice was charged with resignation and growing enthusiasm. "What do you want and when do you want it?"

"I want medical records, military files, police records—everything. And I want it as soon as you can get it here. Start interviewing people, too. Talk to Danzig in prison, and anyone connected with Prince. But be careful," he warned.

After a few more instructions and suggestions, Drew hung up. He readily admitted to hustling Jim Levitz, but he felt a little like he'd been hustled, too. He realized he'd just engineered himself another career shift. Now that he had someone to do the legwork and help with the rest of the research, he'd have more time on his hands. But for what? He'd never had a hobby, and he didn't want travel. He'd seen enough of the world already.

Maybe he'd find a place in the country after all, start on that adventure novel Elizabeth had accused him of writing. A fleeting image of her cabin, its windows bright and welcoming through a curtain of snow, crossed his mind. He ruthlessly dismissed it. He couldn't allow any more fantasies about the future—especially when they regarded Elizabeth. He had to keep his mind trained on the investigation. One slipup could mean his life—or hers.

Elizabeth treadled until the yarn between her fingers and the wheel was evenly twisted. As soon as her fingers had touched the rollag of soft, fluffy wool from Dorcas's first shearing, she'd been able to see this sweater in her mind. It would be special, different from those she made for the shops in Chicago and Minneapolis.

The inspiration had been a godsend. Whenever thoughts of Drew intruded on the cabin's too-quiet interior, she found comfort in the whir of the spinning wheel. Since meeting him in Forest City five days ago, she'd stayed up late every night.

It was natural, inevitable, even that her long-dormant need for closeness had bubbled to the surface at Drew's warmth. The only surprise was that her reserve hadn't melted sooner. Isolated though she was, there were still eligible men in her life, men who would have fit right into her world. But none of them had ever made her heart beat faster. Gene Larson was good-looking, nice, and boring. At fifty-plus, Jed Smith was too old to start a family, and she wanted a little girl to teach as Claire had taught her. Then there was Cal Hoskin....

She shuddered involuntarily. Lately she hadn't been able to think of Cal Hoskin without wondering if he was guilty. Or wondering what Drew's investigation might mean to her careful plans.

Lily was learning how to spin, and once she in turn taught the other women at the Colony, Elizabeth would at last have enough yarn to meet the ever-growing demand for her creations. Then she'd be able to increase her flock. Gene Larson had a black Targhee and two lovely spotted Jacob rams....

But all her plans depended on the Colony's assistance.

Her concentration faltered. For once, spinning wasn't the answer. She stood, wondering how ovine romance was progressing. Gene's Corriedale ram, Samson, had been with the ewes a week now, much to Whiskey Jack's disgust. He'd been banished, with the ewe lambs, to the low pasture.

She stopped in the kitchen long enough to pack a lunch and put it into a backpack along with her journal. At the door she paused to grab a jacket and tuck the bottoms of her jeans into thick wool socks before lacing up her boots.

Outside, the breeze chased woolly white clouds across a bright blue sky. The first killing frost had finally arrived two nights previously, but today the sun was summer-warm. She stripped off her denim jacket and tied it around the waist of her bulky, indigo-dyed sweater.

The five ewes and Samson were halfway to the top of the hill, enjoying the last of the green grass the rains had brought. Elizabeth walked to the top, spreading her jacket on the ground next to the wide trunk of a cottonwood. Its leaves were just beginning to turn gold.

When she heard an engine in the distance she looked down to see a flash of dark red through the trees. Drew's truck. A short blast of the horn confirmed that Drew had spotted her on the hilltop. She stayed where she was with an air of calm, but her heart betrayed her by beating faster as the truck disappeared into the trees on its way to her cabin.

Just as she'd known he would, Drew came to find her. She closed her journal and watched him walk up the hill, admiring his sure-footed stride. In jeans and a red-and-black buffalo-plaid shirt, he looked like a natural outdoorsman. Elizabeth smiled when he paused to pat Genevieve on the head before coming to join her.

"Hi." He wasn't even breathing hard from the steep climb.

"Hi. Would you like some lunch?" The words tumbled out before she could stop them. She was the one who sounded breathless, she realized with disgust. She gestured to the brown bag at her side. "I have enough for two."

He grinned. "Is this to make up for the lunch we missed the other day?"

She smiled back, remembering his invitation. "I'm afraid it's just a cheese sandwich," she said as he took the half she proffered and sat down beside her. "I have a thermos of water in my backpack."

He rummaged through the pack and found the thermos, filling the plastic cup that they would have to share between them. The small intimacy seemed somehow comfortable.

"You don't eat meat, do you?" he commented as he bit into the sandwich.

"You may be an *ex*-journalist, but you still have a reporter's knack for observation."

"For what I do, I still need it. But it doesn't require much genius to notice that you avoid meat. This is at least the fourth time we've shared a meal now, and I know the signs." He offered her the cup of water before taking a long swallow. At her questioning look, he explained, "Juliet—my youngest sister—is a vegetarian. Drives my dad crazy."

"Why?"

Drew paused just long enough to pique her interest. "He's a butcher."

"Mmm, yes." She allowed herself the happy laugh that had been building ever since she saw him coming up the hill. "That would create some friction."

"Friction? That's a very mild term to apply to my father's temper. Why don't you eat meat, Elizabeth?"

She didn't miss the way he'd turned the subject back to her, but today personal questions didn't bother her. Nothing did. The world seemed perfect, and she decided it must be the weather—or the company. "It wasn't a conscious decision at first. It isn't easy to keep meat fresh without electricity, so I got used to going without it. But I'm sure your sister wouldn't consider me a vegetarian. It's hard to farm or ranch and maintain those kinds of ideals."

"Juliet would like you anyway."

Elizabeth knew it was unlikely she'd ever meet Drew's sister, but she warned, "Just don't tell her that when Lily Freeman brings over a butchered chicken, I make soup."

"You're teaching Freeman's wife how to spin, aren't you? Silas said something about her lesson that day I was there."

She paused before answering, realizing that Drew had come after all to ask her questions about the Colony. She'd agreed to help him, she reminded herself, thrusting aside a ridiculous sense of disappointment. "I can't spin enough wool for my needs," she explained. "Lily wanted to learn, and she's willing to teach the other women from the Colony."

Drew nodded toward the ram standing several yards away from the rest of the flock. "Speaking of wool, why does that sheep have paint all over its chest?"

"That's Samson, the ram I borrowed. His brisket wool is marked with greasepaint so that I'll know when he breeds one of my ewes. If I know the days she was covered, I can predict when she'll lamb," she finished with a blush, expecting a teasing remark. When he changed the subject completely, not even mentioning the Colony again, she was surprised as well as grateful.

They talked for several minutes before slipping into companionable silence. Drew leaned back against the trunk of the cottonwood and stretched out his legs. He said lazily, "It's certainly a peaceful scene, isn't it? Quite a change from Chicago."

Elizabeth felt the smile freeze on her face. She knew he'd only meant to make conversation, but the reminder of her former life was like a dash of cold water. "Yes. There's something about sheep that brings out the kindness in people." Before he could comment she changed the subject. "Would you like some more water?"

Drew accepted the cup she handed to him. "What, no merlot?"

She laughed, relieved that he'd allowed her to divert the conversation. "Not this early in the day."

"What happened in Chicago, Elizabeth?"

The abruptness of his question caught her completely off guard. He'd probably planned it that way, she thought. After all, he was the expert when it came to interviewing. "You said you already knew," she accused.

"I know what was in the papers. But I know you, too, and the person you are now wouldn't have done anything like that. Have you changed that much?"

"Oh, I've changed all right," she said without bitterness. "But not in the way you think."

Drew sat up, no longer the indolent picnicker. His eyes were intent as he asked, "The stories about you and Patrick Gallagher weren't true, were they?"

"Not all of your colleagues are as dedicated to seeking out the truth as you are, Drew," she said with a lightness that was forced.

"Tell me what happened."

Elizabeth hesitated. Even Claire had never known what really happened in Chicago; she could hardly believe she was thinking of telling Drew. But the noncondemnation in his dark eyes invited her to speak.

"Patrick Gallagher retained my PR agency on a consulting basis. I was the account manager, the liaison between Gallagher's people and our own," she told him. Now that she'd begun to talk, it wasn't so difficult to tell him how it had started.

"One of the publicity events we arranged for the candidate was a press breakfast at a lakeshore hotel. I was there with Gallagher the night before to go over some of the details. With a knowledge of our schedules and a few well-chosen photos, someone was able to make it look as though we were having an affair. We weren't, but that didn't matter."

"Who did this to you?"

"The campaign manager for the opposition," she answered blandly.

Drew's gaze searched out her secrets. "He was more than that."

She had to look away to tell him the rest. "I thought he loved me." Her fingers caught in a clump of cool grass. "We decided to keep our relationship quiet for appearance sake. At least, that was the reason Barry gave." She shrugged. "It was partly my fault. I should have resigned from the account. But I was ambitious in those days, and my ambition blinded me to the fact that Barry was using me."

Drew swore. "What kind of man would do that to you? It must have been hell, with your mother's death so soon afterward."

Could she tell him about that, too? Yes, she decided. "She died of heart failure, but I think it was shame that killed her. One particularly nasty interviewer intimated that the sins of the mother had been visited upon her child. The story didn't get printed, but afterward she just gave up on life."

"I don't understand," he said. She realized he'd moved closer while she'd talked, until he was sitting just inches away.

"I'm illegitimate, Drew. My mother fell for a sweet-talking insurance salesman from Chicago. He didn't stay long. My grandparents disowned her, and she raised me alone. We moved to Chicago when I was sixteen so she could get a better job. No one knew me there, and it was almost a relief." Drew's hand closed over hers in a silent gesture of comfort.

"When my mother died," she continued, "I came here. I was glad to get away from the reporters. And the memories."

"And I brought them all back. God, Elizabeth, I'm sorry." He reached out to stroke the back of her head, and she drifted into his arms. She felt safe against his solid warmth, close enough to breathe in the "new" smell of his shirt. He must have bought a whole wardrobe of flannel shirts for his stay in Nisswa, she thought, smiling.

When Drew's lips brushed her temple, she knew the gentleness was meant only to soothe her, and her spiking response caught her by surprise. She wondered if her mother had felt this way about her father, that a week or a day with him—or even just a kiss—was worth the heartbreak.

"I'm sorry I hurt you," he said. As he spoke she could feel the warmth of his breath against her cheek.

"The only part that hurt was knowing you thought I was some kind of—"

He silenced her by placing his fingers over her lips. "I never thought that. Nothing I read fit with what I already knew about you. You are the fairest, finest woman I've ever met."

He moved his fingers to her chin and tilted her face until her mouth was millimeters away from his. For several long moments they sat like that, so close that a mere shift in position would close the distance between them. Still he didn't make the final adjustment that would bring her lips to his. Elizabeth could have closed the distance herself, but she wanted the decision to be Drew's. He was the one who was still hesitating. She no longer felt any need at all to hesitate, she realized.

When his lips finally settled over hers, her mouth opened instantly, trapping his sigh of satisfaction. This kiss didn't explore, tease or challenge as the others had. The passion was there again, but this time something sweeter flowed between them as well. It was pure and perfect, and the wonder of it nearly stole Elizabeth's breath.

She could hear the gentle tinkling of Genevieve's bell yards away, smell the crushed grass beneath them, feel the breeze stirring the loose strands of her hair and weaving it between them like a golden web as his lips slowly moved over hers. Never had she felt so at peace. Even after Drew left her to go back to Chicago, this moment would be hers forever.

Drew's hand trailed along her throat, bared by the rollneck of her sweater, then down. Even through the thick wool, she could feel the heat of his palm, and her body responded instantly. When his hands trailed to the hem, she assisted him by moving away far enough so he could slide them underneath.

The bark of the tree was rough against her back, but she hardly noticed. Her hands kneaded his wide shoulders, feeling the movement of muscle beneath the soft flannel shirt. When Drew's palm closed over her breast, she gasped and he made a sound of satisfaction deep in his throat. Their lips rejoined in another soul-baring kiss.

Dimly she realized the tinkling bells were growing more insistent. Then the clatter of an overturned rock and a high-pitched child's whistle warned her they were about to have company.

"Drew, someone's coming," she whispered urgently.

But he was already leaping to his feet, pulling her up beside him and straightening her sweater. She searched his expression, wondering if he felt as frustrated at the interruption as she did. His face gave nothing away as he watched the hillside.

Drew willed his body to return to a normal state. He was tempted to punch whomever had dared to interrupt them, but when he saw a brown-haired boy around seven years old, the impulse cooled. Beside him, Elizabeth smiled as the boy's piping voice greeted every ewe by name.

"This is Luke, Lily Freeman's brother," she said when the boy finally reached them. He halted about five feet away, his hands deep in the pockets of his denim overalls. Drew calculated quickly, barely hearing the rest of her introduction. Silas Freeman had to be almost sixty. If this was his wife's brother, she must be years younger than Freeman himself.

"Lily's waiting for her lesson," Luke announced.

"Is it that late?" Elizabeth asked, moving to follow Luke. Drew looked at his watch, startled to discover it was half past three. He hadn't been aware of the breeze shading to cool, or of the sun lowering in the sky. Everything had taken second place to Elizabeth and what she'd told him about her past. He understood now why she'd thought he'd lied about his injury in order to seduce her, and why she was afraid of being used.

When they passed the flock, she clapped her hands, and the sheep obediently fell into step behind them. Normally he would have enjoyed her discomfort as she delicately explained to Luke why the newest member of her flock was sporting a streak of paint across his woolly chest. Instead he was too busy cursing himself.

He'd come here today to ask for her help. After nearly a week of hanging around Nisswa, hoping to run into someone from the Colony, he'd decided he needed Elizabeth after all. He wasn't using her, he told himself. He only wanted to ask for an introduction to one or two of the Colony's members.

But the question had gone unasked, and he realized that in the three hours they'd spent together he hadn't more than mentioned the Colony. Instead he'd nearly made love to her underneath the branches of the cottonwood tree.

He vowed to keep a tighter grip on himself. He'd been lucky twice today, first with Luke's timely interruption, and now with a chance to meet Freeman's wife. The man himself was an enigma, but Drew might be able to trace him through Lily. The election in Chicago was just a little over six weeks away, and he had to start somewhere.

Now all he had to do was convince Elizabeth to let him stay and speak to her friend.

Chapter 8

If you've never seen someone spin before, why don't you stay and watch?" Elizabeth asked as the three of them climbed the porch steps.

Drew was careful not to let too much of his pleasure show on his face. He wondered if Elizabeth realized she'd handed him the opportunity he'd been seeking. "I'd like that," he said as he held the door open for Luke. But the little boy stood his ground on the porch.

"Can't he stay outside with me instead?" Luke asked Elizabeth. Drew bit back a groan. Elizabeth knelt until she was level with the boy's eyes.

"I baked cookies this morning, Luke. Why don't you have some of them now, with your special tea?" she suggested. "Drew can come out later." She looked up at Drew for confirmation, and he nodded, albeit reluctantly. If entertaining Luke was the price he had to pay for talking to Lily, so be it.

Luke looked ready to negotiate a while longer, so Drew quickly added another enticement. "I think I've got a Frisbee in the back of my truck. If you'll wait for me we could play catch."

"A Frisbee?" Luke's brow furrowed a moment, then cleared. "I remember now. Tommy Harper's big sister had one. I lived next door to him before Silas came and took us away."

"Luke."

The word was admonishing without being harsh, but it was an interruption all the same, and just when things had started to get interesting. Drew looked toward the voice, over Luke's tousled brown hair and into the cabin. The woman who had spoken was even younger than he expected. "Wipe your feet before you come any farther," she told Luke.

Drew had the feeling that wasn't exactly what Lily Freeman had intended to say before she'd spotted him in the doorway next to her little brother. He hesitated for a moment at her look of apprehension, then Elizabeth took charge, grabbing Luke's hand and walking past him into the cabin.

"Oh, good," she said cheerfully. "I see you already have the teakettle on. Thank you, Lily." She turned to Drew as he closed the door behind him. "I'd like you to meet a friend of mine from Chicago. His name is Drew Carter." Drew barely noticed the slight stress on the word *friend*, but it apparently wasn't lost on Lily. Her anxious look faded, and it wasn't until then he remembered the men who'd attacked her in the woods. She had reason to be cautious.

"Drew, this is Lily Freeman," Elizabeth continued as though unaware of any undercurrents. "She's one of my neighbors."

"How do you do?" Lily said politely. She barely raised her head, but in that brief glimpse Drew saw that her eyes were as bright a blue as Luke's. Her hair was a shade darker than her brother's and pulled back into a severe bun that was incongruous with her schoolgirlish appearance. She wore a long dark skirt and a rose-color sweater that looked like one of Elizabeth's designs. Drew almost smiled, guessing that Lily probably had no idea how valuable the gift was. On the other hand, he had a feeling that she valued it simply because her friend had made it for her.

"It's nice to meet you, Lily," he said sincerely, and he sensed that her reservations eased a bit more. She sat down at the oak table.

"Help Luke with his coat while I make the tea," Elizabeth told Drew as she crossed to the kitchen. "I'll make enough of Luke's tea for all of us. Maybe you'll even like this kind, Drew."

At her words, Drew looked up from holding Luke's arm steady to find Elizabeth watching him, her eyes filled with silent laughter. Warmth shot through him, and he would have sacrificed anything—even this opportunity to talk to Lily Freeman—to be alone again with Elizabeth.

"Don't you like tea, either, Mr. Carter?" Lily's question snapped him back to reality. The look on the young woman's face was almost conspiratorial.

"No, I drink coffee. Preferably strong and black," he said as he hung Luke's coat behind the door.

"Oh." Lily looked down again. "I don't drink coffee or tea. But the tea Elizabeth makes for Luke is nice."

"Only because it's half maple sugar," Elizabeth teased as she set the cups and teapot on the table next to a plate piled high with cookies.

Drew noticed that Lily took as many cookies as Luke did. It didn't surprise him that her taste ran to sweets. She looked barely out of the schoolroom herself. He wondered what on earth she was doing married to a man like Silas Freeman.

While Lily ate cookies and quietly scolded Luke for filling his pockets with them, Elizabeth explained the steps she'd followed to teach Lily to spin, first using a hand-held spindle, then a wheel. As she spoke she set up an oddly familiar spinning wheel on top of the table.

"This wheel spins worsted, which is much finer than yarn. Lily's only been using it for about a week now, and already she's got the hang of it. She's a natural."

The young woman beamed at Elizabeth. "It was the way you said it would be. I practiced every day and one day it just came to me, like an inspiration."

"Would you show Drew?"

"All right." She rubbed her hands on a napkin, then reached down to the basket beside her for a loose rope of wool, which Elizabeth called a roving. While Lily attached the wool to the wheel with a piece of spun wool, then started to spin, Elizabeth described the process of drafting, or feeding the loose fibers to the wheel where they were twisted into worsted yarn.

"I'd like to try it some time," Drew told Elizabeth. "Would you teach me?"

He could see his question had startled her, but before she could answer, Luke piped up. "Men don't spin. That's women's work."

"Actually," Elizabeth told Luke, "It was a man who made this type of spinning wheel famous. He traveled to many countries and took it everywhere he went."

At her explanation Drew realized why the wheel had looked so familiar. He'd seen one like it in a famous photograph taken by Margaret Bourke White. "Mahatma Gandhi," he said, and felt as pleased as a little boy when Elizabeth rewarded him with a smile.

"That's right. It's called a *charka*. He used it to spin cotton for cloth, and it became India's national symbol."

Lily's fingers hesitated. She looked up from her work, her expression troubled. "Don't tell Silas. He wouldn't like me using something infidel."

"Of course I won't tell him," Elizabeth said softly. Drew didn't miss the look that passed between them over Luke's head.

"Why don't you go on outside, Luke," he told the boy. "I'll be out in a few minutes, and we'll play catch with the Frisbee."

"All right." Luke slithered off his chair.

"Don't forget your jacket," his sister warned as he yanked open the door. Luke obeyed silently, then risked another warning glance to tell Drew to hurry. "It'll be dark soon," he added.

After Luke had gone, Drew watched Lily spin for several minutes. Elizabeth took the dishes into the kitchen, and he wondered if she'd left them alone on purpose. He decided Lily was too wary to approach directly, so he asked casually, "Why did you decide to learn how to spin?"

"Because Elizabeth needs more yarn," Lily said simply. "She's going to show me how to weave, too, so then we can make homespun cloth. It's good to be self-sufficient."

"You and the others grow your own food, too, don't you?"

"Yes. We make or grow almost everything," she said with a touch of pride.

"Why?" Drew asked. He wondered if it was merely his imagination, or if her fingers had faltered momentarily at his question. He tried again. "Why not just buy what you need?"

"We don't want to be dependent on someone else to get by. When the final confrontation between good and evil comes, and all the cities are in flame and ruin, we'll be able to survive on our own until the Lord lifts us up to rule."

Drew felt a chill at her fatalistic words, so odd coming from one so young and seemingly naive. "Do you really believe that?" he asked. He heard Elizabeth come up behind him and felt her warning hand on his shoulder.

"Why don't you go out and play with Luke now?" Elizabeth interrupted.

Drew shook his head all but imperceptibly to let Elizabeth know that he wasn't through with his questions, but Lily protested herself.

"It's all right, Elizabeth," she said. "Silas says we should witness to people."

"Did your husband tell you about this final war or confrontation?"

"It's the word of God—Armageddon. Everyone knows that," she chided him. "Even Luke. Silas says only those who follow the word of the Lord will be spared. The other infidels will be lost in the chaos."

"Why didn't you tell me about them before?" Drew demanded as soon as Lily and Luke had left.

Elizabeth continued chopping vegetables even though she was surprised at the underlying anger in his voice. She'd assumed Drew would stay and eat, but now she wasn't sure. He was impatiently pacing back and forth on the other side of the kitchen counter. She knew he'd hoped to drive them home, gaining an opportunity to see inside the Colony, but Lily had refused his offer of a ride, much to his, and Luke's, chagrin. After ten minutes of playing Frisbee, Drew had the boy's utter adoration.

"I did tell you," she replied calmly, dumping the chopped vegetables into a cast iron skillet heating on the stove.

"You didn't tell me they were so young. They're just kids."

"You wanted to know about the adult men. I told you there were children living at the Colony, but you didn't seem interested."

"I didn't know then that Freeman had married one of them." Still pacing, he pushed an impatient hand through his hair. "I assumed Luke was at least a teenager. And Lily...she must be forty years younger than Freeman. What was her maiden name?"

"I don't know."

"How old is she, anyway?"

"Twenty."

"And Freeman?"

"He's sixty-two, I think," she answered reluctantly. She didn't enjoy having questions fired at her like cannonballs. She sent him a reproachful glance, and Drew responded by slowing down.

"Doesn't that strike you the least bit strange?" he asked, his voice gentler.

"It did at first," she admitted. "But Lily and Silas have a relationship that is more father-daughter than anything else. Her parents were killed in an accident when Luke was only five. Silas was a friend of her father's, and he adopted Luke, but Lily was eighteen."

"So he married her instead. Why did you leave this out earlier?"

"I didn't think delving into their private lives was important."

"Well, it is. If I'm going to get past that gate, I have to know these people—the way they think, the way they live."

"I don't understand why that's necessary. We'd already decided the murderer was Cal Hoskin." She stirred the sautéing vegetables and added cracked wheat and bits of cheese.

"That it was *most likely* Cal Hoskin. It could be Lewis Cole, or one of the Stoltz brothers or very likely Freeman himself."

"Marrying a young girl doesn't make him a murderer."

"No, it doesn't. But it doesn't disqualify him, either. He also happens to be a zealot, and zealots murder all the time." Elizabeth looked sharply at Drew and he added, "I won't involve you any further. Now that Lily and Luke know me, I can get inside the Colony to talk to the others."

Elizabeth shook her head. "It won't be that easy. If it hadn't been for the attack on Lily and myself, the Colony probably still wouldn't be ready to accept me," she told him as she handed him the plates and silverware.

They didn't talk about the Colony again during supper, although the subject hovered between them like a curtain marked Do Not Enter. The embrace they had shared on the hilltop now seemed like a distant dream.

Neither of them ate much, and finally Elizabeth wondered if it wouldn't be better to talk about it after all. But before she could speak, Drew reopened the discussion himself.

"You didn't tell me about Lily and Silas. I guess we're even then, because there's something I didn't tell you." The statement stopped Elizabeth in the act of trailing her fork across the plate.

"That day you found me in your pasture—" he paused for a moment before baldly stating "—I fell and hit my head because I was running. Someone took a shot at me."

"No," she protested. "I would have heard it."

"Even during a thunderstorm?"

"I'd forgotten about the storm," she admitted. She closed her eyes in an attempt to reconstruct that morning two weeks ago. "It was over by noon, so I put the sheep in the low pasture for a few hours. I was bringing them in when I found you there." She opened her eyes to find him regarding her solemnly. "Are you sure you heard a shot and not just thunder? You were pretty delirious."

"Absolutely sure. I wasn't delirious until I hit my head," he pointed out. "My truck stalled around 9:00 a.m., and I spent almost an hour trying to get it going. Then I saw the mailboxes up the road, and I figured that if I walked up the driveway I'd find help. I passed your driveway without seeing it," he added. "The storm hit before I got to the house."

"But the Kresge farm has been deserted for months."

"It wasn't deserted that day. The first shot ripped through the bushes behind me. I didn't wait around to see if there was going to be a second. I crossed the road to your side and climbed over your fence."

"How? It's mesh-wired and barbed in places."

"I can't remember." He grinned. "Hell, it could have been electrified with a moat on the other side and I still would've made it over. I ran through the woods until I came to open pasture. That's when I tripped and knocked myself out."

"And then I found you."

"After what seemed like days. I thought you were an angel. I was imagining all kinds of crazy things at that time."

"But not the shot."

Drew shook his head slowly.

"And you think it was one of Silas's men?" she asked.

"No one would have been out in those conditions unless he had to be. You told me yourself it was too early for hunters."

Elizabeth's eyes were troubled as she admitted, "Doc Wilson doesn't own a gun. And Tom Wheeler stays on the other side of the lake." Even though she was beginning to accept Drew's explanation, she argued, "Why would they shoot to protect land that doesn't even belong to them? You could have been killed."

"I think it was just a warning. If they wanted to kill me they've had plenty of opportunities in the past few days. They don't know why I'm here, or they'd probably try it."

His words turned her cold. "How can you talk like that? As though being shot at isn't any more unusual than having a flat tire."

Drew shrugged. "I'm just being realistic. If I'm right about the Colony, they've already killed to protect their secrets. You're the one who insists that they aren't dangerous."

"Why don't you call the FBI? They handle things like this, don't they?"

"I talked to a friend with the Bureau, and I got the distinct impression that if it weren't for our friendship, he'd have called my theory a pile of crap. He said he needed hard evidence, so here I am."

"Then talk to Jed Smith. He could help—"

"No!" Drew interrupted. "No one else can know about this, Elizabeth." When she shook her head in bewilderment, he explained. "I'm already an outsider here. If anyone, including Smith, knew I was going after one of their own, it might make things difficult for me." He added, "Only three people know why I'm here—you, Paul Brewster's attorney and Jim Levitz, my assistant in Chicago. That's the way I want to keep it. Do you understand?"

She nodded reluctantly. He didn't remind her of the gunshot; he didn't need to. She kept picturing him lying in the woods wounded—or dead. "I'm worried about you."

"I've been in tighter spots," he reassured her. "If I can get in and get out with the right information, I'll be able to call the FBI and my job will be over with. Except for the book," he finished with a grin.

His cool acceptance of the risks made her angry. "Are you here to find out who murdered your friend, or to get a story?" she asked.

His dark eyes flashed at the question, but he answered calmly. "Both, I hope. I have to expose Prince and the white supremacists who support him. By doing so, I'll find out who killed Paul Brewster. Are you trying to say one goal is more noble than the other?''

"To fulfill the first you need to be an investigator. But when you try to find out who killed your best friend, you're acting as a man. I just want to make sure the man knows what he's doing.''

With Elizabeth's words echoing in his mind, Drew silently helped her with the dishes. He'd hoped her reaction to the shooting would prove who was more important to her, the Colony or him. He wasn't quite sure where her sympathies lay, or why it mattered so much.

"What are you going to do next?" she asked as he stacked the plates.

"Hang out. Let them continue to think I'm a city slicker looking for a piece of the country to run to on the weekends.''

"I'd like to help.''

"Even if it means telling me about your neighbors?''

"Yes," she said firmly.

The expression in her eyes caught him by surprise. Her cooperation meant more to him than the information itself, he realized. Before he could stop himself he'd reached out and settled a kiss on her cheek. It was brief and chaste and highly unsatisfying. "I'd better go.''

"Drew." Her voice stopped him at the door. "Why don't you stay a while? I could make something for dessert, and we could talk.''

"I have to leave." He searched for an explanation. He could hardly tell her that the afternoon on the hill had proved that he couldn't trust himself around her. "Jim Levitz is looking up a few things for me in Chicago," he said finally. "I'm expecting him to call tonight.''

But he didn't open the door, and Elizabeth didn't seem any more anxious for him to leave than he was to go.

"About the Colony members..." she began hesitantly.

"Yeah?''

"Maybe I could find out more. I could ask Lily—''

"No!" he interrupted harshly. If the length of the room hadn't separated them, he'd have been tempted to shake her. His hands clenched helplessly at his sides. "I don't want you doing anything that isn't part of your normal routine. We can't afford to arouse anyone's suspicions. Freeman's wife has her loyalties.''

"So do I."

Her quiet words rocked him—because he was acting like a man instead of an investigator, he realized. "I've got to go now." The roughness of his voice surprised him.

"To take that phone call."

For a moment he didn't know what she was talking about. He covered the lapse by checking his watch. "Yeah, I'll have to hurry to make it back in time."

He went out the door, feeling like he'd just told the whopper of his life. He knew Elizabeth had wanted him to stay, knew what would happen if he did. The phone call was only an excuse to get away before he gave in to the overwhelming impulse to lock out the rest of the world and carry her to bed.

He was losing control, he thought as he yanked open the door of his truck and got in. He needed to concentrate on the investigation, but his mind wouldn't let go of Elizabeth. He drove through the dark, his headlights picking out the trail ahead, but he saw none of it.

Instead he saw a cottonwood tree on a hill, blue skies and late-afternoon sunshine. He saw the highlights in Elizabeth's hair, the way the breeze moved over it and lifted several silky strands from her thick braid. He saw them making love on a carpet of green grass sprinkled with golden coin-shaped leaves.

When he'd told her that she was the finest woman he'd known, he'd meant every word. She was fine and pure and honest, and she deserved someone who was willing to give her a lifetime. He didn't believe in forever anymore, and especially not for them. He knew what she'd think about him after he'd turned the Colony inside out.

He forced his mind back to the investigation.

He'd quizzed Luke thoroughly while teaching him to throw the Frisbee, but the boy didn't remember what his last name had been before Silas adopted him. Armed with that information Jim could look for adoption papers or a marriage license. It was the only way to get to Silas Freeman. Or was it?

He slammed on the brakes. What if he'd been shot at that first day because he was about to stumble onto something important? The answer was waiting for him two miles back on the dead-end road. *The Kresge farm*. It was his best chance for learning something about the Colony without involving Elizabeth.

He swung the truck around, wincing as the boughs of a roadside pine slapped against the window. As soon as the headlights spotted the mailboxes that marked the driveway to the Kresge farm, he switched them off and relied on moonlight. He knew he should go the rest of the way on foot, but if he was going to get shot at again, he wanted to be able to leave in a hurry.

The dark tunnel of hedges ended at the base of a horseshoe-shaped, cobbled drive leading to an elegant white house. He hadn't made it this far on his first visit, and the sight of the solid old house with its peeling paint was oddly reassuring. He passed it and parked between a pair of skeletal corn cribs.

With the help of an unlocked cellar window and a small flashlight he'd found in the truck's glove compartment, he searched the house first. He checked every room up to the attic and found nothing but dust and mouse droppings. The outbuildings—barn, granaries, a small toolshed—were also empty.

The last building was a long, dilapidated machine shed standing at the edge of a field gone to fallow. The wide double doors were bolted and padlocked, but the hardware was shiny and new. The discrepancy made Drew's heart beat faster. A second, standard-size door in back of the building was also locked. He continued to the opposite side, where an old-fashioned wooden corncrib was attached.

He turned the small block of wood that held the slatted door closed and went inside. Like everything else, the corncrib was empty. Disappointed, he was making his way back to the door when a rotten board gave beneath his feet. He grabbed at the slatted wall to keep from falling. The flashlight dropped from his hands, falling between the slats and rolling onto the machine shed's dirt floor.

Drew peered through the slatted connecting wall. The flashlight's narrow beam illuminated one corner of a stack of new lumber. If he'd been paying more attention, he'd have noticed the scent of freshly cut wood before now. His mind ticked off the possibilities. The most obvious was that Kresge's heirs were using the shed for storage. But the obvious didn't satisfy him. He tried to reach the flashlight, to turn its beam so he could see more, but his forearm wouldn't fit through the slats. He gave up with a curse, realizing that the light had to stay behind, like a calling card that announced his visit.

As he crossed the yard to the truck, he wondered what to do next. Elizabeth might know if any of the Kresges were still using the shed. It would only take a few minutes to stop and ask her.

But when he turned at the mailboxes he kept going, past the sumacs that marked Elizabeth's driveway and toward town, trying not to think of the cabin in the woods and the woman who called it home.

He came and went from her life like a determined bee flitting between the two worlds of flowers and hive, Elizabeth realized as she rocked back and forth and tried to concentrate on the white sweater in her hands. Like a buzzing insect, he managed to annoy her, too. It would have been far easier for her to deny her attraction to him if he didn't fit in her world at all. But he seemed at ease in her cabin, almost as though he belonged. Why had he left tonight, after she was a breath away from coming right out and asking him to spend the night? She didn't believe his explanation about a phone call.

Her world had already changed since he'd stumbled into her pasture that rainy afternoon two weeks ago. She found herself looking at her neighbors, even Lily, with new eyes, wondering if they were guilty. The possibility frightened her, but she had to know if Drew was right. He'd told her not to get involved, but how long could she stand on the sidelines and watch without choosing sides?

The Colony wouldn't reveal their secrets to Drew; he needed her help.

Ten days later Drew was on the dead-end road again. Albert had introduced him to several of Kurt Kresge's heirs, who knew nothing about the lumber in the shed. He'd proved to himself he could work without Elizabeth. Yet here he was. He'd thought he could stay away, but he'd obviously been wrong.

He'd replayed the scene under the cottonwood tree at least a dozen different ways in his mind, the only difference being that none of the new endings he'd given to the episode featured an interruption named Luke. No, he saw the scene end the way he wanted it to, with Elizabeth's ivory skin in the sunshine, the scent of crushed grass beneath them as they made love. *Oh, how he wanted her.*

All the reasons he shouldn't leaped into his mind: they were too different, she was too distracting, the election was less than five weeks away...and he was afraid. Something told him that making love to Elizabeth would be an irrevocable step. And definitely the wrong one to take with a woman whose life was so closely tied to the people he was trying to put in prison.

He told himself that he was here to ask one simple question about Lewis Cole, whose police records were in yesterday's information packet from Jim. But the truth was that he was here because he couldn't stay away any longer. His vow to keep away was worthless.

As he slowed down to turn into her driveway, he saw Lily and Luke Freeman walking toward him. He looked at his watch and realized it was time for Lily's lesson to end. He stopped just past the sumac bushes, now bright red with fall color, and waited. "Can I give you a lift home?" he asked.

"No, thank you, Mr. Carter," Lily answered while her brother eyed the truck with undisguised admiration. Drew hopped down from the truck in what he hoped was a neighborly gesture.

"Please call me Drew," he told Lily with an easy smile. He turned his attention to the boy. "Sorry we couldn't play catch for very long the other day, Luke. How about now?" Luke looked up at Lily, and Drew turned his efforts back to her. "I can bring him home in a little while," he offered. It was the perfect opportunity to get past the Colony gate—if Lily agreed.

She was shaking her head. "I don't think so, Mr.—Drew. Luke has chores before supper," she said pointedly when the boy looked ready to protest.

"Tell you what," Drew said as he reached into the pile of blankets and sports equipment Jim stored in the back of the truck. "You can keep this, Luke, so you can practice. Then next time we'll play catch again." He handed the boy the fluorescent orange disk. He was sure Jim would approve of the diplomatic gift, just as he was afraid Lily wouldn't. She surprised him by looking as charmed with the present as Luke did.

Encouraged, Drew tried again. "Sure you don't need a ride?"

"No, thank you. We must be going. Thank him, Luke, for the toy." She nudged the boy, who dutifully expressed his gratitude. They left then, and Drew watched them with a mixture of amusement and disappointment as they walked down the road.

When he pulled up behind Elizabeth's ancient truck a few minutes later the sun was lowering in the west, its beams highlighting the surface of the pond where two Canadian geese paddled. The beauty of the late afternoon held him still for several moments at the base of the porch steps. He heard a bell, then the bleating of sheep, and he knew Elizabeth must be home. He felt as nervous as a teenager picking up his prom date and almost wished that she'd be out in the pasture somewhere. Before he started up the wooden steps he reminded himself that, unlike a teenager, he could exercise a little control. He had to.

"I thought I heard your truck," Elizabeth said as she opened the door. Drew looked unsure of himself, she decided, or at least as unsure as a man could look when he was dressed like a rugged outdoorsman. Every time she saw him, he seemed more at ease in the flannel shirts he'd taken to wearing.

She wanted to tell him what she'd found out, but not right now. She was too glad to see him to spoil everything by discussing the Colony. Instead she told him, "I was just about to go for a short walk before sunset. Would you like to come along?"

She could see his hesitation. She'd only asked him to go along on a walk, for heaven's sake. What was there to dither about? Unless he was thinking of her invitation the other night. She flushed.

"Sure."

"You'll go?" she asked. Like a bemused teenager, she realized. She didn't wait for his assent but headed for the low pasture and the section of woods bordering the lake. He caught up with her and waited while Elizabeth opened the gate, wondering why he'd come.

She didn't have long to wonder. They hadn't even crossed the pasture into the woods before he asked casually—too casually, "Have you ever seen Lewis Cole carrying a gun?"

"I don't know," she answered, trying to decide where Drew's question was leading. "Most of the men do from time to time, but I can't recall specifically seeing Cole with one. Why?"

"He has a felony record, a weapons charge. Convicted felons can't carry firearms legally."

"I should have known."

"About Cole?"

"No, that you followed me here only because you needed information."

He laughed harshly. "Lady, if you had any idea of what I need...."

She looked at him sharply. She was about to ask for an explanation when they reached the edge of the woods. There the path narrowed, and they had to walk single file, leaving her to silently question his meaning.

The late-afternoon sun was weaker here, filtered by a lacework of leaves and blocked by an occasional tall evergreen. Autumn's colors—reds and yellows and browns—contrasted with the dark green pines. They tramped on without speaking, the only sound the rustling leaves at their feet. The constraint between them made Elizabeth walk faster than usual.

She stopped abruptly when she spied a spot of dark green, almost hidden by fallen leaves. "Oh, look." She knelt down and pulled away the dead leaves. "It's a wild orchid. I've never seen one bloom this late before. The rain must have fooled it into thinking it was spring, and the leaves kept it protected from frost. Can you see it?" She looked up at Drew, smiling at her discovery. Her elation quickly faded at the expression in his eyes. He stared at her with a longing so fierce it took her breath away.

"It's the color of your eyes," he said, and she looked back down at the tiny lavender-and-white bloom, trying to hide her sudden confusion. "Aren't you going to pick it?" he asked.

"No. It would die before I got it home," she said quietly, her fingers rubbing a smooth dark green leaf with regret. When she looked up again, his expression was neutral, and he was holding out a hand to help her to her feet.

"We'd better get back before it gets dark," he said, releasing her hand as soon as she stood.

"All right." His dark eyes were enigmatic, and she gave up trying to search out his secrets. "But I came to get some dye stuff. Autumn is the best time for lichen."

He followed her from tree to tree, watching as she used a pocketknife to scrape bits and pieces of lichen into a plastic bag. When she exclaimed over a particularly large specimen, Drew asked her incredulously, "How can you even touch that stuff?"

"This?" She held up a piece of something that looked like a mossy toadstool, grinning at Drew's immediate expression of distaste. "And here I was beginning to think you were actually adapting quite well to the rural life."

"I draw the line at things that look like they've been growing in my refrigerator." They laughed, and any remaining awkwardness vanished as they circled back to the pasture. Elizabeth told him that lichen made one of her most colorful dyes. She pointed out other plants on the way, pausing at the base of an oak to pick a handful of acorns, explaining that they made a rich dark brown. The color of Drew's eyes, she noted silently. She showed him the squirrel's nest in the branches above, and a set of raccoon tracks farther along the path. Drew listened to her explanations, adding a comment or asking a question here and there.

"It smells good in here," he said, his voice carrying over her shoulder.

"Pine trees and dead leaves." Elizabeth turned to smile at him on the path behind her. "That doesn't sound very appealing, does it? Yet I wait all year for this. Autumn is my favorite season." She stopped to take a deep breath. His gaze dropped to the vee of skin above the neckline of her sweater, and her breath caught instantly. He glanced away.

"I like fall, too," he said, as though the moment never happened. "Although I can't say I noticed that trees were particularly aromatic in Chicago. About all we could smell were diesel fumes, unless the wind shifted to the south. Then, there was the stench of slaughterhouses."

"Where did you live?"

"Just off Halstead Street, in Greek Town. Not very many trees there."

"I suppose not. But it must have been fun living there—like a big extended family."

He grunted noncommittally, and started walking, leaving Elizabeth to stare at the back of his head where thick silver and black waves of hair curled vulnerably against his neck. She dared another question as he paused to hold a branch out of her way.

"What was it like growing up there?"

"Not so much different than living anywhere else. Dad didn't want us to be immigrants' kids, so we didn't hang around the neighborhood much." His voice was gruff, his back stiffly straight as he walked ahead of her.

They came to the edge of the woods, and Elizabeth fell into step beside him, unwilling to end her questions. "Did you and your father argue?" she asked carefully.

"Constantly." He grinned, and even in the twilight Elizabeth could see the bitterness that edged the corners of his mouth. "Dad was a hard man to live up to. He volunteered for Korea—did two tours even though he had three kids and a wife waiting for him to come home. By the time I was a teenager, he had three more kids and my grandmother to support. He couldn't afford to send any of us to college. The army was the key to a better life, he told us."

"So did you join?"

"No," Drew stated flatly. He glanced at her as though judging her reaction. She kept her expression carefully neutral and hoped he'd continue. "Even if I'd been drafted, I wouldn't have gone. I was in college when my older brother Tom was stationed in Danang. I agreed with Uncle Sam—that one family member in a combat zone was enough. My father didn't. He wanted me to do the right thing."

He bent to pick up a rock and toss it across the pasture before continuing, "The irony was that I ended up in Southeast Asia anyway as a reporter. Maybe I was subconsciously trying to please my father. Or maybe I needed to prove to myself that I was a man." He shrugged. "I don't know why I'm telling you this."

The admission gave her the confidence to ask another question. "Is that how you got the scars?" He turned his head sharply. "On your abdomen," she clarified. She felt herself blushing furiously and was thankful for the twilight. "I noticed them the first night you were here."

Drew's teeth flashed in a white smile. "No, they're from a car bomb in Paris. I was unlucky enough to be walking down the street at the wrong time, but lucky to be in a country with first-class medical facilities."

Elizabeth felt a flicker of anger at his matter-of-fact tone. "So you kept right on taking risks to please your father. The author bio in your books said you were everywhere from Saigon to Kabul."

"I didn't do it because of my father," Drew said. "I wanted to make a difference, to be where important things were happening."

"Oh? Important things happen here in the States, too. Isn't that why you're here in Nisswa?" He didn't answer. By now they'd reached the gate, and he opened it for her.

"If Cole was carrying a gun," she ventured tentatively, "that would be reason enough to call in the sheriff, wouldn't it?"

"Yes." Her frisson of relief disappeared quickly when he added, "But Cole might not be the man who killed Paul Brewster. If the sheriff suddenly drives up here to arrest him after all this time, the rest of the Colony will figure that they're being watched."

"And the first person they'd suspect would be you." Elizabeth sighed as she climbed up the steps to the cabin. She didn't know what she wanted more—to have the nightmare end quickly, or to have Drew stuck here in Nisswa for a few more weeks.

Chapter 9

Drew stood in the cabin's doorway and watched Elizabeth light the lamps. He'd accepted her invitation for supper, but now, faced with the cabin's familiar lamplit intimacy, he had second thoughts.

He'd already crossed the line tonight, he admitted, as he watched Elizabeth pause to add another log to the fireplace. Flames licked at the wood, picking out the highlights in her hair and turning them to spun sunshine. What had possessed him to tell her about his past? It wasn't as if he'd had a difficult childhood. Until he'd confided in her tonight he hadn't even guessed how much his father's unbending attitude had ruled his life.

And how it still ruled him, he realized as he closed the door.

He blocked that particular epiphany from his mind and joined Elizabeth in the kitchen. "You've been baking bread." He sniffed appreciatively at the scent that wafted from the two crusty brown loaves cooling on the countertop.

"I took them out of the oven just before you arrived," Elizabeth told him. "Want some to tide you over until supper's ready?"

"Sure." While he got the butter and honey from the cupboard, Elizabeth sliced a large hunk from one loaf. It was still warm enough to melt the butter. After slathering the fragrant bread with honey, he perched on the counter and ate the gooey treat, feeling as young as Luke Freeman. At his invitation Elizabeth leaned over to take a bite. The gesture reminded him of the time she'd eaten melted marshmallow from his finger. His body reacted instantly to the memory, and he fought the response as she went to the pantry.

When she came back she told him, "When you're finished with that, you can help me with supper."

"What are we having?"

"Do you like Indian food?" she asked. He nodded, and she said, "Good. In that case we're having a curried *dahl* and potato stew."

"What if I'd said no?"

"Then I would have left out the spices, and we would have had lentil soup with potatoes." He made a face and she laughed, the sound filling him with warmth. He enjoyed this, being together in the kitchen in absolute domesticity. Then he reminded himself that there was no room for moments like this with a murderer only three miles down the road.

"Get off the counter so I can get at the silverware," she told him, playfully slapping his thigh. The light touch reverberated through him, and he slid down, landing on his feet several inches away from her. He edged farther away, and her teasing look faded.

She glanced away, pulling out the drawer and reaching for a knife. When she looked up again, her face was solemn. "I asked Lily a few questions this afternoon," she said.

It took Drew a moment longer to shift gears. When the meaning of her words sunk in, he was furious. "I told you it was too dangerous." He reminded her how unpredictable survivalists could be, how important it was to keep from arousing their suspicion. When he'd finished his tirade, she looked at him with an expression of smug inquiry.

"Well," she asked, "don't you want to know what I found out?"

Yes, he did, and that made him angrier. He wished he could tell her to take her damned information and stuff it, that he wasn't interested, but the damage was already done, and he needed to know. "What did you find out?" he asked heavily.

"Lily said the men aren't getting along, that they argue all the time."

Drew's curiosity overcame his reluctance. "About what?"

Elizabeth rinsed the potato she was peeling in a bowl of spring water. "Lily didn't know exactly. It sounds like a power struggle to me. They fight over who should give orders, who's worthier, that kind of thing. And—" she dunked another potato "—Hoskin and Cole fight over Jolene."

"I see." This particular tidbit of information gave Drew an uneasy feeling. He remembered the way Hoskin looked at Elizabeth, and his stomach churned.

"That's not all." She dried her hands and turned to face him. "Lily's maiden name was Prescott."

It was the key he needed. He was torn between excitement, amazement and anger that Elizabeth had done this for him. "Why didn't you tell me sooner?" he asked.

"I only found out this afternoon. I should have told you while we were out walking but . . ." She looked down.

"You thought I was using you," he finished for her. He caught hold of her hands, cold from the water, and told her. "If I was only using you I wouldn't be so worried about you. Promise me you won't ask any more questions, Elizabeth."

"But I think that if I talked to Cal—"

"No!" he thundered. "I don't want you near Cal Hoskin. You don't play with a man like that, Elizabeth. If he caught on to what you were doing . . ." He couldn't finish.

When she winced, he looked down to see that he'd tightened his grip on her hands. "Sorry," he said, smoothing the soft skin in apology. "Since I'm the one who got you into this, I feel responsible. I'm only trying to look out for you. Will you make that promise?" She countered his question with her own. "If you're looking out for me, who's looking after you?"

"Me? I have a guardian angel," he joked. "I'll be fine." But the concern in her eyes didn't fade, and he grew serious. "Do I have your promise?" He squeezed her hands, and she nodded. "Say it," he commanded.

"I promise." Her lips trembled, and he forced his gaze back up to her eyes as a shaft of unexpected desire pierced him. "It's just that I keep thinking about that shot," she said. "They could have killed you."

He pulled her against his chest, silencing her worries. She was so small in his arms, like a bird, he thought, or that tiny wild orchid. He wished he could draw her inside him and keep her safe. Keep them both safe. His thoughts conjured up an image of them entwined in the shelter of her brass bed. He groaned, unable to stop his body from reacting to the picture.

How many days had it been since he'd kissed her? Ten, twelve? Too many. He'd been foolish to think that staying away would make his desire cool. He hadn't forgotten a thing. Not the wildflower scent that reminded him of the night he'd listened to her bathe. Not the amethyst sparkle of her eyes, or the texture of her hair, or the maddening way she wore it in a braid that prevented him from burying his fingers in it.

His hands went to the thick braid of silk, grasping it and tugging back lightly until her face tilted up to his, her lips just inches away. His fingers crushed the rope of hair as he tried to imagine what it would feel like trickling through his hands like liquid sunlight, or trailing across his chest as they made love.

He groaned and took her mouth in a kiss meant to quench his desire. She tasted like the honey they'd shared, pure and sweet, and the freedom she allowed his questing tongue brought him to the edge of control. He tore his mouth away.

"What's the matter?" she asked, the hazy desire in her voice telling him that she'd lost control as quickly as he.

"That wasn't a very good idea." He reluctantly put her away from him.

"Why not?"

"Because I'm investigating your friends."

"Didn't I prove that my loyalty lies with you?"

"Yes. But there are other reasons why we shouldn't—can't—get too involved with each other." He smiled and said, "You destroy my concentration, for one. And right now I need every bit of concentration I can get." He ignored the look in her lavender eyes, handing her the spoon and telling her solemnly, "The stew's scorching."

Elizabeth managed to rescue the stew, but she couldn't rescue the conversation Drew had ended so abruptly. She wanted to quiz him about the other reasons keeping them apart, but his silence as they finished preparing supper told her the topic wasn't welcome.

After they sat down to eat, Drew asked her a series of questions about raising sheep and wool production. She answered each question politely, thankful that they were speaking, at least. She told him that a couple ewes were showing signs of settling into gestation, and that led to a discussion of lambing. As she described the late nights watching the triumph of birth and suffering through the occasional losses, the uneasiness passed.

While Drew finished drying the dishes, she started to unpack a cardboard box of canned goods that had been sitting on the end of the counter since Lily's visit earlier that afternoon.

"I didn't know canning was one of your talents," he commented as he wiped the last piece of silverware and put it away.

"It isn't. Lily brought these as payment for her lessons."

He held two of the jars up to the light. "Hmm. Corn and...beef?" He looked at Elizabeth, a teasing grin on his face. "If I'd known you had canned steak around here I wouldn't have settled for soup."

Elizabeth smiled and wrinkled her nose. "I doubt it tastes anything like steak. Think you could reach up and put it on the top shelf for me?"

"Sure." He opened up the cupboard door, exposing row after row of jars, and started to laugh. "Jeez, you've got enough beef here to feed a platoon of marines. Why don't you just tell Lily you don't eat meat?"

"I don't want to seem rude," she admitted. "Beef is probably the most valuable canned item she can give me. Besides, I might eat it someday. On the other hand—" she grinned and handed him another jar "—maybe I'll trade it for something else."

"You must have been teaching Lily a long time to earn all this."

"Oh, we barter for other things, too. Garden produce, wood, labor—" she stopped when she sensed his sudden tension. "What's wrong?"

"Nothing's wrong." He reached out and gripped her upper arms, a broad smile on his face. "You just found my ticket to get inside the Colony."

She shook her head in bewilderment, and he explained, "I've been telling everyone in town that I'm looking for a piece of land. I'll offer to barter my labor to Silas Freeman in exchange for an acre or two. He said they were busy. They'd probably welcome the help. I've spent enough time here with you so that it would seem perfectly logical that I'd want to build near you."

The phrase *near you* echoed in her mind, making her heart sing, until she reminded herself that Drew intended it to be a ruse, not reality. "I don't think that will work, Drew."

He let go of her arms. "Why not?"

"If you wanted land near me, why not buy it from me? Or from Kresge's estate?"

"I tried. They aren't selling."

His words surprised her. Perhaps he was serious about buying land after all. Once he had it, would he come back here for vacations? Don't be silly, she told herself. He just wanted to make it look good for his investigation. "Even if Silas was willing to part with some land," she informed him, "he wouldn't deal with a man he didn't know. You're still a stranger to them."

"Not for long. I know you, and I've met his wife and Luke."

"It will take more than that. It will take time for them to accept you."

"I don't have time," he said, impatience edging his voice.

Elizabeth shook her head helplessly, wondering why she was arguing with Drew's determination. Selfishly, she wanted him to be around longer, and working for the Colony might accomplish that. But even more, she wanted him to be safe. If they somehow figured out he was lying.... She refused to dwell on the possibility. The safest course would be to ensure Drew wouldn't be alone. "You'll need my help," she told him.

"No." His refusal was flat. "We've been through this already today, Elizabeth. I don't want you in this any deeper. I can finish without you."

"Without me you won't even get inside the gate, Drew." For several long moments they stared at each other angrily, only the ticking of the ship clock on the windowsill breaking the silence.

"All right," Drew said at last. "What have you got in mind?"

"Next week I'm going to the Colony to get wood for the winter," she told him. "You can go with me then."

For the next half hour they sat at the dining table, putting together a simple plan. On a piece of paper torn from her journal, Elizabeth sketched a rough layout of the Colony. Drew folded it and stuffed it in his pocket, glancing at his watch. "It's getting late. I'd better get back to town." He stood and stretched, avoiding her searching gaze.

"Expecting another phone call?" she asked.

"Something like that."

"And if I asked you to stay?" she ventured, never letting on how much the question cost her.

"I'd say no."

"Because of your investigation of the Colony." She sighed. "What if we'd just met, Drew? What if there wasn't any investigation?"

"Then I'd still say no."

"Why?"

"That's pretty obvious. We're not right for each other, Elizabeth. You're an idealist. You look for the good in everyone, even where there's only evil. I'm too old for you, too cynical. Most of all, our life-styles are just too different."

"You're not old, and you're definitely not cynical. You've spent the past few years of your life exposing fraud and fighting for justice, which makes you quite an idealist, too, even though you tend to see only black and white. You're right about our life-styles—they are different. Why don't you give mine a chance? Take the time to appreciate the differences?"

"I don't have time." His blunt answer told her it was no use to argue.

"Then I won't waste any more of it. Good night, Drew."

The day they'd planned to go to the Colony came without another word from Drew. She knew he was still staying at Albert's. When Doc Wilson stopped by to give her some wild rice he'd gotten from one of his reservation patients, she'd shamelessly asked about him. Doc told her he'd seen Drew at Willie's Bar playing pool.

Drew playing pool? she marveled as she unlatched the pickup's gate. Perhaps he was adjusting to Nisswa's slower pace after all. Or perhaps he'd try anything if it meant avoiding her.

She was almost sorry she'd agreed to help him get past the Colony's gates. The Indian summer day was too beautiful for such perfidy. The autumn leaves were at their peak, and the sky was a bright, cloudless blue. Her flannel shirt matched the sky—if only she could match her mood to the day as easily as she could her clothing.

She was loading a box of apples from her orchard onto the pickup's bed when Drew pulled into the clearing minutes later.

"Ready to go?" he asked. Without waiting for her answer, he swung the second box onto the pickup's bed, reaching for an apple and biting into it with a loud crunch. He was obviously without second thoughts or nervousness. Instead of being re-assured, Elizabeth's doubts multiplied.

"Drew, this isn't going to work."

"It has to work. It's the only friendly way I can get inside that gate. And I'm going to get in, even if I have to do it the unfriendly way." He bit again into the apple. "Are you coming?"

He held the driver's door open for her, and with an air of fatalism Elizabeth got inside and started the engine. She could feel Drew's searching gaze for several long moments as they bumped along the track to the road.

At last he spoke. "What's eating you?"

"I feel like a Trojan horse."

"Pull over." He spoke calmly but Elizabeth could hear steel behind the words. She pulled to the side of the track and stopped.

"I thought your loyalties were with me. If you're having second thoughts, tell me now."

"They've never been anything more or less to me than neighborly."

"Oh, yeah? What about Cal Hoskin? He'd eat you for breakfast if he got the chance," he said, finally exhibiting some edginess.

She was certain Drew was exaggerating, but Cal Hoskin did make her uneasy. Was he the one who'd killed Paul Brewster?

"There's something else," he interrupted her meanderings. "I had Jim Levitz do a computer search on Lily Prescott. There's no record of a marriage. Or an adoption."

Her stomach clenched. "Maybe they got married in a different state."

"Jim checked. He also checked in Canada. He didn't find a marriage license, but he did find something. Lily's parents were killed four years ago in a car accident along with a man named Oliver. Four years, not two. Lily was still sixteen, not eighteen. Now, do you still feel like a Trojan horse?"

She put the truck into gear and drove on without answering. Had Lily lied to protect her husband? The last of her illusions about Silas vanished, and Elizabeth was more determined than ever to find out the truth.

The dread in the pit of her stomach grew heavier as she neared the gate, the critical point in their plan. Typically, someone would be waiting for her here. If not, she would signal her arrival with a honk of the truck's horn. But this time she had a passenger, and they might not be admitted at all.

"Luke's coming," she said with relief as the boy ran to the gate and opened it. Drew called out a greeting as she drove through. Luke waved, relocked the gate and hopped onto the bed of the truck. Shortly after they passed the windbreak trees that sheltered the farmyard, he jumped out and ran the rest of the way.

Women milled on the back porch of the white four square house, smiling their welcome. Elizabeth smiled back, while surreptitiously pointing out to Drew the smaller, newer house next to it where Hoskin and Cole lived with Jolene. She swung around the circular driveway, pulling up beside the woodpile and sawmill in the center of the yard. She could see Silas walking up from the barnyard, breaking into a trot when he recognized her passenger.

"If you need me, I'll be in the house," she told Drew before they got out. He handed her one of the boxes from the back, and Luke manfully reached for the other. She walked slowly to the porch, waiting for Silas to reach Drew, who was standing by the pickup's tailgate. When she heard Silas boom out a greeting and saw the two men shake hands, she relaxed and let Sara Stoltz lead her into the farmhouse kitchen.

Her business inside the house didn't take long. She declined a cup of tea, watched Lily show the women how to hold the wool cards she'd brought with her in her backpack, and promised to come back in a few weeks for a spinning demonstration. When she went back outside, she knew immediately that something had gone wrong.

Cal Hoskin and Lewis Cole had joined Silas, and the three formed a semicircle in front of Drew. The bed of the truck was piled high with cut wood. Out of the four men, only Drew appeared relaxed. Silas moved as jerkily as a bantam rooster, while Lewis Cole nervously combed his fingers through his dark hair. Cal Hoskin looked like a lion ready to pounce. And he was carrying a gun, she realized with a jolt of uneasiness.

"If you change your mind, just let me know," Drew was saying. He walked to the door of the pickup, apparently oblivious to the stares directed at his back. She realized his nonchalance was a sham when he opened the door for her and said "Slide over," under his breath.

She complied quickly, sliding around the gearbox and letting Drew take the wheel. Frustration emanated from him in waves. She didn't speak until they were almost to the cabin.

"Park in front so I can split the wood and stack it on the porch," she said. Now that she'd broken the tense silence, she ventured, "He said 'no,' didn't he?"

"Are you going to say 'I told you so'?"

"Of course not. I wanted you to succeed. I just think you needed to move a little more slowly, that's all. Maybe in a month or two—"

Drew didn't wait for the end of her sentence. Her words were drowned out by the slamming of his door. She scrambled out the passenger's side and walked to the back of the truck, where he was angrily tossing wood to the ground.

"I can't stay in this jerkwater town all winter, dammit," he said as he flung another piece of wood to the ground. "The election is less than a month away. If I can't stop Prince from here—" his sentence was interrupted by another thunk of wood "—I'm going back to Chicago."

Elizabeth realized it was his anger talking, and stifled the hurt his words caused. "I'm sorry it didn't work out the way you wanted it to," she said simply. She laid a hand of comfort on his arm, but he shrugged her off with the next toss of wood.

She stepped back and watched as he vented his anger on the wood. He stopped when he couldn't reach any more of the load without standing on the pickup's bed. He looked at Elizabeth, his chest heaving. She thought she caught a glimpse of regret in his dark eyes, but he turned away before she could be sure. She wanted to ask when he was leaving but she didn't dare.

"Where's the ax?" he asked bluntly.

"There's a single-bladed ax and a maul in the shed. But you don't have to—"

"I know I don't have to. Right now I need to." His voice softened. "Just leave me alone for a while, all right?"

Elizabeth retreated reluctantly. The cabin seemed cheerless and cold, and she built fires in both the range and the fireplace, her movements numb. She fixed herself a light lunch, resisting the impulse to take Drew a sandwich. Then she washed and dried the dishes and put them away before retreating to the loft, where she tried to spin away her lassitude.

As usual, the motions of spinning helped her see things more clearly. She realized now that being with Drew for a few weeks wasn't enough to warm the rest of her days. She wanted more. She wanted all of him—his laughter, even his impatience, but most of all, his love. She was convinced their differences complemented each other. But would she ever have a chance to prove it to him?

Only one thing was certain. Whether he was here or in Chicago, he wouldn't give up until he'd found justice for his friend, Paul Brewster. And for that she loved him most of all.

Gradually the repetitive motions of spinning calmed her. The *thunk, thunk* coming from outside was a rhythmic counterpart to the whir of her spinning wheel. When she felt completely composed she put a hand out to stop the wheel.

She went downstairs to the window, where she could see Drew splitting wood with a fierce concentration. His movements weren't at all awkward as they'd been when he first started. Unaware of her gaze, he removed his red-and-black plaid shirt. The medallion gleamed on his bare chest, and she felt awareness tug deep inside her.

She would ask him to stay.

Drew tossed aside his sweat-damp shirt and started on the next piece of wood. Newly split firewood was stacked neatly underneath the porch roof next to the railing. He'd found his rhythm early on, and the wood seemed to cleave itself each time he brought down the ax. He concentrated on his skill, the clean bite of the ax through wood, the smaller number of blows it took to split each subsequent piece.

With every blow he vented his frustration, and with every new layer of split wood added to the pile, he felt a corresponding rise of satisfaction. He understood now why Elizabeth had found solace in her spinning. Concentrating on physical effort freed the mind.

And still he couldn't decide. *Stay or go?* Elizabeth was right—sometimes goals clashed. He knew it was more important to stop Prince. One man's life didn't compare to an entire nation's best interests, even though the man had been his best friend. Or as close to a best friend as he'd ever had time for. The next blow of the ax pounded away both guilt and regret.

Going would mean leaving Elizabeth. That shouldn't even be a factor in his decision, he told himself. He knew there wasn't a future for the two of them, because hers was tied up too tightly with the Colony's. She relied on them for fuel and food and companionship, and she was including them in her plans to expand her business. When the Colony disintegrated, her world would change, and she would blame him.

His father would tell him to go. Alex Carter had sacrificed his friends and family often enough to do the right thing. Yeah, and now he was sixty and alone. If two people with six kids and forty years of marriage couldn't make a go of it, what was left for him and Elizabeth? He finished splitting the piece of wood in front of him in a single blow.

He heard the door open and turned to see Elizabeth coming down the porch steps with a steaming mug in her hands. "Here." She held it out to him. "It looked as though you could use a coffee break."

He thought she was speaking figuratively until he smelled the rich aroma. "Coffee?" He dropped the ax and reached for the mug with a mixture of pleasure and surprise. He wanted to kid her about feeding his caffeine habit, but her thoughtfulness touched him too deeply for teasing.

"I asked Sarah Stoltz if I could borrow some today," she told him.

"Thank you for thinking of it." He sipped gratefully at the hot liquid. "I'm surprised you didn't decide to throw it at me instead. I'm sorry for the way I acted earlier."

Her eyes filled with a sympathy he didn't deserve. "You put too much pressure on yourself," she said, and he realized she was right again. She added, "You need to follow your instincts more often instead of rationalizing everything."

The words brought a smile to his face. "Thanks for the coffee," he said. "Right now my instincts tell me I should kiss you."

She returned his smile, and he kissed her lightly on the lips. He wasn't ready for the jolt of reaction that nearly made him lose his grip on the mug of hot coffee. She stared at him, her lips parted, and he decided there were aches that no amount of physical labor could assuage. He drained the mug, hardly noticing how the contents scalded his throat on the way down. He set the empty mug on the porch rail and reached for her, but she stepped away. He grabbed his shirt instead, pulling it on without buttoning it and without meeting her eyes.

"Are you staying?" she asked.

"I haven't decided."

"In that case, I'd better let you get back to work," she said in a light voice that didn't quite mask her hurt.

"Elizabeth." His voice stopped her when she would have re-treated up the steps. "Help me decide." He gently pulled her toward him and lowered his head to kiss her, putting all the frustration, all the wanting he felt into that one kiss.

"Won't this just make it harder?" she asked when he re-leased her.

"Yes." She was right about that, too. He stepped away. But as he did, their hips brushed, his aching groin coming into full contact with her warmth. A strangled gasp burst from his throat.

She looked up at him, but the shock he expected to see in her eyes wasn't there. He reached out to pull her head against his shoulder, trying to escape from the heat in her eyes.

"Stay with me." Her words were a warm tingling by his ear making the floodgates holding back his desire tremble. Even as his body swelled with a rushing torrent of need, his mind was clouded with indecision. She took over, grasping his hand and leading him up the steps into the cabin, then to the alcove where the brass bed waited.

"Are you sure this is what you want?" he asked. The words tore reluctantly from him, but he had to give her another chance to be sensible. Neither of them was capable of making a sound decision now. The dam he'd placed on his emotions strained as he waited for her answer.

"Oh, yes." Smiling, never taking her gaze from his face, she peeled back the covers from the bed. An eddy of shock swirled through him as he realized that she was taking the decision into her own hands. He struggled for control, but it was swept away at the sight of her undoing the buttons on her shirt. He watched until he could stand it no longer, then he reached out and fin-ished parting the edges of the sky-blue flannel to reveal the old-fashioned, white cotton camisole she wore underneath. The cotton knit molded to her curves, showing him that she was as aroused as he.

"It's not satin and lace," she apologized.

He smiled and pushed the flannel shirt over her shoulders, letting it drop to the floor. "You're the sexiest woman I've ever seen," he told her, his voice husky with suppressed emotion, "no matter what you wear."

He reached out to touch the soft skin that swelled above the camisole's scooped neckline, and he heard her catch her breath. With a shaky laugh, she told him, "My turn."

She unbuttoned his shirt just as slowly as she'd unbuttoned her own, and Drew let himself be tugged along by the current. But her hands on his belt weren't quick enough, and he took over, unbuckling it himself. At that moment he knew that he had turned his back on logic and was following his instincts. For once, he was going to do what felt right to him, and to hell with the rest of the world. He stripped off his jeans, then hers, before tumbling them both onto the mattress. The smell of wildflowers surrounded them.

He stretched out beside her and told her honestly, "You can't imagine how many times I've fantasized about being with you like this."

"Here in my bed?"

"In your bed, in the bath, on top of the hill—it's a good thing I haven't seen the inside of your barn yet, or I'd probably have visions of making love to you there, too." As he spoke he let his hands explore her skin the way he'd dreamed of doing.

"You can go with me when I shut in the sheep tonight," she promised, a hint of laughter coloring her words.

"Got a hayloft?" He trailed a finger above the camisole's neckline.

"Yes." Her answer was barely audible, ending on a gasp.

"Good." He rolled on top of her. "Then we'll be comfortable."

Their legs tangled, and he thought again how incredibly soft she was. He could feel the pressure build with every touch, every kiss. When he removed the last of their clothing, leaving nothing between them but skin and warmth, the floodwaters rose even higher. His lips tasted the soft skin of her breasts before returning to her mouth for a drugging kiss.

Control was a life raft caught on a swollen river, drifting away with the current farther and farther out of reach. He had just enough presence of mind left to ask, "Elizabeth? Do you need to use the bathroom?"

"What?" Her voice was a confused whisper.

"I didn't bring anything with me," he admitted awkwardly. "Are you okay, or do you need to get something from the bathroom?"

He saw wavering indecision cross her features as the meaning of his words penetrated. He knew even then that she was considering the circumstances of her own birth. That knowledge brought him quickly back to solid ground.

"It's all right," she told him.

He knew her words were truthful, but he'd seen that brief moment of hesitation. He had to press, for both their sakes, even though he'd already guessed what her answer would be. "You're on the Pill?"

Disappointment colored Elizabeth's eyes before she closed them, shutting him out. "No," she admitted. "But it's probably not the right time of month to—"

"Shh." He pressed his fingers to her lips. "We can't take that chance, Elizabeth. The consequences are too great." Her eyes snapped open, and the accusation in them shocked him. "I couldn't do that to you," he finished shakily. He knew he was right, and he didn't question his decision—but why did being noble make him feel so rotten?

She tried to wriggle from his arms, but he wouldn't let her escape. She was angry, embarrassed and frustrated, and he knew he couldn't leave her like this. "We don't have to stop, you know," he told her, capturing her wrists in his hand.

"No? But—"

He silenced her with his lips, putting all the tenderness and caring he felt into the kiss. After a few short moments of resistance, she opened her mouth and responded. He released her hands. The waters rose again, but this time he was firmly in control. There was no other thought in his mind except to bring her pleasure. He trailed his lips over her breasts, her stomach, memorizing her taste.

Her fingers combed wildly through his hair, and she moaned. The breath of sound made him realize how completely she trusted him. That knowledge gave him the strength to resist the tempting thrust of her hips, the wild promise in her hands as they explored the base of his spine. He lifted his head, seeing the pale skin of her stomach rosy from the scrape of his whiskers. His voice was husky with tenderness. "Remember all those fantasies I mentioned?" She nodded. "One of them is about to come true."

He bent his head to show her and she rewarded him with a gasp of pleasure.

Chapter 10

When Elizabeth awoke, it was dark. She had no idea how long she had lain with her arm and leg thrown across Drew's body. Her natural sense of time had fled during his loving. She'd fallen asleep, her body utterly sated, but her heart aching to know all of him.

Now she was awake and restless and longing for that final intimacy. She smiled. Drew wouldn't thank her if she woke him and tried to seduce him again. Instinctively she knew she had the power to make him forget his honorable intention to protect her. But he wouldn't forgive her, and that's why she wouldn't carry through with her longings . . . this time.

Before she could change her mind she quietly withdrew her arm from his chest and felt around in the dark for her clothing. Her jeans and shoes were easily located, but she had to give up on her camisole and panties. And the shirt she'd picked up was Drew's, not her own. She decided to slip it on rather than open the squeaky dresser drawer.

She'd only be gone a few minutes, she promised herself as she rolled up the sleeves of the flannel shirt. After stopping in the kitchen long enough to confirm by the ship clock that it was still early evening, she left quietly through the connecting door to the barn, where she hurried through her chores.

When she opened the door to the vestibule that connected barn and house, the darkness inside had given way to the warm glow of kerosene lamps and a fire in the fireplace. Drew was standing at the gas range, shirtless, fiddling with the burners and swearing bluntly. She watched him for a few seconds, admiring the sleek movements of his muscles and smiling at his rumpled hair, before announcing her presence. "You're up."

He started, dropped a match and bit off another curse. "I was hoping to surprise you with supper. But I can't find a can opener and these dad-blamed burners won't cooperate."

"That's not what you were calling them when I came in." She took the box of matches from his hand. "Let me try. The propane tank is probably low."

He edged away as she stepped closer to the stovetop. His movement wasn't lost on her. "You have to set the knob on high first. Like this, see?" The ring of blue flame leaped to life, but Drew stayed in his corner of the kitchen. She wondered if he was afraid of a gas explosion—or afraid of her.

"I think I've got it now," he said lightly, stretching out his arm for the matches.

"The can opener is in here."

He stepped back as she reached in front of him to open a drawer. "Thanks," he said politely. "I think I can take it from here."

"Then I guess I'd better go change so you can have your shirt back." She hoped he would tell her to stay, to keep the shirt. Or better yet, that he would take it off himself and lead her back to the bed. He didn't. Disappointed, Elizabeth went to retrieve her own shirt from underneath the bed.

In the bathroom with the door closed between them, she regretfully removed Drew's shirt. Why was he backing away now, after their lovemaking? Had her abandoned responses turned him off? She looked in the mirror at her swollen lips and the whisker-scraped redness of her cheeks. She splashed cool water on her face but didn't stop there, rinsing her torso with an icy cold washcloth as though she could erase whatever had offended him.

When she came out, the table was set, and Drew was filling bowls from the pot at the stove. "Soup's on," he told her with a smile that didn't reach his eyes.

She silently handed him his shirt, and he slipped it on and buttoned it quickly. She tried to match his aloofness, but all the while she ate she grew more and more puzzled by his attitude. What was he feeling? she wondered as she cleared the table. Guilt over taking her to bed? Regret? Or was his mind already back on the investigation? His closed expression told her nothing as he joined her at the sink to do the dishes.

When she couldn't stand the silence any longer, she folded the dishtowel she'd been using and asked bluntly. "Are you going back to Chicago?"

"I don't know," he said as he wiped down the countertop. "I should. I've got to stop Prince."

She waited until he looked up. "What about me? We can't pretend nothing happened today, Drew."

"Yes we can, and that's exactly what we're going to do." He wrung the dishcloth tightly in his hands.

Elizabeth stared at him in disbelief. "Just because we didn't—" she struggled for a neutral term "—completely consummate our relationship doesn't make what happened unimportant."

He leaned one hip against the counter indolently, but Elizabeth could see tension in the way his hand gripped the edge of the countertop.

"Your honor is satisfied, so there's nothing more to be said. Is that it?" she demanded. He remained stubbornly silent. "Or did I do something wrong?"

"No, dammit," he exploded, launching himself from the counter. "You did everything right. *Too* right." He stopped as though afraid he'd said too much. Quietly, he added, "I'm the one who did something wrong. The point is we can stop it now without suffering any consequences."

"Ah, *consequences*," she mocked. "That dreaded word again. Did it occur to you that I'm an adult woman, old enough to make my own decisions? That I'd considered the consequences and was willing to take them?"

"You may be willing, but I'm not." He reached out and held her upper arms, forcing her to look into his eyes as he said gently, "I'm only thinking of you, Elizabeth. This is a small town. People will gossip."

Frustrated, she pulled away. She grabbed the teakettle from the stove and reached for the stoneware water jug. It was empty. She slammed her hand against the side and uncharacteristically swore.

"What's the matter?"

She drew a shaky breath, seeking control. "I need a cup of tea, and I'm out of spring water, that's all." She glanced at him and knew that he saw through her to the real cause of her frustration. She looked away nervously. "I was going to have Silas and his men add a gravity pipeline from the spring to the house, but—" She stopped when she realized she was babbling.

"I'll get the water." He took the heavy jug from her hands and went outside.

While she waited for Drew to return, she asked herself if she'd meant what she said about being willing to take the consequences. She knew the answer was yes. Before he'd asked her about birth control, before she'd invited him to her bed, even before then, she'd thought about a child. Drew's child. A little girl she could teach to spin, a girl with his dark eyes, a part of him that would stay behind when he left.

Only now did she realize how utterly selfish the impulse was. When Drew made his decision to leave or stay, she didn't want anything to hold him back. Whatever he decided, she would live with it.

Drew walked slowly up the hill to the springhouse, breathing in deep lungfuls of the frosty air. He glanced back over his shoulder. At night the homestead was achingly beautiful. Moonlight reflected off the pond and lamplight shone warmly from the cabin's windows. He looked away.

It would be easy to stay here, to lose himself in Elizabeth and forget his responsibilities. But he couldn't do that. He had windmills to tilt, a mission to fulfill, a book to write. He had to save the world from itself—or at least from men like Phillip Prince and Silas Freeman.

He closed the door of the springhouse and started back down the hill. The stoneware water jug was heavy, and he wondered why Elizabeth hadn't installed a pipeline before this. If Freeman and his men were willing to do the work for her, it was only logical— He halted, and then started running.

He burst into the cabin and set the jug on the counter, grinning at Elizabeth's startled expression. "I just thought of a way to get inside the Colony," he announced. "You can hire them to help me to put in the pipe from your spring."

She looked at him blankly. "Don't you see?" he asked. "If I work beside them for a while, they'll grow to trust me."

"But, Drew, the pipeline would only take a couple of days."

"Then we'll think of something else. How about a new barn?"

She laughed. "I don't need one. At least not until next winter."

"Is it the money? I'll lend you—"

"Money is no problem," she interrupted, turning away. He caught her by the shoulder and turned her back to face him.

"Then what is it? You wanted to help me before. Why not now?" He didn't add that this new plan would require him to stay. He saw the knowledge of that in her eyes. Was that why she was so reluctant? "Will you help me?" he asked.

She looked at him steadily for several moments while his heart beat in a wild pattern.

"All right," she said at last. "I'll do it."

Their plan was simple, and within an hour they'd settled on the details. Elizabeth wanted a garage, built near the gravel road so that she could get out when it snowed. At first Drew had argued with her. "Wouldn't it make more sense to widen your driveway?" he'd asked. "Or buy a four-wheel drive vehicle?"

"I don't want a wide driveway. It would be too easy for people to find their way back here."

"You'd rather have them stumbling through your pasture and getting hurt," he teased. "Like I did. Or is it that you're too sentimental about Claire's truck to buy a new one?"

His warm teasing had made her falter. He acted as though the afternoon had been erased from his memory and they were simply friends. But they'd gone too far for that, and she wondered if she could be near him for the time it would take to build the garage without making a fool of herself. She reminded him, "If I buy a new truck, or hire a road crew to widen my driveway, you wouldn't get your chance to work with Silas." He'd given in quickly after that, and they'd finished their plans a few minutes later.

The garage would be log constructed. Elizabeth knew that the project would take several days. She told herself that she hadn't chosen the project for that reason, but as she saw Drew to the door, she wasn't sure her motives were pure. The fact was she was glad he was staying.

"I was thinking," Drew said, not quite meeting her eyes as he reached for the doorknob. "The Colony would be more

likely to accept me if they thought you and I . . . Well, if they
believed that you were my woman. Will you play the part? Just
for appearance's sake, of course.''

Her nerves jumped at his words.

He waited for her response, one broad shoulder leaning casually against the doorjamb, his hands thrust carelessly into his
hip pockets. She nodded, not trusting herself to speak.

"Good." He surprised her by bending down to seal their
bargain with a kiss. They could just as well have shaken hands.
The kiss was friendly, sexless, and as she watched him walk to
his truck, Elizabeth couldn't help wishing that he'd pulled her
in his arms, carried her to the bed, and made her his woman for
real.

When Drew turned onto the dead-end road two weeks later,
the sun hadn't yet risen above the tops of the trees. When he
and Elizabeth had gone to the Colony to arrange the work on
the garage, he'd wisely kept to the background, letting her do
all the talking. Freeman had estimated it would take a week to
finish the garage. Drew hoped it would be long enough to get
past their defenses. The election was only eleven days away, and
Prince was leading in the polls.

The days since had dragged by, with only the afternoons to
look forward to. He spent those at Elizabeth's, arriving an hour
or so before Lily's spinning lessons and leaving shortly after
nightfall. He timed his visits for two reasons. The first was so
Lily would see them together, adding credibility to their supposed relationship. The second was because she provided a safe
chaperon.

Somehow he'd managed to stay out of her bed for two weeks,
but he wasn't superhuman. The stress of waiting for Freeman's men and wondering how Jim Levitz was handling Prince
in Chicago, compounded with the tension of being near Elizabeth day after day and denying his sexual response to her, was
tearing him apart.

He turned into her driveway with a sense of fatalism, slowing down as he passed the almost hidden site she'd chosen for
her garage. As the woods thinned, he could see the sheep in the
low pasture. He recognized the one that had nipped at the seat
of his jeans a couple days before, the one Elizabeth called
Whiskey Jack.

He'd stayed long enough at the cabin each afternoon to help her with the sheep, leading them from the pasture to the paddock before Lily's arrival and feeding them after she left. If Luke was with her, he and Drew carded wool or played with the Frisbee. Once Drew had even tried spinning himself, with results that had kept the two women giggling the rest of the afternoon and earned Luke's temporary disfavor. He helped in the kitchen, he fixed the windmill, he cleaned the barn and spread the manure over the garden. Every day he understood a little more about the Colony's life-style. And every day Elizabeth's cabin felt a lot more like home.

She worked beside him most of the time, and it was all he could do to keep from taking her in the hayloft or laying her down underneath a tree in the pasture. He poured all his energies into work and somehow managed to keep his sexual frustration at bay. Now temptation would be under the same roof.

He parked the truck behind Elizabeth's battered pickup, grabbing the box full of papers on the seat next to him and following the powerful scent of her boiled coffee into the kitchen. The scene was cozily domestic. The table was set with a vase of asters in the center, the plates piled high with food, but Drew's gaze passed over them and settled on Elizabeth.

"Good morning," she greeted. She was wearing a cotton turtleneck. The prim neckline didn't begin to make up for the way the thin red cotton audaciously hugged her curves.

"Morning," he returned, deliberately omitting the "good."

"Silas and his men will be at the site any minute. You've got just enough time for breakfast."

"I ate in town," he growled as he looked around the room for a place to stash his things.

"Let me guess. A cup of black coffee, a sweet roll and a cigarette."

Drew tried to keep the surprise from showing on his face but failed. "How did you know?"

"That you started smoking again? It doesn't take a journalist's instincts to notice that your clothes have smelled like cigarette smoke for the past two weeks. I happen to know that Albert prefers chewing tobacco."

He hoped she'd blame his renewed habit on the stress of waiting for Freeman. He knew better. He'd bought the first pack the night he left her place sixteen days ago—the night after they'd spent the afternoon in bed, two whole days before he'd found out from Silas that the men wouldn't be starting until now. Unfortunately, nicotine hadn't blunted his urges one bit.

"I suppose you want me to quit," he challenged.

But she wasn't about to be drawn into a fight. "If you want to kill yourself, that's your prerogative, as long as you don't go around dropping any live butts in the barn. What are you doing with that box?"

"It's full of notes on Prince and the Colony. I can't very well leave it sitting in my truck if I'm going to drive it down to the construction site. Is there somewhere I can keep it away from prying eyes?"

"Well, the loft always used to be safe," she said.

Drew didn't rise to the bait. If she'd changed her mind about wanting an argument she was too late. He wanted to be at the site working when Silas Freeman showed up. He was coming down the ladder from the loft when she asked the question he'd hoped to avoid. He should have known Elizabeth's directness wouldn't let him off easy.

"Are you moving in?"

"I thought it would be more convincing," he said, heading for the door.

"You could have asked," she said dryly. "Do you really think they'll believe that I'm your woman?"

He shrugged, his hand on the doorknob.

"Then you'd better take time for breakfast. Don't you think our supposed relationship would be more convincing if you arrived five or ten minutes after they did, so they'll be sure to see you coming from my place?"

He smiled and pulled out a chair. "You're a woman of subterfuge after all, Elizabeth Johnson."

Elizabeth cleared the table and started on the dishes. She never cooked a breakfast this large for herself, and now she realized why. It was too much work. But throughout the extra chores her mind held on to one thought. Drew was spending the night. And the night after that and every night until he found out who killed Paul Brewster. With luck, it would be time enough to put her plans to work.

Without the desire that she surprised now and then in Drew's eyes, she would have believed him when he claimed his thoughts were only for the investigation. But those unguarded moments proved that he wanted her as much as she wanted him.

She had no qualms about using that wanting as the starting point for her campaign. She had every intention of demonstrating that they had a future together, and she intended to start tonight.

A woman of subterfuge, indeed, she thought with a grin.

Drew had never worked so hard in his life. Sure, he'd stayed up forty-eight hours plus to file a story, even risk life and limb to get an interview, but this was different. This was blister-raising, back-wrenching, sweat-producing labor. He'd discovered an entire collection of muscles that had never been challenged by a game of racquetball or a morning jog, or even by the hour or two of chores he'd been doing for Elizabeth every afternoon.

He felt a little like the skinniest kid on the bench trying out for the first string. He'd had to push twice as hard as the others to prove himself, but it was working. The skeptical glances that greeted him two hours ago had changed to grudging looks of respect.

Except for one. Out of the crew of five men, Cal Hoskin alone remained unimpressed by his efforts, even though Drew pitched in wherever he was needed. He shoveled dirt, cut trees and brush, and unloaded logs and tools from the flatbed truck. Luke dogged his steps nearly everywhere, until a sharp word from Hoskin sent the boy running back to the truck.

Because of his experience as a carpenter, Silas Freeman was directing the crew, but it was Hoskin who made sure Drew always got the heaviest, dirtiest job. Drew had felt a satisfying flicker of vengeance when the two men got into an argument over who should set up the portable sawmill. It deteriorated into a shouting match, and when Hoskin cursed at Freeman, Drew was certain the older man would explode. Red-faced and sputtering like an enraged drill sergeant, Freeman made it clear that the one thing he would not tolerate from his "platoon" was cursing.

When Freeman called for a break, Drew sank to the ground with relief, resting his back against a large pine log. He heard a woman's voice and spun around to see Elizabeth, her arms wrapped around a large paper bag. He hadn't even noticed the old pickup's arrival.

"I thought you men might like some coffee," she said to the group. Drew grinned to himself while she took a large thermos out of the bag, along with a basket of muffins and cookies. He hadn't had the nerve to tell her yet, but she made terrible coffee—pitch-black and muddy with grounds. Right now it was just what he needed. While the men milled around the pickup's gate that acted as a makeshift serving table, Elizabeth walked over to where Drew sat.

He held out his hand to take the mug she offered, automatically wincing when the hot surface seared his palm like a branding iron. Her gaze immediately went to the angry red strip of skin that crossed his hand.

"You should be wearing gloves," she said quietly. She sat and reached for his free hand, running her fingers over the tender flesh. Her touch burned, and not because of the blisters. Drew snatched his hand away.

"No," he said, quietly but firmly. "I don't want them to think I'm a wimp. Do you see anyone else wearing gloves?"

"Is that what this is about?" she asked. "Some kind of macho hazing ritual?" She looked toward the other men, who were perched on the back of the flatbed truck, eating and drinking and talking. Only Hoskin watched them. Drew wondered if Elizabeth could see the enmity behind his stare.

"In a way," he admitted. "I want them to accept me. They won't do that unless I can prove I deserve their respect."

"How did it go this morning?"

"Slow," he admitted with a grin, "but I'm learning." He glanced over at the men again and saw Luke reaching for another cookie. "Speaking of learning, shouldn't Luke be in school?"

"The children are taught at home by Genna Stoltz, Robert's wife. Luke's the oldest boy. Silas must have decided he could come along today."

Drew sipped thoughtfully at his coffee. Elizabeth's next words caught him completely unaware.

"Where are you going to sleep tonight, Drew?"

He choked on a mouthful of coffee, coughed and said hoarsely, "I haven't thought that far ahead yet." It was a blatant lie, but Elizabeth never had a chance to challenge it as Cal Hoskin approached them.

"Time to start," Hoskin announced with his usual economy of words.

For once, Drew was grateful for the man's interruption. Elizabeth's question had done more than just shock him. It had brought an instant—and arousing—image of them together in her brass bed. He wondered if her directness was designed to unsettle him. "We'll talk later," he said under his breath after Hoskin left.

"Silas told me the men will drive home at noon for their dinner. I can bring you some sandwiches here, or you can come up to the cabin."

"I'll come up," he told her, wondering what he might be getting himself into if he did. "Elizabeth," he said, stopping her when she would have walked away. He knew the men were watching and decided this was as good a time as any to establish his "relationship" with her.

"Yes?"

"You forgot something." He took advantage of her momentary confusion by pulling her into his arms and dropping a brief kiss on her lips. Her eyes blazed with anger, and he knew she'd guessed the purpose of the gesture. Before he realized her intentions, she reached up and tugged his head down, threading her fingers through his hair and kissing him soundly while the men hooted and cheered.

"See you at noon," she said coolly, while his insides burned like a brush fire.

He watched her walk back to the truck, admiring against his will the determined straightness of her back. Then he realized he wasn't alone in his observation. Cal Hoskin was staring at Elizabeth with an expression that could only be called lust. Drew swallowed back his instant rage. He reminded himself that he was treading a narrow path. A single step out of place and someone—Elizabeth—could get hurt.

When Drew dragged himself in the door that night, Elizabeth bit back a gasp of concern. She knew that he wouldn't welcome any acknowledgement of his condition. "Wash up," she told him briskly. "I'll have supper ready in a few minutes, and afterward you can take a hot bath."

"Yes, ma'am," Drew said with a tired grin that didn't quite reach his eyes. He disappeared into the bathroom, staying there so long that Elizabeth almost went in and got him. At last he came out. "Sorry," he said. "I feel like I'm moving underwater. I can hardly lift my arms."

"Can you eat? I opened up some of Lily's canned beef." She set a serving dish of stroganoff on the table in front of him, and he smiled.

"Ah, Russia. I wondered where we were traveling to tonight." She looked at him quizzically and he explained, "You've cooked a different ethnic dish for almost every meal, from ratatouille to the *huevos rancheros* we had for breakfast. I can't remember when I've eaten this well." He patted his flat belly. "I can get fat in twelve different languages."

His words brought a smile to her lips. She knew there was no danger of Drew getting fat. He'd worked hard during the past two weeks, and even under his clothing she could see the play of toned muscle as he moved.

While he was on his third helping, she got the tub out of the pantry and filled it. "You go ahead and soak," she told him when he finished eating. "I'll do the dishes tonight."

He didn't argue, and that alone told her how tired he was. She'd filled the tub in front of the fireplace so she could move freely around the kitchen while Drew bathed. As she washed dishes, she kept an eye on him to make sure he wouldn't fall asleep in the water. This time the sight of his body brought out feelings of tenderness rather than passion.

When he was done soaking she helped him out of the tub and handed him a towel. He quickly wrapped it around his hips and waited implacably for her to go to the barn before drying himself off. She didn't know whether to be amused or upset at his newfound modesty.

By the time she came back inside the cabin the tub had been emptied and stored, and a clean shirt hung over the back of the chair where Drew's duffel bag sat. Drew was lying on the sofa. He'd managed to pull on his jeans, but his feet and torso were bare. The ever-present medallion glinted on his chest in the firelight. He was fast asleep. Shaking her head, she covered him with the softly colored afghan from the bed. The evening hadn't gone quite the way she'd expected.

She sat in the oak rocking chair, reaching into her workbasket for the special white sweater she'd been working on since the week after Drew had arrived. Tonight she would weave in ribbons of icy blue around the yoke, leaving the ends dangling loosely. During the past few weeks she'd completed enough sweaters and scarves to take to the shops in Minneapolis and Chicago for the Christmas season. She should deliver them as soon as she finished this project, but she didn't want to leave Drew. They'd be apart soon enough, unless she could convince him to stay.

A soft snore from the direction of the sofa made her smile wryly. Drew probably wouldn't even notice if she left. At least she hadn't given in to a ridiculous impulse to knit a sweater for him. She wasn't that hopelessly besotted, she assured herself.

Hours later, when her head started to nod, she set aside her knitting. She checked on the sheep one more time before adding another log to the fire and putting out all the lamps. When she walked by the sofa, Drew stirred and stretched, throwing aside the afghan and rubbing a hand over his bare chest. The gesture made her catch her breath.

"What time is it?" he asked.

"About ten-thirty. You'll have another busy day tomorrow—you should get to bed."

Drew sat up and laughed. "After sleeping all evening? No, I think I'll run into town and call Jim. Then I'll probably work for a while. Is it okay if I use the dining room table, or will the light keep you awake?"

"The light won't bother me," Elizabeth said, trying to keep the disappointment from her voice. It it hadn't been for her reaction to the sight of his bare chest, she could almost fool herself into thinking he was merely the polite houseguest he sounded like. Silently she handed him his shirt.

No, the evening hadn't gone at all the way she'd expected.

Drew got back to the cabin about two hours later and shut the door quietly behind him. He'd tried calling Jim both at home and at the newspaper's offices. Because it was a Friday night, he'd even phone Jim's girlfriend, Dina. It had taken a considerable amount of persuasion on his part, not to mention outright sneakiness, to get the number from the police department. And all for nothing—Jim wasn't with her, either.

The trip hadn't been completely wasted though, he decided as he walked to the fireplace. It had at least gotten him out of the cabin before Elizabeth finished undressing. He'd watched her pull out a white cotton nightgown from the dresser and sit on the edge of the brass bed to unbraid her hair in the lamplight. He'd never seen her with her hair open, and he knew he couldn't watch without wanting to bury his hands in the bright silken strands and push her back onto the bed. He left before the sight became too hard to resist.

Hell, he didn't know why he kept resisting, he thought as he stared at the dying flames. Elizabeth's lavender eyes hid nothing, and he knew that she would have welcomed him into her bed. Being in that bed once had been a beautiful mistake—any more than that and it would become a habit. And a damned sight harder to break than this one, he thought as he took a pack of cigarettes out of his duffel bag. He went outside to the porch, carefully keeping his eyes turned away from the alcove where she slept.

He leaned over the rail, ignoring the chilly night air as he tamped the cigarette impatiently against the back of his hand. He had a feeling that it was going to take a lot more than a hit of nicotine to erase the vision of waking up next to Elizabeth in the morning.

"You were gone early this morning," Elizabeth commented as she passed Drew the plate of sandwiches she'd made for their dinner. "Did you get a lot of work done last night?"

He'd helped her with the sandwiches, his usual laughing and teasing self, but the laughter never reached his eyes. She knew he was as tense as she was.

"Actually, I did. Jim wasn't home, so I went through Paul's notes again." He reached for another sandwich. "I'm getting a better picture of how groups like the Colony organize. They share a common base with members of the Klan and other white supremacist groups through a church called Christian Soldiers. They believe that white Protestants are actually God's chosen race, the lost tribes of Israel, while the world's governments are run by the descendants of Satan."

"That's ridiculous."

"To you and me. But they've developed an elaborate conspiracy theory with pages of documentation to support it. They want to return the country to Biblical law, violently, if they have to," he added. "Paul estimated about two thousand adherents live right here in Wisconsin. Fortunately, they're too stubbornly independent to band together and start training militarily. Right now their goal seems to be getting sympathetic politicians elected to office.''

"Like Phillip Prince. Do you think you'll be able to stop him in time?''

"Not unless his campaign self-destructs between now and the first of November. He's leading in all the polls." Drew sounded resigned.

"Doesn't that bother you anymore?"

He shrugged. "If I have to, I'll go after Prince once he's in office. First I want to know who killed Paul Brewster."

He sounded like a man out for vengeance. She pushed away her half-eaten sandwich. "You slept on the sofa last night."

Elizabeth could see that the change of subject caught him by surprise. He finished the last couple bites of his sandwich before he spoke. "I didn't want to wake you."

"Are you avoiding me?"

"Yes." If he'd meant to shock her right back, his blunt answer had certainly succeeded. "I can't afford to be distracted from the investigation. I've told you that before." He didn't give her a chance to object before asking, "Would you do me a favor?"

"Maybe." She was reluctant to drop the conversation so quickly, but Drew was already on his feet.

"Since I didn't hear from Jim yesterday, I'm expecting a package today. Could you drive into Forest City and get it for me? I don't want to leave the construction site. The post office closes at noon on Saturdays, but the lobby with the boxes stays open." He dug into his pocket for the key. "It's 36."

He was out the door and on his way before Elizabeth had even agreed to help. She sat with the key in her hand—still warm from his body—and listened to his truck drive away.

Drew grimaced as he sipped the thermos capful of coffee. After sitting since Elizabeth had made it at noon, the grounds settled to the bottom of the cup like delta mud.

He took another sip, then looked toward the lumber pile where the other men sat, wondering if he should cadge a cup of coffee from Richard Stoltz. This morning the two of them had hauled logs to the sawmill, and Richard told him briefly how he'd overborrowed to pay for farm equipment and seed and ended up losing the farm. He and his twin brother were quiet, pious men, but Drew suspected it was because of the farm, and not ideology, that they'd stayed on under Freeman.

This afternoon the Stoltz brothers sat together, away from the others. As Drew watched, Robert tipped the thermos they were using and poured the last drops into his cup. Drew's gaze moved on. And stopped.

Luke, who'd been underfoot all afternoon, had climbed up on the back of the truck and was reaching for the rifle Cal Hoskin had left leaning against the cab.

"Luke!" Drew leaped up, dropping his cup. Hot coffee sprayed over his jeans, but he didn't notice. He vaulted a log and scrambled up the flatbed while five pairs of eyes looked on. Once there, he wasn't sure what to do. Luke looked at him steadily, dressed in overalls, a miniature version of Silas Freeman. The rifle hung slackly from the hand at his side.

"Could I see the gun, Luke?" Drew asked calmly.

"Sure, but it's not mine," the boy answered. Drew's hands shook as he took the weapon from the seven-year-old. He looked down at Freeman, who rose to his feet and walked over to the side of the truck.

"Is something the matter, Mr. Carter?" Silas asked.

Drew reminded himself to be diplomatic, but his heart was beating too fast for caution. "Yeah. You oughta keep this locked up somewhere. Or at least out of Luke's reach." He handed the gun to Freeman.

To his surprise, Silas Freeman threw back his head and guffawed. The other men joined in, filling the clearing with laughter, while Drew watched, dumbfounded. "What's the joke?" he asked.

Freeman, his eyes still twinkling with mirth, turned to Luke. "Show him, boy."

Luke reached out and took the gun from Freeman and shouldered it with ease. "See that branch over there with one leaf still on it?" He announced his target just as a pool shark calls his next pocket. And then he pulled the trigger.

The blast echoed through the woods and rang in Drew's ears long after. Almost with detachment he noticed that Luke had destroyed the leaf and branch. The boy looked up at him, his blue eyes expectant. Drew said, "Nice shot." He hoped no one noticed the hollow ring to the words.

He looked back at Freeman, who was brimming with pride at Luke's accomplishment. "First time he's fired an AR-15," he said. "He has his own .22 rifle. I taught him how to shoot it myself." Drew masked the sickness that rose inside him at Freeman's words. "There's more important things for a boy to learn than that garbage they teach in the public schools," Silas went on. "Ain't that right, boy?"

"Yes, sir," Luke said solemnly. He handed the gun back to Freeman and leaped from the truck bed. Numb with shock, Drew didn't move until Freeman ordered, "Break's over, men—everybody back to work."

When Elizabeth heard Drew pounding up the steps to the cabin she knew that something was wrong. It was late, almost midnight, and she hadn't seen him since supper when he'd told her about Luke and the gun. But it was her news for him that had sent him immediately to town and telephone. There'd been no word from Jim Levitz; the post office box was empty.

When he flung open the door, his face lined with anger, she stood. Her knitting dropped unheeded to the floor. "What happened? Was Jim home?"

He didn't pause, but kept right on walking to the chair where his duffel bag still sat, tossing his answer over his shoulder. "He's in the hospital. The fool kid asked too many questions, and Prince beat him up."

"At least that won't go over very well with the voters," Elizabeth pointed out.

"Yeah, that's what I'm hoping."

"You're leaving?"

Drew didn't answer. He didn't need to; he'd already started to throw overnight things into a small shaving kit. Elizabeth looked away. She'd thought living each day with the eventual threat of Drew's departure was bad enough, but this sudden leave-taking was even worse. She shook her head to clear it and realize Drew was talking.

"...so I'm driving to Milwaukee tonight and taking the first flight out."

"But what about the Colony? And Paul?" *And me,* she kept from adding. "Are you coming back?"

Drew turned to look at her then, and he relaxed visibly. "I'll be back late tomorrow night or sometime Monday morning. Tomorrow's Sunday, so Freeman's crew won't be working," he told her. "You said you needed to take some things to your buyer. Why don't you come with me?"

"I boxed everything up and sent it today while I was at the post office. I didn't want to leave while you were here," she said woodenly. "Besides, I'd have to find someone to watch the sheep, and Lily would be the only one I could ask on such short notice."

"No, that wouldn't do. I don't want anyone from the Colony to figure out where I've gone. Prince may know now that I'm here. If so, you could be in danger, too. Couldn't you call Gene Larson from Milwaukee?" he asked.

She shook her head. "I'll be fine," she assured him. "As long as you come back in one piece."

"That's a promise." He dropped his overnight kit onto the seat of the rocking chair and pulled her into his arms for a fierce hug. He kissed her then, with a desperation that shook her.

After the door had closed behind him, Elizabeth could feel the tears gathering at the corners of her eyes. Could a man kiss with that much intensity if he wasn't in love?

Chapter 11

Drew rapped lightly on the door to Room 419 before entering. Not recognizing the puffy-faced man in the bed nearest the door in the semiprivate room, he was about to try the curtained bed by the window when a familiar voice said, "Hey, Carter, great duds."

Perplexed, Drew looked down at his jeans and plaid flannel shirt before it hit him. The swollen-faced, bandaged patient was Jim Levitz. Drew hid his shock. The unrecognizably puffy face broke into something that resembled a grin, and Drew said lightly, "Forget how I look. You should see yourself." The only thing recognizable about Jim was his shaggy hair.

The younger man groaned. "No thanks. As long as I can't see the damages, it doesn't hurt. What are you doing here?"

Drew sat down in the straight-back visitor's chair next to the narrow bed. "I called your girlfriend last night to find out where you were. She told me that she and a couple of her fellow officers found you in the basement of your apartment building's parking garage." Drew leaned closer to assess the damages. "Mercy, Jim, what a mess. Two shiners, a missing tooth . . ."

" . . . three broken ribs, one bruised kidney, and a partridge in a pear tree," Levitz finished in an off-key chant.

"Cut the comedy. You could have been killed." Drew settled back into his chair and crossed his arms over his chest. "What happened?"

"Didn't Dina tell you? Prince followed me home from an interview I had with one of his dad's army buddies. He caught up with me in a parking garage, and two of his goons played paddywhack on my face while he asked questions. I guess I wasn't careful enough about covering my tracks."

Drew felt a twist of guilt for putting Jim in this situation. If he hadn't hurried off to Wisconsin... He thought of Elizabeth then, and dread swept over him in waves. Was she in danger, too? "What questions? Did they link you with me?"

"Nah, I don't think so, although they figured out I wasn't investigating on my own. They wanted to know why I was snooping into Prince's past, and who was directing me. I told them I was an enterprising young reporter looking for a lucky break. They gave me a break all right." He winced as he shifted in the bed.

"Did they buy your story?"

"After a while. I think it took about twenty minutes, although it seemed like longer." Drew swore, and Jim pointed out, "Hey, the funny part is that it was the truth—I *am* looking for my lucky break."

"There's nothing funny about it. How'd you end up here?"

"Dina and I were planning to catch the last show at Second City. When I didn't show up she came looking for me with a couple of friends."

"Thank God."

"Yeah." Both men fell silent. Then Jim grinned, gaptoothed. "I forgot the best part."

"What's that?"

"You haven't heard?" Jim's head snapped back against the pillows. "Jeez, Drew, don't they get the news in Nisswa?" He tucked his hands behind his head and grinned cockily.

Even with the purplish bruises and missing tooth, Drew recognized the look of triumph. "Well, don't leave me hanging."

"The cops caught up with Prince's goons last night. By this morning one of them was telling everybody who'd listen that Prince had hired him to do me bodily damage."

When Drew didn't react, Jim said, "Don't you get it, man? Prince's reputation is shot. Not only that, but I have it from an inside source—" he stressed the phrase "—that Phillip Prince,

Esq., spent two extremely uncomfortable hours in jail until he was bailed out this morning." He grinned again. "It pays to have friends on the force."

Drew looked at the vase of red roses on the utilitarian night-stand next to him. "I can see that."

"Just a little tribute for a hero. It'll be all over the papers tomorrow—Racist Politician Beats Up Jewish Reporter. We did it, Drew. We got Prince out of the election. Too bad it happened on the weekend, or it'd be out in the afternoon edition. At least it's been a slow news day today. It'll be on the front page tomorrow, mark my words."

Drew sighed heavily. At least Jim was taking it well. Hell, he suspected the kid would let Prince's henchmen break his ribs all over again for another story. Then he smiled, remembering his own excitement at his first headlines. He couldn't blame Jim for feeling over the moon, and he hated to bring him down to earth. "Prince wasn't the one who pulled the trigger," he reminded Jim. "We still have to find the man who shot Paul, and we don't want Prince giving him any warnings."

"Don't worry. There's no way he could connect me with you or Wisconsin. How's it going?" Drew told him briefly about his plans to infiltrate the Colony, carefully omitting any mention of Elizabeth. "How are you and Elizabeth Johnson getting along?" Jim asked archly.

Drew stared at Jim. "What makes you ask?"

"My reporter's instinct. I'm a born investigator, Drew." Jim's words were followed by another wide grin. Then he turned serious. "When you called about those articles in the morgue, I got the impression there was more to it than you let on. You really care about her, don't you?"

A picture of Elizabeth flashed through his mind. "Yeah," he admitted gruffly. Now that Prince was out of commission, he had all the time in the world to infiltrate the Colony. And to be with Elizabeth.

Later, when he was in a taxi heading back to the hospital with the cheeseburger and chocolate shake Jim had requested, his thoughts returned to Elizabeth. He ran a couple of errands on her behalf leaving the hospital, although he was beginning to wonder if he should have made either purchase. His thoughts were interrupted abruptly as the taxi swerved to avoid a bus.

Horns honked, tires screeched, and Drew braced himself for an accident. Miraculously the cab driver squeezed between two other cars, then slammed on the brakes when a group of teenage girls ran across the street. Drew's head snapped back against the ripped vinyl seat. He didn't remember Sunday afternoon traffic being quite this bad.

"Were the Bears at Soldier Field today?" he asked the cabbie.

"Nah, it's always like this." The jowly faced man looked at him via the rearview mirror. "Where ya from?" he asked conversationally.

Drew nearly guffawed at the question. With an ironic smile he answered, "Wisconsin."

Elizabeth was in bed when she heard Drew's truck coming up her driveway. Every tense muscle in her body relaxed at the sound. She'd spent the night blaming a pillow that wouldn't plump and sheets that kept twisting around her ankles, until finally she'd admitted that it was her thoughts and not the linens that kept her awake. The fear that he wouldn't come back after reacquainting himself with city life grew stronger as the night passed. She should have remembered his determination to find Paul's killer. It was late, but he was here.

The truck's engine ceased, and she waited for him to enter. When the silence remained unbroken for several minutes, she threw back the covers and reached for the afghan that draped over the brass bedpost before padding across the wooden floor in her bare feet. She stepped out onto the porch and gathered the afghan around her as the night chill penetrated her cotton gown. Her gaze went immediately to the truck. When she saw that it was empty, she frowned and scanned the darkness, calling Drew's name softly.

"Over here."

He was standing halfway up the east hill, looking down toward the pond and orchard. Moonlight reflected off the pond's glassy surface and highlighted the silver in his hair. Elizabeth stayed where she was, watching him walk toward her, his breath a cloud of steam in the freezing air. He looked reassuringly familiar in flannel shirt and jeans, and his navy down vest reminded her how cold the boards were beneath her feet. He stopped one step below her, and they faced each other at eye level in the night silence.

Drew opened his mouth to speak, then glanced down and caught sight of her bare feet. Elizabeth never knew what he'd been about to say. Instead he told her, "Get inside, woman, or you'll catch pneumonia."

His gravelly command made her smile, warming her like no fire could have. "Pneumonia's unlikely, unless you picked up some germs at the hospital." But she complied, leading the way inside the cabin, where only a faint glow remained of the fire she'd stoked a couple hours ago. "How was Jim?"

"He looked like hell, but he was as cocky as ever and flying high on excitement. They'll release him in a few days. The doctors want to keep an eye on his kidney function." The tiredness in his voice caught at her.

"And Phillip Prince?"

"I don't think we'll have to worry about him anymore." He told Elizabeth about the beating and the evening news broadcast, which had focused on Prince's past as a Klan leader.

"What if he connects Jim to you and warns Silas?"

"He's going to be too busy fending off reporters and civil rights groups to worry about ASP or Freeman. An awful lot of people are watching him right now, and he wouldn't want to tip his hat." He pulled off the down vest and hung it beside Elizabeth's jacket.

She realized that they hadn't moved from the doorway. She walked to the fireplace and threw on another log in lieu of lighting a lamp. As the bark caught fire, orange light brought attention to the lines of exhaustion on Drew's face. "Can I get you anything?" she asked. "Some food?"

"No, thanks. I'm too tired to eat. I pulled over past Green Bay and slept for an hour, but it didn't do me much good."

"Why didn't you just find a motel room and get a decent night's sleep?"

"Everything's full because of hunting season. Besides, Freeman wouldn't like it if I showed up late for work in the morning." Elizabeth squelched her impatience—she knew how important it was for Drew to impress Silas. "What about you?" he asked as he bent to remove his shoes and socks. "Anything happen here?"

"No. Everything's fine. Why don't you go to bed before you fall over?"

"Good idea." He straightened slowly and smiled. She felt a rush of tenderness. He was more than just sleepy—until this moment, she'd never seen him without an edge of impatience and alertness.

"Drew?" she prompted, tugging his arm and heading him in the right direction. He smiled again and followed her obediently to the brass bed. When he sat on the mattress and pulled her down beside him, she caught her breath in surprise.

"It's good to be home, Elizabeth." He reached up and touched her cheek.

Home? She wondered if he even knew what he was saying, but she didn't have a chance to dwell on his choice of words. An instant later he was kissing her, his mouth open and hungry, and she responded with equal fervor.

As he lay down, he pulled her beside him on the tumbled sheets, and she renewed her memories of him: the flavor of his lips, the rough edge of his jaw against her skin, the heat of his hands scorching through the fabric of her gown. Response flashed through her like a lightning bolt.

His fingers kneaded her breasts, and she clenched at the solidness of his shoulders because everything else seemed to slip out of control. The moment had a sense of unreality about it, and she could hardly believe Drew was here in her bed. He bent then to nuzzle the peak of her breast, his mouth hot and moist through the thin cotton, and reality was the electric fire sizzling through her limbs.

Somehow Elizabeth managed to remove his shirt, and her hands massaged the corded muscles along his spine. He rested his head between her breasts, and she drew him closer, until she could feel his heartbeat against her belly. As her hands continued to stroke his strong back, his heartbeat slowed.

"Drew?" She lifted her head to look down at him. He was asleep.

Without disturbing him, she reached down to draw up the quilt. Her senses were still in uproar, and she was certain she would lie awake until morning. Besides, the pleasure of seeing him in her bed—his features softened by sleep and the fire's glow—was too new to leave room for fatigue. But when the morning sun spilled across the cabin, would he remember calling it home? she wondered, as she gradually let go of consciousness herself.

* * *

When Drew opened his eyes, it was barely light. A quick glance at his watch confirmed that it was already 7:30. The days were getting shorter, reminding him he still hadn't found Paul's killer.

He threw back the covers, realizing as he did that he'd spent the night in Elizabeth's bed. Or a fraction of the morning, he corrected. He remembered flying out of O'Hare, then driving through the woods at an ungodly hour, and finally seeing Elizabeth standing on the front porch in her white gown.

While his mind had centered on how much he'd missed her and how good it felt to be back, they'd talked about mundane subjects that he couldn't even recall now. But he knew he'd kissed her, caressed her...and then fallen asleep. Which would go a long way toward explaining why his body felt curiously heavy in certain places, he thought irritably.

He stood and grimaced at his rumpled jeans. He could smell coffee boiling on the stove, and through the open bookcase he saw Elizabeth working in the kitchen. Her hair was tied back loosely with a string of yarn, and it was as bright as the sunlight shining in through the east windows. Last night her hair had been free, limned by moonlight and streaming around her shoulders. And he'd been too damn tired to enjoy it, he remembered with a flash of ill temper.

He spotted his socks and shoes by the sofa and retrieved them on his way to the kitchen. "Morning," he mumbled.

"Good morning. Pour yourself a cup of coffee and sit down. I'll bring your eggs in a minute." Her smile was different this morning, brighter somehow. He *had* fallen asleep last night, hadn't he?

"Scrambled or fried?"

The question kept him from speculating further. "Scrambled."

He took the mug of coffee into the bathroom with him. He came back out a few minutes later, his eyes searching the room. "Where's my duffel bag?"

"I unpacked it this morning. Your overnight kit must still be in the car. Your underwear is in the upper middle drawer of the dresser, shirts and jeans on the bottom," she said without looking up from stirring the egg mixture.

He put on a clean shirt after checking the middle drawer. The sight of Elizabeth's camisoles and panties snuggled up next to his shorts made him uncomfortable for some reason. For Pete's sake, he reminded himself, they're just clothes.

"What kind of jam would you prefer? Strawberry or wild grape?"

"Listen, I don't have time for breakfast," he said on his way to the door.

"You'll be sorry by suppertime. I may not have time to fix anything at noon. I'm expecting Gene Larson to come over and get Samson today."

The door thrust open in Drew's face as a deep voice called, "Knock, knock. Anybody ho—*Oh.*"

The big blond man on the other side of the doorway stared at Drew, a red flush creeping up from the collar of his chambray shirt. His blue eyes reflected embarrassment until he looked at Elizabeth. "Sorry. I saw the sheep in the pasture, and I figured you were up. I didn't realize you had company."

Out of the corner of his eye, Drew saw Elizabeth smile. "Gene Larson, Drew Carter," she introduced succinctly. "Come in and sit down, Gene."

Drew slipped aside to let the taller man enter, watching with narrowed eyes as he hung up his jacket next to Elizabeth's and dropped familiarly into a chair. Realizing he was standing in the doorway like a hesitant bellboy, Drew went and sat down across from Larson.

"Change your mind about breakfast?" Elizabeth inquired as she came over with the coffeepot. "How about you, Gene? Want something to eat?" Was it Drew's imagination, or had her voice warmed a few degrees?

"I ate already," he said, "but if you've got extra. . . ."

"Of course. As long as you like scrambled eggs."

"Love 'em." After Elizabeth left, he turned to Drew. "I never turn down this woman's cooking," he said with a boyish grin that set Drew's teeth on edge. "You must be that writer fella the postal clerk told me about. Found a place to live yet?"

"As a matter of fact—" Elizabeth plunked down a plate covered with food in front of him before he could tell Gene exactly where he was living.

"More coffee?" she asked Drew. "Or are you still in a hurry?" Her eyes mocked him.

He shook his head, and she turned to pour another cup for Larson, who'd already downed most of the food on his plate. The man could probably outeat a lumberjack—he was certainly built like one, Drew thought acidly. Next to him, Elizabeth looked as fragile as a flower. He stabbed his fork into the eggs.

He'd barely eaten half when Larson pushed away his plate with a sigh of satisfaction. He then started telling Elizabeth about the crossbred Finn-Lincoln ram he'd purchased from a breeder in Wausau. He stopped to explain the technical terms to Drew—which only made Drew feel like more of an outsider. He delayed leaving until he realized Larson—who'd settled back with a third cup of coffee—wasn't going anywhere. When Elizabeth got up to refill the coffeepot he stood and followed her into the kitchen.

"I'll be home tonight around five."

She knew that, of course. He'd been home every night at dusk. The words were for Larson's benefit ... and so was the scorching kiss he planted on her lips before leaving. For the grinning man at the table, he spared a brief "So long" on his way out the door.

Eight and a half hours later, when Silas Freeman boomed out "Quitting time!" Drew was the first to move. He dropped the end of the log he and Richard Stoltz were carrying to the portable sawmill.

The afternoon had crawled, at least until he'd seen Larson's black pickup drive past with Samson in back only an hour ago. He'd made more mistakes than usual, and several times he'd caught a gleam of amusement in Hoskin's eyes, as though the man guessed why Drew's attention was elsewhere.

He reached into his shirt pocket for his cigarettes, only to remember he'd finished the pack long before Larson's departure. He'd been certain the truck would drive past when Lily arrived for her spinning lesson, but Larson had stayed another hour after that.

Didn't Elizabeth realize that spending the entire day with an eligible male could jeopardize the care he'd taken to make Freeman and the others see them as a unit? he wondered. His frustration had burned hotter as the day grew longer, until he realized it wasn't directed at Elizabeth. For some inexplicable reason, he was angry at Gene Larson.

The man had been friendly, going out of his way to include Drew in every conversation. He was the sort of man Drew had in mind when he'd decided that Elizabeth needed someone like herself. Larson spoke her language, he was patient, he knew

sheep and homesteading—and then Drew realized he wasn't
angry at all. He was jealous. He set the toolbox on the flatbed
with more force than was necessary, and Cal Hoskin shot him
an amused glance.

Drew hardly noticed. All he could think of was the fact that
once he left Nisswa, the way would be clear for Larson. He saw
Lily standing beside the truck's cab, waiting for a ride home,
and he was tempted to ask her how Elizabeth felt about Larson, but he resisted the impulse. He waved at her before spinning away in his own small truck.

Drew stomped up the steps to the door, and Elizabeth held
her breath, certain he'd break right through the weathered
wooden boards. But he opened the door cautiously, and she
guessed he made the noise to warn her in lieu of knocking.

"You live here now. You don't have to knock," she told him,
pointing out, "You didn't bother to knock at noon."

"I noticed Gene Larson didn't knock, either," he said.

"He's a friend, Drew," she said, watching his expression
carefully as she stirred the dish heating on the stove. Was
Drew's dark look jealousy? She bit back a smile of silly pleasure as his disconcerting gaze traveled over her slowly. She knew
her face was flushed from the heat of the stovetop, and a tendril of hair kept trailing across one cheek. She pulled the straying hair back behind her ear, and he looked away before going
into the bathroom to wash.

Things didn't improve over supper. Drew gave her only the
briefest of answers to her questions about the construction, and
finally she gave up. She decided to try a more innocuous subject.

"Do you like the stuffed grape leaves? I found a jar in Forest city on Saturday."

"They're delicious," he said flatly.

She ignored his lack of enthusiasm and pressed on. "Are they
like the ones you had when you were growing up?" He looked
at her blankly. "They're Greek," she reminded him.

"My father wouldn't allow any of the old traditions in our
house."

She ignored the curt reply and asked, "Did you see him when
you were in Chicago?"

"No," he said without looking up. Elizabeth decided that was her last attempt at conversation, much as she wanted to know about Drew's family.

Drew stood beside her to help with dishes, but he could have been a thousand miles away. The clatter of the plates was unnaturally loud in the silence. When she came back from checking her sheep, he was sitting at the oak table, papers spread all around him. She was curious, but she held her tongue. She wasn't about to retreat to her knitting without saying anything, however, so she asked, "Coffee?"

"Yes. Er, make that a no. I've got enough work here to keep me awake without resorting to drinking caffeine."

"Tea, then?" His assent was a surprise, and Elizabeth smiled secretly as she fixed a pot of mint tea. Maybe his tastes were changing after all. She used the ceramic pot and added enough water for several cups. The shared teapot was a perfect excuse for her to sit at the table with Drew while she updated her business records. Now that the ewes were settled it was time to start calculating lambing dates and making plans.

She took the slim record books from the bookcase and carried them to the table along with the tea things. Drew didn't look up from the papers in front of him, but the atmosphere gradually eased into companionable silence. A long time later, as Elizabeth poured the last few drops of tea into her mug, she looked up to find Drew watching her, his eyes enigmatically dark. Her hand stilled, and a ripple of unexpected desire went through her.

"I'm sorry," she said, her voice husky. "Did you want the last cup?"

"No. I was just thinking about these notes Jim gave me on Phillip Prince. Want to look at them?"

"Please." Elizabeth suspected that wasn't what he'd been thinking about at all, but she wasn't about to refuse his olive branch, or pass up a chance to see what investigative work was like.

"These are transcripts of the interviews Jim had with Prince's acquaintances," Drew said as he handed over a thick manila folder. "This one is all family background, and that's a copy of his military file."

A photograph slid onto Elizabeth's lap, and she set it back on the table. She held up a sheet that listed classes and grades from Prince's junior year at Texas A&M University and said,

"But these things must be confidential. Isn't it unethical to violate someone's privacy like that?"

"You think Prince cares about ethics? Besides, his campaign released most of these documents to the press when he entered the race for Congress."

It was more than curiosity that prompted her to ask, "If this is all common knowledge—except for the interviews, of course—then why are you bothering with it, especially now that Prince is out of the race?"

"I still haven't found the connection between Prince and Freeman. There has to be one, if Freeman was so willing to commit murder on Prince's account. And since Freeman draws a blank, I have to concentrate on Prince, although it's starting to seem purposeless."

"Not quite," Elizabeth said as she shoved the papers and photographs toward him. "It's given you an excuse to avoid me, hasn't it?"

"Avoid you? This may come as a surprise, but the world doesn't revolve around you." Drew stood and impatiently shoved the loose papers into a pile. "You've been living alone so long out here in the sticks that you think everything centers around you."

The words were cruel—deliberately so. But Elizabeth didn't back down. "That's not true," she said with quiet emphasis. "It's just that I've learned to look out for myself after all these years. I can read the weather, and usually I can tell which way the wind's blowing. This time it seems to be blowing nothing but hot air." She rose to her feet and faced him. "Why don't you tell me what's really bothering you?"

She recognized dark anger in Drew's eyes and felt a surge of triumph that she was able to break through to him at last. Her triumph was short-lived. She had only a split second's warning before he moved. He reached out and gripped her arm, and his lips crushed hers. Passion flowed between them, instant, wild and sweet. She moaned. His lips softened for an instant, then he broke away, leaving Elizabeth gripping the back of a chair for support.

She didn't stop him as he walked out the door.

Drew woke just before dawn. It was the cold that roused him, not the faint light coming in through the kitchen windows.

Usually the fire in the black iron stove was crackling by now, with the smell of breakfast lingering in the air. Today there was nothing but cold ashes and an empty table.

He sat up, instantly awake. He looked toward the alcove to see the quilt neatly drawn over the brass bed. He stood, wincing as his muscles protested against another night on the soft sofa. Elizabeth must be sleeping in the loft. Childishly, neither of them had used the bed last night. He groaned as he remembered the things he'd said to her. Wondering why she'd overslept, he walked over to the steep stairs that led up to the loft.

"Elizabeth?" he called up. When she didn't answer, he climbed until he could see that the pallet of quilts on the floor was empty.

He'd slept in his jeans, and now he paused only long enough to put on his boots and pull on a flannel shirt, buttoning it haphazardly as he went out the door. The sun wasn't quite up over the hill, and the pond's surface was mirrorlike, reflecting the sheep grazing in the high pasture. He checked the barn, then walked around the fence and started up the east hill, his boots soon wet with hoarfrost. He found her at the top, bundled into her denim jacket with her back against the trunk of a tree, watching the sun rise over the lake.

Drew ignored the show of pinks and golds in the sky and crouched beside her. "Come back to the cabin. I'll fix you some breakfast."

"No, thank you."

He sighed and sat back against the tree. With just his shirt-sleeves, he was cold in the morning air. He thought longingly of the warmth of the cabin and a cup of coffee—even Elizabeth's. But it was time to talk.

"I do like it here, you know," he told her.

"Then stay with me when it's over."

"Damn it, Elizabeth, don't you see? I'm going to be telling the world about your neighbors. People you care about. Do you think we'd ever have a chance with that between us?" he asked harshly.

"My loyalty is to you now, not to them."

"I'm not talking about loyalty, I'm talking about your life. It's going to be different afterward. Your neighbors may end up in prison, and all your plans for the future, for your business, will change. How long do you think it would be before you hated me for changing your world?"

"I've finally accepted the fact that change is natural, Drew. Things will change whether you stay or not. And I'd rather face the changes with you."

"No. You say that now, but the investigation will always be there between us. Even more so when it's over." Drew rose to his feet. It would be easy to take what Elizabeth was offering, but he knew how differences could eat at a relationship, and he wanted theirs to last a lifetime. Nothing less than forever was good enough. He started down the hill, the sky above him changing from pink to blue as the sun rose higher.

"Drew." He stopped at the command in Elizabeth's voice.

"I still want to make love with you," she said. The words snared him, rooting him to the spot halfway down the hill. He stood there, his legs unsteady, until she caught up with him.

She reached out and touched his arm. He pulled away, but not in time. She'd felt the tremors. "You're afraid. Why?"

"You don't understand," he said, his voice rough.

"I want to. Tell me," she said. She reached out again, and this time he let her hand rest on his arm. He waited for the shaking to increase, but it melted away under the warmth of her touch. She renewed him like the dawn. She made him strong. And she made him want her.

"Dear God," he said, and then he was the one taking the initiative, hauling her tight against him. A brief look of pleased surprise chased across her features, then her passion rose quickly to meet his. Their mouths tasted each other hungrily as their hands explored each other's textures: the silk of her hair, the scrape of his beard, the brush of her eyelash against his cheek, the boldness of his arousal against her hipbone. Elizabeth swayed against him, and Drew nearly dragged them both to the ground.

"No," he said hoarsely. "Not here. Too fast." His sentences were choppy, his breathing ragged. "Let's go inside," he told her.

They crossed the grassy hollow to the cabin arm in arm. When the door closed behind them, Elizabeth turned to him, her teeth biting into her lower lip. "Remember when you asked the other day if I was protected?" The words rushed past her lips. "I haven't done anything to remedy the situation."

Her shy honesty endeared her to him. "I have," he said as he removed her jacket and hung it on the hook by the door, then took her into his arms again. This time he kissed her tenderly, his lips brushing the corner of her mouth. She put her palms on his chest and held him halfway, her cheeks flushed as she asked, "Not at Nisswa Drug?"

Drew smiled at her consternation. "Of course not. I wouldn't want the whole town talking about it. I stopped at a drugstore in Chicago," he told her, rubbing his thumbs over her bright cheeks.

"You knew then? You planned this?" she asked.

"No," he admitted, laughter forgotten. "I didn't plan this at all."

"Then why did you stop at a drugstore?"

"I think my subconscious just took over. Look, do we really have to rationalize this?"

"No. I like your subconscious mind better than your rational one." She reached out and slid one finger down from his breastbone to the button of his shirt. In his haste to find her, he'd left most of the buttons undone. She undid the rest.

The last button popped at her touch, and her hand trailed lower. Drew caught her wrist. "I think we said something about going slowly."

"You did, I didn't. I'm tired of waiting."

Her words renewed the urgency he'd felt on the hillside minutes before. He lifted her up in his arms and carried her to the alcove, setting her down on the brass bed. He bent and removed her boots, then his own, before sitting beside her. He kissed her deeply, groaning in pleasure when her mouth opened to welcome him.

He reached behind her neck to pull at the yarn tie that held her hair, and the free strands fell like silk over his hands. He ran his fingers through it again and again, memorizing the feel and color. He wanted to see it spilling over her naked shoulders, covering her breasts, and he reached to pull her sweater over her head. She raised her arms for him, and he quickly did away with her sweater and the cotton camisole she wore underneath.

She was so beautiful it hurt to look at her. Sunshine poured through the east windows, past the open bookcase, and caught in the length of her hair. He kissed her and bore her gently back against the mattress. The rest of their clothes vanished, a piece at a time, until flesh covered flesh and there was nothing left between them at all.

It felt right. He had no room for second thoughts or last-minute regrets. Time didn't matter, even as the sun rose higher and he realized he would be late for work. He concentrated instead on the moment, the silken feel of her skin sliding against his, the shimmering length of her hair, the feminine strength of her hands as she kneaded his shoulders. He kissed her deeply before going to the bathroom for his overnight kit.

When he returned, he stopped at the foot of the bed and told her in great detail how beautiful she was lying in the sunshine, making love to her with words and a look. Flushing at his praise, she held out her arms to him.

In one fluid motion he eased himself onto the bed and into her softness. Her lavender eyes opened wide with surprise and pleasure. They greeted the morning together, her soft cries mingling with his guttural ones as the sun filled the room.

When Drew's truck pulled up to the cabin shortly before sunset, Elizabeth was taking clothes from the line strung across the porch. Normally, using the hand-powered washing machine was an odious chore. Today, however, the tedium had been spiked with an odd amount of pleasure at seeing Drew's clothing mixed with hers—a constant reminder of how their laundry had ended up jumbled together in the first place, in a rumpled pile next to the bed.

When she saw Drew's broad smile she thought at first he was remembering, too. He took the wicker laundry basket from her hands, picked her up and whirled her around before setting her back on her feet. "Well," he prompted, grinning. "Aren't you going to finish the laundry, woman?" She looked down at the clothes-filled basket to see a green glass bottle lying on top. "It's merlot," he told her unnecessarily. "From your favorite vineyard."

"What are we celebrating?" she asked, with a knowing smile.

"Freeman invited me to go home with them at noon tomorrow for dinner."

Elizabeth's smile faded. She told herself she should be happy for him, but a half-dozen conflicting emotions buzzed in her head—surprise, concern for his safety, shock that he may be leaving soon and, yes, pique that the investigation could so easily overwhelm what had happened between them that morning. "That's wonderful news," she said, trying to imbue her voice with the proper amount of enthusiasm.

"Here, let me take that." He reached for the basket and set it on a chair when they stepped inside. He crossed to the kitchen and set the bottle of wine on the counter and started opening drawers in search of a corkscrew.

"Where did you get the wine?" Elizabeth asked lightly.

"I brought it back from Chicago," he told her. "There's a case of it in the truck."

"A whole case? And you've been keeping it a secret since then?"

"I was saving it for a goodbye present."

She felt as though she'd been kicked in the stomach. Drew looked up, his hands busy with the cork, and saw her expression. He swore. "I really put my foot into it, didn't I?" he said. "I'm sorry. Elizabeth?"

She didn't stay to hear his apology. She left the cabin and headed for the hillside above the pond where Drew had stood early yesterday morning after returning from Chicago. It seemed like ages ago. She leaned against an elm, grateful for the hard trunk supporting her back. When she heard him calling her name, she slid down until she was hidden from view. She gazed westward, watching the last dying rays as the sun set behind the hill.

They'd made love as the day began, with no promises or vows, no declaration of feelings passing their lips. But the words had settled in her heart. Now the day was ending with the reminder that Drew was here for one reason only—the investigation. When that was finished, he'd leave. He'd leave, and she'd get a case of wine.

She heard the crackle of leaves behind her and knew that he'd found her. "Come back to the cabin," he said. "It'll be dark soon."

She ignored his outstretched hand. He sat down beside her, leaning back against the tree trunk, squinting into the sun's fading light as he spoke haltingly. "Last year my parents got a divorce after forty years of marriage. They waited until Juliet turned eighteen, because they didn't want to hurt us kids. It was like waking up and finding out I'd been living a lie for thirty-eight years."

She felt a rush of sympathy at his confession, but she didn't understand the connection. "What does your parents' divorce have to do with us?"

"They were alike, Elizabeth. And they had six kids, six good reasons for staying together. Still they couldn't make it. With so many differences between us, how can we possibly succeed where they failed?"

She didn't bother to argue that the differences were minor compared to their similarities. She suspected he already knew that, even if only in his subconscious. Instead she reminded him, "I didn't ask you to marry me. Can't we just take things slowly, see what happens?"

He looked at her bleakly. "I need to be sure, Elizabeth. And I can't think straight until the investigation is over."

"Then I'll wait," she told him. "Like Penelope at her loom, forever if I have to." She stood and held out her hand. "Now, how about some merlot?"

They entered the cabin just as the last hint of sunset faded from the sky. Neither spoke, but by mutual agreement they crossed to the alcove. Drew lit the lamp, and Elizabeth sat on the edge of the bed. He undressed, and she watched the golden lamplight flicker over his broad shoulders, his flat stomach with its network of scars, the thickly corded muscles of his thighs. Physical labor had honed his body to perfection. As he stepped out of his dark blue briefs, Elizabeth realized he was giving himself to her in the only way he knew how. And she would return his gift with her own.

She unbuttoned her shirt, standing to slip off her shoes and socks and jeans, dropping them on the wooden floor. The tails of her open shirt covered her to the middle of her thighs. She started to remove her panties, but Drew reached out to stop her. "Wait," he said. He walked to the kitchen, graceful and unashamed at his nakedness. She saw him pluck the bottle of merlot and a glass from the countertop before returning.

He filled the glass and set the bottle on the nightstand. In a ceremonial gesture, he drank from the glass before handing it to her so she could do the same. She touched the glass to her lips and swallowed, feeling the soft, rich heat of the wine travel down her throat. He took the glass from her and set it on the nightstand next to the bottle.

He kissed her almost chastely then, his hands on her shoulders keeping a short distance between them. Only their lips touched, but Drew's lips were eloquent. He tasted of wine and man, and the kiss deepened by degrees until it was chaste no longer. A tingling heat spread over her body, as though the wine had seeped through her limbs. She stepped closer, and he slipped the shirt from her shoulders.

The tips of her breasts brushed against the dark hair on his chest, teasing them into aching hardness. Another small step and his knee wedged between her legs, his arms curving around the back of her waist. One last step and she could feel his desire, full and hard, against the soft skin of her belly. The knowledge that she could arouse him so completely sapped the strength from her legs. She sagged, pulling them down to the mattress.

He slid her practical cotton underwear down her thighs, taking time to stroke her skin and plant wet kisses along the way. His lips rejoined hers in a voluptuous kiss while his caressing hands moved to her breasts. She felt the calluses on his palms that he'd earned from his work on her garage.

She touched him the same way, letting her hands linger on the smooth skin of his shoulders before threading her fingers through the hair on his chest, tangling in the chain of the medallion before trailing down his abdomen. She paused to trace the faded network of scars with the tips of her fingers.

Drew gasped and shuddered with pleasure when her hand dared farther, but he grasped her by the wrist and placed her hand on his back, telling her in a rough whisper that he wanted their loving to last all night. He teased her earlobe with his teeth. Her response to the sweet caress gathered, then tumbled throughout the rest of her body.

They were so right together, she thought with a hazy smile. Making love was different than it had been this morning—rich and softer, like the vintage merlot. He'd shared part of himself with her, and she felt closer than ever to convincing him that they were meant to be together. Every touch, every kiss multiplied and echoed throughout her senses.

"All night," he said again, the words lost against her lips as his mouth covered hers.

Drew wiped up the last bit of gravy from his plate with a piece of bread and shoved it into his mouth before he could change his mind. He was determined to please his hosts by eating every last crumb, even though the large hunk of fresh beef sat in his stomach like a block of cement. He'd grown used to Elizabeth's mostly vegetarian cooking, and the meal at the Colony was heavy and unimaginative by comparison.

"That was great, ladies, thank you." He included all the women in his thanks, reserving a special smile for Sarah Stoltz. He'd learned that she did most of the cooking. Like the men, the women worked together, but each had her own niche. Sarah's was cooking, Genna's was the children and Lily's was gardening and canning. Jolene's was...well, the cat-eyed woman had her own niche, and her avid gaze made Drew uncomfortable.

"I knew you'd appreciate a good meal, boy," Silas boomed. "That Elizabeth doesn't eat any better than—"

"Silas," Lily chided as she began to clear the table. Like the other women, she'd been up and down throughout the meal, while the men sat and ate. Drew didn't even have a chance to set down his fork before Sarah Stoltz appeared at his shoulder with a piece of apple pie.

"From Elizabeth's orchard," she told him. Drew's stomach protested, but he smiled and gamely attacked the oozing pastry.

When the meal was over the men pushed back their chairs and filed outdoors. Drew paused in the kitchen to thank the women again. When he stepped out onto the screened back porch, he could hear someone speaking on the other side of the arbor vitae that grew just outside. Hidden from view, he stopped when he recognized Lewis Cole's voice.

"I think we should ask him to join. We could use his help to move the guns, and with him on our side, Elizabeth won't complain about the traffic and noise across the road."

"More important, we need a seventh man," Silas Freeman answered. "As the Book says, 'Select from among you seven men.' It's Cal that we must convince. For some reason he's taken a dislike to the man."

"He's forgotten that he was once an outsider himself," Cole said.

"Money is his god. He is not a man of honor, and we shouldn't have brought him into our circle. If we hadn't needed someone to..."

The voices faded away and Drew nearly cursed aloud with frustration. He knew now that the Colony was running guns, knew that he was the man they wanted to add to the circle. But what had they been about to say regarding Hoskin? And why would Elizabeth complain about noise? Unless...

The Kresge farm was across from her. He remembered the new lumber hidden in the shed and wondered if it had anything to do with the Colony's plans.

Drew hurried out the screen door when he realized the men were milling around the flatbed truck, waiting to drive back to Elizabeth's. And he hadn't had a chance to look around on his own.

"Heading back already?" he asked as he approached them. "I thought I might get a chance to see your operation."

Cole and Freeman exchanged looks. "Some other time, son," Freeman said. "We have to start early and work hard if we're going to finish tomorrow."

"Tomorrow?" Drew hid his surprise. He hoped the invitation to join them would come soon.

Back at work on the garage he had more time to think. And count. There were five adult men at the Colony. If he was going to be the seventh man, then who—and where—was the sixth? *Another secret to unearth, another reason to be careful.* And the Kresge farm was the key.

Chapter 12

Elizabeth ducked behind the trunk of a large oak until she heard the flatbed truck with Freeman and his crew drive past on their way to the Colony. She knew she wouldn't have long to wait and she was proved right when, less than a minute later, Drew crossed the road. She stepped out to meet him.

He strode toward her, his expression fierce. "I told you to stay at the cabin. What are you doing here?"

"I wanted to come with you. And I have something to show you." She reached into her backpack and pulled out a photograph. "I found it under the table this morning after you'd left. You must have dropped it the night we argued. I don't know why I didn't notice it until today."

"We have been rather... busy... during the past forty-eight hours," Drew teased, bringing an embarrassed smile to her lips. He looked down at the photo and handed it back with an air of dismissal. "It's part of Prince's campaign hype. That's Phillip Prince, Sr.'s company in Korea."

"Look closely at the man next to Prince's father. Doesn't he look like Silas Freeman?"

Drew looked again, showing cautious interest. "It could be," he admitted. "There's something familiar about the set of his shoulders." His finger ran over the names listed at the bottom, and stopped. "The man's listed as F. Oliver," he said excitedly. "Francis Oliver was the name of the man killed with Lily's parents. It's got to be Silas. He must have faked his death and taken a new identity."

He continued to scan the list of names. "Look at this— *Missing from photo.* One of the names listed is J. Smith. Isn't Jed Smith a vet?"

"Yes, but the J. on that photo could stand for John or Joe or Jim. Smith is an awfully common name. I know you don't like Jed, but there's no reason to think he might be involved, is there?"

"No. But I've seen him out this way two or three times now, and it seems odd that he'd patrol this road when his headquarters are thirty miles away."

"Jed lives just outside of Nisswa," she told him. "And since Lily and I were attacked in the woods that time, he drives out here quite a bit."

"I'll call Jim tonight and have him check this out," he said, handing the photo back to Elizabeth. "Right now, we'd better get moving. Those men eat fast, and they're in a hurry to finish before it starts to rain."

She glanced up at the slate-colored sky. "It can't rain. I brought a picnic." She indicated the canvas backpack.

"A picnic? This isn't exactly a day trip. We won't have time."

"It's just sandwiches. We can eat them on our way back."

He didn't comment. Elizabeth half expected him to forge ahead of her up the overgrown driveway, but he matched his steps to hers. From a distance the farm building looked as perfect as a calendar photo, but details of neglect—peeling paint and boarded windows—came into focus as Drew and Elizabeth neared.

"It's sad to see the house looking so abandoned," she said, shaking her head. "You should have seen it when Thelma Kresge was still alive."

"It's still sound on the inside."

She looked at him sharply. Drew had told her last night about his earlier visit and his reason for returning. "Are we going inside today?"

"We'll start with the shed first. That's where I saw the lumber. If we can't find anything there, we'll look around."

They walked through dry, overgrown grass to the dilapidated machine shed. The back door was still padlocked, but

Drew pulled a slender metal tool from his pocket. "I came prepared this time."

"Standard equipment for investigative authors?" she asked dryly.

She was answered with a grin and a click as the lock snapped open. Drew swung open the door, but the cloudy day didn't allow much light inside. Elizabeth removed her backpack, fished around inside and pulled out a flashlight. "I guess it's a good thing I came after all," she said pointedly.

Drew accepted the flashlight with an unrepentant grin. "I guess so."

The flashlight's beam didn't penetrate more than a few feet of the gloomy interior. They tried the switchplate near the door, but the lights didn't respond. Drew ran the beam of the flashlight over the walls and floor. None of the exterior neglect was evident inside. The dirt floor was as solid and even as a cement slab, and the corners were free of cobwebs. But it was the walls and ceiling that caught their attention.

The new lumber had been used to create a dropped ceiling and solid walls; the side with the slatted corncrib was covered completely. Each new wall was covered with a thick layer of foam material.

"Soundproofing," Drew said as he used the flashlight to examine it closer.

The humidity outside made the air inside the shed close and heavy with the smell of sawdust. Elizabeth stayed close to Drew as they walked to the end of the long building. There, the flashlight beam struck a white-covered heap in one dark corner.

Drew pulled off the white sheet, and Elizabeth's knees went weak with momentary shock at the sight of stiffened bodies. A closer look revealed that the "bodies" were lifelike silhouettes of cardboard and plywood. She bit back a gasp of relieved laughter, and released the front of Drew's chambray workshirt, which she didn't even remember grabbing.

"Sorry," she apologized. "What are they?"

"Targets." Drew panned the beam around the back wall. "This is a shooting range."

She trailed her hand over a scattering of dark circles on the wall, then snatched it away when she realized the circles were bullet holes. "But why? When Silas and Cal taught me how to use the rifle, they set coffee cans on a fence behind the barn. What's the big secret? I don't see any guns."

"From what they said yesterday about traffic and noise, my guess is they're going to start bringing other supremacists here. Sort of like a military training school," he told her grimly. "The guns must be at the farm. I'll find out when I'm on the inside."

Elizabeth shivered. "Let's leave. *Please,*" she added as Drew put his arm around her shoulders.

"Sure. I've seen enough."

Even the heavily overcast sky was welcome after the dark, windowless shed. When they reached the base of the cul-de-sac in front of the house, Elizabeth slowed to take one last look.

"I've always loved this house," she confessed. "It's sad that the farm is being used for something so ugly."

Drew smiled indulgently before walking over to the base of a towering oak. "Let's stop here and eat. We've got a few minutes."

Elizabeth silently thanked him for giving her a chance to chase away the horror of their discovery with pleasant memories. As she unpacked the food, she described the way the driveway looked in the spring when it was lined with fragrant lilacs, and told him how Kurt Kresge had painted the house's gingerbread trim a different color every year just to please his wife. As the minutes passed, she forgot about the machine shed, and simply enjoyed the moments with Drew.

He reached out and touched the corner of her mouth with a finger.

"Mustard," he told her.

"But I don't put any—" He stopped the rest of her sentence with his mouth, a hungry kiss that seemed to go on forever.

"We've got to get back," she reminded him when she could find her voice to speak.

"I know," he said, and kissed her again. "If we're late, we can go back the way you came—through the woods. If they get there before I do, they'll think I walked from the cabin."

She smiled. "And just why would we be late?" The end of her question was muffled as Drew's lips swooped down in another ravenous kiss that sent desire spiralling through her. She wrapped her arms around him, and he laid her back onto the thick grass.

"I can't believe we're doing this," she said.

"It's crazy," he agreed, actions belying words as he nibbled along the open placket of the shirt she wore under her jacket.

"After last night, I didn't think—" she paused to gasp as he nipped at her earlobe "—you'd have any energy left."

"Still think so?" he asked, pushing his hips against hers and letting her feel for herself how much energy he had.

They groaned simultaneously, and then silence ruled for several long moments as they looked for new ways to please each other.

"Damn," he mumbled against her neck.

"What's the matter?"

"It's starting to rain."

As soon as he spoke a cold drop fell against her forehead. "Ugh," she said, and tried to duck under his sheltering body. They laughed until the skies opened up and drenched their amusement.

"Come on, let's go!" Drew shouted as he pulled her to her feet and grabbed her backpack.

They ran down the long driveway and across the road, slowing their steps when they entered the woods so that they could listen for Freeman's crew. "They're not there," Drew said.

"They won't come back until it quits raining," Elizabeth told him.

By the time they reached the cabin, they were drenched to the skin and breathless with laughter. Elizabeth went to the barn to make sure the flock was sheltered. When she entered the cabin, Drew already had a blaze going in the fieldstone fireplace. She smiled at the sight of the galvanized steel tub standing off to one side of the orange flames.

"I thought we'd better warm up," he told her. "The bath is purely for medicinal reasons, of course." He managed to keep a straight face, but the crinkles at the corners of his eyes betrayed him.

"Of course." Elizabeth tossed her wet jacket over the back of a chair and started to unbutton her shirt. The rest of their clothing followed, dropped carelessly to the floor or strewn across furniture. Between laughter and kisses, they tried to arrange themselves comfortably in the cramped metal tub. Water sloshed over the sides and onto the wooden floor.

"This is impossible. It's too small," Elizabeth complained.

"Not if you sit in front of me. Hold still." Drew picked her up and arranged her so that she was leaning back against his chest. He picked up the bar of soap and started to lather her skin. "Remember the night you bathed in the kitchen while I was in bed?"

"Yes. I told myself that you were like quicksand, that if I would just quit fighting my attraction to you I'd be able to break free." She could feel the rumble of Drew's laughter behind her back.

"While you were fortifying yourself against me, I was imagining what it would be like to be in the water with you, how your hair would feel trailing against my skin."

As he spoke, he undid her braid, letting the ends of her hair cling wetly to his chest and shoulders. He continued to describe his fantasies, in a rough, arousing whisper against her ear. His voice entranced her, rubbing along her nerve endings while his hands stroked her wet skin. The room was filled with whispers and sighs and the crackle of the fire as the water cooled around them.

They stood only to discover that the towels Drew had set near the tub were soaking wet. He used one to sluice away most of the water from their skin before stepping out of the tub.

"Stay there," he told her and he went to the sofa. He took the blanket folded neatly over its cushions, then held the soft folds open for her. She stepped out of the tub and gasped in surprise as Drew picked her up, trailing blanket and all, and stood her in front of the fire.

"We'll dry soon enough here." He rubbed the blanket over her until her skin was tingling, then let it drop to the floor. His silver medallion winked in the firelight in invitation, and her hands reached out to his chest.

With a groan of satisfaction he lowered her on top of the blanket. Still reeling from hearing his fantasies about her, she was acutely aware of every touch, even the whisper of his warm breath against her flesh. He bent to kiss her breasts. The medallion rested on her belly, its coolness slithering across her skin every time Drew moved his head.

It trailed up between her breasts as he rejoined his lips to hers for another long kiss. When he lifted his head she captured the medallion in her hand and held it toward the firelight, looking for an inscription that wasn't there. "Who gave you your Saint Christopher?" she asked.

Drew rolled to his side and looked at her with amused indulgence as he trailed a hand back and forth over her hip. "Someone very special," he said.

She knew he was only teasing, but the words stung. She let the medallion fall from her hand.

"Elizabeth?" Drew moved over her, until he was looking into her eyes. "Does it matter to you?"

"Yes. Maybe it's silly, but the thought of you wearing another woman's gift when you're making love to me..." Embarrassed, she let her words trail away.

"It's not silly at all, and I'm sorry I teased you. My mother gave it to me before I went overseas on my first assignment. She thought it would keep me safe."

"Are you Catholic?"

He shook his head. "She is. My father let her keep that, at least. I've never been in one place long enough to think about going to church. I've learned to look for God inside people's hearts."

He reached out and laid his hand between her breasts, where her heart was beating rapidly. "Why do you wear it?" she asked.

"I don't know. Because it reminds me of my mother, my family, I guess."

So he was capable of putting down roots after all, Elizabeth thought with a secret smile as she pulled him closer to her.

Hours later a knock on the door startled Drew awake. He and Elizabeth were lying in a tangle of covers after spending the afternoon in bed. He could hear the concern in her voice as she asked, "Who could it be this time of the night?"

"And when your driveway is clogged with mud," Drew added. He hadn't been able to get to town to call Jim. He pulled on his jeans and went to open the door, looking back to see Elizabeth pull the sheet closer around her.

Shock went through him at the sight of Cal Hoskin standing on the porch. When Hoskin's gray-eyed gaze looked past him into the cabin, Drew moved to block the view of the alcove. He wasn't about to invite the man inside with Elizabeth flushed and sleepy from hours of loving.

"What do you want, Hoskin?"

Hoskin thrust a damp paper bag at Drew. "Remember," he said in a deadly soft drawl, "I'm gonna be watching you, too." He turned on his heel and left.

"Was that Cal Hoskin?" Elizabeth asked as Drew went back to the bed. "I couldn't hear what he said."

Silently he opened the bag and dumped its contents onto the bed. A small flashlight and a crumpled and faded cigarette wrapper tumbled onto the covers. The flashlight was the one he'd lost the first time he'd investigated Kresge's shed. He guessed the wrapper was from the pack of cigarettes he'd been carrying the day he arrived. Hoskin could have found it anywhere between the road and Kresge's driveway. Or in Elizabeth's pasture, he thought, feeling sick.

"I think it's a warning," Drew told her.

"Then he knows?"

Drew shook his head. "If he knew for sure, they would have done something before now. I don't think he's happy about Freeman's plans for me to join. I just hope he doesn't convince Freeman to keep me out."

The rains kept up for another twenty-four hours, postponing the completion of the garage. The suspense of waiting nearly drove Drew insane. He made love to Elizabeth over and over again, trying to console himself in her warmth. Even so, two questions plagued him. How much had Hoskin guessed? And would he tell Silas?

Drew paused to wipe the sweat from his brow. It was the last Saturday in October, but here on the garage's roof and surrounded by tar paper, it was almost as hot as a day in July. The two days of rain had left behind a lingering humidity that was unusual for the date, and waiting for Hoskin to make another move kept him knife-edge anxious.

He'd be glad to finish and get back to the cabin. An icy lakewater shower actually sounded good. Most of the men were cleaning up below; just he and Richard Stoltz worked on, nailing sections of tar paper to the roof's surface.

He bit back a curse as he missed a nail—the fourth for the afternoon. At least he was improving. The last two near misses hadn't landed on his thumb like the first two. He promised himself that if he missed another, he would shout the loud curse that had been building up ever since he'd opened the door to find Cal Hoskin on Elizabeth's doorstep. He'd shout it out loud, and to hell with Freeman's sensibilities.

No, he wouldn't. He wouldn't do anything to jeopardize his chances of getting back inside the Colony. After two days of waiting for the ax to fall and trying to lose himself in Elizabeth, his feelings for her were all mixed up with the investigation. Glimpses of the future taunted him, until he wondered if she was right after all. Maybe they did have a future together.

But not until he found out who killed Paul Brewster.

A drop of sweat ran into his eye, blurring his vision. *Thunk!* The hammer landed on tar paper, narrowly missing his thumb. Drew growled. He shoved the handle of the hammer underneath his belt, and yanked off the flannel shirt that was more suited to the date than to the weather. A couple of the other men had removed their shirts and tied the sleeves around their foreheads, to keep the sweat out of their eyes. Drew followed suit.

Richard Stoltz watched him, then looked away quickly. Drew supposed he looked fierce enough to frighten a mercenary, and he bit back a bark of laughter when he remembered that the Colony made mercenaries look tame.

Twenty minutes later, he pounded the last nail into the roof with a sense of accomplishment. He climbed down the ladder to join the others, who'd finished loading the sawmill on the flatbed, and were now gathering up the last of the scattered tools.

Silas Freeman and Cal Hoskin stood waiting at the bottom of the ladder. Unease flickered through Drew when he glanced at the truck. The others fussed with the load, trying to look busy, and Lily had arrived early from her spinning lesson. Drew dismissed the uneasiness, assuring himself that this was probably the moment he'd been waiting for. Freeman was going to ask him to become one of them. *Or had Cal Hoskin told him about the flashlight?*

But Freeman didn't speak at all. His narrowed gaze was directed at Drew's chest, and Drew realized he was staring at the silver medal of Saint Christopher. Discomfited, he untied his shirt and slipped it on.

"Tell Elizabeth that she can give the cash for her garage to Lily on Monday," Freeman said. The words were cold, even hostile. Drew glanced at Cal Hoskin, who was grinning widely.

"I'll bring the money over myself," he said, masking his dread.

"No. Elizabeth will bring it. Heathens are not welcome on our property."

Heathens? Then Drew remembered the Saint Christopher medal. How could he have been so careless and stupid? He knew that Christian Soldier adherents regarded Catholics in the same light as Jews and non-Christians.

Freeman faced Drew with an expression that looked like regret. "I was going to counsel you to make an honest woman of Elizabeth. But I cannot wish her married to a son of the Babylon whore. Goodbye, Drew Carter."

Drew looked past Hoskin's grin—even wider now—to Lily. She was standing nearby, but she refused to meet his gaze. She waited for her husband to reach her, then followed him, head down, to the truck.

Elizabeth knew something had gone wrong as soon as she saw Drew walk through the door. "What's the matter?" she asked. "Didn't you finish?"

"Oh, yeah, I'm finished all right." He slumped into one of the wooden chairs.

"What happened?"

Drew unbuttoned his shirt and pulled out his Saint Christopher medallion. "I managed to offend them by wearing this."

"Oh, God." Elizabeth realized immediately what had happened.

"Yes, but the wrong god, according to Silas." He ran his hands tiredly across his face. "Exactly twenty-four hours ago I ate at the same table as that man. Today he looked at me as though he hated me. And only because he thought I was Catholic."

Elizabeth sat down across from him. "Do you think he hated enough to kill Paul Brewster?"

"I'll never find out now, will I?"

His look of defeat pierced Elizabeth, leading her to suggest something she never would have considered before. "Lily came today to make plans for Monday. I'm going there in the morning to give a spinning demonstration. We picked that day because all the men except Richard will be gone."

She could tell the moment Drew realized what she was suggesting. His eyes sparked with challenge. "You can smuggle me in."

"Don't forget Richard will be there," she reminded him. "We'll have to be careful."

"We'll plan everything down to the last detail," Drew assured her.

He was true to his word. By Sunday night they'd planned everything. Elizabeth would smuggle Drew past the gates in her pickup. While she was inside with the women, he would start with the machine shed and work his way east, building by building. When he finished, he would go back to the pickup and signal Elizabeth by tying a handkerchief on the handle of the truck's passenger door. Assuming Richard would be at the farmhouse to eat at noon, they planned to leave the Colony no later than eleven-thirty.

If Drew found the evidence he sought, they'd go back to the cabin just long enough to change vehicles and pen the sheep. After stopping somewhere so he could phone his friend at the FBI, and so Elizabeth could make arrangements for Gene Larson to tend her flock for a few days, they would drive to Milwaukee. Drew had insisted on this last part of the plan. He said it would give them time to be together while he met with the FBI, but Elizabeth suspected it was to get her away from the area, so she wouldn't have to watch her neighbors being arrested.

The plan was solid, but Elizabeth still worried. She tossed and turned in bed that night. When she rolled over and plumped her pillow for the countless time, Drew reached out and pulled her back against his chest.

"Relax. We'll be fine tomorrow," he told her.

"I know. It's just that I can't help wondering what will happen to Lily."

"She'll be all right. I don't think the women are involved in anything sinister. They'll just be questioned and released." He rubbed a hand over the tightly knotted muscles at the back of her neck. "Something else is bothering you."

Elizabeth smiled wryly. During the past six days Drew's hands had learned her body's secrets, yet she hesitated to tell him what was really keeping her awake. "What happens after Milwaukee? To us?" she asked.

Behind her, his hands stilled. "I think it would be best if I gave you some time to adjust to the changes."

Elizabeth swallowed, on the verge of asking him to stay. Instead she told him simply, "I need *you*, Drew. Not time."

"Let's just see what happens when it's over," he told her, his voice straining. "Until then...." He turned her over and kissed her deeply. She tried to resist the response that was already starting to seep through her limbs, but it was no use. She wrapped her arms around him and held on tightly.

Monday, the first day of November, dawned cloudy and cold. The weather had changed almost overnight, as though it were an omen. They reached the first stumbling block while they were still a quarter mile from the gates.

"Oh, no," Elizabeth said softly.

"What's wrong?" Drew hissed. He was crouched next to her in the cab of her pickup, hidden beneath a pile of rolled fleeces.

"Cal Hoskin is on guard duty. I recognize his army jacket," she said under her breath. "I'm turning around." She reached to shift down.

"No!" Drew's hoarse whisper stopped her. "Hoskin's already seen you. You'd look suspicious if you turned around now. Keep going."

"I'm not used to lying, Drew. What if he sees through me?"

"You'll do fine."

Elizabeth pulled into the driveway with the heavy knowledge that Drew trusted her to get them both safely through the gate. She wasn't sure if she could pull it off. Normally, Hoskin would have the gates open by now to wave her through, since her visit was expected. But today the gates stayed closed.

She rolled down her window and tried to smile naturally. "Hello, Cal. They're expecting me at the house."

"Lily said you'd be here. What you got in there?"

Elizabeth looked over at the fleeces, her heart in her throat. She was sure that Drew's hand or foot must be showing. She was relieved to see nothing but paper-wrapped bundles of wool. "Fleece," she told him. "I was afraid to put them in back in case it might rain. Besides, it's pretty dirty back there." She stopped abruptly before making another excuse, realizing that she was being too defensive, too chatty.

"It's too cold. It might snow later, but it sure ain't gonna rain."

Elizabeth looked at him blankly, until she remembered that she'd used the weather as an excuse. "But it looked so cloudy," she said, then wished she hadn't. Making small talk with Cal Hoskin was a completely new experience. She smiled nervously, and was immediately sorry when she saw the interest in Hoskin's gray eyes sharpen.

"That city dude gone back to where he came from yet? He's sure got Silas in a snit."

"Soon. He'll be going soon."

Hoskin leaned forward, his arms folded casually along the top of the door's rolled-down window, so close that Elizabeth could smell the stale sweat from his body. "Well, then I guess you'll be needing a real man—soon."

Drew didn't move a muscle or make a sound, but Elizabeth could feel his fury all the way across the cab. She surreptitiously put the clutch in, ready to throw the truck into gear. "I don't need any man," she said coolly.

Hoskin tipped his head back and laughed. "Stop after you get through the gate. I'll hop on back and ride with you." He went to unlatch the slatted steel doors, and Elizabeth braked obediently after she passed through.

Neither she nor Drew dared break the silence during the short drive to the farmstead. Elizabeth felt a clammy trickle underneath her sweater, and she wondered if Drew was sweating as freely as she was. Probably even more so, since he was wearing a flannel shirt and a down vest underneath all that heavy wool.

What if Hoskin offered to help her take the fleece inside? That was another glitch they hadn't prepared for. Her worries escalated until Hoskin pounded on the glass behind her as she drove past the barn. She stopped, expecting to be discovered at any second, but he leaped out of the truck's bed and jogged to a nearby tractor. She returned his wave and continued around the circular driveway, pulling up a short distance from the big house.

"This is insane," she said under her breath. "Hoskin just left on one of the tractors." She wished she could feel relieved.

"I can hear it. What in hell is he doing here?"

"Should I go to the house and find out, then come back here?"

"No," Drew dismissed her offer. "The women might follow you outside. Just stick to the plan and hope nothing else goes wrong."

She reached for the canvas backpack she'd stored under the seat. Inside were the spindles and cards she'd planned to use to teach the women. She hoped her hands would quit shaking by then. She walked around to the passenger side and unloaded a fleece. Drew stayed in a crouch, keeping his head below the dash.

"I'll give you a few minutes to get into the house and get started. I want to be sure the women are busy before I start going through the buildings," he told her. "You'd better wipe that scared cat look off your face before you go inside."

"I hardly feel like smiling."

"Then don't. But quit glaring in this direction and talking. They're probably watching from the windows." Elizabeth confirmed this with a glance as Drew reminded her. "I'll signal before 11:30. Is the yard clear?"

Elizabeth looked around. "Yes," she hissed through her teeth. She wished she could tell him to be careful. She grabbed the remaining bundles of fleece by the encircling twine and shut the door.

Drew left the protection of the pickup shortly after he heard the tractor's engine fade into the distance. In one all-encompassing glance, he surveyed the yard.

In the center of the circular driveway was an old windmill and pump house, and not far from that, the sawmill and woodpile. The farm buildings were clustered around one side of the circle, the two houses on the other. The farmyard was as neat as a pin, nothing like the chaotic rubble of the streets in Lebanon where he'd finally gotten his fill of being a reporter. But it was dangerous just the same, and this time he wasn't just an observer. This time, if anyone decided to shoot, he'd be the target.

He dashed to the machine shed, his heart pounding the way it had whenever he'd crossed a bombed-out square or walked in front of a line of sandbags. The doorknob turned freely, and he was both relieved and disappointed. With Freeman's passion for secrecy, it wasn't likely they'd leave anything important without locking it. Natural light filtered eerily through the thin green fiberglass panels of the roof, dimly illuminating an ancient baler, a hulking combine and other farm machinery Drew couldn't identify. His footsteps crunched loudly on the gravel floor, echoing in the vast interior. Sheer walls of fiberglass sheeting rose from floor to high ceiling. There were no secrets here.

A small tool shed took longer because there were so many nooks and crannies, including a cramped office area. He wasted a precious half hour breaking into a file cabinet and searching through manila folders that produced nothing more incriminating than cattle-breeding records.

It would help if he knew what he was looking for. Guns and ammo, certainly, but would there be any written records of the group's paramilitary activities? He dismissed the granaries and a large wire corncrib and went on to the chicken house, a two-story white frame building.

As soon as he opened the door, the smell of ammonia burned his lungs. He spared only a quick glance for the entry, cluttered with feed sacks and burlap bags full of wood shavings, before climbing the rickety wooden stairs. When he pulled open the sliding wooden door of the second floor roost, pandemonium greeted him. Feathers and dust clouded the air, and startled chickens squawked and flapped their wings, clumsily flying or running away. Drew shut the door behind him before any of the hens could escape.

"Shh, hush now," Drew said, feeling foolish. Elizabeth talked to her sheep—he'd even done it himself—but chickens? When the hens settled, he walked around the large rectangular room, fighting back a sneeze. His heartbeat quickened at the sight of a smaller room, until he realized it was only a nesting area. Disappointed, he went back to the landing, checking his watch. He realized he had little more than a half hour left to search, and he had yet to investigate the barn and the small house.

He went down the squeaky stairs to the first floor. This time he rapped on the door first, hoping the chickens would heed the warning. It worked. White-feathered hens sat and watched him passively when he stepped into the room. Like before, he walked around the roosts and feeders, peering into the closet-like nesting area before going back to the entrance. He looked over his shoulder, ready to leave, when he got the feeling that something wasn't quite right. This room seemed smaller than the one above it.

He walked across the wood shavings covering the floor until he reached the back wall. Like the other three walls, it was built of raw boards with no visible opening or hinge. He pressed each wooden board in turn. About midway, one of the boards moved slightly. He placed both palms on it and shoved. A narrow section swung open, just three boards wide, and he stepped into darkness. The door closed behind him, leaving only a crack of light from the other room to soften the blackness. He felt for a switch along the wall and gave up. When he stepped cautiously forward, a light pull brushed his face. He tugged and a dim bulb lit the small room.

A large worktable stood to one side, covered with scattered tools. Drew spared it only a brief glance before walking to the pine crates stacked along one wall and taking up nearly half the room. The ink stamped on the sides proclaimed them to be agricultural equipment, but he knew better. He picked up a screwdriver from the table and pried one open. He nearly shouted with elation at his discovery.

Guns. Semiautomatic assault rifles, to be more exact. He took one from the crate to examine it and discovered he was wrong. Thanks to a young Israeli soldier, he knew enough about guns to see that this one was *fully* automatic, capable of delivering multiple rounds with a single pull of the trigger. Death in a split second.

He turned to look at the worktable behind him. At last he knew how ASP could afford to contribute thousands of dollars to a politician's campaign. Here, a simple piece of metal, a trigger sear, was added to the guns, turning the weapons from deadly to deadliest. It also made them as illegal as hell—and valuable on the black market.

He checked several other crates, quickly prying them open and closing them carefully afterward. A couple contained rifles and pistols that hadn't been converted yet. Others didn't hold guns at all, but were filled instead with accessories: flash suppressors, telescopic sights, paratrooper stocks, bayonets. Even more sinister were grenade launchers and timing devices for explosives. Except for the conspicuously absent ammunition, it was a veritable candy store of weaponry.

It was the hard evidence he needed to call in the FBI, and it meant that Elizabeth's neighbors were going behind bars. But it still didn't link the Colony directly to Phillip Prince or to Paul Brewster's death. His throat was tight with anger and disappointment . . . and fear.

He remembered the numbers from Paul's notes: two thousand white supremacists in cabals of seven men and their families, in Wisconsin alone. *Two thousand.* It was an army. He had to get out of here and take Elizabeth with him. If only he had another half hour to search the barn and the house for information on Prince or Brewster. He looked at his watch and cursed. It was 11:25, and Elizabeth was bound to be worried.

He turned to leave, and then he heard it.

The door creaked again, and Drew went into a crouch between the crates and the wall. He peered around the edge of his cramped hiding place. The bare bulb shone down on the dark blond head. . . . Cal Hoskin.

"No, no. Hold the wool fibers farther apart. Like this," Elizabeth corrected, smiling. An observer would have thought she was enjoying herself, talking and giggling with the women, sharing her knowledge. Perhaps she would have if she hadn't been painfully aware of how easily the women's sweetness masked the evil espoused by their men.

The unfamiliar weight of the watch on her wrist was a constant reminder that this wasn't just a spinning circle, although she didn't let her nervousness show. She paused by the two youngest Stoltz girls, who were carding fleece, and demonstrated again how to bunch the carded wool into a sausage-shape rollag ready for spinning. After that, her attention strayed once more to the pickup outside. She looked at her watch. It was almost 11:30, and Drew still hadn't signalled.

From her position by the parlor window, she didn't have a good angle, and perhaps the handkerchief was out of sight. She hadn't expected to be ushered into the rarely used front parlor, but, as Sarah explained, the kitchen was crowded with food for expected supper guests. Elizabeth wondered if the guests were the reason why Hoskin hadn't left. If so, the other men were probably somewhere around the farm, too.

Maybe one of them had found Drew. She looked again at her watch, then around the room at the women. "Lily, would you take this?" she asked. Lily set aside the wool she was teasing and reached for the spindle Elizabeth held out, her gaze curious. "I need to get a drink of water from the kitchen," Elizabeth explained.

She went to the sink, but not for a glass of water. The window above it faced the outbuildings and her pickup. The pickup's door handle was bare, and except for a skinny yellow cat slinking toward the barn, nothing moved under the cloud-filtered sun. Where was Drew?

"Looking for something?" She whirled around to see Jolene. "Or should I say 'someone'?"

"I don't know what you mean," Elizabeth said with a stiff smile.

"Come off it. I know you're after Cal. It isn't enough you got one man. Now you gotta come sniffing around here, too."

Elizabeth felt a desperate laugh clogging her throat. "I came in to get a glass of water," she said, picking up the tin mug that sat beside the tap.

She could feel Jolene's narrow green eyes watching her. Just when she was sure the woman would notice her shaking hands and comment, Jolene said, "Well, just see you don't." She turned to go back to the parlor. With one last glance out the window, Elizabeth followed.

Lily had set up the *charka* and was now showing Sarah how to use it. Elizabeth moved to help one of the teenaged Stoltz girls who was still fumbling with a drop spindle. "Let's all watch Lily now," she said.

The women and girls formed a tight little circle around the gateleg table that had been pulled into the room's center. It was impossible to see out the window from here. Elizabeth gathered up cups and saucers and offered to make more coffee and tea. When Sara Stoltz half rose from her seat, Elizabeth stopped her. "No, you stay and watch. I don't mind clearing up."

As soon as the women were back in their circle, she paused at the chair where she'd left her backpack. Her jacket was on one of the beds upstairs, but she could at least take this. She balanced the cups in one hand and reached for the pack's strap with the other. No one looked up when the cups rattled, not even Jolene.

She set the dishes in the middle of the table and let herself quietly out the back door. She went to the truck first, careful to avoid passing in front of the parlor window. The handkerchief wasn't there, but Drew could have forgotten it. She peered in on the passenger side. The cab was empty.

She quickly crossed to the barn and went inside, calling softly up into the haymow. No one answered. Next she tried the chicken house. She rapped on the inside door before sliding it back. Most of the hens sat on the roost in the middle, while others poked around the feeders. Nothing else moved except the dust motes swirling in front of the windows in the weak midday sun.

"Drew?" she called. No one answered.

She turned to leave but stopped when she heard a slight sound. She looked back to check. It was probably just a hen scratching one of the metal feeders, although it had seemed to come from farther away.

Then she saw the crack of light in the back wall.

Relief quickened her steps, but she took time to glance out each window as she passed to make sure no one from the house had followed her. When she looked back toward the wall, the crack of light had vanished. She decided it must have been the sunlight playing tricks on her, until she noticed that a couple of the boards were askew. She placed her palm on the rough wood and pushed, and the section of wall opened inward. She stepped inside.

"Drew, are you in here?" she called into the darkness and waited.

She felt, rather than saw, motion in front of her. She heard a click, and blinked at the sudden source of light above her head. She collided with a strong chest and felt a masculine pair of arms hold her steady. Her relief changed to horror in an instant when she realized the arms weren't Drew's.

"Well, if it isn't little 'Lizbeth," Cal Hoskin drawled.

"Cal!" She tried to extricate herself from his hold, but his arms only tightened. The room was stuffy, and the smell of Hoskin's sweat choked her. She managed to force her voice into a natural tone. "I'm so glad I found you," she lied. "Jolene has been looking all over for you. We all have been . . ."

His lips curved into a smile that held no warmth at all. "And just why're you looking for me?"

Did he believe her or not? His fingers still bit into her arms through her sweater, and she tried vainly to edge away. "We need you to lift some boxes onto my truck. Come back to the house with me and I'll—"

Hoskin's bark of laughter interrupted her. "Why don't we stay here instead? Just you and me?" He brought his face closer to hers and she turned away.

"You're hurting my arm," she told him.

"Well, why didn't you say so before?" he said pleasantly and released her. Elizabeth stood uncertainly for a moment, her limbs numb with fright. When she realized she was free, she spun around and searched wildly for the panel of wood that led back into the chicken house, ignoring the slivers that pierced her flesh. Behind her, Hoskin chuckled at her desperate efforts.

At last her hand closed over a block of wood. She pulled and it opened, but Hoskin caught her by the shoulder. She gasped and turned to face him. This time his smile was genuine—and it frightened her even more.

"You're afraid, aren't you, 'Lizbeth? That's okay, it'll make things more interesting."

He tugged her against him, but she anticipated the move and led with her knee. She knew she'd connected with her target when he howled with rage, and his back slammed against the door. It swung open again as he advanced. He pulled back a fist.

"Bitch."

The word was softly spoken and more threatening because of it. Elizabeth braced herself for the blow.

Chapter 13

Please, not Elizabeth, Drew begged silently as he heard the door to the roost slide open. When she called out, he cursed mentally, and every muscle poised for action. The irony of the situation mocked him. Here he was, surrounded by hundreds of guns, all inaccessible, all unloaded. Except for the one he'd noticed in Cal Hoskin's hand.

If he revealed himself now, he and Elizabeth would both be in danger. He'd die before he let Hoskin harm her. But with a secret this dangerous to protect, it was unlikely Hoskin would spare either of them. There was no way out, unless he could get Hoskin's gun. Or unless . . . *Elizabeth could bluff her way out.*

He listened with a mixture of amazement and admiration as she lied through her teeth about needing help at the house. He tensed with outrage at Hoskin's crude invitation, then sagged with relief when he heard Hoskin relent. But relief was cut short by the slam of the door and Elizabeth's soft gasp. His body went taut with anger. He didn't waste another moment, launching himself like a panther from the shelter of the crates.

When he saw Hoskin reach back to strike Elizabeth, he felt a roar of rage rip from his throat.

All hell broke loose. Drew's leap knocked Hoskin to the ground, and Elizabeth screamed. The gun flew out of reach and into the shadows. Dust and feathers from the outer room billowed through the doorway, followed by three or four squawking chickens, flapping their wings in fright.

But Drew was barely aware of anything except the sound of ragged breathing as he and Hoskin rolled on the wooden floor, both trying for enough leverage and space to deliver a blow. Instinctively he knew Elizabeth was all right, and out of the corner of his eye he could see her searching on her hands and knees for the gun. *If he could just hold Hoskin off until she found it in the dust and confusion.*

Hoskin was bigger and heavier, but Drew was fueled by rage, and that made it a dead heat. Hoskin managed to throw him off, but before the bigger man could get to his feet, Drew used both fists to club him and send him back to his knees.

Hoskin growled and butted his head against Drew's shins, sending him hurtling backward into the worktable, scattering tools and parts everywhere. The blow against Drew's spine sent a temporary numbness down his legs, and he slid to the floor helplessly. When Hoskin charged like an angry bull, Drew evaded him by rolling under the worktable. He stood up on the other side and faced Hoskin across the table, his chest heaving as he took deep gasps of air.

Past Hoskin's shoulder Drew could see Elizabeth still searching the shadows for the gun among the scattered parts and tools. He reached up to turn on the bank of fluorescent lights swaying above the table and the shadows vanished.

He dragged his gaze away from Elizabeth and looked back at Hoskin. Balanced in his hand was a wickedly sharp awl. Drew reacted instinctively, gripping the tabletop and shoving with all his might. It hit Hoskin's midsection just as his arm snapped back. A blur whizzed by Drew's head, and he heard the sickening thunk of metal biting into wood behind him.

The upended table was no longer a barrier. Hoskin was on the floor and Drew closed in. He'd gone only two steps when he saw Hoskin's hand slip into his boot.

"He's got a knife," Elizabeth warned, as Hoskin got to his feet.

Over Hoskin's shoulder, Drew could see that Elizabeth at last had the gun. He stared into Hoskin's eyes, giving Elizabeth time to stand and aim. He waited for the shot. The knife flashed as Hoskin crouched, ready to leap. Sweat ran down Drew's forehead and stung his eyes, but he didn't dare blink.

"Shoot!" Drew yelled. His shout didn't even faze Hoskin, who was staring at him with the concentration of a cobra.

"I can't," Elizabeth cried. "He's between you and the gun. I might hit you."

Drew moved and Hoskin moved with him. "Just shoot, dammit!" he told her. He'd throw himself on the knife if he thought it would bring Elizabeth to her senses. But somehow he knew she wouldn't budge.

It was a three-way standoff: Elizabeth waiting for a clean shot, Drew trying to get out of her sights so she could aim, and Hoskin, knife in hand, watching Drew's every move and mirroring it. All the while chickens paced around the room, clucking nervously.

"What is going on here?" The door swung open wider and Silas Freeman stepped through. His voice boomed, but nothing was as loud as the sound of the pump-action shotgun locking into readiness. At this range Freeman could probably blow all three of them away, Drew realized.

"Why don't you ask him?" he said, pointing at Cal Hoskin. "Elizabeth and I found out that Cal has his own plans for the merchandise in those crates." Drew's words seemed to release Hoskin from his spell of rage.

"That ain't true, Silas. I found them snooping around in here."

"Put the knife down, Cal," Freeman ordered. Drew relaxed until Freeman added, his voice hardening, "Then tie these two up."

"Silas," Elizabeth interrupted, "Drew's right. We saw Cal acting suspiciously and followed him out here. He as good as told me not to say anything to you." Another deft lie, Drew applauded silently.

"Is that true, Cal?" Freeman asked.

With a movement like a cat's, Hoskin spun around and faced the older man, knife in hand. He laughed. "If it wasn't for you and your damn tribunal, these crates would be on their way to Canada." He feinted toward Freeman and the older man jumped back.

"Just what I thought," Hoskin sneered. "When it comes right down to it, you're too chicken to pull the trigger. That's what you needed me for, wasn't it, Silas? Lew Cole had the connections and the know-how, and dumb ol' Cal here had the muscle. You never even needed that gun you carry. All you had to do was point me instead. 'There's a little problem down in Chicago,'" Hoskin mimicked. "'We want you to take care of it for us, Cal.'"

At Hoskin's words, Drew tensed. His hands itched for a gun, until he realized that would be vigilante justice—no different from the kind Freeman decreed and Hoskin delivered. He listened as Hoskin continued.

"Well, ol' Cal ain't as stupid as he looks. I'm tired of being your bad boy for nothing. This time the money is mine. That mealy mouthed politician sure don't need it anymore."

"We'll send it to another righteous man who wants to restore this country to the laws of God and the Lost Tribes of Israel. Only then will—"

Hoskin cut him off. "I'm sick of listening to that bull."

While the men argued, Drew edged his way toward Elizabeth, hoping they could get between Freeman and the door. When he reached her side, he squeezed her hand reassuringly. The brief contact strengthened his determination to get them out safely. He nodded toward the door, still slightly ajar, and reached to take the rifle that was now hanging loosely from Elizabeth's other hand. Before his palm closed over the barrel, Freeman's voice rang out.

"Hold it right there."

Drew froze. With Elizabeth standing beside him he wouldn't take any chances. "Now drop the rifle on the floor," Freeman instructed.

As soon as Freeman bent to pick up the rifle, Hoskin lunged. Drew pulled Elizabeth out of the way as Freeman swiftly brought the barrel of his shotgun down hard on Hoskin's hand. The knife landed on the floor with a clatter.

"Leave it!" Freeman ordered when Hoskin would have bent to retrieve it. His gaze shifted between the three people in front of him. He stood with a gun in each arm, like a western gunslinger. "None of you move. Don't think I won't shoot. I killed soldiers in Korea, and I'm still fighting for this country's future. Cal, you're either with me or against me."

Three people waited for Hoskin's answer.

"Aw, hell, Silas." Hoskin grinned affably. "Of course I'm on your side. It's these two you oughta be gunnin' for."

Freeman apparently agreed, because he turned to Elizabeth and said, "I'm sorry, but we can't interrupt our plans at this stage. We'll have to keep you here until tomorrow."

"Jeez, Silas, don't be stupid. Shoot 'em."

"It wouldn't be right, even done in the Lord's name."

"You didn't worry about *right* when it came to that reporter. 'Course he wasn't white. Bet you never shot a white man before. Or a woman." Drew's jaw clenched. "Okay, put 'em up in front of your damned tribunal tonight if you want. Fact is we'll all vote to shoot 'em anyway. Just don't expect me to do your dirty work this time."

"Take them downstairs," Freeman ordered.

Hoskin lifted a trapdoor set into the floor where the table had stood. He grinned. "Ladies first."

Drew could feel Elizabeth shudder. He tightened his arms reassuringly, until Hoskin pulled her from his grasp.

Dampness pressed in on Elizabeth, making it difficult for her to breathe. The room was dark, with a dirt floor and rock walls, and it smelled like mildew. It felt too much like a tomb for her peace of mind. Judging from the crates and sandbags in haphazard piles, it was a bunker of some sort. She leaned back against a wooden crate, wishing she was back in Drew's arms. Hoskin had pushed him to the floor several feet away.

"Bind them," Freeman ordered as he tossed a roll of duct tape to Hoskin.

"But—"

"Do as I say. The tribunal will decide whether to shoot them, not you."

Hoskin obeyed, wrapping Drew's wrists and ankles expertly. Drew sat calmly while Hoskin worked, and Elizabeth tried to draw strength from his stoicism. When it was her turn, Hoskin's brisk efficiency changed to idleness. He moved slowly, brushing his hand over her legs before wrapping the tape.

Nausea filled her. She looked away, and tried to concentrate on what Drew was saying to Silas, his voice low but urgent.

"Let her go," Drew insisted. "She has nothing to do with this. I forced her to come along."

"But she knows."

"She's known enough for years to bring the IRS down on you, and yet she'd never done it. You're her neighbors, and she wouldn't do anything to jeopardize your operation." He saw then that she was listening, and he looked at her intently. "Isn't that right, Elizabeth? Tell Silas you won't say a word about this to anyone."

Elizabeth didn't answer. She had no intention of leaving Drew behind. Without her presence, Silas would no doubt give Hoskin leave to kill Drew without suffering a qualm. Hadn't he cold-bloodedly ordered Brewster's death? She didn't speak, but her eyes telegraphed her thoughts to Drew. *I'm staying.*

Drew's expression clearly retorted. *Don't be a fool.* Elizabeth lifted her chin stubbornly. Her resolve didn't falter, not even when Hoskin trailed a hand down her arm to her wrist. She saw Drew's eyes turn black with rage. Jaw clenching, he looked away and appealed to Freeman again. "When Lily finds out that you've done this to her friend, she'll be upset."

"It's not a woman's place to question what her man does."

At last Hoskin finished with Elizabeth's wrists and stood up. Freeman made a quick gesture. "Gag them."

Freeman trained his gun on Hoskin while he worked, as though he didn't trust the younger man to do his bidding. Elizabeth didn't know what unnerved her more. The feel of Hoskin's fingers on her cheek, or the shotgun Silas kept pointed at them both. Hoskin saw that her terrified glance was directed toward the gun and smiled.

"You don't need that gun anymore now, Silas," Hoskin told him. "Your prisoners are wrapped up all nice and tight."

"Oh, yes I do. It will be you who faces the tribunal tonight, Cal Hoskin."

The threat in his words chilled Elizabeth, but Hoskin's smile never faltered. He just led the way upstairs, Freeman's gun at his back.

When the trapdoor dropped into place, the cellar was filled with darkness. Something scraped across the wooden floor above them. One of the crates, Elizabeth guessed, pulled in place to keep the trapdoor closed—as if she and Drew had any way of escaping from their bonds. The strong tape held her as firmly as handcuffs. She inhaled sharply when she felt something brush the back of her hand. Then she realized that Drew had sidled closer.

She sagged against him. Without the feel of his solid warmth next to her, she knew she would have gone mad. He rubbed his elbow against her side, signalling to her to turn around. High on the wall, three small windows let in slats of afternoon sun.

Later, when he pantomimed that he wanted to look at her watch, she moved her arms to the side so he could see, although it was unlikely he could read the tiny numerals in the semidarkness. The gold watch had been purchased for its elegance, not its utility. The part of her that was once Liz Eden seemed even further away now than before. But, she'd dug the watch out of the jewelry box to wear, so she'd be assured of the synchronization of their plans.

She didn't need a watch to see what time it was. The narrow strip of light coming in from the windows told her not much time had passed since she left the house to look for Drew. She wondered if the women had any idea of the ugliness taking place across the yard from their spinning circle.

In a few more hours it would be time for her sheep to be in the paddock. By now she and Drew should have been on their way to Milwaukee. She tipped her head back against the crate behind her and let the tears flow. Drew made a sound at the back of his throat, and she raised her head to find him looking at her, his expression anguished. She tried to smile, but the tape that covered her mouth prevented her. She let her eyes carry the message and hoped Drew understood.

He did. He leaned his head forward until their foreheads touched. He used his face to caress hers, his whiskered cheek endearingly rough against her nose and chin. Elizabeth knew then, without any spoken words between them, that he loved her. A shaft of sweet joy pierced her, and for a moment, her surroundings were forgotten.

Hours passed like days as they watched the rectangles of light crawl from the middle of the floor to the opposite wall, mirroring the sun's movement across the sky. Drew had tried to loosen the tape around his wrists by rubbing it against the corner of the crate, but it only twisted. Elizabeth could sense his frustration. She knew he still hadn't accepted their fate. Her own bonds were uncomfortably tight, and no matter which way she shifted, her body felt tender from the contact with the hard floor.

Thud. Thud, thud.

When Elizabeth heard the irregular pounding she thought at first that it was her heart. When Drew halted his efforts with the tape, she realized that he'd heard something, too. They looked at each other, hope and fear mingling in their eyes.

A shadow darted in front of the window and she recognized Luke Freeman's childish form. The boy was bouncing a ball against the outside wall of the chicken house, unaware of the drama inside. An unearthly noise filled the cellar. She tensed until she realized it was coming from Drew's throat. Following his clue, she moaned loudly behind the square of tape. They sounded like a pair of banshees, but the thudding continued unabated.

Drew stood awkwardly and hopped over to a ceiling-high stack of crates. He shouldered the stack and three of the crates tumbled down and shattered noisily. The thudding outside stopped abruptly, and Drew and Elizabeth began their chorus of moans again.

A small white face flashed in front of the window. Could Luke see into the shadows? Elizabeth wondered. The face disappeared, and she sagged with disappointment.

When thirty minutes passed in utter silence, they knew Luke wasn't coming. Perhaps the noise had frightened him. Or perhaps he'd told an adult—the wrong one—about what he'd seen.

The sun set, and the cellar grew cold. Elizabeth and Drew sat as close together as possible, taking comfort in each other's nearness. She dozed off now and then. Between heartbeats she thought of dying, and when her contemplations threatened to give her nightmares, she constructed elaborate fantasies, imagining herself and Drew in places that were sunny and warm and miles away. She thought longingly of the lined denim jacket that she'd left behind at the big house. She shivered, and Drew moved closer. His down vest was open in the front, and she snuggled against his chest. Close to his heartbeat, she slept.

Elizabeth woke stretched out on the dirt floor, her head and shoulders cradled on Drew's lap. His head was bowed forward in sleep. Was it her imagination, or had the darkness grayed a bit? She lay still for a moment, her gaze traveling around the room, wondering what had woken her. Then she heard a scraping sound. *The trapdoor.*

She looked up to see Drew's eyes snap open. He, too, listened intently as the noise came again, the sound of wood rubbing against wood as the crate was moved away. Her feelings warred between relief and fear. Was the visitor a rescuer—or an executioner?

She straightened, noting the protectiveness in the way Drew shielded her with his upper torso. The trapdoor creaked open. A flashlight beam advanced down the ladder stairs, traveling over the broken crates before settling on the two of them. As the flashlight neared, Elizabeth tried to discern the identity of its carrier. When she realized it was Lily, jubilation swept through her.

"Luke told me you were here," Lily whispered urgently as she knelt beside them. "I didn't dare leave until now. The men have been talking all night." She produced a kitchen knife from the folds of her skirt and started sawing at the tape binding Drew's wrist.

"How many men? Where are they from?" Drew asked as soon as his hands were free and he'd pulled off the tape covering his mouth. He took the knife from Lily and used it to cut through Elizabeth's bonds.

"Twenty or thirty—I don't know exactly. Some came after we'd finished eating and some went home for the night. Most are from Potawatomi County, the others come from all over," she whispered. "They meet once a month. They were supposed to meet in Forest City this time, but it was changed. I don't know why."

Drew worked as gently as possible, but Elizabeth's cheeks and wrists still stung from the tape. She didn't care. Her relief was too great to notice pain.

"You must go quickly," Lily told them. "It will be light soon. Silas hid your pickup in the machine shed, and the men's cars and trucks are blocking the doors."

"Then we'll go on foot," Drew said. "The sound of an engine might wake someone up anyway." While Elizabeth stood to stretch, he bent down to cut the tape around his ankles. He looked up to ask, "When are they planning to ship the guns?"

"Tonight, I think."

"Where?"

"I don't know." Lily's voice was edged with fear.

"You must have overheard them," Drew pressed.

"She's telling the truth," Elizabeth interrupted. "And she's right. We have to leave quickly." She turned to Lily. "These men are very dangerous. Even Silas."

"I know," the young woman admitted quietly. "I saw the guns upstairs, and I heard them planning to take you into the woods and...they were going to make it look like a hunting accident." She looked away. "He is my husband, but I had to disobey him. Leave quickly before he finds out I helped you."

"Come with us," Elizabeth urged.

"I can't." Her blue eyes filled with tears.

Drew squeezed Elizabeth's hand and added, "When Silas finds out we've been freed, he'll suspect everyone here, especially you. We'll take you somewhere safe."

Lily shook her head so violently her brown hair slipped from its tidy bun.

"We're going to call the FBI, Lily," Elizabeth said gently. "What Silas did was against the law."

"I know." Lily's voice was barely a whisper. "I won't tell him where you've gone, but I can't go with you."

"Why not?" Elizabeth asked.

"Because I'm going to have a baby," she confessed in an impassioned whisper. Her eyes begged Elizabeth to understand. "His child. And I can't leave Luke."

Elizabeth was too shocked to argue further. Drew pulled her to her feet. "We have to leave now. Lily, you go first. I'll be behind you with the flashlight. We'll wait until you get inside the house before we leave."

Elizabeth gathered up her backpack from where Hoskin had thrown it before he'd tied her wrists. She looked longingly at the packets of dehydrated food scattered across the floor. She and Drew hadn't eaten in hours. Working quickly, she stuffed as many as she could into the pack as they made their way to the stairs.

The chicken house was blessedly warm after the damp cellar. They moved quietly past the roosts, disturbing only a few of the sleeping hens. When they opened the exterior door, a blast of icy air greeted them. Snowflakes fluttered like ashes to the ground, melting as soon as they landed.

The farmyard was deserted in the predawn light, except for ten or twenty trucks and cars parked in front of the machine shed and next to the small house. Like Freeman's, many were painted in camouflage colors. Nearer to the chicken house was a small moving van. After a low-voiced question from Drew, Lily confirmed it was going to be used to transport the guns.

The three figures moved away from the white wall of the chicken house to the shadows of the woodpile in the center of the yard. Elizabeth hugged Lily, tears stinging at the corner of her eyes. "I'll see you soon," she said, hoping it was true. "Would you see to the sheep for me?"

"Yes. Your cabin will be just as you left it," Lily promised. She left the protection of the woodpile and started across the yard. Elizabeth shivered at the sight of the lone figure walking toward the dark house.

Drew crept up behind her and wrapped his arms around her. She leaned back into his warmth gratefully. "She'll be all right," he said softly, his breath brushing her ear. "So will we." He dropped a light kiss on her earlobe.

Then he stiffened.

At first Elizabeth didn't understand what made him react; then she saw it, too. A man carrying a gun walked around the front of the house. From where they crouched they could see what Lily couldn't—that his path would intersect with hers before she reached the back door.

"Can't we do something?" Elizabeth whispered urgently.

Drew was edging toward the smaller pile of scrap wood before she even finished her sentence. He grabbed a couple pieces of kindling and fired one toward the windbreak before retreating to his place beside Elizabeth.

The wood landed short of the windbreak and made a dull thud when it hit the lawn. The guard spun in his tracks and took off for the trees mere seconds before Lily would have crossed his line of sight.

Elizabeth didn't tear her gaze from Lily's back until the door closed behind her. She turned to Drew, who was watching the guard, his body tense. The man was checking the high grass that marked the edge of the yard. At least eighty feet of open lawn lay between them and the windbreak.

"We'd better circle behind the barn while he's busy—"

Elizabeth grabbed Drew's arm, cutting off the rest of his words. "Look!"

The guard had found the piece of firewood, and his head swung round to the woodpile. They crouched deeper in the shadows, out of sight. When the guard started coming their way, Drew cursed under his breath.

"Get behind me," he whispered urgently.

She moved slowly, afraid to make a sound. Drew hefted the second stick of wood in his hand, and she realized what he planned to do. She eased the pack from her back and opened it, searching for a weapon of her own. Her fingers closed on the handle of a wool comb. The guard was so close now that she could hear his cautious footsteps in the dry grass. Before he could spot them, Drew leaped up.

Violence exploded around her. Locked in a brutal embrace the men stumbled against the stacked wood, and it crashed down on top of them. Elizabeth bit back a scream as one of the heavy logs hit Drew on the head. The makeshift club skidded from Drew's weakened grasp. The blow provided the other man with a respite, and he scrambled on his hands and knees, searching the ground for his rifle, caught under a log inches from his outstretched hand.

His hand grasped the gun, and Elizabeth didn't think twice before striking out with all the strength she possessed. The wicked metal teeth of the comb sunk into the fleshy part of the man's palm. He screamed in agony. She let go of the handle and looked at the blood welling up around the comb's teeth with a sense of revulsion.

"Come on, we've got to get out of here," Drew's voice barely penetrated her stare of horrified fascination. The guard's features were distorted with pain, but Elizabeth recognized him as one of the men who'd attacked her and Lily a year ago. A shout from the direction of the house finally broke through her horror. She grabbed her pack as Drew pulled her to her feet.

"Head for the trees. Don't wait for me," he added as the guard started to rise. The bang as the porch door slammed shut was followed by an even louder bang. *Gunfire.* Elizabeth heard Drew's footsteps behind her, and when she would have turned to look, he yelled at her to keep going. They crashed through the long grass and underbrush into the sheltering trees of the windbreak. Too soon they emerged in open pasture.

She ran, Drew's footsteps loud in her ears, mingling with the sound of blood pounding through her veins and the staccato harshness of their labored breaths. Elizabeth was sure she couldn't run any farther—her legs felt leaden and the gate was too far. She concentrated on interim goals—past that tree, over that rock—until finally the gate rose before her. Adrenaline spurred her climb, and then she was jumping to the ground below, Drew now two steps ahead of her. They crossed the steep ditch, and at last they were in the woods.

Here, snow clung in thin, slippery patches, bright white in the dawn light. They slowed their pace just enough to be safe, wordlessly agreeing that direction wasn't as important as distance. Elizabeth knew that the men would soon follow, and Lily's warning about a "hunting accident" rang in her ears.

Drew slipped on a snow-covered log, and Elizabeth reached out to steady him. The sight of blood on his sleeve brought her up short. Her fingers grabbed his arm. "You're wounded."

"It just grazed the skin. Come on." Drew pulled from her grasp. "We have to keep going or we'll never make it to your place before they do."

But she was already sliding the backpack off her shoulders. "I have something in here to stop the bleeding." As she spoke, an engine backfired in the distance.

"We don't have time."

"Drew, they'll be there waiting for us. Even if we hurry we can't beat them on foot."

"So what do you suggest? Just hide out here until they find us? We have to get to my truck. We can't make it far enough on foot. You heard what Lily said. Half the damned county will be looking for us."

Elizabeth didn't listen. She was too busy pulling away the edges of his torn shirtsleeve. What she saw made her stomach roll, but she spoke calmly. "They expect us to do that. We're going north instead."

"It's a dead end," he said patiently. "What are we supposed to do, dive off the rocks into the lake?"

"We're going to Doc Wilson's."

Drew protested, but Elizabeth stood her ground. "Every minute you argue, you lose more blood," she reminded him. He bent his head to look at the red liquid dripping from his fingers onto the light dusting of snow, then looked away.

She followed his gaze. A few feet farther, another spot of red stood out against a dusting of snow. Wherever they had crossed snow, footprints and blood marked their path. Drew swore. "Can we trust him?"

"Yes." She tightened the roving of wool around the wound. It wasn't the most effective of bandages, but it was something, at least. "We don't have a choice. We can't cross the lake, and Silas and his men will be waiting for us to the south." She wanted to wipe away the blood on his forehead, to kiss the lump left by the falling wood, but there wasn't time.

"Let's go then. And stay away from the snow."

They headed deeper into the woods.

Doc Wilson's cabin, like Elizabeth's, was far from the road. But at least the doctor had the good sense to install electricity, Drew noted with a sense of detachment as he listened to Elizabeth pound on the cabin door. He kept his eye on the overhead wire as he slumped onto the cabin's front steps, using it as a focal point to help him concentrate on staying awake.

Bam! Bam! Bam!

The pounding sent a ripple of nausea through him, and he swallowed it back. Thank God for Elizabeth. She'd been right about his arm. It was worse than he'd admitted, but at the time his fear for her had kept him from voicing his own concerns. He'd started feeling the loss of blood halfway to Doc's, and she'd alternately cajoled and hounded him into keeping up with her fast pace.

As they ran, the sounds of angry shouts and gunning engines had carried through the forest. They'd avoided the road and kept to the trees. Without Elizabeth, he never would have made it. In the woods she was like a nymph, darting from the shadow of one tree trunk to the next, always sure of her direction, never stopping. To him it all looked the same. Except for the pines, the trees were bare, leaving a jumble of branches and an endless carpet of damp leaves spotted with treacherous patches of snow.

Bam! Bam! Bam!

The pounding on the door reverberated with the pounding in his head. He sat, his spine as straight as possible, hoping that he wouldn't lose control. He had to stay conscious. Elizabeth had gotten them through the woods, but they still had a long way to go before they were home free. *And the odds definitely weren't on their side.*

He'd hoped that they could hole up here and hold off their pursuers until help came. But Doc's log cabin didn't look nearly as sturdy as Elizabeth's. Besides, they couldn't drag another person into this, especially when chances were their efforts would be in vain. In all likelihood, any reinforcements that arrived would be on Freeman's side of the battle. No one knew they were missing. Jim Levitz might figure it out—in a few days. By then it would be too late.

Bam—

Drew waited, but the pounding had at least ceased. He could hear Elizabeth talking to someone, but he couldn't understand what she was saying. Her voice kept fading in and out as the pounding in his head grew louder. He tried to concentrate on her voice, and his brow furrowed.

Then he could feel her hands on his, helping him to stand and pulling him through the cabin's dim hallway to a brightly lit room. He could smell whiskey, and he wondered how that could be since the bottle the white-haired man handed him still had a cap on.

He twisted it off, dimly aware that someone was tearing away his sleeve and ordering him to drink. He felt the cap roll from his fingers, heard it skitter across the floor. He held the bottle to his lips and tipped it back. He expected blessed oblivion, but at the same moment the alcohol burned his tongue and throat, he felt something bite into his upper arm.

Hands eased him onto his back—he'd ended up on top of a table of some sort. He fought for a minute when he remembered he had to stay awake, but it felt so good to relax that he couldn't help himself. He saw Elizabeth's face above him and smiled weakly. She looked the way she had the day she'd found him in her pasture.

"Angel," he said, the strength of his voice surprising him. He realized then that he needed her. *Always.* He tried to tell her so, but he wasn't sure if she heard him before the room's light faded to gray.

Chapter 14

Elizabeth watched helplessly as Doc Wilson probed the torn flesh of Drew's upper arm. She knew the man had been drinking—she'd smelled it instantly—but his eyes were clear as he assured her he could operate. She watched him now, looking for signs of ineptitude, but his hands seemed steady, his long fingers nimble.

She'd winced at Drew's obvious pain when Doc had first opened the edges of the wound to check for the bullet. But alcohol or pain or exhaustion—or a combination of all three—had sent Drew mumbling into unconsciousness. She was thankful for that, because Doc didn't have any anesthesia. Seeing Drew helpless was nightmare enough; she couldn't have borne seeing him in pain.

"The wound isn't so bad after all," Doc told her, his gray eyes kindly when he saw her tortured expression.

Elizabeth tried to return his reassuring smile but failed. She watched until he started to close the edges of the torn skin, then she got up and left the small office. After going to the bathroom, she entered the kitchen, certain Doc wouldn't mind if she looked for something to eat. She wouldn't do Drew any good if she was weak on her feet from hunger.

But when she entered the kitchen, she forgot all about food. There, on the table against the wall was Doc's radio. Excitement bubbled within her until she sat down and stared at the jumble of dials and switches. She didn't even know where to begin.

On her first attempt, she was rewarded with an earful of static. Next she tried combinations of switches and dials, hoping to discover how to transmit. Her movements grew more frantic until a strong pair of hands covered her own.

"Don't." The voice was endearingly rough.

She looked up, her gaze traveling slowly over the white gauze bandages on his shoulder and forehead before meeting his dark eyes. Drew looked wonderful, or at least wonderfully alive. His skin was almost as white as the bandages, and lines of pain edged his mouth, but he was walking and talking and breathing—and she loved him. For a moment she forgot about the radio.

"Don't what?"

Drew pulled her hands from the switches and dials and set them in her lap. "Don't radio anyone." At her questioning look, he told her, "I recognized a couple of the men who were outside the farmhouse. Mel Bofry was one of them. We don't know who we can trust. Anyone with a CB could hear us."

Elizabeth sighed, knowing he was right. If Mel Bofry was involved, there were bound to be others in Nisswa who secretly sympathized with the Colony. She told him about the man she'd recognized, and admitted, "Half the men in the county have CBs in their pickups. Including Silas."

"Exactly. They've probably already figured out we're not headed for your cabin. We have to leave before they start coming north."

Elizabeth stood, ready to argue. But before she could open her mouth, Doc entered the kitchen and chimed in gruffly. "Oh, no you don't, son. I just wasted half a bottle of my best bourbon whiskey on you. I don't want you running around and dying on me."

Drew snorted. "I'm not going to die unless that godawful rotgut catches up with me before the supremacists do. I explained the situation to you, Doc. If we don't get out of here now, they'll come looking. For all three of us." He nodded toward Elizabeth, and Doc backed down.

The old man grumbled, "I could use a little excitement in my life." He looked at the two faces in front of him and relented. "Go. But take my truck. The tank's almost full." He ignored Drew's outstretched hand and gave the keys to Elizabeth.

As she and Drew went out the door, Doc stopped her. She looked at him, puzzled, when he reached to the hall tree for his hat and set it on her head. "You're not as ugly as I am, but it'll be better than nothing," he said.

"Thank you." Elizabeth kissed him on both of his lined cheeks before tucking her blonde braid up under the hat and leading the way outside.

Drew found out Elizabeth had no intention of letting him drive. "No," she said flatly. "I have the keys—" she held them out of his reach "—and your right arm is in a sling. You can't handle a stick shift. You can hardly even stand up," she pointed out.

He straightened after realizing he was swaying on his feet. "When we get to a main road I can get all the rest I need," he argued, but she stood her ground next to the large white pickup, blocking him from the door. He knew she'd stand there until nightfall if she had to. "All right," he growled, opening the door. "Get in."

She clambered up and he went around to the passenger door. The engine started with a powerful rumble—quite a change from Elizabeth's temperamental vehicle or the four-cylinder engine in Jim's truck.

It stopped spitting snow shortly after they left Doc's. The road was surprisingly deserted, until they spotted a man lurking in the brush near Elizabeth's driveway. Drew slumped low in the seat and watched Elizabeth. She kept her eyes straight ahead, but he could see her throat work as she swallowed. He knew how she felt. His throat was tight with strain, too.

"Do you think they're still waiting for us to show up at the cabin?" she asked after they'd driven past.

"Let's hope so."

He tipped his head back against the seat and watched as the treetops grew farther apart, signaling that they were nearing the intersection with the county road. When Elizabeth gasped and her foot lifted from the gas, he knew they were in trouble.

Cautiously, he lifted his head to peer over the dash. Two pickups, one of them Elizabeth's, were parked across the gravel road a couple hundred yards ahead of them, just before the road joined the county highway. On either side steep, weed-choked ditches separated the road from fences and fields. Ten or fifteen men—all armed—swarmed around the trucks and the ditches, positioning themselves.

"A roadblock," he said unnecessarily. He felt his heart sink to his stomach. So this is how it would end. He slumped back down out of sight, ready to tell Elizabeth to do the same. She was driving slowly, heading closer to the roadblock.

"Buckle your seat belt," she said.

"What are you going to do?"

"The only thing I can." She shot him a determined smile. "Hang on."

Drew's head jerked back against the seat as she slammed down on the accelerator. She shifted gears when the rpm needle entered the red zone, and he was reminded crazily of Paul Newman and Robert Redford jumping off the cliff in *Butch Cassidy and the Sundance Kid*. With Doc's white hat, Elizabeth made a good cowboy-cum-robber. But this wasn't the movies.

The men looked almost stupidly at the white pickup bearing down on them. At the last moment, Elizabeth yanked the wheel sharply to the right. Drew braced himself for the impact. The pickup slammed into the ditch, and he prayed they wouldn't roll over. He watched her battle with the steering wheel as she guided the pickup up the steep bank. Long dry grass and brush scraped the vehicle's underside.

At the top they faced another obstacle—a taut wire fence that followed the edge of the field all the way to the county highway. He glanced back at the men, seeing that they were already scrambling to get in their vehicles. He knew they wouldn't have time to follow the fence to the road.

But Elizabeth had other ideas. She headed straight for the fence and Drew started a string of curses that ended abruptly when he realized that the fence had snapped up behind them and they were still moving.

The men swung the trucks around in pursuit, the first one—Elizabeth's old pickup—taking the road, the other heading for the ditch behind them. As he watched, a man poked out of the window of the second truck, gun raised.

"Get down!" Drew ordered, hoping that the man wouldn't be able to get off a clean shot while traveling through the steep ditch.

Elizabeth slouched in her seat as the truck bumped diagonally across the plowed field to the county road. "There's another fence up ahead," she warned.

But Drew was more concerned about the men behind them. "They're through the ditch," he told her.

They headed for the same fence Elizabeth had crossed, but instead of snapping up behind them, the wires caught underneath the pickup. Steel fence posts popped out of the ground and trailed behind the slowing vehicle. Drew cheered, but his triumph was short-lived as gunfire exploded around them. He could hear shot smack against Doc's truck seconds before they plunged into another ditch.

"We're almost there," Elizabeth told him as she downshifted. The engine screamed when she guided the pickup up the steep-sided ditch toward the county road.

Drew looked back again. Elizabeth's old pickup, crowded with gun-toting supremacists, was waiting at the intersection as a loaded logging truck passed. The driver of the behemoth truck blasted its air horn in warning, but Elizabeth didn't wait. Drew felt Doc's pickup shudder as she gunned the engine and pulled out in front of the huge truck bearing down on them.

The air horn blasted again, so close Drew could feel it vibrate through his body, and brakes screeched behind them. He waited for the impact, but it didn't come. Elizabeth drove as fast as possible on the twisting road, using both lanes to negotiate the curves, and Drew silently blessed her cool-headed skill. The driver of the logging truck stayed on their tail, his lips moving in pantomime curses. Somewhere behind him were the two trucks driven by the Colonists and their cohorts. The logging truck made an effective albeit unwilling shield. They were safe for now.

Or were they?

As they topped a hill Drew caught a glimpse of flashing lights ahead. He quickly switched on Doc's CB radio and turned the dial until he found the police band. It didn't take long—he recognized Jed Smith's voice immediately.

"... a stolen Ford pickup, white, license number—"

"Oh, no." Elizabeth's face was pale as the APB continued.

"It gets worse," Drew told her.

"How?"

"Smith—or one of his deputies—is coming down the road right now. We'll meet him any second. Turn off the next chance you get." He'd barely finished speaking when the patrol car and its flashing lights came into view at the top of the next rise. "See the sign that says Sherwood Forest? Take a right there," he ordered. "Don't slow down until you have to."

"But—"

"Just do it." Drew glanced back to see the logging truck still behind them and decided it just might work. When they reached the turn, Elizabeth jerked the wheel to the right. At the unexpected move, the truck driver behind them slammed on his brakes and came to an excruciatingly slow and noisy halt. Drew could see the livid driver waving his fist as they bumped down the narrow gravel road.

Elizabeth glanced up in the rearview mirror. "The truck's blocking the turnoff. Jed can't get in."

"He'll be back on our tail any second," Drew warned as they drove into the trees. "Let's hope we can lose him in here." He could hear the siren coming closer behind them and Smith's voice on the radio giving out the location.

"What is this place?" Elizabeth asked. "I've noticed the sign before, but I've never been back here."

"Take a left here," Drew told her before explaining. "It's a lake development—summer cabins."

The gravel road curved and narrowed as they headed deeper into the trees. Tiny cabins were barely visible among the pine and hardwoods, and the network of driveways and trails were marked with rustic street signs bearing names such as Friar Tuck Way or Little John Lane. Most of the cabins were closed for the winter, docks pulled out of the water, windows boarded over. The area had a deserted, ghost town feel.

Looking for a working telephone was too risky, Drew decided reluctantly. He wouldn't take any chances with Elizabeth beside him. He rolled down his window and listened for the siren. The only sound was the pickup's engine and the sputtering radio. He leaned back against the seat and breathed in the cool lake air. "Smith sounds mad. Think we lost him?"

"I hope so, because I'm lost myself. It's a maze back here."

"Turn left up ahead." She complied. "Now take the next two rights. We should be at Maid Marion's Trail, which will take us right to a county road."

"How did you know about this place?"

"I did a lot of driving around when I was trying to stay away from your cabin," he confessed. "Do you think you could go a little faster? I'd like to get to the highway before Smith's deputies come after us. I'd hate to get caught back here."

"I forgot about the deputies," she said. "Do you suppose they're involved with Silas, too?"

"Could be. Smith certainly is. We know that Doc didn't report the truck as stolen. Even if the deputies aren't involved, they'll be out looking for a stolen pickup. And who knows how many men Freeman's got after us. From now on we have to stick to the back roads."

They arrived at the highway, and Elizabeth turned right. Drew instructed her to turn off at the next gravel road. "We've got to get out of Smith's jurisdiction as soon as we can," he added.

"We'll never make it to the state line, or even to the next county."

"I know. We're going to the reservation. It's the only place we can be sure we won't run into any sympathizers for Freeman's cause, and since it's federal land, it's outside of county jurisdiction," Drew explained.

"To get to Eagle Lake Reservation from here, we'll have to drive around the state park. It's almost thirty miles," Elizabeth protested.

"Are you suggesting we go back and use the shorter route?" She shook her head and stared straight ahead. Drew could see tension in every line of her body. "We're going to make it, Elizabeth."

"How can you be so sure? Silas has probably got patrols everywhere, including this road." As soon as she spoke, a pickup appeared around the curve in front of them. Drew's breathing stopped until the truck was well past.

"Just a hunter," he said. He didn't point out that hunters would be driving the same kinds of vehicles as the supremacists. Elizabeth already knew that.

"I wish we could go faster," she said, braking to take another sharp curve.

"Hungry?" Drew offered her some of the dehydrated food he'd found in her backpack. "It tastes like dog food, but it's filling."

"No. I don't know how you can eat at a time like this." She turned to look at him. "What on earth are you smiling about?" she demanded.

"I was just thinking that Freeman and his men will probably be so busy looking for us that they'll get a late start loading those guns."

"Do you think the FBI will be able to catch them in the act?"

"I hope so. But in case they don't get there in time, it just so happens that I got the license number of the moving truck."

Elizabeth started to laugh, and Drew joined in. It felt odd to be laughing in the middle of nowhere when their lives were in danger, but he knew the tension of the past few hours needed an outlet. Her eyes were still sparkling like amethysts when he unbuckled his seat belt and slid over to plant a kiss on her cheek.

"We *are* going to make it," he told her with conviction.

For another forty-five minutes, Elizabeth drove, sheer nerves keeping her alert. Drew was asleep, his head cradled on her lap. Her right leg was starting to go numb, but she didn't wake him, not even when they reached the border of the Eagle Lake Indian Reservation. She realized how exhausted Drew must have been to let down his guard enough to doze.

It wouldn't have taken this long to reach the Reservation, but when she'd spotted a camouflage pickup with two men coming up behind them at a ridiculous speed, she'd panicked and turned off the road. She'd gotten lost and ended up backtracking several miles. It seemed ironic that she—who'd lived in Potawatomi County for five years—needed Drew to direct her. She realized just how out of touch she'd let herself become, with her beat-up, unreliable pickup and her isolated cabin, and she vowed to change.

She parked in front of a long, low building with a sign out front designating it as the reservation's community center. Drew woke up the moment she cut the engine. "We're here," she said as he sat up. "A little late, but safe and sound."

"Thank you." He leaned over and kissed her. "Why don't you stay here in the pickup while I get things straightened out?"

Elizabeth's protest died on her lips. Now that she no longer had to devote every ounce of energy to staying alert, she felt tiredness steal over her. She agreed to wait, and when Drew returned several minutes later, she was already half asleep.

"Elizabeth, this is Charlie Littlehawk. He's the local law." Elizabeth looked past Drew to the slender young man standing outside the pickup and drowsily acknowledged the introduction. "Charlie has offered to let us use his home to rest up. We'll follow his Jeep."

"Did you get in touch with the FBI?" she asked as soon as they'd pulled out of the parking area.

"Not yet. We'll call from the Littlehawks' place. Charlie says they have a phone."

Elizabeth followed the Jeep past a group of residences that ranged from little more than shacks to mobile homes to modest one-story frame houses. Charlie Littlehawk pulled up in front of a double-wide mobile home, and they followed him inside. He introduced Elizabeth and Drew to his wife, Madeline, who was about Elizabeth's age. Her dark eyes widened as her husband related their ordeal.

While the men used the phone in the kitchen, Madeline led Elizabeth to the master bedroom. "Would you like to shower and lie down for a while?" she asked shyly. "I have some things that might fit you."

Elizabeth accepted gratefully. The sweat of fear and stress clung to her, and the smell of the cellar bunker was still fresh in her mind.

"Here." Madeline took a soft yellow sweatsuit from a dresser drawer. "I think this will do," she said. Although the two women were equally slender, Madeline was several inches taller. Elizabeth took the clothing and thanked her.

A few minutes later, she walked down the hallway to the bath, taking a towel from the linen closet Madeline pointed out. She could hear voices in the kitchen, and she was tempted to listen to Drew's phone conversation, but the thought of running hot water beckoned. She undressed quickly and stepped underneath the spray before it had a chance to warm completely. The cool water refreshed her, and as it slowly turned warm against her skin, she felt the last of her tension slipping away. She wondered when the FBI would arrive and make their arrests. As soon as it was over, she could get her life back to normal.

Only it wouldn't seem normal at all, she realized as she shut off the water. She could live without the Colony down the road, even without Lily and Luke. But Drew Carter had worked his way into her life so utterly that she couldn't imagine being without him. She reached for the towel and wiped the moisture out of her eyes, not at all certain it was merely tap water. She dried herself and dressed, realizing as she blotted the ends of her hair that she didn't even have a comb. That reminded her of the wool comb she'd used on the supremacist, and she was gripped by a fist of revulsion until she reminded herself that they were safe here.

Still toweling the ends of her hair, she went back to the bedroom, pausing in the doorway when she saw Drew stretched out on the bed. He was fully clothed, both pillows behind his head. His jeans and shirt were rumpled, his jaw dark with whiskers, but he was smiling, his eyes crinkling at the corners.

"Hi." He patted the mattress beside him, and Elizabeth sat down, trying to use her fingers to bring some order to her tangled hair.

"What did the FBI say?" she asked. "Did they believe you?"

"They're getting a team together this very minute. I told them not to count on help from the county sheriff's department." Her fingers stilled in their task of separating strands of wet hair. "Let me," Drew said, pulling her hands away. "Do you mind if I use my comb?"

"No, of course not." *We've shared more than that,* she wanted to add. But personal conversation could come later. Now she wanted to know what would happen to the men who'd tried to kill them. "Did you tell the FBI that Cal Hoskin as much as admitted killing Paul Brewster?"

"I told them everything," he said. "It's going to be all right." He combed her hair behind her ear and paused to kiss the sensitive lobe. It was almost enough to make her forget where they were.

"I feel awful imposing on the Littlehawks like this," she admitted.

"Don't." As Drew carefully pulled the comb through her hair he told her that Charlie Littlehawk was glad to help because Mel Bofry was among the mob that violently protested the reservation's treaty rights to spearfish on Eagle Lake the previous spring. "He figures a couple more of Silas Freeman's buddies were in on it, too," Drew added as he took the towel from Elizabeth's hands and squeezed the last drops of moisture from her hair one section at a time.

With Drew's hands gently massaging her scalp, it was easy for Elizabeth to forget the terror of the past twenty-four hours. When he finished, she leaned back against the headboard and closed her eyes. "Thank God it's over," she said.

Drew lifted a pillow from behind him and arranged it beneath her head. "I'm sorry, Elizabeth."

Her eyes snapped open. "Why?"

"Things will be different when you get back."

"I know. It's going to be a lonely winter." She looked at him steadily, hoping that he knew she wasn't referring to her neighbors. He didn't say anything, and Elizabeth finally looked away. She'd already fought too many battles that day. She felt the last of her energy seeping away as she leaned back into the pillow. Drew turned toward her and rested a hand lightly across her rib cage, and she smiled at the familiar weight.

"When do we have to go back?" she asked. She was just aware enough to notice her choice of words. Not *when can we,* but *when do we have to.*

"The FBI wants to get there soon enough to interrupt the shipment. It should be all over with tonight."

Tonight. Such a short time left for them to be together. Elizabeth looked over at Drew, who was watching her, his dark eyes serious. She'd done her best to convince him that they belonged together, but whether or not to stay was Drew's decision, since he would be the one making the most changes. She felt a deep ache starting inside her rib cage that even the warm pressure of his arms couldn't assuage.

"Hey—why so quiet?" he asked, pulling her closer until she was nestled against him spoon fashion. The position reminded her of the nights they'd slept together in her brass bed. Would she wake up in his arms tomorrow morning, with the sunlight streaming past the curtains, or would he leave for Chicago tonight?

"I'm just tired, I guess," she said.

He kissed the back of her neck, and a reassuring warmth stole over her. "I think we could both use some rest," he murmured against her ear.

She smiled, wishing she weren't so sleepy. Drew's breath brushed the damp hair at her temples, making her tingle with awareness even as it soothed. An hour ago, she'd been wide-awake while he slept. Now it seemed to be his turn to stand guard. "You don't sound very tired," she accused. A yawn slipped out at the end of her sentence, removing the sting from the words.

She felt him chuckle against her back. "I am," he insisted, but she barely heard him, already drifting into sleep.

Drew listened as Elizabeth's even breaths told him she'd fallen asleep. If she knew what he was going to do, she'd demand to go along, and he couldn't allow that.

His friend at the Bureau had told him what to expect, and it wasn't just a simple matter of reading suspects their rights and slapping handcuffs on them. When the FBI had cornered a particularly militant supremacist group in Seattle a few years back, they'd used two hundred combat-equipped agents in a fiery confrontation that lasted several hours. He didn't expect anything like that to happen tonight, but he still didn't want Elizabeth present, where she could get caught in the middle of a shoot-out, or where she might see one of her neighbors arrested or injured.

He'd had a hard enough time convincing the Bureau to allow his own presence. They hadn't reckoned with his determination to get *all* of the story, including the ending. He'd offered a simple exchange—the notes on ASP and Phillip Prince that he and Jim and Paul Brewster had already gathered, for his presence at the confrontation. He'd been sternly reminded of the penalties for withholding information from the FBI, but he'd held fast. The FBI didn't give in until Drew pointed out that he was familiar with the Colony's layout and its members. He'd also warned that he'd be there without the FBI's permission, if it came to that.

It wasn't an idle bluff. He'd derailed Phillip Prince, solved Paul Brewster's murder, but there was still one more thing to do. He had to tell the rest of the world about the evil that some men espoused in the name of God—and how easy it was to get caught up in the idea that everything in the world was either good or evil, black or white. And to do that, he had to be there to the end.

He'd briefly considered letting someone else tell the world about the dark side of Elizabeth's neighbors, but no other writer had worked beside them or shared their table. Drew understood their light side, too. He had to write the book himself and hope Elizabeth would understand.

It would take the FBI several hours to get everyone assembled and into Wisconsin. Until then he'd stay right here beside her. Who knew how long it would be before he got another chance to hold her in his arms and watch her sleep? The familiar vision of the log cabin nestled in the snow, its windows warm and welcoming, tempted him. He allowed himself to imagine what it would be like, living there with her.

He watched her as the hours passed, drifting in and out of sleep himself. He heard the children's voices when they came home from school, and their mother telling them to hush. He heard the muffled sounds as the Littlehawk family gathered for supper. His stomach reminded him that it had been hours since he'd eaten the packet of dried food in the pickup.

Without waking Elizabeth, he lifted his wrist to check the time. Not long now and he'd be where he always wanted to be—in the thick of the action. He'd done his best work under fire, so to speak. *So why wasn't he looking forward to it this time?*

Drew already knew the answer. Because it hurt like hell to leave Elizabeth. Even angelic and innocent in sleep, the sight of her made his body tighten. She lay on top of the covers, her pale hair fanning out on the pillow behind her. He moved away, careful not to disturb her. He reached down and covered her with the bedspread. She stirred for a moment, and he actually hoped that she would open her eyes and see him, stop him from leaving. Then sanity returned.

She had her place in life, and he had his. Right now his required that he turn her life upside down. His dark gaze swept once more over Elizabeth's sleeping form. It was time to leave. But there was still something he needed to say to her.

"I love you."

The words sounded impossibly loud in the room's stillness, but she didn't stir. He pulled the door closed behind him before he could give in to the urge to wake her.

Chapter 15

When Elizabeth awoke, it was night. For several moments she lay disoriented, then memory rushed back in a dizzying whirl: the bunker, their escape, the tension-filled ride to the reservation where they'd at last found help. She realized she was in the Littlehawks' bed. And she was alone.

"Drew?" Even as she called his name she knew he wouldn't answer. She reached over to touch the pillow next to her. It was empty and cold.

She sat up, reaching blindly for the lamp she remembered seeing at the side of the bed, nearly knocking it over as she fumbled around for the switch. She found it and turned it on, blinking as the sudden brightness stung her eyes.

She looked at her watch and her heart plummeted. Eleven p.m. Until that moment, when she realized how late it was, she'd hoped that Drew was in one of the other rooms with the Littlehawk family. Now she realized that the trailer was utterly silent. Everyone was sleeping. *Or gone.*

Had Drew left her without a word of goodbye? Last night, in the basement bunker, she'd been so sure that he was trying to tell her he loved her. But today he hadn't talked of love or even of leaving. Of course, fleeing through the countryside wasn't exactly conducive to loving words or fond farewells, but he could have said something after they'd arrived here. Unless he didn't love her after all.

She refused to believe that. She drew back the curtain, surprised to see a layer of newly fallen snow—and even more surprised to see Doc's pickup. Drew must have gotten a ride to the cabin from Charlie Littlehawk so he could get Jim's truck. Was there a chance she could still catch him before he left for Chicago? It was late, but she had to try. She tossed aside the bedspread.

Her clothing was neatly arranged on a chair by the door, and she realized Madeline Littlehawk must have laundered it for her. She put on everything except the damp wool sweater, which Madeline had thoughtfully kept out of the hot dryer. Elizabeth hung it over the back of the chair, opting to leave on the pale yellow sweatshirt. She laced her boots quickly and left the room, standing for a few moments in the hallway to let her eyes adjust to the darkness before picking her way through the unfamiliar trailer.

Two children shared a second bedroom, another slept in a third, and Madeline Littlehawk was sleeping on the living room sofa. Her husband and Drew were nowhere to be seen. If Charlie Littlehawk wasn't back yet, perhaps Drew would still be at the cabin by the time she got there—unless the young law officer was on duty, or staying with friends. She'd taken the only other bed, she realized guiltily.

She silently opened the door and slipped outside. Winter had paid an early visit sometime while she'd slept. The cold took her breath away, and when she stepped down, snow reached above her ankles. And it was still falling. She dashed to the pickup, praying the keys were where she'd left them. She lifted back the floor mat, and her hands closed triumphantly around cold metal.

She started the truck and drove away, wishing belatedly that she'd left a note of thanks for the Littlehawks. She turned up the heater and switched on the headlights. The beams revealed a dizzying pattern of snow, and she hoped she could find her way through the unfamiliar Reservation roads to the gravel county road where Tom Wheeler lived. From there she could make her way home.

She blessed Doc's four-wheel drive for the second time that day and wondered if it was time to buy her own. She hated to think of what Freeman and his men might have done to Claire's truck, or to her cabin...*or to her sheep*. She pressed harder on the accelerator.

Anyone who was prepared to kill two humans—who'd already killed—would hardly stop at arson, or any other crime. Silas Freeman's anger, coupled with frustration at losing his prisoners, could have turned to vengeance.

What awaited her? Had Drew arrived at the cabin only to find it in ruins? He wouldn't have left her to face it alone, she told herself. Still she pressed on.

Drew crouched against the barn's stone foundation. He was out of the bitter wind, but more important, he was out of sight. Across the Colony farmyard were the two houses, their outlines blurred by the falling snow. The unexpected storm had kept the supremacists from delivering their weapons. Unfortunately, it also prevented most of the members of the FBI's hostage and terrorist SWAT team from reaching Nisswa.

Somewhere behind him was Special Agent Miller. After meeting Drew and Charlie Littlehawk at the reservation, Miller had turned the community building into a command center. Unfortunately, they had precious few to command.

Only ten of the men now scattered around the perimeter of the farmyard were with the Bureau. Filling out the ranks were two U.S. marshalls with three of their deputies, and Littlehawk, along with his assistant. Conspicuous by their absence were Sheriff Smith and four Potawatomi County deputies, currently under custody in their own county jail. The fifth deputy, now acting sheriff, was with Miller. Eighteen men in all. A nineteenth remained behind at the Colony's gate in place of the guard, who was bound and unconscious.

It wasn't nearly enough manpower. They didn't know for sure how many survivalists were left in the house along with the Colony members, but judging from the pickups and cars still parked in the farmyard, the opposing side numbered more than twenty. And counting firepower, the SWAT team was vastly outgunned.

While waiting for the Colony's inhabitants and visitors to finish the nightly chores, the eighteen men, along with Drew, had gathered behind the windbreak. The tall evergreens protected the farmyard, but the SWAT team had sat freezing on the other side. Drew had plenty of time to think then, and he'd used thoughts of Elizabeth to keep him warm. He even allowed himself a couple fantasies of the future.

The SWAT team moved in when the supremacists gathered at the big house. Efficiency made up for their small numbers. Men were stationed at every point along the yard's perimeter. Drew was farthest away, with Miller and Goodyear, the deputy-turned-sheriff, but this time he didn't mind being well behind the front lines. He wanted to get the job over with and leave.

His attention was drawn away by Agent Miller, whose monotone voice droned into a two-way radio behind him. It could have been a day at the office for all the emotion he showed. "We're going to use the bullhorn now," Miller said. "Since these men don't recognize the authority of the federal government, Deputy—that is, *Sheriff* Goodyear is going to do all the talking."

Drew looked back toward the house. Even this late, the windows still glowed with warm light, and he could see people gathered around the dining room table. It looked like a family holiday. The peaceful scene was shattered by Goodyear's amplified voice, informing the house's occupants that they were surrounded, to come outside and give themselves up. *Just like in the movies,* Drew thought for a second time that day.

A face appeared at the window—a woman. Snow and distance obscured her features until the curtains were abruptly drawn by a second figure. Even through the snow, Drew recognized Freeman's stooped silhouette. One by one, lights were extinguished and curtains drawn. Moments later, the yardlight came on, flooding the area with a light bright enough to make Drew blink in surprise. Miller cursed behind him.

"What now?" Drew asked. No one answered. The deputy-turned-sheriff repeated his message for the house's occupants. He'd barely finished when a loud gunshot pierced the cold air. The waiting was over, Drew realized. "Tell your men to hold their fire," he urged. "There's women and children inside."

"The shot wasn't ours." Before Miller finished his reply the night exploded. Bursts of gunfire and flashing light came from the farmhouse windows, drowning out the reports of the marshalls' service revolvers and the scattered shots from the FBI commandos.

"They've got a goddam arsenal in there."

It was the first time all evening he'd heard Miller raise his voice. Drew didn't waste time pointing out that he'd warned them. Instead he reached back and grabbed the bullhorn.

"Tell your men to hold fire for a minute," he shouted at Miller. The agent complied, using his two-way radio. As soon as there was a brief pause in the fusillade from the house Drew called out Freeman's name. At the sound of his voice, the farmyard fell eerily silent. The snow thinned enough so that Drew could see the house clearly.

"Silas, I know you're not going to quit fighting now for what you believe in." Drew's voice carried across the farmyard. "Let the women and kids go. It'll be safer for them in the barn."

Freeman's response didn't require a bullhorn. "We'll take care of our own."

"He's crazy," Miller said.

Drew handed him the bullhorn. "He's not crazy. He just operates under a different logic than you or I do. And he's a determined man."

The raucous blasting of guns started all over again, and Drew pushed himself flatter against the side of the barn. Next to him, Miller raised a rifle to his shoulder and, with a single shot, shattered the bulb of the yardlight.

"We can't afford to have any of our men picked off," Miller yelled in explanation.

Through the darkness Drew saw a lone figure step out the back porch door—a woman, her skirts billowing in the wind. Before he could turn, Agent Miller was already calling for his men to cease their fire. Even squinting Drew couldn't identify the woman's bulky outline. Then a second figure stepped out from behind the woman's skirts. His broad shape was easily identifiable. *Cal Hoskin.*

No one dared shoot as Hoskin pulled the woman—Drew thought it was Sarah Stoltz—across the front lawn. Drew couldn't figure out what Hoskin had in mind. Every sector of the farm was covered, and Hoskin had to be aware of that. He wouldn't be able to get very far unless he dragged the woman along with him, and even then he'd be followed.

Hoskin swung his rifle toward the smaller house, and started shooting out the basement windows. Drew realized in a flash that Hoskin had no intention of dragging a hostage with him. He was creating a diversion. Before Drew had a chance to warn Miller that he suspected the Colony's cache of ammo was inside, the windows erupted with fire. The earth shuddered beneath their feet, and a huge rumbling drove out all thought. All eyes turned toward the flames that towered dangerously close to the main house.

Drew shut out the screams and the explosions and the fire. In the dancing shadows, he saw Hoskin throw the woman to the ground and run for the windbreak, the rifle in one hand, a handgun in the other. The man had sacrificed his allies so that he could get away.

Behind Drew, Miller tried frantically to rouse his team on the radio. Drew grabbed the agent's arm, pulling away the receiver to warn him. His words were lost as another round of explosions rocked the night. He didn't wait to see if Miller had understood. He couldn't let Paul's killer get away. He ran for the trees where he'd last seen Hoskin.

Elizabeth guided Doc's truck into her driveway by instinct. The path was almost obliterated by snow, but she recognized the stand of pines and brush that hid the garage. She considered taking the truck back to Doc, but she dismissed the idea as quickly as she'd thought of it. Tomorrow would be soon enough. And soon enough to see what had happened at the Colony.

She parked in front of the cabin, too tired to walk from the shed. The pickup's headlights illuminated the snow that decorated the porch railings and roof. It looked safe and serene, like a Currier and Ives Christmas card. The snow was unmarked by tireprints or footprints, and the cabin's windows were dark. She'd missed Drew and Charlie Littlehawk by hours. Spirits sagging, she trudged directly to the barn.

The snow in the paddock bore faint hoofprints all the way down to the pond and back, and she knew the sheep had been

corralled even if they hadn't been shut in the barn. She turned
on the battery-powered lantern just inside the barn door. Sheep
blinked sleepily at the light, and a couple bleated plaintively. All
were present and accounted for. The ewes probably hadn't
gotten their special rations, but they seemed healthy as she ran
her hands over the woolly bodies, talking back to them softly.
She didn't know what time the snow had started, or how long
they'd been enclosed, but chances were they probably hadn't
been pastured that day.

She climbed the ladder up to the haymow, intending to throw
down a bale of hay, when she spotted a bundle of clothing in
one corner. Then the bundle moved, and Elizabeth realized it
was human. The lantern's beams didn't illuminate the corner
very well, but she had a pretty good idea who crouched there in
the hay bales and loose straw. "Luke?"

The bundle stirred again. "Yes, ma'am." The boy turned a
white face toward her. His voice was small and frightened, and
Elizabeth felt a rush of concern. If Luke was still here, what
had happened? Why wasn't he at the Colony with Lily and the
women?

"Don't be afraid," she said. "I'm not angry. But Lily might
be if you've missed your bedtime."

"She told me to come here and watch your sheep."

"Thank you for taking care of them, Luke." The boy didn't
move and she realized he was still frightened. Her unease grew.
"Is your sister all right?"

"Yes, ma'am," answered the small voice. "But she told me
to come back here."

"Why?" She waited tensely for his answer.

"I don't know." The words wavered. "Silas was mad at her."

Elizabeth sat down on a mound of straw next to Luke, and
she lightly touched his bent knee. "Did he hurt her, Luke?" He
looked away, and she reached out and lifted his chin with her
finger. His eyes were dark blue and wide. "This is very important," she told him. "Did Silas hurt Lily?"

"He hit her. Hard. And then he told her to go to her room.
Aunt Sarah let me take her some supper. That's when she told
me to come back here."

Luke had missed the FBI's arrival. Why hadn't Lily come for
him? Had the FBI broken their word and arrested her along

with the men? A deep, faraway rumble interrupted her speculation. Elizabeth knew it came from the Colony.

"Lily!" Luke yelled and jumped to his feet. Elizabeth rose on her knees and grabbed him by the sleeve before he could run to the ladder.

"It's just thunder, Luke," she told him.

"No, it's not. It's snowing out. It doesn't thunder when it snows."

She couldn't argue with the stubborn logic of a seven-year-old. "Then I'll go see what it is," she said. "But you stay here like Lily told you. Okay?" She handed him the lantern. "I'll leave the lantern for you. Your job is to feed the sheep. Think you can do that for me?"

Luke nodded and sat down on a bale of hay. Elizabeth smiled reassuringly at him as she climbed down the ladder, and Luke smiled back. She wished she could quell her own fears as easily. Did the ominous noise mean the FBI was there now? What on earth was happening?

She entered the cabin through the connecting door, then found her way through the dark room to the table where she always left the lantern. She lit it hurriedly, her fingers shaking and her mind gone numb. All she could think of was that she and Luke were alone, and that something horrible was happening just down the road. Her first reaction was to get the gun, but she couldn't remember where she'd left it. Since the day Drew had told her about Paul Brewster's death she hadn't kept it above her door. She squeezed her eyes shut and tried to remember.

The loft. She didn't stop to consider her actions, but reacted automatically. She brought the rifle downstairs and dashed to the pantry for ammunition. The box had never been opened, and she fumbled with it, scattering bullets over the floor underneath the oak table.

The sound of the bullets reminded her that for several moments she hadn't heard anything. She paused. And then the rumbling came again. Her breath caught in her throat. She went to the front door and pulled it open, running to the porch steps, ignoring the snow that covered the tops of her boots. To the north the night sky was stained with an eerie orange glow.

She ran back through the cabin and opened the door to the barn, ordering Luke to stay put, before hurrying back to the table. Her ears still ringing from the explosion, her fingers numb, she tried to remember how to load the rifle. She forced herself to calm down, and at last she succeeded.

She pulled on a jacket before going outside this time and went to sit on the snowy top step of the porch. She watched and waited, the rifle clutched protectively in her cold hands. *What was happening?* she asked herself again. She knew she had to go find out. Drew would tell her not to get involved, to put the gun back and stay away.

She realized then with sickening certainty that Drew wasn't on his way to Chicago. He was at the Colony.

She ran to the shed and saw the red truck still parked there. All thoughts of hesitation vanished as she strode to Doc's pickup. She didn't see the dark shape that slipped from behind a tree until she'd opened the door. The moment the pickup's dome light came on she noticed a stealthy movement out of the corner of her eye. She responded instinctively, spinning around and raising the rifle to her shoulder. It never made it. A strong arm snaked out to block it, and she saw Cal Hoskin's face illuminated in the dim circle of light. He smiled.

They battled silently for control of the rifle. Her hands were on the stock, but Hoskin's left hand gripped the barrel firmly, preventing her from raising it any higher than his waist. She could see an assault rifle dangling from his right hand and a pistol stuck in his belt. As Elizabeth's muscles strained she realized that at this range, with the rifle pointed at Hoskin's belly, she didn't need to aim. All she had to do was squeeze the trigger before the opportunity was lost . . . if she dared.

"So the little pigeon that flew away came back. I saw the tire tracks and knew it must be you since your boyfriend was already at the party down the road.

Drew *was* there. Her concern must have shown on her face because Hoskin's smile grew wider, his teeth white in the dim light. "If you're running off to see him, it's too late." His eyes glittered with amusement. "He tried to follow me here, but I stopped him."

A wave of fear weakened Elizabeth's grip. Hoskin took advantage of the opportunity, pulling hard and dragging her closer. One of her hands slipped from the rifle's stock, and she grabbed wildly to keep from losing the gun.

"Why don't you come with me, 'Lizbeth?"

"No!" She thought about screaming, but she didn't want Luke running outside to see what was wrong. No one else would hear her over the scattered explosions and sirens. *Sirens?* She heard it again: the wail of a siren coming closer down the dead-end road. She hoped Hoskin was enjoying his game of cat and mouse too much to notice.

He laughed and loosened his hold so abruptly that she almost fell. His hand was still on the barrel, but he allowed her to regain control. He leaned his own rifle against the side of the truck, freeing his right hand. She knew that with both hands he could snatch the gun away and turn it on her whenever he chose. She stared into his eyes as she slowly put her finger back on the trigger and edged the barrel toward his stomach. *Why wasn't he stopping her? Was he insane?*

"Carter's dead." Her fingers froze. "So are the men with him. Why don't you come along with me and be a good little hostage?" he drawled.

"If everyone's dead, why do you need a hostage? I'll just give you the keys to the truck and—"

"No! You're pretending not to hear the sirens, when all along you know I need you to make a run for it. You're coming with me. Unless you really are going to shoot me, that is." His voice was challenging, his eyes bright as he let go of the gun.

He *was* crazy. He enjoyed the game he was playing with her, liked the feeling of daring and control it gave him. Hoskin's motivation wasn't just money, and it was more than power. This was a man who liked living on the razor's edge.

Still she couldn't pull the trigger. Images of Drew's body, riddled with bullet holes, haunted her. She tossed the gun into the snow several feet away.

"Get in the truck." He grabbed her arm. Then the triumph in his eyes vanished as a harsh command rang out from the trees.

"Let her go, Hoskin."

Elizabeth recognized the deep, gravelly voice with a relief that made her legs weak. She was so overjoyed at proof Drew was alive that she forgot about Hoskin. She took several steps for-

ward, until cold metal against her neck stopped her. She'd forgotten about the pistol, too.

Drew stepped out from behind a tree ten feet away. "I said,
let her go."

Hoskin laughed. "You can't add, hero. You don't even have
a gun. I've got a gun *and* the woman. You got zip. Why should
I let her go?"

"Because you can take me instead." Drew stepped closer.
Elizabeth glanced toward her rifle, half-hidden in the snow between her and Drew. He'll try to reach for it, she thought, her
body tensing in readiness.

Hoskin pretended to consider Drew's offer. "You'd be too
much trouble. Besides, there are certain . . . fringe benefits to
traveling with a woman."

Drew moved swiftly, reaching for the rifle in the snow. Elizabeth pulled from Hoskin's grip just as a shot rang out, ob-
scenely loud in the snow-covered hollow. Drew's hand closed
around the gun, but he never rose. She screamed and ran to
him. She heard a second shot and thought that at least they
would die together. She hugged the warmth of his prostrate
body, and his breath stirred her hair.

Drew opened his eyes. "Angel?"

"You're alive." Her words were little more than a whisper.

"So are you." He captured her face in his hands for a hard,
swift kiss. They turned back to look toward the truck. Hoskin's body was prone in the snow, deathly still. Next to the
pickup, a small figure stood, Hoskin's rifle still held to his
shoulder.

"Oh, God," Elizabeth said when she recognized the boy. She
rose to her knees. "Luke."

The gun dropped from the boy's fingers with a thud, and he
ran to Elizabeth's outstretched arms. "Silas is going to be mad
at me," he choked out between sobs.

Drew sat up. Their gazes met over Luke's head. "It's all
right, Luke. No one's going to be mad," she soothed as she
stroked the head burrowed into her shoulder.

"He'll be okay," Drew told her.

"I know. What about you?" Her eyes ran over his form.
"It's a miracle Hoskin didn't hit you."

"Oh, but he did." At Elizabeth's shocked look, Drew unsnapped his down vest. "My mother believes in Saint Christopher. I put my faith into this."

"A bulletproof vest?"

"A flak jacket, courtesy of the FBI. I put it on before we went into the Colony. Good thing, too. I felt the bullet glance off here." He touched the top of his shoulder, the one that wasn't already bandaged. "It felt like a fist. Or a bionic mosquito."

"What if he'd hit you in the head?" she asked, clutching Luke tighter.

Drew reached out and touched her cheek, brushing away a tear she didn't know had fallen. "Don't talk about it." But then he violated his own warning. "I don't think I've ever been more afraid of dying. I hadn't told you how very much I love you."

"I love you, too."

Mixed with her joy was sadness. What would happen to the child in her arms? Luke pulled away, rubbing his eyes with the heels of his hands. "Can we go home now?" he asked.

Elizabeth turned to Drew for the answer. He shook his head slightly and said, "You stay here with him. I'll go." He rose to his feet.

"No." Elizabeth stood and faced him, a stubborn lift to her chin. Luke was at her side, holding tight to her hand. "I'm not letting you go anywhere without me." She expected an argument, but Drew shrugged in resignation. He walked toward Doc's white truck, bending down to pick up the rifle Luke had used.

"Is he dead?" Elizabeth asked quietly when Drew removed the pistol from Hoskin's outflung arm.

"No. He's unconscious and bleeding. The bullet hit him in the side. You'll have to help me get him in back of the truck. The FBI had an ambulance standing by, and I saw it on my way here."

"There's a fire truck, too. I heard the siren." She led Luke to the other side of the truck, shielding his view of Hoskin's body and helping him up inside before going back to assist Drew. When they joined Luke in the truck's cab, the boy slumped against her. Elizabeth wrapped an arm around his shoulder and pulled him closer, hoping he wouldn't go into shock.

As they drove toward the Colony the glow in the sky became brighter. They had to wait for a second fire unit at the Colony's open gates. As soon as they passed the screen of the windbreak, a man separated himself from the crowd and limped toward them. Drew got out to meet him, and Elizabeth followed, Luke clinging to her hand like a limpet.

"You must be Elizabeth Johnson," the man said as he approached. "I'm Special Agent Miller with the FBI." Before Elizabeth could do more than nod to acknowledge the introduction, he turned to Drew. "I'm glad you're all right," he said. "I was going to send some of the men after you, but we've had our hands full here. What happened?"

While Drew briefed Miller and led him and a paramedic to the injured Hoskin, Elizabeth's horrified gaze traveled around the Colony. The yard was utter devastation. The small house was engulfed in flames, and next to it the farmhouse roof had caught. Flames flickered behind an upper story window. She could feel the heat from the fire on her face, and the smell of smoke and spent ammunition seared her lungs. Two fire trucks were parked by the houses, but the occasional explosion as more ammo caught fire kept the firefighters from advancing too closely.

Figures darted here and there, and shouts of command mingled with the cries of the injured and the roar of the fire. Elizabeth spotted a white-haired figure bending over a prone body. She pulled Luke closer. "Isn't that Doc?" she asked as Drew and the agent rejoined them.

"We couldn't keep the old man away," Miller admitted. "For a while we thought he'd end up a patient himself. He trotted all the way over here through the woods."

Another group of people, heads bowed, stood near the ambulance. Elizabeth knew that among them were the Colony members even though she couldn't make out their faces in the flickering light. As she watched, several of the figures were led into a waiting van in handcuffs.

Luke tore his hand from hers. "Lily!" he screamed and ran toward the ambulance. Before Elizabeth could go after him, a figure broke away from the crowd and embraced Luke. Relief flooded through her as she recognized Lily.

Elizabeth walked toward the woman and boy slowly, wanting to give them time alone, reluctant to face her friend. Would Lily blame her for this? She stopped in her tracks when she saw Doc drape a blanket over the body in the snow.

"It's Silas. He's dead." Elizabeth looked up to see Lily's tear-streaked face. Her hair hung limply and a dark smudge—or a bruise—colored one cheekbone. "God must hate me."

"Why?"

"Because I'm happy."

Lily didn't look happy. Her face revealed utter desolation, and Elizabeth pulled her into her arms.

An hour later Drew found Elizabeth leaning against the side of the barn, her jacket and borrowed sweatshirt streaked with grime. He touched her arm and she gave him a watery smile. "Let's go home," he said gently. "Doc's with the ambulance. I don't think he'd mind if we took his truck."

People, mostly firefighters and FBI agents, milled around the site. Lily, Luke and the other women and children had been taken to Forest City for the night where they would be questioned and released. The men were being held in the Forest County jail pending extradition or trial. Fire still consumed both houses, and Drew could see Elizabeth's exhaustion as the orange light of the flames flickered over her face. He reached to fold her into his arms but she held herself stiffly away and started to walk toward the truck.

"It's so ugly," she said. "Everything will be gone except the outbuildings." He realized the depth of her involvement when she added, "I hope they send someone to take care of the stock."

"I'm sure someone will think of it," he said. He ached with guilt. It was happening just the way he'd feared, but he vowed not to let it turn her against him. "I know it's ugly. I'm sorry it had to end like this." He told her how Hoskin had set off the ammo to get away.

As they walked to the pickup the snow started again. "Maybe it will snow all night long and cover everything," she said, a wistful note in her voice. They stopped to watch the flames. She leaned closer, and when her arm went around his waist Drew felt a relief so strong he nearly shouted with gratitude. He hugged her fiercely, and they walked arm in arm the rest of the way.

When they reached the truck, Elizabeth put a hand out to finger one of the bullet holes in the side. "Doc's pickup has sure been through a lot in the past eighteen hours. I should offer to buy it from him." Drew smiled at her attempted joke and held the door open for her.

"You'd actually change your loyalty from that old beater of Claire's?" he teased as he helped her up into the cab.

"It's about time, isn't it?" she said as he sat beside her and started the engine. "I realized today how isolated I'd let myself become from the rest of the world." She paused, then admitted, "I think it affected my judgment, at least where the Colony was concerned."

As they left the Colony behind Drew reassured her. "No one could have known, Elizabeth. The danger of people like Freeman and his men is that they don't seem very different from anyone else."

She shuddered visibly. "Even so, I plan to get out and mingle more with my other neighbors."

They were silent for a few moments as they turned into Elizabeth's driveway. When they passed the new garage, Drew ventured, "As long as you're so amenable to changes, how about a telephone and electricity? And a driveway," he added as they bumped over a particularly large rut.

"I've gotten along fine without electricity, and you know how I feel about the driveway when I'm out here all alone."

"What if you weren't alone?" he asked carefully.

Elizabeth turned to stare at him. "What are you saying?"

"Well, I need electricity for my computer and coffeepot."

"Your coffeepot?"

"I hate to say this, but your boiled coffee stinks."

She pretended to be affronted, but she was smiling broadly. Drew's tension eased. "I suppose you want a telephone so you can order in pizza," she said.

"Actually, I need it to call my coauthor."

"And the driveway?"

"If I'm going to be busy writing and midwifing lambs, I won't have time to shovel snow. I know you're capable of doing everything yourself, but I will not have my wife out here digging through drifts," he teased as the truck pushed through a snowdrift. "Call me old-fashioned but—"

Her hand over his mouth silenced him. "Are you sure?" she asked.

He playfully nipped at her fingers until she pulled them away. Then he grew serious. "I'm sure. The bullet brought me to my senses, Elizabeth. We may be starting out with a couple strikes against us, but I think love is worth the risk." He parked the truck in front of the cabin. "Will you marry me?"

"Yes." Her assent was lost as Drew captured her lips with a deeply satisfying kiss. When they parted, he realized with surprise that his breathing was uneven.

"I love you," he said, then kissed her once more. He was shocked at how quickly his body responded to Elizabeth after the evening's trauma. He edged away, afraid he might offend her, but she threaded her hands through his hair, holding him closer. Her sweet taste and loving hands brought him to the edge of control.

"I love you and I need you," she said. "Tonight."

As she kissed him, Drew felt the power of love beam through him like bright sunshine. He realized then that they needed to reaffirm that love, to make a pledge to the future, in order to put the ugliness behind them. With a promising kiss, he set her away from him and opened the door. "Come on. We're home."

He helped her slide across the seat, but instead of setting her down on the ground, he swept her up into his arms and started up the porch steps. "Let's go get snowed in," he told her.

Their laughter was the first step on the road to healing.

Epilogue

Genevieve baa-ed softly and shifted. Elizabeth knelt next to her in the straw that bedded the lambing pen. She smiled at the small awkward bundle of wool that bleated in protest at losing her place at her mother's teat. The lamb was three days old, the last to be born. It was the first week in March, and the small barn was crowded with temporary lambing pens. Elizabeth's ewes had given her eight lambs, all healthy.

In seven months there would be another birth, she told herself, and smiled in anticipation. She looked up as the door between the barn and house opened. "Hi," she greeted as her husband joined her, standing next to the pen with his arms resting on the rail.

"How's the mother doing?" he asked, reaching down to pull her to her feet.

"Genevieve's a born mother. She's doing splendidly."

"I meant you," Drew said, his palm flat against her abdomen. Elizabeth's breath caught at the adoring expression in his eyes.

"I'm fine," she said.

"No cabin fever yet?"

"No," she grinned back at him and went into his arms. Even with only five ewes, lambing was hectic, and she was glad just to be able to stand quietly with Drew's arms wrapped around her. As for cabin fever, they'd been virtually stranded by a string of late-season storms since early February. Mail service had been sporadic, and they'd made few trips to town.

Even so, the winter had gone quickly. Thanksgiving was spent in Chicago with Drew's family, all gathered together for the first time in years to celebrate with the newly married couple. Drew and Elizabeth had spoken their vows at the Potawatomi Courthouse the week before the holiday, with Charlie and Madeline Littlehawk as witnesses. Elizabeth wore the white sweater with ice blue ribbons for her wedding day, and again on Thanksgiving. Her nervousness about meeting Drew's family had disappeared by the time they all gathered around the huge dining room table. Grandmother Carter made *spanokopita* to celebrate, and even Drew's father, who'd been invited at the last minute, ate heartily. Elizabeth felt like a part of a big family at last.

There'd been no question about where they would spend Christmas. A blizzard struck the day before Christmas Eve, and they'd spent the next few days snowed in at the cabin. The newly purchased generator had failed, and so had the back-up system for Drew's computer. Even so, it didn't take long for Elizabeth to convince him that being snowbound had its advantages. She was certain that was when she'd conceived. She smiled against the front of Drew's sweater.

"I thought we might try to make it into town tomorrow," he said, tipping her face up to his. "I have a business appointment."

"Did you finally convince Jim to come and visit?"

"No." Drew gave her a hesitant smile. "A few weeks ago I wrote the executor of the Kresge estate. The children and grandchildren have agreed to sell us the farm. I didn't want to tell you until I was sure."

Elizabeth was stunned. "You mean we'd live there?"

"You said you'd always loved the house. And we'll need the room for the babies," he said persuasively, his hand going again to her belly.

"Hmm, yes, with all that soundproofing and insulation the shed would make a wonderful lambing barn," she said, teasing him. Her breath caught when he trailed his fingers lower.

"I was talking about *our* babies." His lingering kiss sent a flash of heat through her limbs. Even after a winter of using every snowstorm as an excuse to spend the day in bed together, she responded to his touch like wildfire.

"Won't you be sorry to leave the cabin?" he asked.

"I'll miss it. Unless—" She smiled.

"Unless what?"

"I thought Lily and Luke might want to live here. I know they're anxious to leave their apartment in Forest City. They'll only be staying there until the trial is over. On the other hand, maybe I won't mention it to her."

"Why not?"

"Well, according to her letters, Gene Larson keeps stopping by and—"

He stopped her with another kiss. "Matchmaker," he accused. His hands moved to cradle her hips, and her legs went weak. She leaned against his strong chest.

"I have a business to think of," she reminded him. "If Lily marries Gene, I won't be losing a spinner. I'll be cementing my arrangements with the county's best breeder."

"You don't need more spinners anyway, not once Madeline Littlehawk starts teaching the women at the reservation."

"I wonder what kind of progress she's made since we saw them last." Her words started to drift as she concentrated on Drew's fingers, which were doing magical things to her bare back. She didn't even remember when he'd pushed aside her jacket or lifted the edge of her sweater....

"I'm not making any progress," he complained.

"Oh, yes. You are," she told him with an inviting smile.

"Come here." He pulled her along by the arm until they were standing below the ladder to the second story. "We never did try the hayloft," he said, his eyes crinkling at the corners.

"It was too cold all winter," she reminded him.

"But now it's almost spring. Or have you lost your pioneer spirit of adventure since I got the generator working again?"

"Of course not." She climbed up the ladder, Drew at her heels.

He picked her up and carried her to a bed of loose straw, setting her on her feet long enough to strip the jacket from her shoulders. He spread it over the straw and regarded it consideringly. "Maybe this wasn't such a good idea after all," he said.

"Oh, no." She grabbed his arm and pulled. "You're not backing out now." He landed in the straw beside her, smothering her laughter with a kiss. He rose on his knees to pull off her sweater and jeans. His eyes lingered on her soft curves, and Elizabeth knew he was seeking signs that her body was already changing from the baby. The air was cool, but she didn't even notice as heat crept up from her feet to her hairline. He smiled at her shyness.

"You're beautiful, and I love you," he said, running his hands over her skin. He quickly pulled his sweater—dark acorn brown, handknitted—over his head, stripped off his jeans and lay beside her.

"I love you," she told him as he joined her body to his. "Forever."

* * * * *

Double your reading pleasure this fall with two Award of Excellence titles written by two of your favorite authors.

Available in September

DUNCAN'S BRIDE
by Linda Howard
Silhouette Intimate Moments #349

Mail-order bride Madelyn Patterson was nothing like what Reese Duncan expected—and everything he needed.

Available in October

THE COWBOY'S LADY
by Debbie Macomber
Silhouette Special Edition #626

The Montana cowboy wanted a little lady at his beck and call—the "lady" in question saw things differently....

These titles have been selected to receive a special laurel—the Award of Excellence. Look for the distinctive emblem on the cover. It lets you know there's something truly wonderful inside! DUN-1

Silhouette Special Edition

Appearing in October
for a return engagement, Nora Roberts's
bestselling 1988 miniseries featuring

THE O'HURLEYS!
Nora Roberts

And making his debut in a brand-new title, a very special
leading man . . . Trace O'Hurley!

In 1988, Nora Roberts introduced THE O'HURLEYS!—a close-knit
family of entertainers whose early travels spanned the country. The
beautiful triplet sisters and their mysterious brother each experience
the triumphant joy and passion only true love can bring, in four books
you will remember long after the last pages are turned.

Don't miss this captivating miniseries in October—a special collector's edition available wherever paperbacks are sold.

OHUR-1

Back by popular demand, some of Diana Palmer's earliest published books are available again!

Several years ago, Diana Palmer began her writing career. Sweet, compelling and totally unforgettable, these are the love stories that enchanted readers everywhere.

This month, six more of these wonderful stories will be available in DIANA PALMER DUETS—Books 4, 5 and 6. Each DUET contains two powerful stories plus an introduction by Diana Palmer. Don't miss:

Book Four	AFTER THE MUSIC DREAM'S END
Book Five	BOUND BY A PROMISE PASSION FLOWER
Book Six	TO HAVE AND TO HOLD THE COWBOY AND THE LADY

Be sure to look for these titles now at your favorite retail outlet. If you missed DIANA PALMER DUETS, Books 1, 2 or 3, or wish to order Books 4, 5 and/or 6, order them by sending your name, address, zip or postal code, along with a check or money order for $3.25 for each book ordered, plus 75¢ postage and handling, payable to Silhouette Reader Service to:

In the U.S.
901 Fuhrmann Blvd.
Box 1396
Buffalo, NY 14269-1396

In Canada
P.O. Box 609
Fort Erie, Ontario
L2A 5X3

Please specify book title(s) with your order.

DPD-1A